MW01174771

DOUBLE HELIX

ANTHONY HYDE

VIKING

VIKING
Published by the Penguin Group
Penguin Books Canada Ltd, 10 Alcorn Avenue, Toronto, Ontario,
Canada M4V 3B2
Penguin Books Ltd, 27 Wrights Lane, London W8 5TZ, England
Penguin Putnam Inc., 375 Hudson Street, New York, New York 10014, U.S.A.
Penguin Books Australia Ltd, Ringwood, Victoria, Australia
Penguin Books (NZ) Ltd, cnr Rosedale and Airborne Roads, Albany, Auckland
1310, New Zealand

Penguin Books Ltd, Registered Offices: Harmondsworth, Middlesex, England

First published 1999
1 3 5 7 9 10 8 6 4 2

Copyright © Anthony Hyde, 1999

All rights reserved. Without limiting the rights under copyright reserved above,
no part of this publication may be reproduced, stored in or introduced into a
retrieval system, or transmitted in any form or by any means (electronic,
mechanical, photocopying, recording or otherwise), without the prior written
permission of both the copyright owner and the above publisher of this book.

*Publisher's note: This book is a work of fiction. All names, characters, places and
incidents either are the product of the author's imagination or are used fictitiously,
and any resemblance to actual persons living or dead, events, or locales is entirely
coincidental.*

Printed and bound in Canada on acid-free paper ∞

CANADIAN CATALOGUING IN PUBLICATION DATA

Hyde, Anthony, 1946–
   Double Helix

ISBN 0-670-87825-1

I. Title.

PS 8565.Y34D68 1999   C813'.54   C98-932267-X
PR9199.3.H92D68 1999

Visit Penguin Canada's website at www.penguin.ca

Every chicken-and-egg farmer knows that no increase, however great, in the cock population will affect the growth of his poultry population. The determining factor in the growth of all animal populations is not the birth rate of offspring, but the rate of female offspring. Only women have babies. And only girl babies grow up to be women.

Even in the affluent countries, the majority of women (let alone men) prefer to have sons. In the overpopulated countries, the preference for males amounts to an obsession. In those countries, a pill, unguent, or injection which, taken prior to coitus, would assure the birth of a son would come as man-ah! from Heaven. . . .

—Clare Booth Luce

DOUBLE HELIX

VENICE

S*he saw him the* first time in the *Piazza San Marco*, walking
through the crowds, with his hands in the pockets of his blue
windbreaker. *A tall young man.* That was the impression. She
never saw his face; by the time her eyes settled on him, he had
already turned, *curly black hair*, and then a little Japanese boy
gave a great shriek and waved his arms so the pigeons that were
settling on him all flew up, with a great flapping of wings; and by
the time Deb turned back, the young man was gone. But—she'd
always remember this—she did turn back . . .

That was the early afternoon of her fifth day in Venice.

She'd loved every minute of those five days. She'd found a great
place to have coffee in the morning, and the newspaper man
would be reaching for an *International Herald Tribune* as soon as
he saw her. Reading it, watching the *vaporetti* bring in the first
wave of day-trippers from the mainland, she would fantasize
about living here. It seemed like paradise. She was already picking
up a little Italian. And even when she didn't understand, she loved
to listen. As well, there were the canals, the boats, the water, and

somewhere there had to be sailing. And there was a big stock exchange in Milan, so . . .

It was a great dream. How incredible, to live in one of these houses with water lapping into the basement. Venice was magic, its own world. And although it was very old, it also seemed new, untried. Walking through the *calle* behind the great opera house— the Fenice—with one little alley leading off to another, she suddenly imagined them as the branches and turnings on one of those charts that show the development of Man, from *australo*-this to *homo*-that. Venice wasn't a dead end, she thought; it was a branch that had stopped, but it was still alive, a lost world waiting to be discovered again, a possibility that had never been truly explored.

But the next day, lost, with rain beginning to fall, she didn't find Venice quite so magical.

Her feet hurt. Her *legs* hurt. She was sick and tired of altar pieces and icons and other tourists, and having the rain drip from her nose onto the map as she tried to figure out where she was. This was supposed to be spring—she was shivering!

And yet that's when she saw the young man again.

He was leaning against the parapet of a little stone bridge, looking down at the *rio*. Deb recognized him at once; *that guy*. Just seeing him, the coincidence, made her pause, and she stood and watched him for a second, wondering what he was looking at, for there seemed nothing to hold his attention, unless it was the old, beautifully varnished launch tied up to a piling about thirty yards along the canal; gleaming in the rain, a rich golden red mahogany in colour, it was the only spot of light in the deepening twilight, and it would have held *her* attention, since she loved boats of all kinds . . . But then the wind blew a hard gust of rain into her face and some real, genuine, twentieth-century Venetians—hurrying home to warmth, coffee and television—bumped against her, *'scusi, 'scusi*, and she was jostled forward onto the bridge.

As she reached the top of the gentle arch, the young man turned around and smiled.

Now *he* had seen *her*. She could have just kept walking, of course; but as his eye caught hers, she stopped. And then stepped to one side, away from the people who were streaming past her. "Hello," she said.

"Hello."

"I don't know why, but somehow I knew you spoke English."

In the dark, leaning back against the bridge, he seemed very relaxed. She couldn't see him that well in the gloom, but he had curly dark hair—he *looked* Italian, actually—and his face was all hard highlights and shadows in the wet and the dark. But his voice was soft, even amused. "Let me guess. You're lost. You *look* lost."

"God. Yes. Yes, I'm lost."

He smiled and, reaching behind him, pulled up the collar of his jacket against the rain, which was falling harder now, swept by the wind along the narrow canal. As he made these adjustments, Deb could see his face better—strong, slanting cheekbones and a firm mouth. For some reason, she was immediately conscious that he was slightly older than she was. In the darkness, however, it was still his voice that defined him—it was very friendly and warm, perhaps a little teasing: as if they knew each other very well already. "Wasn't it Henry James who said that was the whole point of coming to Venice? To get lost."

"But not *tonight*. Not in the *rain*."

He laughed. "You're right. Where do you want to go?"

"Anywhere . . . any place I recognize. St. Mark's, say."

"My grandfather was born here. It must be in my genes—as long as I don't think, my feet will find it all on their own. Come on."

Then, hunching his shoulders, he turned and crossed to the other side of the bridge, gave one quick glance back to see that she was following, and headed into a dark *calle*—when she caught up to him, Deb found it was so narrow they could barely walk side by side. They didn't talk. Now, it actually started to rain quite hard. In two minutes, Deb was wet and miserable. She ignored the mysterious doors that opened in walls and the little gaps that offered glimpses of gardens and the small gleaming windows that flashed other people's lives. After a time, she realized she was walking with her head down, and had a sudden, panicky thought—he could be leading her anywhere. And who was he, and what had he been doing on that bridge? It was almost as though he'd been waiting for her. She gripped her purse more tightly. But almost at once she told herself not to be an idiot, she was being stupid, paranoid... although, as a *calle* branched away to the right, she thought of slipping into it, dashing off... But he turned just then, looking down at her with a smile; and a moment later, she thought she recognized where they were, yes, American Express was right over there... and then she *did* know where she was. They stepped under the shelter of the colonnade around St. Mark's. She looked across the floodlit square, almost deserted now, even by the pigeons, in the rain.

"So here you are," the young man said.

"Thank you. Look, that was very kind—I shouldn't have..." She felt suddenly guilty at being so suspicious, when he'd gone so far out of his way to be kind.

He smiled, and then blinked quickly as the rain ran into his eyes. "It was a pleasure," he said. And then he grinned: "Maybe you could reward me for my gallantry—and let me take you to dinner."

Deb laughed. "Would it still be gallantry then?"

"No. It would be a cunning ploy."

Deb thought, just for an instant. Then shook her head. "I don't think so. I'm too wet—too tired. Not tonight ... but maybe tomorrow."

"I'd like that. Where are you staying?"

Deb cocked her head to one side. "Maybe you should let me call you."

"Of course, if you like. I'm at the Excelsior."

The wind gusted, and Deb screwed up her eyes against it. She stuck out her hand. "Thank you again. It was very kind." And she turned away; but as she turned, she realized that he hadn't—that he was standing there, watching her; and she felt, she *knew*, that he would watch her all across the square, until he lost her in the rain. And she turned around slowly, to face him again. There was a little distance, now, between them. Deb tried to smile across it, but the rain was driving into her face, and she could barely see, the way it kept running into her eyes. But she said, "That was dumb."

"What was dumb?"

"Not telling you where I'm staying."

He shrugged. "I don't know. You've never met me before, you're alone—"

"I'm at the Hotel Zurich. And I haven't even told you my name. Deborah. Deborah Graham."

"My name is Giacomo Valli," he said.

"Giacomo . . ." It was a strange name to her, but once she said it, she liked the sound of it. Still, she felt a moment's embarrassment, because he'd realize that she found it strange. "Your English is so perfect," she said.

"Of course. It should be. I was born in Toronto."

"That's incredible."

"Why is that incredible? Weren't you?"

"No . . . yes, I mean I live there now—" She was taken aback—

"Listen, I know a little place, Deborah—we could just have coffee."

No. She shook her head. She couldn't change her mind. And she looked horrible—no. And yet she couldn't say it, in fact she felt totally strange, and it took all her strength to finally say what she *wanted* to say, "Call me tomorrow. Please." And then she turned and ran and she didn't look back—she didn't dare to—though she was utterly certain that he stood there, watching her, until she was gone.

Would he call?

The next day, there was no point in kidding herself, that was the only item on the agenda, though Deb told herself not to be an idiot, he wasn't going to call at nine in the morning, so she might as well have her usual *latte* and read the *Herald Tribune* . . . though she wouldn't have wanted to take a test on what was in it. She was back in the hotel by ten. She could wash out some stuff. After so much walking these past few days, her feet could do with a rest anyway . . . And it wouldn't be a bad idea, if she could work out the time change, to make a few calls home . . . But she hadn't even sorted out her pantyhose when he called—it was just past eleven.

"I hope it's not too early . . ."

"No. Of course not."

"I was afraid you might go out for the day—"

"No. Really. This is—fine."

She'd closed her eyes—she couldn't look. And when he asked her if he could take her to dinner, she had to bite her tongue to stop herself blurting out "yes" before he was finished. They finally hung up and she fell back on the bed and gasped—she'd been holding her breath the whole time.

It's just a date.

That was ridiculous, of course.

Something had happened.

But remarkably, when Giacomo arrived—just before seven—all her anxieties vanished and she was left with a pure, exhilarating excitement. She wasn't in the least self-conscious and the whole world of *dates* seemed, in some absolutely definitive way, to have been left behind. They went to a bar for a drink, then to a restaurant run by two Americans—Giacomo claimed they were the best cooks in Venice—and of course everything was easy because Giacomo's Italian was so quick and fluent, but there was also a slight formality to his manner—a *deftness* as he led her into the room, a small gesture of his hand restraining the waiter so she had time to decide—that gave her a definite status and importance in the eyes of the Italians. It wasn't quite deference, but rather a special attentiveness. She liked it; she had to live up to it in a way, but that didn't seem to require her to be anything other than herself. It was all very easy. She didn't feel she had to put anything *on*. At a certain point, realizing all this, she was silent for a moment, and he cocked his head and smiled. "Everything all right?"

"Yes. Thank you. I'm enjoying this."

"I'm happy that we met."

"I am, too."

And he reached over then and took her hand, just for a second, but long enough for her to squeeze back; and after that, it seemed, they couldn't stop talking, they had to tell each other everything. Again, it was all so very easy. She suddenly knew answers to questions she'd only vaguely understood before:

"So you have a history degree, but you're a stockbroker?"

"Do you disapprove?"

"No, I'm just curious. Well, maybe I do disapprove—maybe you're wasting yourself. Are you?"

"No. I'd hate to be an academic. I don't trust them. And I can't be wasting myself if I'm enjoying myself. Unless you're a puritan."

"But maybe *you're* the puritan. You feel just a little guilty. All that money."

"That's backwards. If you're a puritan, the money makes it okay, money is always moral—those old banks, just like churches. It's the enjoyment part that makes the guilt."

"And you do enjoy it?"

"Yes."

"Because . . . ?"

"I like making the decisions. You make up your mind, and then you *do* it—it's not just talk. You always put yourself on the line."

"And you win or lose?"

"Yeah."

"So you're a bit of a gambler?"

"Maybe. Okay—especially because I win more than I lose."

He laughed. "I don't have much money, but where do I sign?"

Giacomo Valli managed, at one and the same time, to be both very confident and yet slightly reserved. It took her a moment to grasp the meaning of this—that he was taking her seriously. She liked that. For one thing, it meant she could take *him* seriously. And he was a serious man, though he took his seriousness rather lightly. Looking at him—tan trousers, a navy blazer, pale yellow shirt buttoned at the neck but no tie—she wouldn't have guessed he was a doctor . . . though his face had a quiet, enquiring intensity that maybe fitted. In any case, when he told her, and saw her reaction, he laughed:

"It's okay. No one believes me. But you are looking at a genuine graduate of the University of Toronto Medical School, Johns Hopkins Medical School, and various strange institutes in Paris and Madrid. I'm afraid I'm a specialist."

"In?"

"The bad news: tropical diseases. The good news: I don't have any."

"You mean . . . those terrible viruses?"

"Are you sure you want to talk about this over dinner?"

"I'm loving my dinner. Yes."

"Well, the truth is, most people in the Third World—which is where the tropics are—don't die from fancy viruses, but the most ordinary kind. Especially the children. Babies get them here, too, but because they're well fed and drink clean water and live in decent places, they just have a tummy upset or a runny nose, and no one even bothers to call the doctor. In Mali, they get severe diarrhea, dehydrate and die." He shrugged. "Of course, it's not as bad as it used to be. Even in Mali. So more of the kids do survive and you have huge overpopulation—a hundred thousand homeless children in Nairobi alone." He grinned. "Do I sound like I'm pitching UNICEF?"

"I was just thinking, thank God I always use their Christmas cards."

"I hope it's not that bad, though these days I'm more of a bureaucrat than a doctor. I'd done a course in Paris—in fact, I was studying some of those fancy viruses—and then I took a job in a clinic in Rwanda. There were five branches, and when I got there, I realized they were in a mess. So, after a couple of months, I put away my stethoscope and tried to organize them properly . . . and I guess I did. Now I spend most of my time pushing paper and playing at 'expert.'"

He worked for the Marsh Foundation, which funded various medical aid projects all over the world. "We do small, innovative things. Then, if they work out, we try to talk the big agencies into taking them over and expanding them."

"And your job is . . . ?"

"To evaluate proposals, decide which ones to back. And I more or less represent the Foundation on the scientific side. I still *am* a doctor, even though I do spend a hell of a lot of time on airplanes. On Friday, for example, I have to go to Hong Kong for a conference."

"It sounds exciting—I envy you. I love travelling. I've been to Hong Kong—once."

"Emerging markets?"

"Yes."

"Morally, I trump you. I'm orphans."

"Not fair! Really?"

"Yes, or . . ." He waggled his fingers. "It's one of those times when you have a text, but a subtext too. Chinese orphanages are full of baby girls . . . who nobody wants . . . except for ladies in Des Moines or Winnipeg, which naturally makes for all kinds of problems."

"I've read about that . . . Chinese people only want boys."

"Don't believe everything you read. They love little girls. But the Chinese government has a 'one child' policy—since they're more or less drowning in people. The trouble is, the Chinese do want sons, because they believe that you have to be buried by a son to get to heaven. So baby girls are abandoned or simply killed. The *lucky* ones end up in the orphanages . . . though they're pretty primitive. The trouble is—no matter what they say—the Chinese government probably isn't so upset about this. Little boys don't grow up to have more babies—only little girls do, and if there's one thing China doesn't need, it's more babies." At this point, however, Giacomo raised his wineglass. "I want something on the record, though . . . I love little girls and the way they grow up."

"I think you're changing the subject."

"Yes. I'm remembering that I met you on a bridge in the rain in Venice, and as soon as I saw you . . ."

"Now, now."

"Oh, no. *Yes.* I knew . . . at the very least, I was going to speak to you. Because if you hadn't, I would have."

"I looked like a drowned rat."

"You looked lovely and lost and . . . found."

"Now you're being Italian."

"Yes."

Afterwards, they walked.

It is, after all, what you do in Venice.

The night was mild, they walked in silence, and Deb had no idea where they were going; she didn't care. Giacomo, too, seemed quietly happy beside her. At a certain point, she slipped her arm in his, realizing as she did so that she'd never before taken any man's arm except her father's. But it was so easy, so natural: like everything else since she'd met him. She glanced up at him, *a tall young man*. But he was actually twenty-nine, four years older than she was, and serious and knowledgeable and doing things in the world—*a tall man*, then. She began to compare him to other men, the other men she'd known, but almost immediately found the idea absurd, irrelevant. No; there was no point comparing him to anyone. She sneaked glances at him. He was good-looking, she thought. But what did that mean? Why did she like his face, so full of planes, his features so strongly etched—maybe another woman would find there a hint of cruelty. A strong face. But strength could be . . . so many things. Strength could be reassuring. Strength could be cruel. Strength could be careless. Strength could be . . . They walked along beside a canal, and for an instant, in the lights of a house, his shadow stretched gigantically. Who was he, *this tall man?* But it didn't make any difference because—this was undeniable—she felt tremendously excited, just to be there, beside him. She tightened her grip on his arm. And all at once realized where they were: ahead, on the water, an old mahogany launch softly shone in the shadows.

"This is where . . ."

"Yes."

The stone arch of a bridge was empty now; there was no one about—only the discreet, gentle witness of the boat. It was very quiet. The water lapped gently against the bridge. And then, from somewhere in this ancient, intricately connected little world, a small wave moved down the canal and slapped against the side of the launch, then slipped beneath them under the bridge. It passed on and the world fell quiet again. And finally, gently, he turned her toward him. She couldn't quite look at him, she didn't have the strength: and so, tenderly, his hands cupped her face and turned her lips up. And yet once her lips touched his, all shyness left her, and she moved into his arms. He kissed her fiercely. When he let her go, she leaned against him. He held her. He held her so tightly but gently, and gently, gently rocked her.

"Deborah," he said, "it's no use pretending . . ."

"No."

"We both know—?"

"Yes."

His lips found a funny little spot between her eye and her ear and he kissed her so tenderly—she could have slept, she felt so at peace.

He eased her back, and smiled. Well, what had to come next? But now she took his face in his hands, looking into his eyes.

She whispered, "I told you . . . I was a gambler."

"Yes."

"But most of time, you know, I don't . . . I don't buy, I don't sell. I never *hedge*—I hate that. It's not my style. I just don't do anything. Not until I'm sure. Then I make my bet."

"Yes," he said, "you have to be absolutely sure."

"Not absolutely, you can't be . . . just as sure as you can be. And when you are, that's—"

"Deb, you have to be sure. In a way, for both of us."

"Yes."

So he kissed her again, but then slipped his arm around her and walked her away, through the narrow *calles* and across the dark *piazzi*, until they reached her hotel. There, almost chastely, he kissed her good night—and so it wasn't till the next day that they actually made love. But even that, in the end, was easy. Deb was sure. Before she fell asleep that night, she was as sure as she could be. When he called in the morning, she was ready, all settled in her mind. She met him in her usual café and then they walked along the Grand Canal. It was a beautiful day. The water sparkled. Taking her hand, Giacomo said, "You can see it from my room— the sun comes streaming in through the shutters."

She said, "I want to see."

So he showed her. And it was as beautiful as he said. The light fell across the bed in golden streaks. He cupped her breast so the sunshine kissed her nipple and then he kissed it. Gently, she kissed his neck. He stroked her hip, and the hairs along his thigh were all coppery in the sun . . . There was just a little awkwardness about the condom. "You should—"

"Of course."

"I'm sorry—"

"No. It's okay."

"It's not—you know. It's just . . . my doctor says . . . I'm a hormonal conundrum."

He traced a finger down between her breasts, and smiled. "Professionally—did your doctor actually say 'conundrum'?"

"Don't laugh. Her name is Nancy Liu. She's Chinese and sometimes she doesn't quite—"

"So you should be on the pill . . ."

"She's tried a dozen combinations. With the last one, I got headaches . . . so I'm not using—"

He kissed her then. He kissed her quiet. He kissed her till her head was swimming. And then he slipped inside her. In the end, it was all very easy.

For three days and two nights, they made love and talked, and talked and made love, and sometimes ate, and for a few weird hours—emerging, blinking like owls in the sun—they even walked around the city. On the second day, he told her that he loved her, and she said that she loved him. He was the second man she'd used this word with; the first had been a great mistake—this, she knew, was right. The whole thing felt right. They went from mystery to intimacy, and back to mystery again . . . and all they wanted to do was explore some more.

By the time he left for Hong Kong, a great deal was settled.

By the time Deb left for home, she knew her life had changed, *would* change, in a hundred ways. She even expected to be surprised. But she didn't expect—no; she truly didn't . . .

TORONTO

CHAPTER ONE

"*D**o you have the* tickets?" Deb asked.

"Jesus," said Rosie, trying to catch her breath—and whispering in her most conspiratorial fashion—"you're right. I'd forget my boobs if I wasn't wearing a bra."

Somehow, without strangling herself, she managed to get her enormous shoulder bag over her neck, and started to rummage.

They were in Mustachio's, on Queen Street; the idea was a drink—which Rosie would need, since she'd overnighted with her mother—and maybe lunch. Then they were going to a matinee at the O'Keefe or the Hummingbird—whatever they called it now: *Something Something* followed by the inevitable *!!!!*

Diving into her raincoat pocket, Rosie finally emerged with the tickets, along with a crumpled wad of Kleenex, thirty-seven cents and half a roll of Tums. "Thank God," she said. She grabbed a waiter and ordered a vodka and cranberry juice.

Deb, who'd arrived first, was already equipped with a Bloody Mary. She took a sip and asked, "How's Greta?"

Rosie made a face—as usual, at any reference to her mother. "I tell you, Deb, I swear I'll never get over her. When she gave me the tickets, she said, 'I'm sure you'll find some nice young man to take you.' Can you believe it?"

"I'm not sure. Sometimes I wonder whether Greta really exists. Maybe she's an urban myth, like alligators breeding in the sewer pipes."

"Exactly!"

Rosie grinned; it was just the sort of thing *she* might have said. Then the waiter came with her drink. She tasted it, then nodded at Deborah's blouse. "I like that, by the way."

"I wasn't sure. What do you wear to a matinee?" But her linen blouse seemed to work with her soft, grey, corduroy trousers.

"Of course," said Rosie, "you have a neck. On me, a collar is like some sort of surgical appliance."

Deb gave her a look. With Rosie, all you did was set up her punch lines, and sometimes it bothered Deb, the way Rosie put herself down. All the same, it was true—she was better looking. And sometimes it made her a little uncomfortable. Worse, she took her beauty for granted, she always had; it was wasted on her. And she definitely did have a long, graceful neck—and, just as definitely, long, graceful legs: the classic Nordic type, as Rosie liked to put it. If pressed, she could complain about her feet (squashed flat, she feared, by too much barefoot sailing) but what secretly bugged her was looking so totally innocent, like one of those hideously healthy girls in an ad for milk, cross-country skis over her shoulder, a moronic white moustache on her lips. To make it all the more aggravating, she had to admit that this image contained a certain amount of truth. The closest she'd ever come to anything kinky was a tomboy streak, whose last expression, a big black motorcycle, still languished at the back of her parents' garage—and even then it was a Kawasaki, not a Harley, so how kinky could that be?

Admittedly, there were advantages to her sort of look. For example, people told her things—she'd certainly made a lot of money buying Harley Davidson *stock*. And, checking out her freckles, they didn't expect certain other things—like the ability to do net present value equations in her head, or the knowledgeable enjoyment of single malt Scotch. But of course that was the greatest pleasure of innocence, the ability to shock. In any case, at that particular moment, she didn't feel innocent at all. Taking a breath, she was suddenly very aware of her breasts inside her bra—they were *very* tender—and unconsciously slumped her back. "Anyway," she said, looking down at the blouse and making a face of her own, "I thought this would be okay—my mother gave it to me for Christmas."

Rosie put down her vodka. "Excellent. I think you've struck the perfect note for our cultural afternoon. You want to look like an aunt—"

"—or maybe you're taking a young cousin out to the movies—"

"—your cousin from God knows where. Winnipeg."

"No. Moose Jaw. That is where the truly classic Canadian cousin originates."

"Jesus," said Rosie, "can you imagine the sort of man who actually *would* take you to a matinee?"

Deb couldn't, and admitted as much—then added, "And I don't really think your mother—"

"Oh, you'd better believe it. This was to be a very hot date. And remember, every time I go out on a date, she figures I should A, fall in love with the guy; B, marry him; and C, have her grandchildren with him. C, of course, is what it's really all about."

Deb was about to speak, but then stopped herself. Rosie could make a joke out of anything; but perhaps, in her own particular situation—assuming it *was* her situation—this wasn't a subject to joke about. Still—did her mother want her to have children? *Expect* her to? She couldn't remember them ever talking about it. Did she want them herself? In the last twenty-four hours, these had all become very interesting questions. And she realized that she'd never thought about any of them before, not really. Maybe, until it actually happened, you *couldn't*. Finally she said, "You don't honestly think that's why she got married—Greta, I mean—why she married your father? Just to have children?"

Rosie took a sip of her drink, then put it down slowly. "Well, it's not easy to get my mind around that, I mean imagining Greta seeing Sydney as a stud. But I expect that's about it. Once I came along, I'd say Sydney's role was pretty much exhausted, outside of the old paycheque, and certain ceremonial occasions." Rosie screwed up her face, being Greta again. "'My dear, I want you to know that every night on our wedding anniversary, your father takes me in his arms.' Ugh!"

"But that's not why *you'd* marry? Just to have children?"

"You're being serious, aren't you?"

"It *is* possible, Rosie."

"Well, I don't know. Actually, I don't mind children, it's the baby part I have trouble with. But it's as good a reason as any. Why does anyone get married? Sex? Give me a break. Shared interests. Jesus! Companionship—sharing our Able Walkers, as we clump around the Seniors' Home? Love? Okay, I still believe, and maybe with the one-hundred-per-cent right guy—but anyway, in my case this is all theoretical. What about you? Why would you marry?"

Rosie, as she said this, leaned across the table—her eyes, her whole expression, even the glass in her hand, positively inquisitorial. Deborah knew she was really asking, Are you going to marry Giacomo? And that, come to think of it, was another interesting question. It was almost a year since Venice—was she? But Deb just smiled; if you were going to be Rosie's friend, you had to learn to keep her in line and this seemed a definite opportunity. Leaning forward herself, she whispered, "Rosie, I want to tell you something, but you can't tell anyone else."

"Yeah. What?"

"Okay. You remember, back in the winter, that time I got sick?"

"Bronchitis, wasn't it?"

Deb nodded. "And of course you know that Giacomo—he doesn't practise—but he is a doctor?"

"Yeah."

"So he gave me a prescription, for some antibiotics. Pills. But he thought, to get it started, I needed a shot and guess where he gave me the shots?"

"Deb, I don't believe this!"

"Rosie, I can't tell you what it was like. There I was, draped over his lap. Very gently he took down my panties and—"

Rosie's eyes widened—but then, seeing the look on Deb's face, she caught herself. "Okay. I deserve that—you're telling me to mind my own business."

"No. I was just *not* resisting temptation. But since you brought up the subject, tell me—what happened last night?"

"What do you mean?"

"You know perfectly well what I mean. I mean *Ronald.*"

Rosie made a face. "Ron-*ald.* My trouble is, I can never find a guy who lives up to my fantasies, who even comes close. I mean, just when you start to think he's perfect, he rolls over, and there it is, a pimple on his ass."

"You don't mean you actually did it with him?"

"Good God no. His face, after a couple of drinks, reminds you of one of those early Technicolor movies, the kind that comes on at three in the morning when you can't sleep and it's too late to phone anyone and you've run out—"

"Of course," said Deborah, interrupting, "maybe you should have slept with him. Why not? Why can't he just be, you know, a fuck? Why does he have to be a *fantasy* fuck? Why can't he just be," Deborah smiled mischievously, "Ronald."

"Jesus! Give me a break! Why couldn't he be Brad Pitt or Keanu Reeves or that Ian whatever his name is on the CBC or—I don't know—even that smarmy little guy who does the weather on CNN, I don't know why but I've always found him—"

"Ugh! He's a fantasy?"

"Listen to her! Who does she meet? I mean, talk about fantasies—the ultimate F word! He's tall, he's dark, he's handsome and he's even called Giacomo! And she meets him in Venice, no less. On a little bridge, no less. On a little bridge in the moonlight. My God, he's even a doctor," Rosie dropped her voice to a whisper "who gives you shots in the bum. Come on! If you were a nurse, it would be a perfect Harlequin romance." She leaned back and then added: "I'm definitely not buying any of the publishers, by the way. Newsprint prices have nowhere to go but *up.*"

Deb smiled. Rosie was a broker, too. Torstar, the company that published Harlequin paperbacks, had flashed though her mind as well. But now her smiled faded. "I told you, Rosie. Venice wasn't like that. Not exactly."

"Not exactly. *Right*. Most of us, dear girl, would settle for roughly. Approximately. *In the neighbourhood*."

Deb was about to say something, but then stopped herself. For three days, she'd been *not* thinking; now, all at once, she was. "Rosie," she said, "you know how, sometimes, the only way you can make something real is to tell someone else?"

"Of course." Rosie leaned forward. "What do you mean?"

Deb gave a little shrug. "Just that—to tell you the truth—I'm having a little crisis as far as all that's concerned."

"You mean—Giacomo? Jesus, Deb, you can't blow this—"

"It's nothing like that." All at once, now it *was* real, she felt panicky. A weird feeling passed over her. Two tables away, a man was leaning down, digging his *Star* out of a plastic bag; a Chinese woman, pushing a baby in a stroller, was passing behind them, out of her sight and then back into it again and then gone again . . . And she was conscious how separate these people were, how separate from each other and herself. Her life was absolutely separate from every other life. She leaned forward and whispered, "Rosie, I'm not kidding this time. This is something I really would like to keep private."

"Who am I going to tell—my mother? Tell what?"

"I think I'm pregnant."

Rosie leaned back. "Oh, dear."

Deb felt a rush of relief and smiled. "Is that what Greta would say?"

But now Rosie was serious. "You're sure?"

Deb shook her head. "No, but a couple of days ago, when I woke up, my breasts felt tender—and they're still tender."

Rosie, sitting back, looked skeptical. "You mean, you woke up and your boobs hurt?"

"Yes, Rosie, exactly. I woke up and my boobs hurt."

"Okay. Just a minute. It takes a moment to get your mind around this."

"You and your mind."

"Okay, but your boobs can feel tender for lots of reasons. PMS. Maybe you're *getting* your period."

"No ... Well, maybe. It just doesn't feel like that."

"Didn't you play squash on Thursday? Who's ever heard of a comfortable athletic bra? And you're big enough—"

"It just doesn't feel like that either."

"So maybe the last time you did it, before he went on this trip to South America, he was just a little teensy-weensy bit rough?"

Deb was amazed—at how much better she felt, now that she'd gotten it out. "Maybe," she thought out loud, "this is why people go on Oprah."

"What are you talking about?"

"Never mind. And no, he wasn't rough. He's never rough, Rosie. Just firm. *Very* firm."

"Firm. *Very* firm. My God, you can be cruel. And he left Wednesday and this is Sunday, so if he'd been that firm, you would have called the cops. So are you late? Except, with you, I suppose you're never sure."

"That's the trouble. I'm so irregular. Sometimes I swear I don't have them at all, and other times they never seem to stop. But I guess in the back of my mind I've been worried."

"If you're that irregular, for Christ's sake, you should be on the pill."

"I tried them—I don't know, they all do something to me. And I told you. My grandmother died of breast cancer. And my aunt— my mom's sister—she got it. I just don't want to take the chance."

"Yeah, I remember. So what have you been using?"

"Well, in the beginning, in Venice, we used condoms. Of course."

"But then you discovered that your wonderful Italian lover actually grew up in Scarborough—on top of everything else—and only lives two subway stops from your apartment—"

"Three, to be exact—"

"Which meant your meeting underneath the Adriatic moon was kismet. So when you got back here and your holiday romance blossomed into true romance, it became an issue. It. Them. Those things."

"Okay," said Deb, "but don't blame him. I mean, at first it was sort of fun, putting them on, but then . . . What the hell, Rosie, I like to feel it—don't you?"

"I know what you mean—at least I think I remember. And latex does have certain inevitable gynecological connotations."

"And we always used foam and the other things."

"Right. And now your boobs hurt. I suppose that's the trouble with foam—and the other things."

"I know. It's dumb. He made me get a diaphragm. The thing is, I hate—"

"Yeah, yeah, don't tell me what you hate, I hate them too. But—listen—are you upset? I mean really upset. Frightened?"

"No, I'm not frightened. But yes, I'm upset. I've had scares before—but not like this. I think this time . . . well, I think I am."

"Have you told him? I guess you haven't if he's in Brazil or wherever."

Deb shook her head. "You're the first to know."

"I think I'll take that as a compliment."

Deb reached out and touched her hand. "You should. I think I was waiting until I could tell you. So thanks . . ."

"Come on. What are friends for?"

"Okay. But I'm just glad you are."

For a moment, they were silent. They hadn't known each other that long, a little over two years—since Deb had first started at Orme Capital. They'd hit it off right away; partly it was the attraction of opposites, partly it was an office alliance, partly it was sharing a similar view of the world—but mostly it was a thousand things never put into words. And now, in fact, this little silence expressed their friendship best. Then Rosie said, "Okay, let's work it out . . . When does he get back from this South American jaunt?"

Deb could tick it off on her fingers. "There's the WHO conference in Mexico City—that's where he is now—and that ends the eighteenth. Two days in Costa Rica. Then a few days in Caracas. And then Brazil—at least a week—but the foundation is putting on the conference there, and he'll probably stay for an extra couple of days, maybe even another week, to help clean up—"

"So you're talking June," Rosie said, "before he gets back." She shook her head. "Too late. Or at least you don't want to leave it that long."

"I know."

"On the other hand, it's not the sort of thing you want to talk about on the phone—"

Deb smiled ruefully. "You're telling me. When he called today, I kept trying to work things around—"

"Deb—I think this is the sort of news you kind of just blurt out."

"Except I can't be completely sure. I think that stopped me. It could just be—"

"Okay," said Rosie, "we have to get that straight right away." She twisted around in her chair, and found her purse—but then she stopped. "Listen, I guess I've been assuming something."

"What?"

"Well, you know . . . that you don't want to have it."

Deb was quiet for a moment, and then she said, "I don't know." She shook her head. "I'm just not sure. I don't know how to put it, but it's not *automatic*. It can't be. At least not for me. Something's happened. I can't pretend it *hasn't*."

"My God. You're in love with this guy—now you're Having-His-Baby."

"Don't be an idiot, Rosie. Yes, I'm in love with him, but it's not like that. It's just . . . I'm not an automatic sort of person. I'm not going to do anything without thinking about it.

"Yeah," said Rosie, "I guess that's you all right. But look"—she leaned across the table—"tell a secret, hear a secret. I got pregnant once. I had an abortion. Maybe, when I'm a little old lady, I'll weep and moan and make a mess in my Pampers about it, but right now I'd say it was one of the smarter things I've done in my life." She cocked her head, thinking for a second: "Understand, I'm not trying to persuade you, just telling you."

Deb smiled—she was, now, feeling a whole lot better. "It's funny," she said. "When I woke up this morning, I remembered something I hadn't thought about in years. I was lying there and my breasts hurt, and I was thinking *Oh no!* And then I

remembered the way my mother used to call me Thomasina—
which always infuriated me, it seemed like such a dumb name—"

"Because you were a tomgirl. Or boy. I'm never sure which."

"Yes. And I was. But even afterwards, it stuck in my mind, the
name, I mean—it became my secret name for myself. Whenever I
had to psych myself up, that's what I'd say. 'Thomasina, you can
do it.' The first time I had to climb up a mast—"

"You climb up masts?"

"Of course. You have to, if you sail. Or you haul yourself up—"

"And you're worried about being pregnant? I don't believe you."

"Come on, Rosie. This is a lot different, and you know it."

"Yeah. I guess it is. Anyway, so that's how you feel—like
Thomasina. Neat—a pregnant tomboy. The question is, what are
you working yourself up to? Having the baby, or an abortion?"

"You're going too fast. I'm just working myself up to being pregnant. I can't believe it. No. I *can*. Or in a funny way I can. All the
same . . ." But the trouble was, she thought, nothing could ever be
the same again. No matter what she did. A baby. One little baby. It
was so ordinary, really. How many women, today, had learned
that they were pregnant? It couldn't be more common. But so
exceptional. So little. But so much. She almost didn't hear as Rosie
rattled on:

"Well, that was the part I was trying to skip over, I admit, the
being pregnant part. But okay. And I know what you mean. The
worst of it is, you're not sure what you feel."

"Exactly," said Deb. "You're supposed to feel so much—"

"Like one of those soft-focus ads. Kodak memories. Getting
closer with AT&T—and that's another one I'd leave alone, let me
tell you. Although I suppose it's pretty hard to short the old
miracle of life."

"Something like that."

"On the other hand, your boobs hurt and you're sick to your
stomach."

"Well, I haven't felt sick."

"*Yet.*"

"No. Really. I mean, I'm still not sure. Maybe I'm getting all worked up about nothing."

"Right, dear girl, that's just what I was doing..."

Rosie, reminded, now opened her purse, and burrowed, eventually producing one of those small plasticized calendars given out by the banks—in this case, the Royal Bank of Canada—ostensibly to mark holidays and paydays, but which are really used by millions of women to keep track of their periods. Rosie's starting days were circled neatly in ballpoint pen. For her part, Deb had given up keeping this sort of record years ago. She was too irregular—it was, she sometimes thought, one of the three things she had in common with her mother, and she usually couldn't remember what the other two were.

Rosie said, "So when do you think..." Deb had gone through it a dozen times, but once more wouldn't hurt. Not that it made any difference. Not now. She wasn't sure. She couldn't be positive—but she *knew* just the same.

CHAPTER TWO

A*ccording to the New York* police, Curtis Price placed his first call to Deborah Graham's office at 10:58, but he was "call forwarded" to the receptionist and Deborah didn't speak to him. As she later explained, she'd been "away from my desk." In fact, she was in the washroom—being sick.

This was a relief—almost; by that point, she'd already suffered through two false alarms.

The first had come early, just as she was riding up in the elevator, a slow, uneasy tilting of her stomach that rapidly became an oily sloshing at the back of her throat. She made it to her desk, but then discreetly fled downstairs, as if to get something from the library. But nothing happened. She felt better as soon as she got into the washroom. She waited five minutes and then went back upstairs.

And yet, as she set to work, she had the feeling that every move she made was slightly tentative. It was as though she was going around with a platter balanced on top of her head. And just after ten, it began to slide off. She'd made a few calls, actually sold two hundred shares of Intel—a reward for patience; she'd been working on Mrs. Oliver for almost a month—but all at once the chatter around her sounded funny and far away, and she was suddenly aware, looking out the window, that she was forty floors up.

She leaned back.

Swallowed.

Rosie—their desks were pushed together—sensed something was wrong and peered around her terminal. "Deb?"

Deb shook her head and whispered: "If this is morning sickness, I can understand why the pill is so popular."

"Oh, Jesus."

Deb got up.

Rosie got up.

Deb said, "*Don't.*" She grabbed up some papers from her desk—camouflage—and headed down the hall.

But, again, nothing happened.

When she got back, Rosie came around and leaned over her shoulder. "Are you okay?"

Deb nodded. "False alarm."

"You're not kidding? You really felt—?"

"Yes. I really felt—"

"But you didn't actually—"

"No. I didn't *actually*—"

"Thank God. I think it's too early."

Deb made a face. "That's a great comfort." But then she managed a smile. "I feel so self-conscious. Go back to your desk. Everyone's watching."

"No one's watching. You're just feeling guilty. Remember, you're a WASP."

"I am not. Or at least—"

"Come on. You were a bad girl and now—"

"Shut up."

"Look, it's the price you have to pay for all that elegance. And it couldn't be more traditional. I mean, falling for a tall, dark, handsome *Latin*—"

"Rosie, you shouldn't read so many books."

Of course she didn't really believe she was a WASP—but it was probably there, working away. If you were pregnant, it certainly proved *one thing*. But she smiled to herself. *You enjoyed every minute of . . . Him . . .* She thought about Giacomo. A good man was hard to find, but she'd done it. He was intelligent, he knew what he wanted to do with his life, he was good-looking, he was funny, he was—well, what more did she want? She tried to think of that— to remember, really, that she was happy. And who cared anyway? She looked around her—thirty or forty desks, a hundred terminals tilted and swivelled to every imaginable angle, somebody yelling about the bank rate . . . Bob Davis, across the room, leaned back in his chair and yawned. Deborah Graham, Deb thought, was the last thing on his mind. "Would he really think anything of it?"

"What?"

Deb hadn't realized she'd spoken out loud. "Never mind."

"Okay, in your state you're allowed to be a little crazy. But look . . ." Rosie leaned forward. "You've got to—"

"I know. Don't worry. At lunchtime, when I go feed Henry, I'll stop off at a drugstore." Henry, Giacomo's cat, was in her charge while he was gone.

"Okay. And the next time Giacomo calls—"

"Don't worry. I'll tell him."

"Promise?"

"Yes, Greta, I promise."

"I probably deserve that, but don't forget anyway." And then, mollified, Rosie peered more closely at Deb's terminal, reading the stocks she had up on the screen. "TMX, ESO, YPF, TPL . . . How romantic! All South American ADRS—you're following Giacomo's trip, aren't you?" She read down to the end of the list. "BLX?"

"It's a Banco something or other in Brazil. Remember? Rio's his last stop."

As she said this, her screen saver came on; Homer Simpson began gobbling up the screen, barfing bits of it out—proof that no one had touched the keyboard in the last five minutes.

Rosie said, "That's truly disgusting."

"It's even worse with the sound." And though Deb was feeling better now, she didn't feel like listening to Homer barf. She touched a key and disappeared him—and then Deb's phone began ringing, so they both got to work.

For the next forty minutes or so, Deb felt pretty much back to normal.

Then, around ten to eleven, she noticed Terry Dillon, their gold analyst, go into his office, and she went off to speak to him. One of her clients had asked her if it would be a good idea to switch out of Barrick, the big gold producer, into Franco-Nevada, a company with a royalty interest in the Barrick mine. Deb followed Terry down the hall—he had a meeting in the conference room—listening to his answer, and right there, in mid-sentence, in mid-stride, it hit her again. Her insides rolled over. And Terry's voice sounded very, somehow, *removed.* "I wouldn't think, given the transactions costs, there'd be much point, but of course either way..." She tried to swallow; her mouth kept filling with saliva. Terry kept on. She felt almost dizzy. "The point is, if you want exposure to gold, you want that mine as..." It was terrible, because she liked Terry, and he was trying to be helpful, but it was like being stuck with a horrible bore at a party. She thought she was going to die. "I mean, it's one helluva mine. I went out there, you know..." She knew, if she didn't get away—"It was fun, actually, gave me the illusion I was still an engineer. Besides..." God knows what she said. It was actually possible that she said something like, "This is terrible but I've just got to pee." And she almost ran... in fact, once around the corner, she *did* run, and when she reached the washroom she shouldered through the door like a halfback going through the line. *Pray God there's nobody in here.* There wasn't. She was gasping. She really felt sick. Looking at the line of sinks, she decided that they were definitely half measures, and went straight into one of the stalls, pushed up the seat and got down on her knees. And of course, for a moment then, she felt better. She caught her breath. She felt relieved. Because... because, after all, this was the ladies' room. She didn't want anyone to come in, but if anyone did come in, at least they'd help—they wouldn't...

Oh God.

She half-heaved. But not quite. And then, horribly, someone did

come in. And to make it worse, she knew—that *strut* of her heels—
that it had to be Alice Berman from reception, which was
grotesque. This was the main ladies' washroom on this floor. Last
year, in a fit of corporate anxiety about Women's Issues, the place
had been enlarged—more stalls, wider counters around the sinks
so there was enough room to lay out your makeup—and these ren-
ovations had fatally changed the room's acoustics, so that privacy
was now the one thing it didn't offer. Every whisper carried. Not to
mention other sounds. So Deb couldn't help but follow Alice's
every move as she went into the last stall, tinkled—her word, and
it was perfect, because everything about Alice tinkled, including
those platinum blonde hair inserts she wore—and then popped the
button off her skirt— "Sugar! Oh, sugar!"—while Deborah waited,
frozen on her knees, a laugh almost strangling her despite everything because she could just imagine Alice in this same position,
the incredible ties and bows that always festooned her blouses
dangling above the bowl. *Thank God for small mercies . . .* and the
relative simplicity of DKNY. But finally Alice left. And then there
was a long, awful silence. She tried to think, but can you actually
think in those moments just before you're going to be sick? A pregnant tomboy. She remembered Rosie saying that. What a predica-
ment. But then she was always getting herself into predicaments.
Right. God, this was awful. Of course, *now,* she could hear her
mother's voice. Predicaments! She remembered the summer she'd
tried out for Little League. Only three years later, no one would
have thought anything of it; but she'd made the TV news—she'd
felt like such an idiot . . . She closed her eyes. She could feel it start,
she leaned forward, but then . . . Oh God, oh God ohgod. It slipped
back. She swallowed. What am I doing here? How do I get myself
into these things? She remembered a party, more or less her first
party—as in date—and how awkward she'd felt, how positively stupid . . . *Well you're here now, you might as well make the best of it.*
That's what she'd thought then, that's what she thought now.
Right. Make the best of it. Really? She felt ghastly. She stared at the
handle of the toilet, slightly shiny with damp, the words "Crane
Limited" pressed into the metal. She tried to think. Could you buy

their stock? Yes, of course you could, CR on New York. They did millwork. Was that what you called it? Even defence stuff. Valves. Oh God . . . *Pipes* . . . And then it wasn't funny, it wasn't even embarrassing, and her only thought was making sure that *absolutely everything* went straight into the bowl . . .

When it was over, she felt better.

Somehow, everything did get into the bowl. When she flushed, it all went down. And she had that wonderful marvellous incredible feeling of *not being sick*.

Thank God!

And then, as she rinsed her mouth and dabbed her face at the sink, she felt all sorts of things, all at once.

Relief, because now she *knew*. Shock—because she couldn't *believe* it. And then excitement, because, believe it or not, she *felt* it. Pregnant, that is. She made herself think it: *Deb, you're pregnant*. And it was extraordinary; she could feel, despite everything—did she have a Certs?— that somewhere, deep inside, she was happy. She could see it on her face, in the mirror. She thought of Giacomo . . . and she longed to tell him.

But then, as she went back to her desk, Deb realized she didn't want to tell anyone else. She wouldn't have known how; she wouldn't have known the right words, the right tone of voice. However it came out, she would have been expressing someone else's feelings, not her own. An excited whisper: *Guess what? I'm pregnant!* A sort of Oh-My-God tone: *You're not going to believe this, but I'm p-r-e-g-n-a-n-t.* Or a nice domestic *I've got a bun in the oven*. Or . . . But it didn't make any difference. Right now, she didn't know what she felt, and anything she said would have been false; she needed time to get used to it. Which made her feel badly, however, almost selfish, when Rosie looked up, a hint of enquiry in her expression; she would have loved to know. But Deb just smiled—not exactly a lie—and then got back to work, pretending that nothing had happened.

But then something *did* happen.

Price called again—at 11:32.

It was on her direct line, and she knew immediately who it was;

Price had a very American voice, low, sincere and confidential, like a man on television. "Hello, Deborah, what news of the Rialto?" And that was typical, never just "hello." That was part of the trouble with Price; everything was always a bit too complicated. But of course she managed to be friendly. Already, his account was flickering into life on her screen. Cash: USD 2,642,894.21. The trouble was... but for months she'd never quite been able to put her finger on it. And despite herself, she always seemed to play along.

"Mr. Price, if you go buying Italian stocks, you do it on your own hook."

He chuckled; he liked it that she'd picked up so fast. "I called earlier, but you weren't around."

"I'm sorry, I didn't get a message."

"That's fine, I didn't leave one. I was just thinking, though, we haven't done much business lately, and there was a little company I was interested in. It's called Xynex. To rhyme with Nynex. Symbol X-Y-N-X..."

It would be the Nasdaq, thought Deborah. She mildly resented Nasdaq, still the Wild West of U.S. stock exchanges—though, if you were politically correct, it certainly proved that scalping was the white man's invention. But she called it up on her terminal. "The last trade was five and a half," she read off, "it's bid at a quarter—a thousand shares wanted. The high was five eights. It's only done eighteen thousand shares."

"It's not very liquid, I know. And I want a lot."

"I really don't know anything about them."

"No reason you should. They came public about three years ago, at twelve, had a run, then headed south."

"To five dollars... You're not kidding."

"Well, it happens. They're one of those little biotech outfits. Cures for cancer, test kits for AIDS, the usual things. But they actually make money out of vaccines, or at least they did. They have some kind of proprietary process—they can do generic things cheap." Then Curtis Price laughed, a nice, soft, easy laugh. "Of course, Deborah, you understand, when it comes to science, I don't have the faintest idea what I'm talking about."

Deb was smiling—despite herself. He was always so very smooth. At their one and only meeting, about a year ago, that's how he'd struck her: very, very smooth. She'd guessed he was close to sixty, but he seemed younger—well over six feet tall and slim, with full, dark hair—he probably coloured it. But it looked good—*he* looked good. He looked like a healthy, rich American who could afford to spend a lot of time in the sun. He had a quick, crinkly smile and behind his heavy, black-rimmed glasses his eyes had been bright and friendly, curious. He'd made a good impression—anyone who gives you a cheque for half a million American dollars creates a good impression—but ever since, Deb thought, she'd been trying to shake that impression off. Now, realizing she was smiling, she made herself stop. Every time she'd spoken to him, it was the same; she'd felt conned. And today it was worse. But she kept her voice even: "I'm sure you know exactly what you're talking about, Mr. Price."

"Flattery will get you everywhere, Deborah. But this whole idea made me think of you because it started out with a sailboat. I gather . . . I saw Walter about six weeks back—you didn't make it south this year?"

At the mention of Walter Manley's name, his voice shifted slightly, took on a quietly confidential tone. He was so seductive; he always knew how to talk to you. But of course it worked and she said, "You're right, I didn't make it to Florida, but last fall me and my dad and a couple of his friends took a Swan 41 down to the Virgin Islands."

"My, my, so you're a real blue-water gal."

Deb thought: "*Woman.*" But as soon as she thought it, she scolded herself; it was a dumb thing to think. But somehow Price brought it out in her. Price went on: "Anyway, you'll appreciate this. This past summer I was down in the Carolinas, just sailing around, and one evening I spotted an interesting boat in a marina, something called a Krogen 38."

Again, despite herself—she *did* love boats—Deb said, "This is a trawler?"

"No—a thirty-eight-foot sailboat, a cutter. But you're right, it's the same company that makes the trawlers—I suppose this is the only sailboat they ever did make. You don't see many of them, and I wouldn't say I like them, but they're interesting. A raised deck design, but better looking than you'd think. I was curious, and of course as I was looking at it, the owner came up on deck and invited me aboard for a drink—you know how that works. His name was Peterson. A geneticist. In fact the chief scientist at a company called Xynex Inc. Just in passing, he told me a little about them, and it was interesting enough that I checked them out later. But I didn't do anything—just filed it away. Then, in the fall, I ran into him again. This was Baltimore, at the boat show—again, just an accident. In any event, Peterson was there with a friend. We all had a drink. It was pretty clear that Peterson was un-happy—he did a lot of grumbling. He said he was going to quit the company, but as he talked, I decided they were actually pushing him out in favour of a younger guy. An Indian. Another geneticist named Nisram Singh."

"He told you all this?"

"Not quite. It wasn't that clear. I'm not even sure he mentioned Singh's name, but I've checked into it since and that has to be who he was talking about. Definitely a rising star. A very bright young man."

"So he has taken over—from Peterson?"

"That's the last part of the story, and what brought it all back. I was in Florida about six weeks ago—that's when I saw Walter—and I picked up a copy of *Soundings* and there was an article about Peterson's boat. Dreadful. The Coast Guard had found it, just drift-ing along in Florida Bay, no one on board . . . That's what the story was about, actually. Were the Coast Guard going to claim salvage? Poor Peterson's disaster was just worked in as an example."

"So Peterson drowned—?"

"Yes, I'm afraid so. They found his body later. He had a lot of alcohol in him, his fly was open . . . the usual story. He was being a gentleman over the taffrail, and went in."

Deb closed her eyes; that was the only fear she ever had sailing.

But having to sit down can sometimes be a great advantage. "God," she said—she couldn't help herself.

"I know. Clip on. Always—but especially when you're alone on the boat."

"Yes." But of course, thought Deb, she didn't.

"Anyway—I suppose it's a little morbid—but that started me thinking about Xynex again. I found out about Singh. And to be honest, I do know a little science, but more importantly, I know people who know a lot, and they say this man is something special. In a way, he's what I'm buying."

But why are you buying him through me?

Why are you buying an American biotech company through a Canadian brokerage house?

And why did you set it up with this kind of story?

That's what Deb thought. What she said was, "Interesting."

"I think so," Price replied. "So let's pick up two hundred thousand shares."

Two hundred thousand . . .

For an instant, Deb's mind went blank, as though the infamous Microsoft hourglass was spinning inside her brain. But then it chugged out the numbers, the commission on a million plus bucks. *Six grand, gross.* Just for answering the phone . . . She took a breath. "That large an order will be more than enough to move the market, Mr. Price."

"Well, what are trading desks for?"

Yes, he was playing her; it must have seemed so easy. *Such a sweet young innocent gal . . .* "Maybe we should spread it over a couple of days."

"Okay." *And because he's a friend of Walter Manley, your dad's old pal,* ". . . and give them a quarter point discretion."

"All right, Mr. Price."

"Good. And look, Deborah . . . I know we don't have the chance to meet often, face to face, but why don't we drop the Mr. Price? I'm Curtis."

That's it. What's a little deal between friends?

And then Deb took a breath and closed her eyes. "Mr. Price, there's something I have to ask you. Are you proposing this transaction on the basis of any information you've received from an officer or director of the company, or anyone beneficially owning ten per cent or more of the company and required to file reports of their share dealings in the company with the United States Securities and Exchange Commission?"

There was a moment's silence. Then Curtis Price said: "No." And then his voice deepened, and took on a particularly confidential tone. "This is not an insider transaction, Deborah. But don't worry, I understand why you felt you had to ask. I'm not embarrassed—and I hope you're not, either."

"Thank you, Mr. Price."

"'Curtis'?" he prompted.

"Curtis."

"Great. You get to work then, and give me a call when you get a fill—even a partial."

Curtis . . .

After she hung up, Deb leaned back in her chair—and realized she was absolutely furious. My God, she'd actually called him on it. She counted ten. But being angry wasn't important, she told herself. Had she done the right thing? Was it, she wondered, even reasonable that she should have a suspicion? It was a good question; because, when you got right down to it, she'd acted on instinct more than anything else. It had all felt wrong. Why? And as she sat there, puzzling it out, she was no more pregnant than Sylvester Stallone. It had felt wrong because of the pattern . . . the whole way the relationship had developed between them; but also because he'd told her so much, brought her into it, made her part of it. And then she realized that this was a turning point.

Or at least it could be.

Curtis Price wasn't buying big chunks of an obscure little company because he thought their stock would go *down*; no, he knew something, no matter what he said. And all she had to do was keep quiet . . . she could even, if she wanted, slip in a little order for her own account, nothing big, just a few thousand shares . . . and the profits would probably pay for . . . what? A trip to Europe, say. In the fall, Giacomo had a conference in Paris; she could quietly tag along . . . It would all be so easy: but she also knew, in the bottom of her heart, that she wasn't even tempted. And even if she had been tempted, was she going to let a man like Curtis Price use her like this? The answer was no. He was playing her for a fool; all along, he'd flattered her and condescended to her, but what it added up to, subtly, was bullying. And she didn't like being taken for a fool and she hated bullies. The trouble was it had worked a little. Which made her even more irritated. It wasn't the money, the commission, but the sheer size of the deal. For a broker of her age and experience, Deborah actually had some very big accounts; her father now taught at RMC—the Royal Military College in Kingston—but he'd started out in Calgary and Dallas in the oil and gas industry and some of his old friends, now pretty wealthy, had come to Deb as clients. Moreover, their accounts were the simplest she had; they knew what they were doing, knew what they wanted—she almost never had to make any hard decisions. Not like this, certainly. But to hell with Curtis Price, she thought. Swivelling her terminal out of the way, she whispered to Rosie: "What do you think of André Tellier?"

Rosie raised her eyebrows, "You serious?"

Deb nodded. "Remember that funny client I told you about? Mr. Smoothy? He just called. And I think something funny's going on."

André Tellier was Orme Capital's compliance officer: a polite term for cop. It was his job to make sure that both the firm and its brokers complied with the maze of laws and regulations laid down by half a dozen jurisdictions—Canada, the United States, the province of Ontario, the state of New York . . . even, at least as a formality, the Vancouver Stock Exchange. It would have been wrong to describe him as the most unpopular man in the firm— but, one way or another, he meant trouble.

Rosie shrugged. "I don't know him any better than you do, I guess. He seems okay. But I've just seen him at meetings, and of course I've suffered through the usual heart-to-heart. Someone told me they really want him on the bond side, but they're waiting for Warren Matthews to retire."

Deb honestly didn't know any more. But she looked down at her desk—at the "ticket" she'd have to fill out for Price's order. And the only choice was to fill it out now or see Tellier.

Five minutes later, after a phone call, she was in his office.

He was about thirty-five, tall and good-looking. As she'd come through the door, he'd slipped into his jacket—an acknowledgement that they barely knew each other. But he had a friendly smile that seemed to invite her to break down his formality; and either because of that, or just because she was so irritated, she said right off the bat:

"André, I want to cover my ass."

He smiled, and leaned back in his chair. "I'm not sure, in these politically correct times, that I could even acknowledge offering such a service, let alone actually supplying it."

Deb laughed—and felt a lot better at once. "I'm sorry—"

"No, no. That's what I'm here for, but . . . Perhaps we should use the other language? *Vous voulez protéger vos arrières.*"

"Not *derrière*?"

"Absolutely not. I assure you, Deborah. This is an expression you can use in the most polite company."

"All right. *Je veux protéger mes arrières.*"

"Very good. You see? You even have a nice accent."

"Thank you."

"Okay. So . . . what do you need protecting from?"

"I've got an American client."

Tellier tilted his head a little to one side. "Always an issue."

Though NAFTA was eventually supposed to deal with the problem, it remained technically true that Canadian brokers were not supposed to have American clients and were absolutely forbidden to solicit them. Of course, this was more honoured in the breach than the observance, but it was one way to lose your licence. And Orme was fairly strict about it. They did a big institutional business in "Yankee" bonds—bonds issued in American dollars by

Canadian governments and corporations that were traded in Toronto and New York—and so they tried to keep on the good side of the U.S. Securities and Exchange Commission.

"Don't worry. I played by the rules. I didn't solicit him."

"Filled in all the forms, ticked all the boxes?"

"Yes."

"Passport number? Social security number?"

"Everything. Here's his file."

Tellier flipped it open, but only glanced at it. "Curtis Price," he said. "Long Island."

"Yes."

"Okay. And if you didn't solicit Mr. Price, how did he come to be your client?"

"Through Walter Manley, another client. Walter's Canadian—an old friend of my father's—but he spends the winters in Florida, and Price is an acquaintance of his. They both like sailing, boats. Walter apparently told Price that if he ever wanted to invest in Canada, he should come to me."

"You checked this?"

"Yes. That's the way it happened. Price called me about a year ago, in June, said he was going to be in Toronto, and could he come and see me. We had lunch, then he came back here—actually that's the only time I've ever met him. We did the paperwork and he gave me a cheque for half a million U.S. dollars."

Tellier pushed the file to one side and nodded. "Always interesting, half a million American dollars."

"Yes. And he sent me another cheque—the same amount—about three months later. Trading, he's more than doubled what he put in. And he's never taken anything out."

"Really? I'm not sure I like that. Do you have any idea where his money comes from?"

"I don't think that's the problem—it's not drugs, or anything. Walter told me that Price's father owned a string of service stations in St. Louis or someplace, and he's been successful in business on his own account, financing things—start-ups, private companies, high-tech stuff. He's not a young man—he's probably in his early sixties. He *looks* perfectly respectable. I don't think he's laundering money or anything like that."

"Okay, so what is he doing?"

"Well, you ask yourself—why do Americans set up accounts with Canadian brokerages? So they can buy the golds, junior oils, paper companies—"

"Our wonderful rocks and trees."

"Yes. But Price has never done that. He's only been interested in American stocks that trade on the American exchanges."

"*Definitely*, I don't like that." Tellier pursed his lips. "And what happens to these stocks? I suppose they go up?"

"Always."

"Ah, well. Stocks that always go up . . . I can't imagine anything more suspicious, can you?"

Deb smiled. Somehow, Tellier had made this easier than she'd expected. She said, "Except you keep thinking, maybe he's just lucky. Because it's never anything obvious. It's never a fast move. He never day trades, but just wait a couple of weeks, even a month, and something happens. A takeover, terrific earnings—something."

"Give me an example."

"Okay. He bought a big chunk of preferred stock in a steel company in Georgia, which I'd actually heard of, because there was a rumour that Laclede was going to buy them out and of course Laclede is owned by Ivaco, which we follow."

"Right."

"But there wasn't a buyout. Instead, the company restructured and redeemed the preferred. In five weeks, Price made three dollars in capital gains plus a seventy-five-cent final dividend payment . . . and out of a pretty conservative investment." Deb added: "It made me wonder, but somehow you don't think . . . I mean, preferred stock and insider trading don't usually go together . . . But it's happened so many time now . . ."

"Has there been anything obvious—regarding you, I mean? Nice cheques in the mail—I've been doing so well, I thought you deserved a little present . . . ?"

"No. That wouldn't be his style. He's *not* obvious."

"No invites to his condo in the Bahamas?"

"Nothing like that."

"Has he ever mentioned another brokerage house—somewhere else he's doing business?"

"No. But there must be something. I'm sure the account he has with me is peanuts. He treats it that way . . . like it was a joke, almost. That's how he talked today."

Tellier made a noncommittal shrug. "Well, after you called, I asked Tyler Deacon to find out what he could about . . . Xynex? That's the name of this new thing?"

"Yeah. I just—again, I can't really say anything's wrong—but this is a lot of money And I have a dreadful feeling that I'm being set up."

"Tell me about this other man, Walter Manley."

For a second, Deb didn't see what he was driving at. "What do you mean?"

"Well, has he held any of the same stocks—"

"No. That's not possible." But, as soon as she said this, she wanted to bite off her tongue. Of course it was possible: Price and Manley could well be working together. How naïve she was.

"If Manley's doing this with him, and he was smart," Tellier went on, "he'd use a different broker, but it's surprising how stupid people can be."

Deb couldn't help herself. It was dumb, but she said it anyway. "I can't believe Walter Manley would be involved in anything illegal. I told you, he's an old friend of my father's . . . he gave me one of my first accounts after I got my licence."

Tellier smiled. "Come on. Everyone who's involved in an insider-trading scheme is a good friend of somebody's father." But then, leaning back, he stretched his hands out flat over his desk and said, "Let's not argue, though. We'll see. But I'll want to check his accounts too—remember, everything started with him."

Deb hated this—but there was no way to argue. She was happy, a moment later, when Tyler Deacon came into the office. He was Orme Capital's biotech analyst. A couple of years younger than

Deb, he was still trying to fit into the corporate mould, and in his dark suit looked as though he was on his way to a high-school graduation. Deb liked him—though she would never have dreamed of buying a stock he recommended. He pushed hair out of his eyes, grinned eagerly at Tellier, and said, "Hi. We on to something hot?"

"No, no, Tyler, you have to tell us."

"Well, I wouldn't say it was Xynex Incorporated. I made a few calls but—"

"No rumours, little stories . . . ?"

"No, they won't start till tomorrow—then it'll be all over the street, how Orme Capital's underwriting a buyout of Xynex by anyone you care to name." He shrugged. "Seriously, I didn't find a thing, but you didn't give me much time and this isn't a stock I follow. They're a real company, though." He grinned. "I've even got a file." He held it up.

"Okay," said Tellier, "just a little."

Tyler Deacon flipped the file open and began scanning through it. "Incorporated Delaware, head office Boca Raton, also a lab there, a manufacturing facility in Daytona . . ." He looked up. "They have a vaccine business, mostly subcontracted stuff, but it gives them—least it used to—a certain amount of cash flow."

"Who owns them?"

He looked back at the file. "Institutional ownership is twenty-two per cent . . . I'd say that's low . . . The control block is held by Norman Danson, prez and CEO, and then smaller blocks by other insiders."

"In fact, it's closely held?"

"Yeah. You couldn't take it over unless Danson went along."

"But if he was prepared to sell . . . ?"

Tyler gave Tellier a happy nod, as though of anticipation, and said: "Then the company's in play."

"But there's no evidence that it is?"

This was, Deb knew, the most obvious possibility: the company would be taken over, at a much higher price than the stock was now trading for, and somehow Curtis Price had found out. But Deacon shook his head. "What about Danson?" Deb asked.

"He's been involved in a quite a few biotech start-ups, though he actually made his money in Silicon Valley, computers . . . He's had a few successes, but not, you know, lately. And I wouldn't say Xynex is one of them. If they've got anything going for them, I couldn't find it. But Danson's an interesting guy. A player, if you like. And pretty slick. Broads, pardon the expression, fast cars, yachts."

"Seriously—yachts?"

"Yeah. Sailboats." He poked through the file. "Xynex Inc. was an official sponsor of one of the America's Cup boats—if you're the prez and principal shareholder, I guess you get to spend the company money any way you like." Tyler looked at André Tellier: "Is this important?"

"*Moi*, I am Hercule Poirot."

"Yeah," said Tyler, "I always knew you guys were really Belgians at heart." Then he grinned and added: "I don't suppose you're going to tell me what any of this is all about?"

"Of course not," said Tellier. "Any other interesting—recent— corporate developments?"

"Actually, there was one thing . . . When you called, I thought I recognized the name from a story—they were getting it off the computer. Just a sec . . ." He darted out the door and Tellier turned to Deb:

"Listen—you have to give me everything you know about Manley."

"I just can't believe it. But yes, of course. *Sailboats.* Walter sails! I sail!"

Tyler came straight back in. "Here it is. An old story off the Reuters wire. But it's not much. Last fall they replaced their chief scientific officer. Nothing really important."

"All right—"

But Deb interrupted Tellier. "What does it say?"

"Well, nothing much really . . . it says that Xynex Inc. is pleased to announce the appointment of Mr. Nisram Singh, Ph.D., as head of research. Mr. Singh has worked for the Food and Drug Administration, SmithKline Beecham, he's a graduate of . . . blah blah blah—

Deb said, "Would you say he's good?"

Tyler, reading, was silent a moment. Then he said: "He's sure got all the credentials. Biria Institute of Technology and Science, Jawaharlal Nehru University in New Delhi, the Centre for Cellular and Molecular Biology in Hyderabad—these are good places to come from; India's big in biotech stuff—and so is the Cambridge Centre for Molecular Recognition, and there's nothing wrong with Johns Hopkins, either."

Johns Hopkins, at least, Deb knew about—Giacomo had done six months' research there. She turned to Tellier: "Price said—"

Tellier put up his hand and stopped her. "That's okay."

But Deb, turning back to Tyler, persisted: "Would you say from that he's anything special? This Singh man—"

Tyler shrugged. "I really couldn't say. I mean, there's not enough here. But he's clearly a top scientist." He hesitated, and shrugged again. "Maybe it's a little surprising. He sounds a lot better than the company." Tyler looked at Tellier: "That it?"

Tellier nodded and Tyler Deacon headed out the door. But then Tellier quickly added, "Tyler—you understand . . . don't do anything about the stock."

Tyler smiled and disappeared.

Deb said, "But I have to do something about it—Price's stock, I mean. I either put the order in, or I have to tell him I'm not going to."

"Right. So make out the ticket, mark it unsolicited, and then bring it here. I'll put it through."

Deb smiled. "Thank you." She was silent for a second, and then she added: "André . . . this—well, it could have been pretty dreadful, but it wasn't as bad as I expected."

He smiled, and got up to shake her hand. "And don't worry about your *arrières.*"

Two minutes later, she put Price's "order to buy" onto André's desk, and five minutes after that she was getting ready to go for lunch—or, to be precise, to give Henry his breakfast.

Rosie said, "And what are you doing on the way back?"

Deb, to her surprise, actually had to think a split second before she understood. And then she remembered: she hadn't told Rosie. About being sick. About being ninety-nine and forty-four one hundredths per cent certain. Not that it made any difference . . . one way or another, she had to do a test.

"Don't worry," she said, "I'll get it."

"And . . . how do you feel?"

Deb looked at her watch, and whispered. "Ten past twelve. How can I have morning sickness now?'

Rosie smiled. "Somehow, I don't think it works like that. And I still say it's too early—it's probably all in your head."

Deb headed out. How *did* she feel? She was pregnant. She was unmarried. But there was no getting around it—she felt like a million bucks.

As long as she didn't have to take it in Xynex stock.

CHAPTER THREE

There was a Shoppers Drug Mart downstairs, but though she didn't make a fuss about it, Deb never bought tobacco stocks—she figured there were plenty of other things that would go up—and Shoppers was owned by Imasco, which was in turn a subsidiary of the huge British tobacco conglomerate, BAT Industries: they purveyed carcinogens under such illustrious brand names as Carlton, Kool, du Maurier and Player's. Anyway, all she had to do was walk across to Commerce Court where there was a branch of Pharma Plus; it was a subsidiary too, but just of Oshawa Wholesale, staid old IGA—although, come to think of it, she didn't buy their stock, either, since it was non-voting.

Still, they had a great hormone aisle, everything from Sheiks to Midol, KY Jelly to Shy. The pregnancy kits, just down from the condoms, were on the same shelf as basal thermometers and ovulation tests. *Confirm, Simplicity, First Response, Answer Now* . . . unconsciously, Deb made a face: the names they gave to women's things . . . *Confidelle*! She was surprised, though, at the number of brands, and thankful—maybe she *should* buy their stock—that Pharma Plus had put up a chart and a rack of pamphlets to explain it all:

Pharma Answers ... How similar or different are the various test kits? All of them are urine tests to detect the presence of human chorionic gonadotropin (CG), a hormone produced by developing fetal tissue ... The wand or stick type of test is basically 1 step- you hold the wand in the urine stream about 5 or 10 seconds ... The well or vial type of test may amount to 2 or more steps. First, you collect a urine specimen in a cup or container, then you use a dropper ...

Deb stopped reading right there. As far as she was concerned, the human female was simply not built to pee into bottles; she went for the wand. *Advance.* The name was okay, and it was made by Ortho, who made birth-control pills, which maybe she should have used. But then being pregnant was the ultimate *should've, could've, might've.*

Except, outside, leaning into the blustery wind blowing up from the lake, she realized that wasn't how she felt. I'm not exactly—I'm not *allowing* myself to—but I *could* ... enjoy this, she thought. And maybe she was enjoying it anyway. It had been nice, the way the lady at the cash had smiled. Just to test things out, she stepped ahead into a little empty space on the sidewalk, and whispered— out loud, so she could hear her voice—"I'm pregnant." And it sounded like her, all right. My God, I am. *Of course you are.* Part of her was aghast. But another part—a tiny part—wanted to giggle. And she realized that somewhere inside she also wanted to call her mother, *which you are absolutely under no circumstances going to do.* She smiled. It was crazy.

Crazy. She walked down to Front Street, and the doorman at the Royal York put her into a cab. The driver, black, was named Yussef Mohammed, so he was almost certainly a Somali, which meant he'd come here as a refugee from genocidal clan warfare ... or at least that would have been the story. He'd been playing a tape— Arabic, fiercely melancholic: probably a passionate love song—but as she settled herself in her seat, he switched it off and turned on the radio, to the CBC. Deftly, he U-turned in front of Union Station, with its spidery web of tracks running all the way to Montreal and

Halifax, Winnipeg and Vancouver, and on the radio a feminist lady began talking on Radio Noon about rape. *Crazy.* Vaguely, as they idled in traffic, Deb listened. "'No' means no. That's something men are going to have to learn." She made a face; come on, she thought. She'd certainly said "no" when she'd meant... something else. "Maybe." Or "I need a little more convincing." Which was fun, after all—the best thing about saying "no" was changing your mind.

"It is a very nice day," said the cabbie. "A very nice pretty day."

She closed her eyes. What if she'd said "no" to Giacomo? Well, in a way she had . . . What if he hadn't called her? And then she remembered his room, and the sun on the bed and his skin...

"Yes, it is," said Deb. "I love the spring."

"Yes, the best time. All over the world, it is the best time."

A moment later, with a blinding flicker, they passed out of the tunnel under the railway tracks, and joined a line of traffic under the Gardiner Expressway. *How I love him,* Deb thought.

"It's such a wonderful change, after the winter," she said.

Then she thought she was going to cry. *No you're not,* not here, not now. *I'd really prefer not to.* She caught herself...

I'm pregnant, though. By him. It seemed such an extraordinary thing to say. It was like something out of an old book, she was *with child.* My God! *Enceinte.* It was pretty silly, really. *Knocked up.* She wanted to laugh—but she knew if she began laughing, she'd definitely cry. *Crazy.* As the lady on the radio blathered on, Deb wondered what the Somali was thinking. She tried to block it all out; what else could you do? Somalis and refugee camps and feminists . . . *She was pregnant.* She wondered—when had it happened? Some women claimed to know when a man made them pregnant; or at least characters in books did. It was always a great romantic moment. *Earthy.* That was the word. She wondered—had Giacomo known?

Of course I knew.

At the time, though. When you did it.

Don't you remember? We'd just come back from the Kingsway. Actually, she thought, that made sense. *We'd seen that film of yours, you know, the one you like so much . . .* Yes. She'd especially wanted to go. *The Year of Living Dangerously.* She'd seen it ten times at least . . .

That's it! You were in love with Mel Gibson . . .

No way! I never liked *him*, I wanted to *be* Sigourney Weaver! At least when I was fourteen. But later, the Linda Hunt character had fascinated her more and more . . .

You're clouding the issue, you know perfectly well what I mean . . .

She did know perfectly well. The sex. The sex that night had been something very special. She'd never felt anything like that before in her life, she didn't know you were *allowed* to feel like that. But had she felt anything *happen*?

No. She smiled, amused at herself. Up to a point, you're romantic, she thought—but beyond that point, you're completely practical. Which was maybe not the worst way to look at things if you were pregnant, so she took a breath and began to get herself together and watched the lake out the window—white sails fluttered like handkerchiefs above the blue water—and in a moment the cab pulled up at Giacomo's building. It was one of the new towers along Queen's Quay, a condo, which Giacomo certainly couldn't have afforded normally, but he rented it from a friend who had a lot of money; he was working for Oxfam in Kenya. Deb didn't like the place that much. The security, which everybody raved about, made it feel like a fort. On the other hand, the man in the lobby, surrounded with all his TV monitors, knew her by name and always had a smile. "Time for Henry's breakfast, Miss Graham?" he asked.

"Brunch," she said, as she opened Giacomo's mailbox. "He's one of those yuppie cats."

She liked Henry, though he had created a small crisis—she was allergic to cats. But then, as she'd several times discovered, there are advantages to having a doctor for a boyfriend, especially since one of his pals from medical school was an allergist: now, rather than having her visit his office once a week, Giacomo gave them to her—though, in the arm, more conventionally than the famous bronchitis injection. With their help, she and Henry had become fast friends. Outside the door, fumbling with her keys, she was already chatting with him. "Hi, Henry . . . it's just me . . ." Usually, he'd be waiting inside, his black-and-white face turned up with an expression of mixed expectation and indignation: how could you have left me alone so long? "I know I'm late . . . you probably slept in anyway, didn't you?"

But he wasn't anywhere to be seen. It was sufficiently surprising that she stood for a moment, the door half open behind her, and simply called, "Henry?" She listened. She could feel the dark, quiet emptiness of the waiting rooms. He still didn't come. And the emptiness, just for an instant, was slightly uncanny, a spell that had to be broken: so she shut the door and stepped completely inside. She sniffed. A stale smell. She went into the living room, and opened the curtains on the big window.

"You're hiding, aren't you? You can't look me in the eye . . . you're ashamed of what your master's done, aren't you . . . Knocking me up—how dare he!"

Looking out, Deb could see for miles, out to the Islands, and across the lake: she watched a Dash-8 sink slowly down toward the airport.

"I know, you sit on the chair, watching us, and you're thinking 'What animals!'" She decided to come in some evening and vacuum—it was crazy, since no one was here, but that's what it needed.

"But you're not fooling me, Henry, you're just jealous because they cut your little balls off . . . Henry? Here Henry . . ."

She went out to the hall and called again through the half-open door to the bedroom—"Henry?"—but she didn't actually look inside because Henry only liked the bedroom when they were all in bed. "Henry . . . you're a cat, so stop being childish." She stuck her head into the den. "Come on, Henry . . . Now that I've had my shots you can rub up against me all you like . . ." Giacomo was slowly taking over his friend's place—big-band albums were gradually displacing vintage Beatles—and this room was now his entirely. A large poster for an immunization project the Marsh Foundation was supporting in Guatemala hung on one wall, and another wall was all shelves jammed with medical books; just inside the door, an Ikea storage setup held his rock-climbing gear . . . and a piece of rope Deb had been using to teach him sailing knots. She wondered what he was doing. He loved his work—in a quiet way, he was very passionate and committed about it. Did you necessarily admire the man you were in love with? Probably not, love being so strange, but it sure helped. She certainly admired Giacomo. He knew what he wanted to do, and why (which, her mother claimed, was the real difference between a man and a boy), although he never made much fuss about it. "You try to help. What else can you do?" In fact, he always claimed that he was really a dilettante, which was why he liked the Marsh Foundation—it was small, and he had a lot of independence. "I can do whatever I want." Of course, Deb knew, he wasn't a dilettante about anything, unless it was fancy cocktails—he was a frustrated bartender—and in fact he was quite capable of working himself into exhaustion. But he was always *interested*, that was the point; he loved it. He hated being bored. He always said he wished he could have stayed a student for his whole life—he'd loved university. And so had Deb. His desk made her think of this now, because it could have been a student's; it was just a slab door stretched between two file cabinets. His computer was running; he always left it on when he travelled—he had a laptop with him, so he could dial in. Now, his File Manager was glowing away on the screen.

"Henry? You're lonely, aren't you? Did you modem yourself to South America?"

And Deb, as she glanced at the monitor, *did* register something— something that wasn't quite right, something she wasn't expecting—but she was too preoccupied with Henry to stop and think about it. She began calling him again. "I agree, I miss him too—he's wonderful and handsome and kind, probably the world's greatest can opener and lover and patter . . . Though, you know, he's just as lucky to have us as we are to have him, in fact I'm not such a bad patter myself . . . come on, now . . . you can do anything you want, anything at all, I promise, now that I've had my shots you don't have to hold back. Lie on my crotch, stick your head into my armpit . . . all your favourite things."

She turned away from the den and went into the kitchen. Feed him, she thought. When it came to food, Henry epitomized brand loyalty. He didn't care one way or another about flavour, as long as it was Whiskas. There was a great pile of tins on top of the fridge, and she selected tuna and whitefish. They had pop-tops; she peeled it back and looked up—the sound usually brought him running. But there was still no sign of him.

And then she shook his box of Cat Chow and that did it, finally he emerged, though tentatively, coming down the hall on tiptoes, looking up at her—asking her something?—instead of marching along with that tromp, tromp, tromp, I-am-going-to-my-bowl look on his face.

"You all right?" she asked. She knelt down and gave him a pat. "You *were* in the bedroom, weren't you? You haven't even woken up yet!"

Ignoring him for a moment, Deb opened the fridge. Yesterday, when she'd come over, she'd made up a big bowl of yoghurt and cucumber; and there were still two slices of pita bread in a plastic bag. She dished some out, then ate at the counter, spooning up the yoghurt with the bread as she sorted through Giacomo's mail— he'd want to renew *The Economist*, he didn't need to join the Columbia Record Club . . . He'd told her to look for his Visa bill and pay it . . . and she found it and slipped it into her purse. Only then did she notice that Henry still hadn't touched his food. She leaned down. "Bowl, Henry! Bowl!" He looked up at her, his eyes wide and patient and calm; he was used to dealing with lunatics. She stuck her tongue out at him. "I know you, you want some of those Cosmic Catnip things . . . but no way, not till you've eaten that. *Some* of it, anyway."

It was quarter past one; the market, presumably, would be heading off in all directions without her. Deb had a last scoop of yoghurt, washed out her dish, and then found a pitcher in the cupboard and filled it at the sink. Henry, weaving between her legs, followed her into the living room. "Look—you should go and eat," she told him. Plants, other people's plants, made her nervous; she was always killing her own. She didn't even know their names, except for the very common ones—she was pretty sure this was a ficus, maybe that was a lipstick plant?—and only ever bought them in Loblaw's, usually in nasty plastic pots wrapped up in gold-coloured foil, because they made her think of her mother. Still, she turned all the pots around and then pulled the curtains, though only the sheers, because she thought they could probably do with more sun.

And then she went into Giacomo's office.

And Henry kept following her.

He was meowing, and it was his cry that finally reached her. Henry's voice, once you got to know him, was pretty distinctive. Most of the time, he just grumbled away to himself; if he wanted something, he badgered. Lonely, he whined.

But this was a voice she'd never heard before.

He was upset.

Henry was frightened. He was *crying* . . .

Deborah froze. And for a moment half of her mind was thinking *he's frightened*, but she was also was seeing the thick, dark leaves of the clivia she was supposed to be watering and the long, spiky leaves of one of the other plants, and then her eyes lost their focus and all she could see was the computer, the monitor. Something was happening. One moment, she was looking at Giacomo's File Manager, the same screen she'd noticed when she'd first looked in, but then, *blip*, the image changed and there was disgusting Homer slobbering his way across the screen as the screen saver came on . . . And she knew something was wrong. She knew something was very, very wrong—but for one instant she wasn't completely sure why.

She turned. *Quickly*. She looked over her shoulder, back into the hall. She could see the bathroom, and the half-open door to the bedroom, and the front door far, far away. And she remembered the feeling she'd had coming in, the dark, quiet emptiness of the waiting rooms.

"Henry," she whispered. "Henry..."

And then she looked back, almost dreamily, to the computer... And understood.

Screen savers, during periods of inactivity, prevent images from "burning" into monitor screens; Homer had come on *because no one had touched the keys in* ... how many minutes? Five minutes, perhaps. Or ten. Probably no more than fifteen. But if you turned that around it could mean only one thing: someone, only a few moments before, had been touching the keys.

And Henry, she remembered, had come out of the bedroom where he almost never spent any time.

She stood very still and turned her head; across the hall, she could see the half-open door.

The bedroom.

Someone was on the other side of the bedroom door. Someone was waiting. Someone had been standing there the whole time.

Henry, delicately, rubbed against the back of her calf.

"Henry."

He meowed, happier now. *So you finally figured it out.* He meowed again.

All the time you've been talking to him, you have to keep talking to him.

"You all right, Henry? Let me look..."

She took a step back. "Did you make a big jump?" she said, in a loud voice, trying to sound natural, but then she was whispering, *"He was in here, wasn't he, doing something at the computer, and he heard me coming in, and then he hid in the bedroom and you followed him ... Oh Jesus."* She cleared her throat—she was so tense. She knew she had to keep talking. "You see?" It was so hard to keep her voice steady. "You probably strained yourself, Henry, that's all."

She bent down quickly, picking him up, and with her right hand reached toward the shelf with Giacomo's climbing gear and grabbed up a piton and clutched it in her fist. *I can't do it.* She meant the front door—she meant a dash across the hall to the door—but she knew she'd never get it open, work the lock—and so she simply stepped back, edging back. Now she was in the hall.

Quickly, she sidestepped into the living room, "Good Henry, good boy." She took a big step back. Now, she could only see part of the hall. *If he opened the bedroom door he wouldn't see her, she wouldn't see him.* Which made her feel safer. Which was stupid. She wasn't safe at all. Still . . .

Her heart was pounding, but steady. *Keep talking to Henry.* As much to keep herself calm as anything else. "I bet you strained a muscle, didn't you? It's all right, just let me look . . ."

She put him down on the couch and stroked him, he was okay now, and then she eased her shoes off—they were only half heels, but, *but . . .* and now the bedroom door was opening.

She could hear it creaking.

Cool air moved over her cheek.

The piton was something like a marlinespike, heavy in her hand. She was holding her breath . . . a mass of shadow fell into the hall . . . and she made herself take a breath. And then it was a little more clearly a man, his shadow, or at least a figure—which stopped.

He's waiting. Listening . . .

"It's okay." *As if she were talking to him.* "It's okay, Henry, it's okay."

And then he moved, and now the light, coming from the office, resolved his shadow clearly on the far wall of the hall, a man, *a man in a peaked cap, a baseball cap.*

A Blue Jays cap. A John Deere cap.

He was coming . . .

But then the shadow, almost magically, disappeared—he'd stepped out of the light—and she barely caught one brief glimpse, *a shiny blue sleeve and shoulder, a jacket* and then that was gone, into the little alcove by the front door. And then she heard the door open . . . "Good Henry, good Henry . . ." and click shut.

Deb held her breath. And then strides took her across the hall to the door and she reached out and turned the bolt. *Thank God.*

She leaned against the door.

Something was moving behind her.

She spun around.

"Oh my God, Henry . . ."

He looked at her, grumbled, and sidled up, back to his usual self.

She slipped down against the door, and for the second time in an hour she wasn't sure whether she was going to laugh or cry.

"Henry," she whispered, "come here."

Funny. For the first time all morning, her stomach felt really okay. Except, now, she was terrified.

She scooped Henry into her arms, and held him. "You've never been to my place, have you?" Her voice had started to tremble. She gave him a pat. "Don't worry," she whispered, "you'll love it."

Henry, happy, started to purr.

CHAPTER FOUR

*T*wo *curiosities:*

It never occurred to Deborah to tell anyone what had happened—she was too shocked. So, downstairs, at the security desk, she was all smiles, as chipper as Kathie Lee Gifford. But it seemed very important, necessary somehow. She didn't want to *admit*—what? She didn't want to face—*something* . . . And then there was Henry—curiosity number two. He didn't like travelling. He didn't like strange places. He didn't like anything different. But he was oddly content in the cab, and hopped down eagerly from her arms when they were finally inside her apartment. He seemed relieved, in fact, happy to be out of there.

Deb sagged down on the sofa. "You okay?" she said, as he began exploring. "You are, aren't you." She let out her breath. "I'm not." *What was happening? Who could that man have been?* She closed her eyes. In the cab, she'd kept everything back; it had taken all her energy simply to hold on. Now, the questions rushed at her. She remembered . . . that hat. The way, on the wall, the shape had suddenly resolved itself. She shivered—it was all so creepy. She opened her eyes and watched Henry rub his chin against the leg of a chair. "Hey . . . you're really making yourself right at home . . . Know what? I'll have to get you a bowl. And a tray . . ." *How long had he been there? What could he possibly want? What had he been doing with Giacomo's computer?*

She stood up—she was a little trembly. And she wanted to change her clothes, to take a bath. She felt awful. *What had he been doing?* He'd been there the whole time.

She went into the bedroom, took everything off, and then put on her Wooden Boat T-shirt. Back in the living room, she opened the drapes on the big window; outside, the blue sky curved away to infinity, or at least Buffalo, and a big patch of Lake Ontario pressed up between the jigsaw of the towers downtown. She could see part of the Island—she and Giacomo shared more or less the same view, he was just a little closer. She took a breath, then stepped back. "Okay," she thought, trying to calm herself, "okay. *No one's here now, just you and Henry.*" Closing her eyes, she settled into the *Samasthiti*, the position she always used to start her yoga. She held it for a moment, then slipped away, into The Tree, an "easy" posture, with one foot against the opposite knee. Rocking a little, she found her balance, didn't let herself go tense; and everything flowed out of her as she felt her foot relax and the earth, two hundred feet below, take her weight—she was always amazed at how it worked. She changed legs. All she thought of now was sailing, going up to the jib with the deck rolling smoothly beneath her. And when the thought passed away, she was just there, absolutely steady. She hung onto it—hung onto it until it became an effort—and then let it go . . . and felt a million times better, the way she always did.

Then the phone began ringing.

She almost didn't answer it—she didn't really feel like talking to anyone. But when she picked it up, she heard Giacomo's voice.

"Deb? Is that you? This is great, I just called my place. I thought you might be still feeding—"

"Giacomo . . . My God, it's good to hear your voice."

"I love this. You're already desperate, and it hasn't been a week!"

"Listen . . ." Deb took a great big breath. "This is awful."

"Hey—are you okay? You sound—"

"You're not going to believe this—I was frightened half out of my mind—but someone was in your apartment."

"Someone was in my apartment? Someone broke in?"

"No, not like that. Someone was there—when I was there."

"You mean . . . one of the maintenance guys?"

"No. I just mean *someone was there*. I was . . ." Deb took a breath. "I was so frightened."

"Look, Deb, I still don't get this. Someone was in the apartment. *Who* was in the apartment?"

"I don't know. Listen . . . just listen for a second. I came in. The first thing was, Henry wasn't around. Usually, he's right at the door when I come in. But he wasn't there. He wasn't in the living room, and then I looked in your office."

"Right."

"Your computer was on."

"I always—"

"Yes, I know you always leave it running. Anyway, it was on—and your File Manager was on the screen."

"Just a minute. You're saying the screen—the monitor—was on?"

"Yes. File Manager was running."

"Well . . . I must have forgotten. I always leave the computer on, but I normally turn the screen off."

"God, I didn't even think of that . . . it just looked the way it always does when I come over—"

"I was in a hurry, I forgot—"

"No, I don't think you did forget. Anyway—that only adds to it—just remember that the screen was on and File Manager was running. That's the point. Think about it for a moment."

"Okay. The screen was on. File Manager was running. You came in and saw that—did you find Henry?"

"Not for a few minutes. I went out to the kitchen and got his bowl ready and called him, and finally he showed up. He was acting strange. Meowing a lot. And then I began watering the plants and he began following me around. I realized—when I went into the office again—something was wrong. He sounded frightened, really upset."

"Frightened? Henry? Surely that implies too great an expenditure of energy."

"Giacomo—listen—he was frightened. And then I noticed your computer screen. The screen saver was running. The Simpsons . . . Homer. Do you get it now?"

The line hummed, and Deb realized she was holding her breath, waiting. And somehow it was so important that he understand. Because? In order to *confirm* . . . but exactly what, she couldn't have said.

Finally, his voice came back, "Yeah, I do get it now. Actually, Homer should have been doing his thing the first time you looked in there. In fact, the screen saver should have started running ten minutes after I last touched the keyboard on Monday."

"*Yes.*"

"Which means that someone must have been at the computer just before you arrived. Well . . . I can see why you'd feel spooked. But—I wonder . . ."

"Giacomo—"

"I'm just trying to think if it comes on—the screen saver I mean—when I dial in. I didn't, as a matter of fact, but—"

"Giacomo—"

"Look, I can see why you were upset, but you know what happened? It was Henry. He walked across the keyboard, that's all. He sometimes likes to sleep on the monitor, just because it's warm—"

"*No, he didn't.*"

"Hey, calm down."

"Giacomo, I saw him."

"Who?"

"The man . . . in the apartment. He was in the bedroom. Hiding. And then—"

"You saw him? You actually saw him?"

"Yes."

"What did he look like?"

"Well I didn't exactly—I mean, I saw his shadow."

"His shadow?"

"When I realized he was there, I hid in the living room. He came out. I could see his shadow—"

"His shadow, but not... *him*."

"Giacomo, I saw him!"

"Just a minute, Deb. You were frightened—of course you were. For crying out loud, you must have been frightened out of your wits. You probably—"

"Giacomo, I saw his shadow absolutely clearly, distinctly. He was... he was wearing a baseball cap."

"A baseball cap."

"Yes, a baseball cap. For Christ's sake—"

"Hey, hey. All right. You saw him, or at least you saw his shadow. But what was he doing? Did he steal anything?"

"No... No, I don't think he did."

"All right. If you actually did see—"

"*I saw him.*"

"Okay. Look, I don't deserve this—"

"I'm telling you, *I saw him.*"

"Sure. You saw him. But who did you see? What did you see? Did you ever see him before?"

"No."

"Could you identify him again?"

"I don't know. No. I don't think so."

"Well, look... I'm sure it was just some maintenance guy from the building—think of the cap—who came in to do something—in that building, you know, they even change your light bulbs for you—and he got curious—because the computer was on—and he began playing around with it, and then he heard you come in and he was embarrassed. You know... I mean he wasn't really doing anything wrong, but it would have looked bad. So—"

"Giacomo, I saw him."

"All right. Agreed. You saw him, and of course it was frightening, but... no harm done. Right?"

Deb hesitated. "I suppose. Yes."

"You're okay? Henry's okay?"

"Yes. Everybody's okay."

"And he didn't take anything."

"No. I don't think he took anything. But . . . I feel awful." Giacomo didn't say anything and Deb said again: "I don't know why, but I feel awful."

Giacomo said, "It must have been really upsetting. I think you should pat Henry . . . and tell him to keep off the keyboard."

Deb hesitated, and then thought, *No*. And then she said, "He's here, you know. Henry."

"Tremendous. It will broaden his horizons. You're okay—the shots are working?"

"Yes. That's all fine." Deb felt herself relenting. "I guess I'll keep him here. I might as well. I'll have to buy him a tray and a special bowl."

"Don't let him bully you. Too much."

"I'll tell him you said so. Not that it will do any good."

Giacomo said, "Look . . . I have to go."

"No."

"Yes. I have to meet a man called, if you can believe it, André Pieyre de Mandiargues."

"And what will you do with him?"

"He is a recipient of a grant from the Marsh Foundation. We'll discuss his interim report. It's about STDS, and how they're transmitted from tourists to the locals. Believe it or not, he thinks there might be something new."

"In other words, you'll have lunch."

"Something like that."

"Lucky you."

"No. You're not here . . . I miss you."

"Okay. I miss you too."

"We shouldn't argue."

"I know. It upsets Henry."

"Okay."

"Okay."

But it wasn't, quite. They said goodbye and Deb hung up—and

realized she was angry. Henry came over and rubbed against her legs. She scratched his ears.

"You better suck up to me. You have a little work to do on behalf of your master." Because he hadn't believed her. Damn! He'd humoured her. "But I did see him, and it wasn't any maintenance man, either. You saw him too, didn't you. He was nasty. *Nasty.*" She remembered how his cap had suddenly formed against the wall. There'd been something menacing about it. There'd been something absolutely *wrong* with the whole business. The way he'd hidden there, waiting, listening, watching. And Giacomo . . . he hadn't believed her, hadn't understood.

Who cared what the man in the cap was actually doing there, what she *felt* was more important.

"Henry," she said, "I miss him and I love him, but right now, right at this very minute . . ." She bent forward, and looked Henry in the eye. *"I'd like to kick him in the . . .* well, maybe not there, but in the ass, anyway." Henry frowned. Gently, just the way he liked, she tugged his ears; he closed his eyes and smiled.

She let him go, feeling a little better. Only then did she remember that she hadn't told Giacomo she was pregnant. Well . . . did he deserve to know? She looked at her watch. She was already late— she could be a little later; she'd made Orme Capital a lot of money this year; besides, Rosie would field any calls. So she decided she might as well do the test. She went into the bathroom. ADVANCE . . . *1 Easy Step . . .* Inside the box was a sheet of instructions and a foil pouch; inside the pouch was something called the "Test Stick," a beige plastic wand about ten centimetres long, one end of which was ridged so you could hold onto it. Two depressions in the stick were covered with a strip of clear plastic; the smaller of these was the "end of test" window—it was supposed to turn red after five minutes when the test was complete—while the larger would show either one red line—*not* pregnant—or two if you were. That seemed easy enough. At the very end of the stick was a third depression, about as big as the end of her little finger and marked with an arrow; it didn't actually say "pee here" but that was the general idea. A little self-consciously, she sat on the toilet and did so. It was possible to do this without getting too much on your hand; more difficult to hold the wand level, so as not to spill anything from the "urine well," and wipe yourself with your left hand especially since the toilet roll was empty and she had to reach around behind her and get the spare one off the back. But she managed. And then carefully set the Test Stick beside the sink. Waiting, she sat on the toilet. She read the French side of the instructions, the good old *"Mode d'Emploi."* It was a lot wordier and they'd used a smaller typeface to fit some of it in, but *l'autre langue* always had its compensations. For example, your period was *"vos règles,"* which—just because it was plural—sounded messier, more like the real thing, even if her own were never especially *règlé* at all. And pregnancy itself was apparently *"grossesse,"* which was also better—she remembered, last summer in Kingston, watching a hugely pregnant woman waddle ponderously across Battery Park; *grossesse,* undoubtedly, was what *she'd* figured it was. Deb sneaked a look at her watch ... three minutes. She was determined to make herself wait right till the end. And if, after all this, she wasn't pregnant ... but she was. "Two pink lines in the Result Window means you are PREGNANT. You can assume you are PREGNANT even if one line is lighter than the other." Actually, both her lines were pretty dark; there was no doubt about it.

Well, well.

She went into the living room, sat on the couch, and looked down at herself. Nothing seemed to have changed. She pressed her hand against her abdomen. It was supposed to get tight, she remembered; but not till later. Which raised a question ... how far along was she? Thinking this, she made a face. *Far along.* What an expression ... at least in relation to herself.

"Henry, I'm not sure I like this."

Henry, having explored, was now sitting in the exact centre of the room, tail neatly arranged around himself. He raised his eyebrows and yawned.

She smiled, but she felt flat, completely different than the way she'd felt outside the Royal York, whispering "I'm pregnant" just to hear how it sounded. And the real reason, she knew, wasn't what had happened in Giacomo's apartment; it was the phone call. She just didn't like— If only he hadn't—

But she didn't want to think about it. And she ought to go back to work . . . or at least phone. So she got up and called Rosie, who in fact had been wondering what had become of her.

"I came home," Deb said. "I decided I might as well do that test."

"And?"

"It was positive. As in, yes, I am."

There was a pause; then Rosie said, "At least you know everything works. You do, he does . . ."

"I was thinking that."

"How do you feel about it? No, no—scratch that. None of my business, and you don't know anyway. But how's the tummy?"

"Okay, actually. But I was thinking, maybe I might take the rest of the day off. Have I had many calls?"

"Not really. I can give them to you—"

"Great."

"Oh, one thing—Mr. Smoothy got a fill . . ."

"Really . . . Not on all of it?"

"Let me look . . ." She went away and came back. "You were trying to buy two hundred thousand, you got fifty. Xynex . . . Xynex Inc. Never heard of it. Should I be buying this stock?"

"Absolutely not, Rosie. Look, go and check on my machine. A number for Price, Curtis. You know how I've got it set up—"

"Just a second." Rosie went away again and came back and gave her the number. They chatted a moment longer; Rosie suggested they go out for dinner, but Deb decided she didn't want to.

"I know what will happen," she said. "You'll tell me all about your abortion, and then we'll go back and forth, should I or shouldn't I, and really—right now—I don't want to think about it."

"I promise, I won't."

"Right. And you'll keep your promise. Every once in a while, though, you'll narrow your eyes and lick your lips and I'll know exactly what—"

"Nuts! I'll see you tomorrow."

Deb hung up and immediately called Curtis Price's number.

A man answered—but she knew immediately that it wasn't Price.

"Could I speak with Mr. Price, please?" Deb said.

"Who is this?"

She hated that. On the other hand—she was calling. She said, "My name is Deborah Graham. Mr. Price is expecting my call."

"Are you . . . do you work for something called . . . just a minute . . . Orme Capital?"

She didn't like this person's tone. She said: "Who am I speaking with? Could you put me through to Mr. Price, please? Or give him a message?"

"Miss Graham? You're talking to a police officer."

"A policeman . . ."

"Yes, so if you'd just answer my question, Miss Graham. Are you—"

"I think I'd like to speak with Mr. Price first, if you don't mind."

"Miss Graham, you know, if I want, I can compel—"

"Look, I don't know who you are, but if there's a problem you can ask Mr. Price to call *me*. Goodbye."

"Miss Graham—look—hang on. I'm sorry . . . maybe we should start this over. My fault. I apologize. I guess I've been a little heavy-handed, but . . ." Deb could hear the man take a breath. "My name is Dean Bannon, Miss Graham. I'm a detective, as I said. Mr. Price can't speak to you because Mr. Price has been murdered. He almost certainly died around noon. According to his phone records, he called an outfit called Orme Capital—is Toronto area code 416?"

"Yes. my God—murdered?"

"That's what I said. Okay now, he placed a call, a brief call, to that 416 number at 10:58, and then a much longer call beginning at 11:32. Your name is beside that number."

"Yes . . . my God. He called me. The second time. He said he called me before but I wasn't there."

"You did speak with him?"

"Yes."

"What about?"

"Well, I'm a stockbroker. His broker. Or one of them anyway. I guess. He gave me an order."

"For what?"

Deb hesitated. "I'm not sure I should . . . he was a client. He bought some stock."

"Okay. I understand. He was a client. I don't want to put you in an awkward position. But—I don't know, maybe you can help here. Almost certainly you were the last person to speak to him alive, except for whoever shot him."

"My God, I don't believe it."

"Listen . . . you're at this number? 416—"

"I'm at home. But I'll be in my office in twenty minutes. That number's my work number."

"All right. Look, I'll probably want to speak to you again. You don't mind? It's possible that you can be very, very helpful."

"Of course. Yes. If I can . . ."

"I'll probably call you then."

They hung up.

For a moment, Deb stood there, stunned. Price—*murdered*. And then she had an eerie feeling—she was back in Giacomo's apartment, with the knowledge creeping over her that someone else was there. But that had to be coincidence, *pure* coincidence. You can't be in two places at the same time, so whoever was in Giacomo's apartment defintely hadn't killed Curtis Price. And so she dismissed it from her mind, and half an hour later was back at work. Good thing, too. Everything got very frantic; during the afternoon, senior people at Orme Capital received calls from the RCMP and an FBI agent at the U.S. Consulate. So Deb worked late that night—it was just one meeting after another.

CHAPTER FIVE

*T*wo *days later, at 10:57 a.m.* (she took a nervous glance at her watch, so she knew the time precisely), Deborah Graham told a lie, and her lie changed everything.

She knew it was a lie, and she told it to a policeman, so there was no escaping the meaning of what she'd done. She'd crossed a line; on the other side . . . well, she didn't know *what* was on the other side. But everything was different beyond that point. It was rather ironic, though; only by telling the lie did she understand an important truth—the truth of how frightened she was: frightened for herself, frightened about what was going on around her; and above all, frightened for Giacomo.

Of course, up to that moment, she'd had plenty of other things to worry about.

It seemed crazy, it seemed absolutely incredible, but Curtis Price, *her* client, had been murdered. It had happened in his home on Long Island. There were no signs of a break-in, and since he had been killed in his workroom at the back of the house, it was possible that he'd known "the perpetrator"—as the police put it; or "his assailant," as *The New York Times* preferred. (On the other hand, he'd been shot once in the head with a thirty-two calibre bullet, which hinted at something "professional," at least according *The Times*). The horrible part was that this must have happened within minutes of his talking to her. MCI's records showed that Price had first called Toronto at 10:58, then again at 11:32—when he'd reached Deb—and had ended the call at 11:38. Barely half an hour later, at ten past twelve, his body had been discovered by a domestic, Maria Olivera, who came in every day to clean and also made Price his lunch.

In a way, these details were almost beside the point, since the police obviously didn't suspect Deb (that was one thing, she thought, she could be grateful for). The trouble was, they didn't suspect anyone else; they very quickly ruled out robbery, drugs or any sort of domestic quarrel as motives, and that left one obvious alternative, Price's business dealings. By the next morning, this had become the great issue: should they, or should they not, tell the police that Deb had been worried about Price's trading? They were under no obligation to do so—the first meeting with the lawyers had settled that pretty clearly. But of course there were "other considerations." In the end, the decision was more or less taken out of their hands, because the police on Long Island checked with the enforcement division of the Securities and Exchange Commission—the SEC, the body that oversees American securities markets—and found that they already had a file on Price. There'd never been a formal investigation of him, but he'd owned a lot of stock in a steel company that had been taken over, and had bought most of his position just hours before the official announcement. So it looked suspicious. And, as it happened, this was one of the first stocks he'd bought after he'd started his account with Deb. Fenton, the head of the legal team advising them, managed to earn them a few hours to work out their response, but there wasn't much doubt about what they had to do. "You just can't lie. Yes, they have no jurisdiction, but you have to think how it looks to the SEC. That's what you want to focus on."

And there was a good reason for this. *Bonds.* Orme Capital's equity trading through New York was important, but it was nothing in comparison to their bond business—as was made very clear to Deb when she enjoyed the rare privilege of a meeting with the Great Orme himself.

"I'm sure you understand, Miss Graham, how important New York is to us."

"Of course—" she'd wondered if she should call him "sir" but had decided not to—"Mr. Orme."

"I forget the precise number , but on the right there are a good many zeros."

The old bastard, she thought, did so know the number *precisely*, to the last cent. "I realize it's a particular specialty of ours . . . the Yankees, I mean."

"So do I, Miss Graham. I hope we all do. And naturally, because of the importance of that trade, we'd prefer to stay in the good graces of the American authorities. But if what you suspect about Price is even half true—especially if it actually has some connection to his death . . . his *murder* . . ." He made an unhappy face. "You see?"

"Yes, sir." *Damn.* In the end, she *had* called him "sir."

"There's no point taking chances. If there are any questions about this man's dealings, the Securities and Exchange Commission will be brought in as a matter of course. Let's keep them happy. Let's look *good.*"

"Absolutely."

"It's one of those times when appearances may be as important as reality, Deborah. Of course you've handled this perfectly correctly—there's no question about that. But go down there, do whatever you can to help, and generally be . . . how can I put this? a nice, pleasant, *Canadian* girl."

"Right."

"And have a good time, of course."

"Yes, sir." Damn! She'd said it again.

In the end, that whole idea—Deborah flying down to New York, in a show of "co-operation"—had been abandoned. Instead, after negotiations through the lawyers, she'd talked to the police on the phone and then faxed them a statement. For a few hours, that almost seemed to be the end of it—but then they said they wanted to speak to her face to face, and would fly a detective to Toronto.

For once in her life, Deb was relieved not to be going on a trip; her home ground just seemed a lot safer . . . at least she didn't have ask where the washrooms were. Because that was something else she had to worry about, and for one awful, queasy moment with Orme, she'd imagined a great lake of vomit spreading across the immaculate surface of his burled walnut desk. That had passed off; another false alarm. But it was a worry . . . although, from somewhere, maybe a magazine at the hairdresser's, or perhaps one of the great media pregnancies—the Kathie Lee Gifford production, the Vanna White event or even one of the Royal arrivals—she'd picked up the idea that half a dozen soda crackers consumed immediately upon waking—*I'll kick* myself *out of bed for eating these things*—settled the stomach. This actually seemed to work. For the first day after Price's murder, she subsisted on Premium Crackers, Campbell's tomato soup—*no coffee*—and finally, in the evening, with her confidence increasing, one-half of a small Hawaiian pizza which (another sign?) she'd absolutely craved. Next morning, waking up, she felt a little off, but the policeman—Bannon, the same man she'd spoken with on the phone—wasn't due to arrive until ten, and by the time she left her apartment, she felt okay. She knew she *looked* okay. Black Ferragamos, with a heel. A Donna Karan suit, dark grey. And to top it all off—after rejecting the inevitable pearls and the almost-inevitable Hermès scarf—the perfect skin of her delicately curved, discreetly bared, swanlike neck.

Rosie was impressed. "You're so lucky. I can never get their shoes to fit." She leaned forward and said: "Mr. Bannon, *Detective* Bannon, *Keanu-Reeves-look-alike* Dean Bannon, arrived about ten minutes ago."

"I was being fashionably late."

"Why not? You're the star. Besides, if you got here early, you'd just drink a lot of coffee, and if there's one thing I hate it's getting up in a meeting full of men and having to go to the john." Deb pretty much agreed, but didn't want to say so; it was so dumb. Rosie went on, "There's someone else with them, I think a dogcatcher."

A dogcatcher was someone from the osc—the Ontario Securities

Commission; they were more or less the equivalent of the SEC and regulated the Toronto Stock Exchange. Fenton, the lawyer, came out to get her and confirmed this.

Deb said, "But you were expecting them to show up."

"Absolutely. This is no problem. They *asked*, all very polite, *could* they please sit in. They know they don't have anything. Anyway, they have less teeth than my grandmother. In fact, I was just deciding that we've probably overreacted, and that I might leave you with him—Bannon, I mean. This cop. Certainly he'd prefer that."

Deb wasn't so sure. "Mr. Fenton, if anything goes wrong . . ."

"Nothing will go wrong."

"But if Price really was doing insider trading through this firm, we know who'll get the blame."

"Deborah, you've nothing to worry about."

"No, Mr. Fenton, *you've* nothing to worry about."

"Okay." He waved a hand. "I'm hearing you. Still—"

"Could we just play it by ear? You stick around until we're sure there won't be any surprises. And then—I don't know . . ."

"Take him for coffee. Something informal."

"All right. Who knows? I might actually be able to help him."

"Exactly. You don't want him to feel he's been wasting his time. And look, don't worry. You're in the clear, the firm's in the clear. You know?"

Deb smiled. "Remember that. Because I'm just going to tell him the truth, the whole truth and nothing but the truth. He can do what he wants with it."

That made Fenton laugh. "Okay. You tell him the truth. But don't be disappointed when he doesn't believe you. They never do. The cops are such liars themselves, they assume everyone else must be too."

They went into Tellier's office, and there was a lot of chair scraping and handshaking, and someone made a joke about the Guinness Book of Records. Lansdowne, the man from the OSC, muttered about co-operation, and "a watching brief," and liaison "with our friends south of the border," and then, as they were about to start, an obnoxious Orme Capital VP named Henderson stuck his head in the door. He looked grave and said very solemnly, "I just thought it would be appropriate, Detective Bannon, to say a few words on behalf of the firm. I want to assure you that co-operation runs right to the top here at Orme Capital—if you need anything, just ask. Frankly, this is the sort of problem we want to put behind us as quickly as possible."

When he left, André leaned forward and murmured to Deb, "Not too bad. I mean, only one *appropriate.*"

Deb smiled. "I noticed. And only one *frankly* and not a single *let me be perfectly clear.*"

Tellier, leaning back, grunted "I'm comfortable with that." Deb smiled—she knew he was trying to put her at her ease. Dean Bannon smiled too. "I have to admit, he reminds me of a guy in the commissioner's office."

"Detective Bannon, there are guys like that all over the world."

Fenton said, "André, they run the world."

In the end, even Lansdowne managed a smile.

So it all started well. And, instinctively, Deb liked Bannon—he didn't at all match the cynical portrait Fenton had indicated. Keanu Reeves? Not really, but she could see what Rosie meant; he certainly looked less like a policeman than a model out of the L. L. Bean catalogue. He was in his early thirties, of medium height, with thick brown hair that would look great ruffled by the wind. His tan slacks, brown tweed jacket and boat shoes left the same easy, pleasant impression. He was completely straightforward. In fact, he began by apologizing.

"The other day, we didn't get off to the best start on the phone. I'm sorry."

Deb said, "It sounded like it might have been one of those days."

"It was. But I'm supposed to be used to it. It's just—well, I shouldn't have talked like that, and I really am sorry."

After all the preliminaries—when he was finally able to get around to it—he was equally direct with his questions.

"Deborah, it's almost certain that you were the last person to speak to Price, with the exception of his murderer."

"I understand that."

"And your phone call is crucial, because it establishes the time of his death."

"Yes."

"Okay. Now you got off the phone about twenty to twelve. His cleaning lady found him at ten past."

"I know. It was in *The Times.*"

"Right. And that seems to narrow it down, but of course there's another possibility . . . namely, was the murderer already with him when he was talking to you?"

Deb made a face; it seemed a grisly idea. "I never thought of that."

"Well, that's probably important in itself. But you see what it means—the killer might have arrived hours before."

"Yes. But—"

"Just a second. Did Price ever put down the phone when the two of you were talking?"

"No."

"Did you ever feel he covered the mouthpiece, and turned away to someone else?"

"No—wait." She closed her eyes, tying to remember as clearly as possible. Then she said, "It just didn't *feel* as though someone else was there."

Bannon seemed about to speak, but then merely tightened his lips and nodded. "All right," he said, "good enough. Another point. And this is sort of about 'feeling' too. Price was found—well, you say you saw the story in *The Times?*"

"Yes."

"With the picture of his house?"

"Yes."

"Okay, so you know how big a place it is. He was in the back. He's got a sort of den, workroom place back there. We don't think anyone broke in. Of course, it's possible that Price opened the front door to the murderer, who then forced him inside, but it's more than likely that he knew the person who killed him."

"I understand."

"Which raises a point, you see. Was he *expecting* that person?

Did they have an appointment? So think about the call again. Did you feel that Price was in a rush, squeezing you in, that he wanted to get off the line and—"

But Deb was already shaking her head. "I'd say the opposite. He wasn't in a hurry. He was—we chatted, really. It was all . . . *normal*. He was just . . . talking on the phone."

"You're sure?'

"Positive."

"Okay." Bannon leaned back a little in his chair, and now casually picked up Deb's statement, glancing over it. Deb felt herself go tense; Bannon was ready for the main event, the question of Price's stock dealings—though he pretended to treat it almost as a side issue, a formality that merely had to be got out of the way. Shifting in his seat, he looked at Lansdowne and Fenton. "I know you're all concerned about that side of it, the deals Price was making, it's your world. But I'm only concerned with Price's murder. I don't really care if there was anything fishy about his stock deals, unless that helps me find the person who killed him."

Lansdowne was short, had thinning hair and a toothbrush moustache; in his too-small brown suit, he looked like a high-school vice-principal. "That's understood. If you turn up something, we'd like to see it, but we're not asking you to do our job. If we think there are grounds for an investigation, we'll get it going."

Bannon turned to Deb. "What do you think about it—was Price up to something?"

Fenton opened his mouth, as if wanting to make a lawyerly intervention, but Deb didn't even look at him. "No," she said.

There was a little pause, as if everyone expected her to go on; when she didn't, Bannon said, "Okay, that's clear enough. But you did want to talk to André here?"

"I was being careful. I'm someone who plays by the rules."

Fenton beamed. "I think—not to put words in your mouth, Detective—that you're really interested in the possibility that Curtis Price might have been part of a conspiracy, some larger insider-trading scheme. And if you could figure it out, that might indicate who killed him."

"Well, that's a possibility."

Deb said, "So far as I know, he wasn't. I had no information that he was doing anything illegal or improper. There was simply a pattern in his trading that I thought I should report to my compliance officer. So I did."

Lansdowne's mouth settled into a line. Fenton beamed some more. Tellier said, "Deborah was simply working to our guidelines, Mr. Bannon. Price being murdered . . . I think it was just coincidence."

Bannon kept looking at Deb. "You can't remember him mentioning any names, in talking about his trades?"

"Apart from the ones in my statement? No."

"This scientist . . . Nisram Singh. From Xynex corporation . . . and the other man he met at the boat show in Baltimore . . ."

"His name was Peterson."

"Almost certainly," Lansdowne put in, "that man was still an insider, even if he'd left the company."

Fenton kept smiling. "Since both he and Price are dead, I expect that's moot, Leslie. But just to be clear about the record—the minute Deborah hung up the phone after that conversation, she was in this office talking to André Tellier."

"Yes, sir," said Tellier.

Bannon held up a palm, as if to quiet them. "Okay, no one's accusing Deborah of anything. But what about Walter Manley? According to your statement, Manley introduced Price to you."

"Yes, but I've checked all his trades, through that whole period. He's never owned a single stock that Price was into."

"But he could have been trading with Price through a different broker."

Deb shook her head. "Of course I wasn't Price's only broker—or I assume I wasn't—but I'm sure I have all Walter's money. You understand, he's a family friend. I know, pretty much, what he's worth, and I'd say he's investing everything through me."

"Well, we can check that."

"And Walter's over seventy, Detective Bannon. It's hard to see him shooting someone."

"Don't worry, Deborah, old people do. Anyway . . . you realize, there are no other names in your statement—according to you, he didn't mention anyone else."

"Well, I don't see anything surprising about that. Why should he? Most clients don't."

"All right—"

"Look," she continued, "Price was a wealthy man. He travelled in the circles that wealthy men travel in. Country clubs and yacht clubs—he owned a very expensive boat—"

"And you like sailing too?"

"That's right. *That* we did talk about. But the point is, the people he knew are the kinds of people who play the market. Some of them own companies, they sit on boards. I expect he heard all kinds of stuff, and some of it from insiders. But that wasn't his game. There was nothing systematic about it. Or at least I have no knowledge that there was."

"Tips . . . that's what it comes down to?"

"I guess that's what most people would say."

"And you can't remember him using any other names?"

"That's it."

It was, pretty much.

Fenton glanced at Deb. "Is it fair to say, so far as Price's actual transactions are concerned, that you've nothing material to add to your statement?"

"I'm sorry, but it really wasn't that complicated. I only met him once, and talked to him a few times on the phone. There isn't much I *can* say."

"I agree," said Fenton, buttoning his suit coat. "And in fact, being a busy man, and having put in a few good billable hours here this morning, I think I'll toddle along." He looked at Deb. "Do you mind?"

"No."

"Sure?"

"Uh-huh."

He got up. It was, altogether, a neat manoeuvre; if there was no reason for Fenton to stay, there could be no reason for Lansdowne to stay, either—especially since Fenton had to clamber over him to reach the door. Lansdowne smiled. "I should be on my way, too," he said. "Just wanted to introduce myself—establish our standing."

He shook hands with Bannon and Deb, and a moment later André's little office almost seem deserted.

"Lawyers," said André.

"Lawyers," said Bannon, with a smile.

Deb looked at him. "I guess, from your point of view this has pretty much been a waste of time?"

"Well . . . I haven't learned anything new. But I've confirmed a few points."

"About the time Price was shot?"

"That, especially."

"Tell me . . . do you believe me when I say I wasn't helping Price in some sort of insider-trading scheme?"

"Yes, I do."

"Good," she said. "Why don't we go and get coffee?"

Deb gave André a significant look, but he must have missed it or misunderstood, because he invited himself along; and of course Rosie had to come—it would have been cruel not to ask her. She was clearly impressed by Bannon, and immediately monopolized him. "Take my hand, Dean. You're only from Long Island—you might get lost in a world-class city like Toronto."

"Now, Rosie," said Deb, "keep it under control."

She was barely able to. In the coffee shop, Deb said, "If you like, we could just make small talk for a few minutes, then get rid of these two, and you could properly interrogate me."

Bannon smiled. "That's okay, though if you don't mind—if I could ask a few questions?"

"Of course."

"Good. In the office, it was all a bit formal." He shrugged. "In fact, I was a little surprised at the reception you guys gave me. I didn't expect it would be such a big deal."

"Dean," said Rosie, "we lead very dull lives. We just love a crisis."

"Rosie's right," André put in. "Every once in a while, if you've got hot-and-cold running lawyers, you like to turn on the tap."

Deb sipped her coffee. "In a way, I was thinking the same thing, but from the other direction."

"I don't understand," said Bannon.

"Well, Price was only killed the day before yesterday. And you're here today. Are you usually so efficient?"

Bannon ducked his head and smiled. "Some cases have—how to put it? A funny kind of pressure around them."

"You mean," said Rosie, "that Price was rich."

"Not exactly. It's hard to put your finger on." He grinned. "Pressure is always hard to put your finger on, but you feel it just the same."

"Is that why it turned into one of those days—when you found him?"

"Maybe."

"Aha," said Rosie, "we're talking politics. Tell me something . . . I read a lot of books—"

André couldn't resist: "While watching television, you mean."

"Unlike some," said Rosie, "I can do two things at once. But shut up—what I was wondering, will the FBI investigate this?"

Bannon shrugged. "Almost certainly, if there's anything to the stock-trading angle."

"Do you think there is?"

He looked at Deb: "I still think you can answer that question better than me. Do you?"

"You mean you didn't believe me?"

"I believed you. But I bet you could flesh it out a bit."

Deb looked into her coffee. "Not really, or at least not very much. I told you. Price travelled in the circles where people are always talking about stocks. Technically, half the stuff he heard was probably illegal, but that's not what he was about. Anyway . . . I'm not sure that's the sort of thing people get killed for."

"Not usually," said Bannon, "but maybe this time. Tell me about Xynex."

"It's a biotech company. I'd never heard of it before."

Rosie said, "What *could* he have known about it? Say they'd discovered some new drug . . ."

Deb said, "Except they're into vaccines mainly. But I guess if they found something for AIDS—"

"That can always move a stock," André said, "but most inside information—the sort of information people trade on—concerns mergers, buyouts, stock buybacks... corporate developments, as we like to say. Some people always do know about that sort of thing, they have to. I don't see why anyone would kill Price just because he did."

Deb said, "You mentioned... well, that this had a funny kind of pressure. And in the paper it said something about how he was killed professionally."

Rosie said, "You're not thinking the *Mafia* could have had anything to do with it?"

Bannon held up both palms. "Hang on. This is murder—which is bad enough. We don't need to make anything more out of it. The professional business... that's the sort of thing journalists like to write. What it means is, he was killed neatly. Actually, professionally—to the Mafia—most often means *thoroughly,* as in both barrels of a shotgun."

André said, "But it's interesting—you were asking about this yourself—that his killer was able to get into the house so easily. They must have known him or—what? Posed as someone? Reading the water meter... a policeman..."

Bannon shrugged. "There could be a lot of explanations—the killer could have pulled a gun at the door, and just backed him up. On the other hand, you're right—it's not the way things usually happen. It wasn't a robbery. Drugs don't seem to have been involved. Price had no known criminal connections ... so the whole thing is odd. Which brings you back to his stock trading..."

"The trouble is, Detective," André went on, "I don't see how that works either. Look—say he did know something. Go to Xynex. Ask them if there *is* something to know. But so what? Price was trying to profit from it. He wasn't going to call up CNBC and give them a scoop—he was trying to make money on this thing—"

Bannon interrupted: "All that's true, but maybe what he was

doing could have prevented *someone else* doing something . . . doing their takeover say."

But André was already shaking his head. "He was trying to buy two hundred thousand shares in that company . . . a lot, but not enough to block anyone."

And then Deb said, "It didn't feel like that, anyway. He was just buying the stock. You talk about a funny kind of pressure, Mr. Bannon—but when I spoke to him, there wasn't any sense of pressure at all."

Bannon pursed his lips, was about to say something—then stopped. "Would you excuse me for a moment?" He got up, went to the front of the restaurant and pulled out a cellphone.

As Bannon began talking into his phone, Rosie turned to André and said, "You have to shut up for a moment. We're going to have some girl talk." She turned to Deb. "So what do you think?"

"I like him."

"Yeah. You wouldn't call him cute, certainly not drop-dead gorgeous, but just the same . . . I don't know, he's *handsome*, wouldn't you say?"

"Very good," said André. "Sometimes, you know, the old words are best."

"Exactly," said Deb.

Rosie ignored them. "*Dean Bannon, NYPD*. It could be the title of a show."

"But he's from Long Island."

"Don't quibble. . . . At the same time, you know, he isn't too full of himself. He doesn't think he's God's gift."

"But perhaps he is," said André.

"Actually, André, I have news for you. None of you are—not quite. I was wondering—"

But André, with a frown, touched Rosie's arm, and looked at Deb. "Hang on for a minute. Tell me something . . . about Price. Did you ever think he had some sort of connection to the government?"

"What do you mean?"

"I'm not sure—but the 'funny pressure' our friend Bannon talks about . . . I wonder what he means by that. And you know, the Mafia aren't the only kind of professional killers."

"Jesus, André," said Rosie, "you're not trying to bring the CIA into this? Talk about making mountains out of molehills. This guy was murdered . . . okay. There could be a hundred reasons. I'm not so sure it *isn't* drugs—let's face it, we all know plenty of people in this business who do a little coke now and then."

Deb was going to say something, but didn't. It all sounded far-fetched; but then the whole business, *someone she knew being murdered*, sounded far-fetched. Just then, Bannon returned . . . and seemed to introduce a more conventional line of enquiry. Turning to Deb, he said: "You only saw Price that one time, face to face?"

"Yes."

"So you didn't really know him personally."

"Absolutely. I've never claimed to."

"I know. But in all his conversations, did he ever mention a woman?"

Deb hesitated. "I don't think so. No. Somehow, though, I know that he wasn't married." Then she said, "I remember. Walter told me."

Rosie asked, "Was he gay?"

"The time he came to your office . . . he was alone?"

"Yes."

"No one, say, might have waited for him? In that reception area you have."

Deb thought for a second. "Actually, I went out to get him . . . and I *think* I walked him out there afterward. I usually do."

Bannon took a photograph from his jacket pocket and handed it across to her. "What about this lady?"

Deb looked at the photo, a snapshot of a beautiful black woman in a bathing suit, lounging beside a pool.

"Let me see," said Rosie, as she leaned closer. "My, my. *Cherchez la femme.* God . . . what a body."

André, across the table, said: "Detective, am I really missing something?"

Bannon chuckled. "Help yourself. You never know, maybe you saw her."

"Doesn't he wish! Wow! If you saw her, Deb, you'd remember."

"Yes. She's very beautiful. And—well—I guess I would. Who is she?"

"His lady friend, obviously."

Bannon said, "She's a doctor, in Baltimore."

A doctor. And Giacomo was a doctor. Which meant absolutely nothing. *Except . . .* all at once, she felt an odd sense of alarm. Of course it was ridiculous. But it was still a coincidence—Price's murder, with all its peculiar overtones, coming at almost the same moment as the appearance of a strange man in Giacomo's apartment. It *had* to be a coincidence. *But.* It was there. *Something.* She said, "Price told me he was sailing on the Chesapeake. And he went to the boat show in Baltimore." *So what if this woman was a doctor? The world was full of doctors.* She took the photo back from André, who sank back reluctantly into his chair. And her voice was calm. "I can't be sure . . . but I don't think she was with him the day he came to see me." *But she was all on edge now, as if she knew this was the start of something bad.*

"It was just an off chance. Anyway . . . something else . . . think back to January. Did you see Price at all?"

"Absolutely not. I told you. I only saw him that once. And I've been over all my files and notes and . . . I don't even think I *spoke* to him in January, let alone saw him."

"You're sure?"

"Yes. Don't you believe me?"

It was okay; she had a right to sound annoyed like that. Though Rosie did give her a look.

"Yes, I do. But it's strange. You see, Price was in Toronto on January 17. We know because he was the kind of man who lived off his Amex card, kept all his receipts, bills, kept track of all his expenses. He stayed at the Four Seasons, and of course all his calls are on the bill. None to you."

"Well, I told you."

"And you don't think that's strange?"

"Not really. He just didn't want to buy a stock."

"Okay. But do you recognize any of these numbers?"

He slipped a photocopy across the table. It was Price's hotel bill; the phone numbers were all underlined. She read through. "Well, I guess that's Air Canada..."

"What about that one?" Bannon, leaning over, indicated a number with his ballpoint. "Nine two two..."

Four three eight seven ... She glanced at her watch—10:57—she needed just a second to think. And then she lied, "No," and this was the lie that changed everything. "I don't think so."

All she could do was stare straight down.

"It's the main number for something called the Marsh Foundation. They're a sort of Third World outfit, medical aid, research, conferences—you know the sort of thing."

"I don't think I've ever heard of them." *Okay. You tell him the truth. But don't be disappointed when he doesn't believe you. They never do. The cops are such liars themselves, they assume everyone else must be too.* She had to lift her head. She had to look at Rosie. As Rosie's eyes grew wider. *922-4387* ... *She could hear his voice, Hi Deb*..."No, I'm sure. I've never heard of them." André, thank God, didn't know of Giacomo's existence, period. "And I'm absolutely certain Price didn't call me." Well, that much was true. And Bannon believed her; *nice Dean Bannon believed it all.*

And Rosie, God bless her, played it perfectly.

She didn't blurt. She didn't gasp. She didn't gape. There was one moment, entirely forgivable, when she looked a little stunned, but no one noticed, and then something determined came into her eyes, a decision, *my friend, okay*, and she reached out for the photocopy and calmly said:

"When I'm a *very* old lady, after I've been married *at least* three times, I intend to become Miss Jane Marple."

Deb glanced at her watch. André, seeing her, took it as a hint, though it was nothing more than terminal nervousness.

"Well, he didn't call *me*," said Rosie, running her finger down the numbers, skipping over the Marsh Foundation. "I'm sort of disappointed. What's that one...?" *As if she was deliberately diverting him.*

Bannon leaned across to look. "Actually I'm not sure. It's the number of someone called Chahal ... a funny name. I called it but we still haven't got an answer. That one ... and that one ... in fact all the rest are long distance." Bannon shrugged. "Of course there's no reason to believe his coming here in January has anything to do with his murder. I was just curious. So far as we know, you're his only real connection in Toronto, but he *didn't* call you. You see?"

Deb couldn't speak, but Rosie could. "You know what I think? I think it's *all* coincidence. Deb was talking to him twenty minutes before he was murdered, so you assume there was a connection. I don't think there was one. I bet nothing he did in Toronto had any importance." She made a face. "We're entirely irrelevant. Damn it!"

Bannon smiled, they all smiled. And then André said: "I've got to go. Back to the wars."

He eased out of his chair and for an instant Deb closed her eyes. "Maybe you could take Detective Bannon back with you. You're going to want to copy some things, aren't you?"

"If I could."

He was smiling. He was believing. *Nice Dean Bannon believed it all.*

"Well, André or a vp will have to sign anyway."

"Okay."

"Well ..."

"It was great meeting you, Deborah. Thanks for everything. You too, Rosie."

They all shook hands, and Deb's face hurt, her face was aching, but she said, "If there's anything more ... just call. Or I could come down. I always love a trip to New York!" *Aching ...*

They all smiled once more; then they were gone. And Rosie was lunging over the table. "*Deb!*"

"Just a second, just a second." Because she was scribbling on her napkin, all the phone numbers, the bits of them she could recall ...

"Deb—"

"*Try to remember that number* ... there was a girl in my class called Chahal. It's not a funny name, it's an Indian name."

Rosie, no matter how excited she was, could never stop thinking. Besides, already, she was holding Deb's hand. "As in Nisram
Singh, you mean?"

Deb was nodding. She was almost crying. But she wasn't crying.
"Except there'll be hundreds in the book..."

"Deb... Jesus. Giacomo... you don't think...?"

She kept scribbling. Then she stopped. She nodded. "Yes." Then
she shook her head, "No!" And then she closed her eyes. The truth
was, she didn't know what to think. She was thinking of that afternoon, the man in the apartment, the weird way Giacomo had
sounded on the phone. And now she was seeing the picture of the
black woman and that phone bill, and hearing her voice as
she lied...

Rosie whispered, "Deb, what the hell *is happening?*"

She couldn't say anything; if she'd opened her mouth, my God,
right there, she would have started to blubber. So she just shook her
head again. And then Rosie was squeezing her hand, and Deb did
finally choke it out, "I don't know, I don't know." She shrugged, or
tried to. "Why would Curtis Price have Giacomo's phone number?"
And then she blurted: "God, Rosie, I'm going to have his child."

CHAPTER SIX

*A*t *3:58, Deborah dialled* the number of Giacomo's hotel. It was only 2:58 in Mexico City, and although the Dow looked to be closing down, the Bolsa Index—which measures the stock market south of the Rio Grande—was staging a rally. Deb watched the numbers flicker away as the phone rang in Giacomo's room. Twelve rings: no answer. The Bolsa was up three-quarters of a point. Annoyingly, the hotel operator didn't come back on the line; Deb had to dial again to leave a message. She left all her numbers. "It's urgent. Please tell him to call right away."

Rosie peered around her terminal; Deb shook her head.

Rosie said, "Don't worry. He's still at lunch—big deal."

Deb didn't answer, but she was feeling queasy in a way quite different from this morning. *Price knew Giacomo.* At least, he'd called the Marsh Foundation. Of course, that had been months ago. Still, Price had now turned up murdered—at almost exactly the same time as someone was showing a very peculiar interest in Giacomo's computer. It could all be coincidence . . . *But.*

Rosie came around to Deb's desk and said, "There're all kinds of Chahals, but I think it has to be this one on Walmer Road."

Between them, they'd managed to remember five of the digits from the number Bannon had shown them, and Rosie had gone through the phone book, trying to match them up. "Somebody listed as 'K. Chahal.' An apartment. One of those old buildings—"

"Yes."

"Deb—"

"It's okay. Sorry."

Rosie said, "Listen, something's going on, it has to be. Maybe you should have told him—maybe you still should. If he ever connects the Marsh Foundation to Giacomo, and then to you—"

"Are you going to tell him?"

"*Of course I'm not.*"

"Okay then. So . . . go make your calls."

They both started on the post-market ritual, calling customers about orders, disasters, the few scintillating successes. And then— at 3:45 Mexican time—Deb called the hotel again. Giacomo still wasn't in his room. She called her apartment, to pick up any messages he might have left there—again, nothing. *What was going on?* Nothing. It was all coincidence. *He's just finished lunch and now he's going for a walk.* Of course. *But why, of all the numbers in Toronto, had Price called that one . . .* And then been murdered. Almost at the same time someone had come into Giacomo's apartment and snooped around—

"Deb? Want to go? Let's get a drink."

Deb didn't move. She let out her breath, scanning the room. It was amazing, after the market closed, how quickly the place emptied out. Only a few figures were still huddled in front of their terminals—mad magicians, staring into crystal balls—while one or two others, hanging on to doorframes, chatted up the select minority who actually had offices.

Turning to Rosie, Deb shook her head. "I don't want a drink. I'm . . . I don't know what I am. I don't like it, that he hasn't called."

"Deb, we never like it when men don't call. It is one of the very worst things about men, their persistent, habitual, *chronic* failure to call. But it simply means he's out somewhere, probably doing his job—why should he be hanging around his hotel room in the middle of the day?"

"I know . . ." She tried to smile. "But I don't understand this. What's happening. Price and Giacomo *knew* each other—"

"Come on. That's stretching it."

"Not much. There has to be a connection. If Bannon finds out, he'll certainly assume there is—"

"I know, and I don't like that either. But it may only *look* bad . . . It doesn't have to *mean* anything."

Deb was silent. She hadn't told Rosie about the man in the apartment, and now, again, debated whether she should. Once more, she decided not to. And yet, she realized, that whole incident preyed on her mind in a special way. Because she'd been afraid. Because it had introduced an element of danger, of violence. *If that man had seen her, what would he have done?* Finally, she looked up at Rosie. "I think," she said, "that I'm going to speak to this Chahal person."

"Why? *Don't*."

"Why not? It probably doesn't mean anything, but it might. Price called him, whoever he is, on the same day he probably called Giacomo."

"But there's nothing to show that Giacomo and Chahal knew each other. Look—just wait. Call Giacomo later. Ask him—"

"I will. All the same . . . I mean, they *might* know each other. Giacomo knows quite a few Indians—there are a lot of them around the aid agencies. Maybe it's very simple. Price was interested in this Nisram Singh, an Indian scientist, a medical guy—he didn't hide the fact, when he was talking to me. So he wants to check up on him. In some way, that leads him to Chahal. Chahal knows Giacomo and tells Price, look, call up this person at the Marsh Foundation, maybe he can help. It could be very simple. Very innocent. It could explain everything."

Rosie thought about it. "*Maybe*," she said.

"Anyway, if I don't do something, I'll go out of my mind."

Rosie reached for her purse. "Okay," she said, "but I'm coming with you."

Deb, to tell the truth, was glad to have her along. They took the subway up to Bloor, then walked up to the Annex, an old and still-desirable area in downtown Toronto—although this particular building, probably put up in the sixties, was perhaps a little past it;

the yellowish façade was worn, and the low, marble lobby—once smart and "modern"—now seemed irretrievably dated. But that turned out to be a piece of luck, in a way; instead of the usual security codes, there was an old-fashioned directory. They didn't even have to use the buzzer; someone was going in, and Rosie, discreetly, caught the door.

"Maybe we should anyway," said Deb. But then she changed her mind. "What if he tells us to go to hell?"

But that was the first surprise—there was no "he" in apartment 627. When they rang the bell, the door opened and a woman appeared. She was about their own age, Indian, with black hair and thick, perfectly shaped eyebrows; she was wearing square, very stylish, black spectacles—the frames were all bevelled and very shiny. She smiled. "Yes?"

Deb was a little taken aback. "Hello . . . I was looking for Mr. Chahal—?"

The woman smiled more broadly at this. "There isn't any Mr. Chahal. I'm Kumari Chahal. I live here."

"Then—I was really looking for someone called Nisram Singh."

"Nisram? But he isn't here. Who . . . ?"

Deb blushed. She was being rude. "I'm sorry, really. My name is Deborah Graham. This is my friend—"

But before Deb could introduce Rosie, a voice—deep, but very feminine—called out from within the apartment. "Who is that, my dear? Invite them in. My God, their feet probably ache as much as my own."

Kumari Chahal smiled, almost apologetically, and turned away, saying something in Hindi, or some language that was decidedly not English. The door had opened a little more; Deb could see that the young woman was dressed in a light navy jacket, white blouse, and a straight grey skirt. She was in stocking feet, and, as she'd turned, her hand had gone to her ear—Deb had the feeling she must have been changing her clothes. When she turned back, she said: "Nisram isn't here . . . though . . . well, sometimes he does stay here. May I ask . . . ?"

"I'm sorry, I'm not doing this very well. I'm a friend of Dr. Valli, Giacomo Valli—"

"Oh yes. Of course."

"You know him?"

"At the Marsh Foundation?"

"That's right."

"I met him once with Nisram, at a party there. This is very nice. We had a long talk."

From inside, the other voice came again: "But tell them to come in, if they are friends of Nisram's . . ."

Deb said, "I'm sorry about this—I must be intruding, but you see the Marsh Foundation called me at work because they had had a fax from Giacomo—Dr. Valli—he's in Mexico, at a conference—"

"Yes, I see."

"Well, he wanted to get in touch with Nisram Singh, but didn't have his number—he didn't know where to find him—but he said you'd probably know."

"I understand—"

"*Kumari*, it's just what we need—some visitors! We have the rest of our lives to spend talking to each other. Are they students? Your friends? Have them in!"

Kumari rolled her eyes. "Would you mind?" she whispered. "Perhaps it would be better. Please?"

"Of course."

She opened the door. "And you are—?"

"Rosie."

"Rosie and Deborah. Good . . ." And then, stepping aside, she called behind her in Hindi or Punjabi—a little exasperated, judging by her tone—and Rosie and Deb followed her into the apartment.

The age of the building, and its general atmosphere, had brought "beanbag" into Deborah's mind—as in the two beanbag chairs she could remember from her childhood, which over the years had gradually moved into the basement, with her motorcycle, and were now living out their lives at her parents' cottage on Bob's Lake. This was reasonable enough, for the building dated to an era when "high-rise" had an almost exotic connotation; but this apartment was exotic in a much more genuine way. For just a second, this wasn't quite apparent, for the layout, in fact, was entirely conventional. A tiny entranceway passed as a hall, and then you stepped into the inevitable "L-shaped" living room, or, more precisely, the "living-dining area." But this was bigger than usual, and the "picture window" actually filled the back wall—and sunlight streamed through it, golden, rich and mellow at this hour of the day. The light seemed to fill the room, all the more so because there was little furniture; only one large sofa, and two matching armchairs, which were covered in a heavy, coarsely woven white fabric, and a third chair, which might have been a deck chair from an old liner, though definitely from the first-class end of the boat: the frame was mahogany, and its cushion was covered in raw silk. And there was a long glass coffee table in front of the sofa—in fact, this almost might have come from the sixties. But it took Deb a moment to notice any of these details, for what swept her up, as though she had been caught in a rainbow, were the rugs, layers of them, as colourful as flowers or stained glass or tropical fish, and so thick and soft that she wanted to kick off her shoes and go barefoot. There were so many—they were laid on top of one another. And a huge one covered a wall.

"What a beautiful room," said Deb.

"Thank you," said Kumari.

"Oh, I don't know. I think it is too bare. And I've taken the only comfortable place to sit." This was the lady who'd been calling to Kumari—and who was sitting, rather spread out, on the sofa. On the one hand, she was as exotic as her surroundings—she was wearing a beautiful sari; on the other, she couldn't have been more down to earth—leaning forward, with an expression of acute pain on her face, she rubbed one chubby foot. "My God," she said, "I am so stupid. A sari is one thing... it's warm enough. But sandals! I am mad. This town, from beginning to end, is nothing but concrete." Piled up around her on the sofa were numerous shopping bags—Holt Renfrew, The Bay, Gucci, Calderone, Sam the Record Man... she'd gone everywhere.

Kumari began making introductions: "Rosie, Deborah—"

"Deborah Graham."

"This is—"

"Oh, never mind! Everyone calls me Auntie. Auntie! Because I have so many nieces and nephews. I am the oldest, you see, and my parents were most unrestrained. Wicked, in fact!" She laughed. "Two brothers, five sisters . . ." Lifting her eyes, she began counting on her fingers. "Yes, that's it, eight including me—I don't want to leave anyone out. And my mother died, you see, before any of us married, and on top of that I was the last to marry. So all the little ones were brought to me first. 'Here's your Auntie, this is your Auntie!'"

Kumari smiled at Deb and Rosie. "I should explain," she said. "This is Nisram's mother, and Nisram and I are going to be married."

"Which makes me her mother-in-law, the traditional ogre of the Indian family. Soon, she will be in *my* family, within *my* power. She will do as I say—won't you!" Auntie laughed as she said this, but then looked serious. "I suppose I shouldn't say that. Not as a joke. Too often it's true. You mustn't get the wrong impression—I was there when Kumari was born. Her mother and me, we are the oldest of friends."

Kumari smiled at Deb and said, "My mother and Auntie went to university together. That's why I'm studying here, you see. Or partly."

"Here? You mean at the University of Toronto?"

"My God, it's different now. Toronto used to be such a nice, clean, English city. Now—I might as well be back in Asia. So many Chinese! So many Koreans!"

"Auntie, you mustn't talk like that. Really."

"I suppose you are right. I should be tolerant. But then, I admit, when it comes to religion, I am hopeless, I smoke, I drink . . ." And, saying this, she leaned forward and took a Benson & Hedges from a pack on the table. She lit it with such vigour that her face disappeared in a cloud of smoke.

Rosie said, "When you say your religion, you mean . . . Hindu." But already she realized her mistake. "No. Sikh."

Auntie's laugh blew the cloud of smoke away. "Yes, thank God. Frankly, Hindus can be just a little unclean, even though one doesn't like to say it."

"Auntie!"

Deb said, "I remember. The five K's? Isn't that right?"

"How ever did you know that?" said Auntie.

Deborah, asserting herself, ignored her. "The dagger, the bracelet—"

"Yes. *Kara*..."

Deb thought a second but then shook her head. "I'm afraid I don't remember the others.

"*Kagha*, the comb, and *Kachch*—it's a kind of underwear. Drawers, I suppose you could say. But I'm surprised you would know that."

"There was a girl in my class at school, her name was Chahal. Jaswant... Kaur—that's the name for girls?"

"Yes. Exactly."

"Once she had to give the class a talk on being a Sikh."

"Poor woman!"

"Yes! But we were just girls... everyone had to do it. One of the boys had to talk about Baden-Powell . . . I knew her especially because her father taught at the Royal Military College—this was in Kingston—and so did my father."

"What did he teach?"

"Jaswant's father taught engineering. He was in the Indian Army."

"My God, the army. I know you think of war and pomp and glory, but really it is all bridges and supplies and forms. RMC—yes?"

"Yes."

"And Queen's... that's the big university there."

"Well, it's not very big."

"But RMC was full of boys, cadets—a good reason to go to Kingston. But of course I didn't. I was—are you listening Kumari? —a good girl."

Rosie, trying to puzzle this out, was being left behind. "So . . . Mrs. Singh... you went to the University of Toronto?"

"Yes. Yes, exactly. I'm an alumnus. Alumna? I can never remember... It was very important—for me, one of the most important things in my life. For one thing, as the oldest, I should by rights have married first, but I didn't. I was last, in the end. But then my family is like that—everything is out of order. Kumari—you can count on that!"

"No, Auntie. I will put *you* in order—wait and see."

"My God, her mother's daughter. And I know what I'm talking about. Because her mother was with me here, we came together. This was in 1953. The year of the Coronation. I don't suppose you remember?"

"Well," Deb said, "I wasn't born."

"How extraordinary. But of course you weren't. None of you were. And it was so exciting. There was television, it was just starting. Everyone was impressed because they flew the film across the Atlantic—I suppose it was a jet, did they have jets then?—and we saw it on the same day."

Rosie, doggedly, sought some conventional order. "You were studying . . . ?"

"Medicine, of course. We wanted to be doctors. Her mother as well. And Kumari. And Nisram. We're all doctors, though Nisram and this one don't actually cure anyone, or even stoop to touch a body. No! All research. Very superior. I don't understand a word."

Kumari said, "And your friend, Deborah—Dr. Valli . . . another doctor!"

"I'm afraid he doesn't touch many bodies, either."

"Auntie, Dr. Valli works for the Marsh Foundation. They sponsor medical research all over the world, projects." Kumari smiled at Deb. "Do they have any in India?"

"I'm not sure, to tell the truth. There's a project in Malaysia—also Bangladesh. A lot in South America."

Kumari nodded. "I know Nisram was interested because his company was supporting a number of clinics—one was in Brazil, another in Baltimore, Maryland." She turned to her future mother-in-law. "They are developing a new rubella vaccine, Auntie."

"Well, it's the sort of thing you can easily forget about, but I expect it is still a problem."

"In Baltimore, I know, the clinic is in the ghetto. Principally, they do abortions—"

"In my heart, I don't approve. But—*but*..."

"And they did a study showing that the best time to test for rubella immunity, and vaccinate if necessary, is when a woman comes for an abortion. They're supposed to get their shots in school, but many of the poor girls miss them. Just a minute, I can show you something..." Kumari got up, left the room—a swirl of lavender smoke now drifted in the golden light, above the carpets—and returned almost at once with a magazine. "Dr. Valli and Nisram went to Baltimore together, and he brought me back this magazine..." She opened it, folded it over, and handed it to Deb. It was a regional "marketing" magazine called *The Chesapeake*—as glossy as *Vogue*, and about as thick, with ads and articles that were pretty much indistinguishable: "infomercials." Kumari said, "It's not really about the clinic, but that's the doctor who runs it."

Deb found herself looking at big photo of the black woman Detective Bannon had shown them: *Doctor in Motion*, read the caption. She looked even more beautiful, Deb thought—sensual but very cool, remote but enticing—though this time there was no bathing suit; instead, a white lab coat was fashionably draped over an expensive black suit. But how many women, in a suit, could show off their figure so well? Deb's eyes blurred; she didn't so much read the article as absorb it by osmosis. The lady's name was Charlaine Daniels. The clinic, housed in a seedy cement-block building that had formerly served as a package store, was her charity work. She was "giving something back to the community." She loved her private practice, but "my clinic work gives me that extra measure of fulfillment." Working with poor people, she said, "reminds me of why I became a doctor in the first place." It was all pretty gooey, though that was probably unfair; it was just that sort of article.

Kumari said, "Nisram said she was very competent. I understand—" she looked at Deb—"that your friend knew her in school."

"I don't think so," said Deb ... though why did she say that? Because, really, she had no idea.

"Let me look," said Auntie, putting on a pair of readers. "Oh well

... very beautiful. Such dramatic eyes ... and, you know, just that sort of figure—the prominent buttocks so characteristic of her race."

"Auntie, really, you must *stop* saying things like that."

"But they are perfectly true, Kumari. Where did Nisram know her? She *is* beautiful. And that is quite a nice suit."

"Auntie, it was Dr. Valli, *not* Nisram, who knew her. They were together in school." She looked at Deb. "I think Nisram was counting on that to get Dr. Valli's support."

"Did the Marsh Foundation help them?"

"In the end, I believe not. They were reluctant to fund a project like that—I think because it was in a U.S. city."

"But you know," said Auntie, "that would be an idea for these ghettos. Treat them as part of the Third World."

"Actually, Auntie, I believe they have thought of that. Some American mayors have requested help from US AID. And I think ...""

But now Deb wasn't listening. Her eyes were moving down the columns in the article, picking out little facts. Dr. Daniels had worked, briefly, for Oxfam—and Giacomo knew hundreds of people there. She'd studied at Johns Hopkins—and for six months Giacomo had done research there. Yes, they certainly could have known each other; Giacomo could have known her, Deb realized, long before she came on the scene. She looked up now. She felt queasy; and this had nothing to do with morning sickness. Charlaine Daniels, undoubtedly, was very beautiful. And Giacomo had never mentioned Baltimore, a trip there, a clinic or Nisram Singh. But then, she thought, why should he? The Marsh Foundation received hundreds of applications for support. Giacomo was always making trips, and why mention this one? What was so special about Baltimore—he'd probably flown in and out on the same day. Discreetly, she turned the magazine over and looked at its cover; the only date was "winter"—which meant it would have been on display any time after Thanksgiving. Was it possible—now she faced it directly—that Charlaine Daniels had been Giacomo's lover before herself? He had mentioned other girls, but nothing recent ... and then, suddenly, she thought of something else.

"Did they mention—when they went to Baltimore—meeting a man called Curtis Price?" And as soon as she said this she turned to Rosie with a look that said "shut up."

Kumari shook her head. "Oh, I don't remember. It was just a trip."

"He was a friend of Giacomo's . . . he had a sailboat, and sailed a lot on the Chesapeake. He was an older man. And he had a girl-friend who was a black doctor."

Deb, saying this, realized it sounded awkward, and she could sense Kumari growing self-conscious. Rosie even gave her a glance. Only Auntie seemed unaware. "I know it's not fashionable to say—you will scold me, I know—but there's nothing wrong with an older man and a younger woman. And I think that is *especially* true if the woman wishes to have a career. I think it settles your private life, you see. You can just get on. An older man is estab-lished. He has already made his way—you don't have to help *him* so much; he can help *you*."

Rosie said, "But I bet Nisram isn't old."

Kumari smiled, "You are right, he is not. And I wouldn't stand for some old man—would I, Auntie?"

"But he is a little older, Kumari," said Auntie. "And what about your doctor, Deborah?"

"Yes. Just a little older."

"Of course, that is the tradition here. The man is a little older, but only a little. You both work. But then you will leave your job when you have your first child. And of course you will have only two children. Yes?"

"Well, I don't think I'll stop working."

"No one does, Auntie. Not any more."

"Of course, I had to. But then I had four. I thought that was good, four. A girl, a boy, a girl, a boy. And even if Sula had not been a boy, I would have stopped. Four was a good *enough* num-ber, if you see what I mean. But think, before family planning, how many would I have had?"

Rosie couldn't stop herself. "How many?"

"Well, my mother had eight, didn't she? And many had more in those days. Mind you, all of hers lived, which wasn't so common—she had so many grandchildren!"

"Auntie, I'm warning you. I'll only have two."

"That is perfectly all right by me—have as many as you want. But you'll see . . . it may not be so easy." Auntie looked at Deb. "Tell me, after you have *your* two, what will happen if you find yourself pregnant with a third?"

Deb's head began to spin; she was, after all, having trouble enough getting her mind around one, let alone two, let alone a third! She said, "I don't know what I'd do. I suppose—well, it would depend on so many things. What my husband wanted. Our economic situation. The first two—I guess!"

Kumari looked at Deb and smiled, as if they were in a pact to humour the old lady. "After two, I will have my tubes tied, Auntie. I'll take no chances."

"We'll see, we'll see. But don't be so certain about it, you may eat your words. Children are wonderful, they are not just a problem, an expense. You can't imagine the joy you brought your mother, how many happy hours we spent talking about you. Your little teeth. Your hair. Your schooling. Your doctors. So, you see, you may have two and then find you *want* to have more. What will you do then? And then—don't scold me!—what if the first two are girls? Don't worry—you'll think about it! Should I have another, to have a boy?"

"Auntie, there would be nothing wrong with two girls."

"Nothing at all. Except neither would be a boy."

"Are you," Rosie began . . . but then broke off, floundering in politically correct confusion. "I mean," she said, "the Chinese—"

"We are in no way like the Chinese," said Auntie. "But I see what you're saying. Actually, we are worse than the Chinese. They only want one. We want two, for our old age—one, and then another for insurance."

"Not 'we,' Auntie—you!"

"Absolutely not. I want nothing. I will express no opinion on the matter. We have already discussed this. I will be the best, most non-interfering mother-in-law any woman ever had, certainly better than what I had to put up with!" Auntie laughed, then looked at Deb. "What about you, Deborah? Do you like your mother-in-law?"

"I don't know her very well—we've only met a few times. But yes. I think so. And I like her husband too."

"And you, Rosie?"

"Actually, I'm just a little behind Deb. I mean, I haven't even met the son yet, let alone his mother. And I think, at this point, I wouldn't be too fussy."

They all had a good laugh at this. Then Kumari said, "Auntie, you've had a real treat."

"So I have. A good chat. Now, of course, you want to be rid of me."

"Not at all. But Deborah wanted to know where Nisram is."

"Heavens, don't ask me. I'm only his mother."

Kumari looked at Deb. "I think I have a phone number, a hotel in Los Angeles. But I can't guarantee anything—I know he's travelling all the time—he's never in his office—and I don't expect to see him myself for at least two weeks."

"Anything would be fine. At least I'd be able to say I'd done my duty."

"That's always the important thing, isn't it? Just give me a minute." She went off, returning with a number written on a card. "That's the number I have, for tonight, and then for the next two days. And that's my address and number. We must keep in touch."

"Absolutely." Deb wrote her own home number on one of her business cards. "It's been wonderful meeting you, really."

Auntie insisted on pulling herself up and shaking hands. "You are wonderful young women," she said, "and it has been a great pleasure talking to you."

Her careful smile, and the slightly formal tone of her voice, were like a proof of her sincerity. Deb realized that they'd made friends; it was awkward to part. And for a moment this even overshadowed the reasons that had brought her there. But finally they said goodbye and then she and Rosie found themselves in the corridor—where the carpet was pure polyester and the light perfectly artificial. It was like coming back to earth. Outside, on the street, Deb could feel her spirits sinking. And then she said:

"Rosie, I have to go to Baltimore. And you have to cover for me."

"Baltimore?"

"Yes. I have to speak to Charlaine Daniels, that doctor."

"Just a minute, Deb. Let's think about this."

"Look—will you cover for me or won't you."

"Of course I will. I'll come with you—"

"No."

"Okay, but slow down a second."

Rosie finally caught up. She took Deb's arm in hers. "I know what you're thinking."

"What am I thinking?"

"You're afraid Giacomo had a thing with this gorgeous doctor."

"No. I'm not thinking that."

"Of course you are. And you want to go to Baltimore—"

"No." Then she took a breath: "Something's going on, Rosie. I'm afraid."

"How? Afraid, how?"

"Because—"

"Deb, what difference does it make? Maybe he was seeing this lady. I guess he did know her in school. But it would have all happened before he met you. That's probably why he went back there. He was giving her the kiss-off."

"Look, Rosie, all right—he knew her. But there wasn't anything between them. I know *that*."

"So why go to Baltimore?"

"You know me... I'm a big Jays fan. They're playing the Orioles."

"Come on."

"You come on. Isn't it obvious? I want to go to Baltimore because something's happening. *These people all knew each other.* And Price was killed. And Giacomo... he's mixed up in it. Somehow." Deb almost told Rosie about the man in the apartment then, how frightened she'd been, and the way Giacomo had pretended— but Rosie didn't give her the chance.

"Okay," she said, "I don't deny it looks a little funny... Price is murdered. Price knew the beautiful Charlaine. Charlaine knew Giacomo and runs this clinic in Baltimore that the brilliant Nisram Singh is interested in—Nisram Singh being the top scientific guy at Xynex Inc., whose shares Price was buying the day he was killed. It all comes full circle."

"Exactly."

"But what you have to do is *call Giacomo,* not go to fucking Baltimore! Call him! Tell him! Ask him!" She'd pulled a cellphone out of her bag, and was waving it around.

"Rosie, I have called him, and I didn't get any answer."

"So call him again." She waved the phone in Deb's face.

"Okay. I will. And if I still don't get any answer?"

"You're assuming things. Because you're all at once afraid you can't trust him and—"

"*No,* that's not the reason." And it wasn't—and maybe no *one* thing was, it was so many things, together. Quickly, before Rosie could answer, Deb headed across the road. By the time she reached the other side, she was almost pulling Rosie along.

Rosie, out of breath, finally said, "Where the hell are you going?"

They'd turned down a side street. Now Deb slowed down; she let go of Rosie. And then, hurrying ahead, she let her arms and shoulder slump, trying to relax. They'd come quite a way. It was quiet here, almost dark, for they were on the edge of the University of Toronto. In the gloom, the lawns were like soft, dark shadows, and she could smell the dew and the fresh leaves on the trees. One of the grey stone colleges loomed ahead of them. Deb waited. When Rosie caught up, she said, "Sorry. Sorry, sorry, sorry."

"Okay. Don't worry about it. I need the exercise."

"Rosie, I'm not explaining this very well, but I'm afraid. *For* him."

"So *call* him. I'm telling you. Here."

Deb took the phone as Rosie thrust it into her hand, but then shook her head. "I'm not sure. It's too complicated for the phone."

"Don't be crazy. The phone is simpler than going to Baltimore, for Christ's sake."

"I'm not sure. I'm not sure I know the right questions to ask—"

"No, you're not sure if you'll believe the answers you get, but the only way to know that is to get them."

Nearby there was a bench. Rosie sank down on it and pulled Deb down beside her. Deborah said, "I just hate the way it all connects up. Price was in Baltimore—he told me that. This clinic is there, this doctor. Giacomo was there. Nisram Singh—"

"Okay," said Rosie, "I'm not saying it isn't a little funny. But what you do is call Giacomo. I think the reason you don't want to—which you're not admitting—is you're worried he did have something on with this lady doctor. And you're pregnant, for crying out loud. That's what you have to add into the equation. Maybe, just maybe, Giacomo was playing some kind of number."

"I'm telling you, that isn't it. I'm just afraid—everything seems to circle around him."

"So phone him. Really. I'm telling you. Right now. On me. After all, if you go to Baltimore and talk to this gorgeous thing, what do you get? An inferiority complex."

"I bet she doesn't look as good as her photographs. Even if she does, I'll find *something* out. I'll *know*."

"Deb, this is dumb. It's that Thomasina thing you were telling me about. When you were a kid. You're only trying to prove something to yourself."

Deb smiled in the dark. It was like Rosie to remember that. "Maybe you're right. God, I don't know. Let me think about it. But if I do go, you'll cover for me?"

"Of course I will."

Deb didn't say anything. For a moment, in silence, they sat there together, then Rosie reached her arm around Deb and gave her a squeeze, and they stood up. In the gloom, they followed a curving path that let them out through a black wrought-iron fence overgrown with lilacs; the smell of the first blooms hung in the air. The night was like that: spring, but already soft and heavy with the coming summer. A little sand, left from the winter, crunched under their shoes as they stood on the sidewalk, but it made Deb think of the beach. They didn't talk. The sounds of the city seemed far off, drawn down to the gentle buzzing of a street lamp, whose wet, hazy light was jumping with moths. They stepped off the curb—

It happened very fast—and was the sort of thing that happens a hundred times a night in every big city. A black Honda CRX—where had it come from?—accelerated down the street and flashed its lights (but then it was the time of evening when drivers start remembering to turn on their lights) and out of this blinding glare raced toward them. The car braked—or at least its tires squealed and its back end swerved—and Deb and Rosie leapt backwards, stumbling and sprawling across the sidewalk. And then the car was gone.

"Jesus!' Rosie said.

The car, Deb thought, had hit her. Yes; ever so delicately, it had brushed her hip. She looked over at Rosie. "You okay?" And then she started to pull herself up—but had to wait a moment, resting on her knees.

"The son of a bitch! Did you see him? Some redneck asshole in a baseball cap!"

A baseball cap . . . in fact, Deb hadn't seen it, but she'd *known*. She got to her feet. She still had Rosie's phone in her hand.

"I'm telling you, he almost ran us over. He could have killed us."

But then Rosie fell silent, and came over as Deb found her diary in her purse, and with a trembling hand found the page where she'd written all Giacomo's numbers. They both listened as the stream of digits sailed through the ether.

This time, they didn't put her through to his room. He'd checked out.

"Are you sure?"

"Yes, Miss. About an hour ago."

"Were there any messages, please. For Deborah Graham."

"No, Miss. No messages."

Deb pushed "end" and Rosie said, "I know you love him, but right now I hate him to bits."

BALTIMORE

Telecommunications in North America are, no doubt, the most advanced in the world—but in the Washington-Baltimore International Airport the only way to get a phone book was to borrow one from the nice young man at the Hertz counter. It listed numerous "Daniels" but no "Charlaines." Among the doctors, however, there was a "Dr. C. Daniels" on North Calvert Street., *Specialist in Obstetrics & Gynecology*. Deb took a breath and dialled the number.

She felt nervous.

She was less certain than she'd let on to Rosie about the wisdom of coming here. But earlier this morning, when she'd called the Marsh Foundation, they'd been surprised to learn that Giacomo wasn't in Mexico—he was due to be there for at least another day. And they had no idea where he was. Which had settled it. She'd driven right to the airport, thinking, *You have to do something*. And then, *What else can you do?* Still—as the phone rang, she was half hoping that she might reach voice mail. But it was a female voice—apparently live, analog and in real time—that finally picked up. "Dr. Daniels, Dr. Read, good morning."

"Hello. I'd like to speak to Dr. Daniels, if I could. Or leave a message."

"It'll have to be a message. I'm not expecting her in for the rest of the day."

"Oh . . ." *Her.* So it was definitely the right Dr. Daniels. "Is she at the clinic?"

"No."

Deb closed her eyes; somehow, it seemed to make lying easier. "But she's not at home. I just called."

"Look, all I know is she's driving to Oxford. Something about a boat. And I've got to cancel all of her appointments, so if you don't mind . . ."

"Thanks. Sorry. I guess I'll call her tonight."

"Fine, then."

Deb put the phone down and tried to work it out. Oxford . . . A boat . . . Curtis Price, she remembered, had sailed on the Chesapeake. But what was going on? Charlaine Daniels had cancelled all her appointments *because* . . . because the police had called her? That would be one explanation for the urgency. But Deb was surprised; she'd assumed that Bannon had already spoken to her, since he'd had her photograph. But perhaps not. If he hadn't, it probably meant that Charlaine Daniels had learned only *today* that Price had been murdered, and indeed if the police hadn't called her before, that made sense; the story wouldn't have been carried in the Baltimore papers, it wouldn't have been big enough. But why the rush—and why to Oxford, to a boat? That was harder to answer; it had never occurred to Deb that Price's boat could have any importance, and there didn't seem much reason for the police to think so, either. Of course, they'd probably know about its existence, although they might well not know where it was. So was it possible that Charlaine Daniels was in a rush to get to the boat before the police?

Deb was framing these questions, and puzzling over possible answers to them, in the airport bookstore, as she thumbed through guidebooks to Maryland. Oxford was in all of them. It was a small town, but with lots of history, home to a man named Morris—the "financier of the American Revolution"—and a certain Colonel Tench Tilghman, an aide-de-camp to Washington who'd carried the news of the British surrender to the Continental Congress. Even more important, Oxford was full of boats—there were at least three boatyards, including one that claimed it was the largest on Chesapeake Bay—which confirmed the general line of her thinking. It sounded just the sort of place Price *would* leave his boat, and its proximity to Baltimore tied in nicely with Charlaine Daniels . . . who was *rushing* there now. But, Deb realized, she couldn't be that far ahead of her; from the airport, Oxford was almost convenient. The young man at the Hertz counter gave her a map and traced an elegant finger—chocolate brown and pink— along her route: "You get out of here, then take the I-97 south, that's to Annapolis—except you don't go into Annapolis, you pick up the signs for the Bay Bridge . . ."

"Right."

"That gets you over to the Eastern Shore, then you swing down route 50 and watch for the turn." He smiled. "It's a nice place to visit in the heat of the summer."

Driving, Deb was a little nervous, since she didn't do much of it— in downtown Toronto a car seemed crazy—and she screwed up getting out of the airport and had to go around again. But finally she worked it out. There was lots of traffic. Washington and Baltimore were separate cities, but barely; only the highway, in a funny way, kept them apart. That morning, coming in on the plane, they'd been put into a holding pattern for twenty minutes or so, and she'd stared down at this landscape, slowly revolving beneath her. The cities were like Lego scattered across the floor of a playroom—the child, for the moment, was watching TV; and when the Chesapeake had come into view, it seemed like a blowsy, wilting iris, ragged and pale. Brown clouds hunched to the north—Philadelphia? Wilmington? She'd decided, finally, that you couldn't see that far, but you knew they were there, and then New York. Looking down, she'd started thinking about the environment, how fragile it was, and for some reason—she still wasn't sure what she'd meant—she'd said to herself, "It has nowhere to go." Now, shifting lanes, she still wasn't sure; but down here, she thought, the environment didn't even exist: *on* the earth, you had absolutely no sense of the earth. The world here was entirely artificial, she was like a pulse travelling through a computer chip. One of millions. How many people lived here? How many people *could* live here? On the plane, the in-flight magazine had contained an article about Baltimore that gave the city's population as seven hundred and fifty thousand, no doubt accurate in some technical sense, but it was crazy. City, county, metropolitan area, state . . . except to the bureaucrats, such divisions didn't mean anything; they were like the charts of ancient mariners, or pictures of the mind drawn up by early psychiatrists. Dots on the map, crowding in on each other, overlapping, blotting each other out. There was a word for it, and she tried to think what it was. Conundrum . . . but that wasn't it. Agglomeration? No. And then she was changing lanes again, as the first signs for Annapolis flashed by. But you couldn't see anything—she was hoping for a glimpse of the Naval Academy. And then she was heading up to the Bay Bridge, which proved to be quite spectacular, miles long and high, so you had a great view, and she got the rush she always did when she was close to the water. There were sails, there was even a gaff-rigged schooner . . . she had to work to keep her eyes on the road. But on the other side the landscape turned into regulation American Highway, gas stations and malls and bungalows, until she hit the turnoff, when it became, in a quiet way, much prettier. This wasn't really countryside; everything was all built up with golf communities and little groups of suburban homes—each with an enormous lawn—but there were still a few farms (fields hardening already beneath the sun) and patches of woods, and a pretty bridge across Peach Blossom Creek.

Oxford, when she reached it, was much the same.

In a few years, real-estate agents and infill would spoil it, but for now it was still a lovely old town of small, clapboard cottages, white and grey, and a few larger houses. It was obviously old—it had been founded in the seventeenth century—and obviously wealthy; the signs on the liquor store and gas station were discreet and tasteful. The whole place had a trim, shipshape, Yankee feel.

And the water was everywhere; there was the Tred Avon River, the Town Creek, the Bay itself. On a quiet inlet, she found the town marina, and stopped a moment, looking at the boats. They were mostly daysailers, weekenders. Nothing *very* big. But she recognized a Tayana, and there was a Dickerson, for sale. And—also for sale—a Glander, which caught her eye because Walter Manley owned one and loved it, partly because it was made in the Keys; since he had a bigger boat, he'd been pretending for years that the Glander was available, but he always asked too much, and she knew he was never going to let it go. It was a great gunkholer and she loved it too—but then she loved yawls, period. She drove on. Zigzagging around, she kept her eyes peeled for a gorgeous black woman . . . who shouldn't be hard to spot, Deb realized, in this very white town. On that first pass, though, there was no sign of her, not on the streets, nor in the big boatyards, Crockett's and the Oxford. But then, trying to work out what approach to take, she went into the Schooners Landing, a restaurant just across from the Oxford Boatyard—the only big restaurant in town—and there was Charlaine Daniels, sitting out on the deck.

There was absolutely no doubt who she was . . . although, Deb realized, she was probably trying to look plain in a lumpy brown sweater and baggy plaid slacks. But it didn't make any difference; Charlaine Daniels was still spectacular. Even in that sweater, her figure was incredible, and her face . . . it *shone*, somehow. *If he fell for her you couldn't blame him, you couldn't blame any man.* There was no way to avoid this thought. But then she pushed it aside. She was probably staring, though, like an idiot. In any case, Charlaine Daniels noticed her, and there was absolutely nothing to do but smile and walk over there and say "Hello, my name is Deborah Graham."

Charlaine Daniels, apparently, didn't find the introduction thrilling. "So?" she said.

"I know who—that is, I know you're Charlaine Daniels. You see, I knew Curtis Price."

Charlaine looked up at Deb, as if she hadn't believed her. "You knew Curtis?"

"Yes. I knew him."

"How?"

Just then a waitress pushed through the screen door that led from the restaurant to the deck. With a smile, she came over. "Hi," she said. She had a tray, with a bottle of Beck's beer and a plastic cup, also cutlery rolled up inside a paper napkin. She set this all down in front of Charlaine, and Deb said, "You're having lunch?"

"Yes."

"Do you mind—?"

Charlaine didn't seem happy about the prospect of company, but she didn't actually say no—she just shrugged.

The waitress smiled. "I'll bring out a menu. And we have a special, an imperial melt, that's Swiss cheese melted over crab. Comes with fries."

As she sat down, Deb said, "All right. I'll have that. And a beer too."

"Beck's?"

Deb nodded. All the tables had umbrellas with "Beck's" printed on them. There were perhaps a dozen altogether, but Charlaine and Deb were the only customers sheltering under them—it was barely noon. The restaurant overlooked a bay, and the deck turned into a dock; in fact, a power launch was moored to it. Beyond this, in a line, huge wood pilings, like stubby telephone poles, poked out of the water; an osprey had built a big, messy nest on the one farthest out, and Deb watched the mother settle onto it. She didn't say anything. In fact, she thought, *I'm not going to say anything*—right away, that is, they were locked in a contest of wills. That time, Deb won. Finally, after the silence had stretched on, Charlaine Daniels frowned and said, "You knew I was here . . ."

"I called your office. Your secretary said—"

"But you're not from around here, are you?"

"No. I'm from Toronto. I'm a stockbroker. Curtis Price was a client. I guess you know . . . what happened?"

"The police called me this morning."

"Detective Bannon?"

"That's right."

"I saw him yesterday."

"You knew yesterday?"

"Yes. The day before." Then, before Charlaine Daniels could respond to this, she added: "Curtis Price kept his boat here, didn't he?"

"I've no idea."

"We talked about it. I do a little sailing. Quite a bit, actually."

"You were on his boat?"

"I never knew him that well. But you—you went sailing with him?"

"What if I did?"

The suspicion in Charlaine's face was clear, and, Deb conceded, it was reasonable enough. Charlaine had only just learned that Price was dead. And it was peculiar the way she, Deb, had turned up like this. Yet the focus was the boat. That's why *she* had driven here this morning, after cancelling her appointments. So Deb asked, "What about the boat? *Is* it here?"

Charlaine shook her head. And then, with a shrug, added: "I thought it was in the boatyard, but he must have moved it." She hesitated, then shrugged. "I don't know why I'm explaining this, but there were some things on it I wanted." Then she added, "Personal things." And Deb thought, *underwear*. Panties, to be exact, probably that incredible lavender shade, or maybe—but then, scolding herself, she thought: *Do not be grotesque.* And smiled. "I understand." And then the waitress came back with her beer, and a plastic cup, and a paper napkin folded around the cutlery. "Thank you," Deb said.

"Uh-huh."

A nice sailing breeze was freshening. The umbrella shook a little. Carefully, Deb poured a trickle of beer into the cup, enough so it wouldn't blow away, and then took a sip from the bottle. Another long silence stretched out. Charlaine Daniels sat there, looking into the distance. She was obviously upset. But she'd been upset before; Deb's arrival had only made her *more* upset. She'd been sitting here, trying to work out what to do—about? The boat.

Because it hadn't been where she'd expected and she was trying to work out what to do next.

Not that Charlaine was happy about it. After a moment, she turned and leaned forward and whispered, almost hissed, "Look, I really don't understand what you're doing here."

"I wanted to talk to you."

"*Me?*"

"Yes."

"Why? I don't see what any of this has got to do with you."

"I was his stockbroker . . . in Toronto that is. I was speaking to him the day he was killed. Just before he was killed, in fact."

"So what?" said Charlaine Daniels. "I still don't see—" but then the waitress came back with their food. Setting their plates in front of them, she smiled and said, "Enjoy your meals." She was quite young, with a ponytail pulled through the back strap of her cap; all the same, there was something soft about her. She was wearing shorts, and Deb could see the soft shadows of cellulite already forming.

Then they all turned, even Charlaine, who had to look back behind her—three old couples were coming out on the deck. They looked incredibly the same. They all wore pants and light wind-breakers of synthetic fabric in soft pastel shades, pastel green, pastel blue, pastel pink. The women had white permed hair and skeptical expressions. The men all wore baseball caps and expressions of infinite patience. "So what do you think of my bootstripe?" one of the men said; the most distinctive of the group, his pants were cinched tight with a beaded Navajo belt, and a Western string tie dangled from his neck. Deb followed his gaze across the water. From here, you could see many of the boatyard's slips, which were all occupied by large fibreglass sailboats. Some came from as far away as Clearwater and Fort Myers, but most were from Wilmington and Philadelphia, or smaller ports nearby like Severna Park and St. Michael's. Deb thought she could see this old man's boat— a big Taswell, named *Tonto*, with a fresh blue double bootstripe. "Of course," the man said, with a chuckle, "it's all tape." Another of the men chuckled along with him, as if this was a great joke, and then they headed for a table farther down the deck, bobbing slightly on their very resilient running shoes.

Deb could no longer see them, but one of the women said, "I think that chair's got my name on it," and they must have all sat down because the waitress went over and began explaining about the imperial melt, which Deb now contemplated herself. Using her fork, she peeled back a layer of melted cheese. The crab underneath was pretty good. Charlaine, with absolutely perfect white teeth, took an immaculate half moon out of her sandwich, tuna on dark rye. But now Deb didn't feel so intimidated, as if Charlaine's fear cancelled out her extraordinary beauty. And somehow that also made it permissible to sample three of the french fries, which were excellent. So she had one more . . . although Charlaine, naturally, didn't seem in the least tempted by the potato chips that had come with her sandwich. Deb sneaked a glance at her. She was, Deb figured, a little older than she was, in her early thirties at least—how long does it take for med school? But she looked fantastic, beautiful, wonderfully sexy and elegant all at the same time. Yet there was no doubt that she was afraid. Not just uncertain or anxious: afraid. And maybe she *was* tempted by the chips, because a pair of glossy mallard ducks appeared from behind the pilings and Charlaine flipped one toward the water. Squawking, the ducks busily paddled toward it. Deb took a slug of her beer and said, "That day—the day he was killed—Curtis gave me a big order for a company called Xynex."

Charlaine was taking another bite, which made it hard to tell if this meant anything to her. When she put her sandwich down, she said, "I don't think I've heard of them."

"A biotech company."

She shrugged. "I'm a doctor. I read a lot of magazines." But after a moment she added, "I don't know, maybe Curtis mentioned them."

Deb felt sure Charlaine was lying. Behind her, one of the old men said, "Betty Ann, you want a beverage? I think I'll have a cup of decaf."

Deb said, "Did you ever meet a man named Giacomo Valli?"

Charlaine said, "Why the hell should I answer your questions?"

Deb shrugged. "Why shouldn't you? Ask *me* one, if you like."

"Maybe I'll take you up on that. Did Curtis ever talk about me?"

"No. Not to me. But he did tell me about the boat. I sail. We used to—"

"So how come you know about me?"

"The police, Bannon, showed me your photograph."

"Shit."

"But that's all. There wasn't anything special about it."

Charlaine, holding the sandwich in her hand—her wrist resting gently against the edge of the table—thought for a second. Then she shrugged. "Okay . . . And yes, I knew Valli, or at least I met him. A doctor. A nice man."

Charlaine, looking down, had some more of her sandwich, while Deb decided this was a clear answer to Rosie's questions. If you'd slept with a man, you just didn't speak of him in that tone of voice. Or at least *she* didn't. She looked out, over the water; the osprey on the piling lifted up its wings in a great stretch. Behind her, one of the ladies was saying, "Can you imagine that? He orders a Caesar and I've got all that romaine coming up in my garden. Never asks *me* to make one." Deb, turning back to Charlaine, said, "He's my boyfriend."

Charlaine gave a little nod. "Congratulations. As I say, he seemed like a very nice man."

"What about a man called Nisram Singh? Yesterday, I was talking to *his* girlfriend. He works for Xynex."

Charlaine sat back. "Okay. So you caught me out in a lie."

"I didn't—I wasn't trying—"

"What difference does it make? There's nothing wrong—"

"I know. I'm not saying there is."

Charlaine, again, gave a resentful shrug. "Everybody knows about it anyway. I work in a health clinic, a community clinic, and they were funding us, they had a special program . . . That's how I met your boyfriend. He works for some foundation, doesn't he?"

"The Marsh Foundation."

"I remember. Xynex was trying to get them involved, too. And, of course, Curtis was interested in them."

"Why?"

"*What do you care?*"

Behind them, one of the old men said, "By the same token, I've had you for fifty-six years and I *still* like you."

Deb looked at Charlaine. "Does this have something to do with what you wanted on his boat?"

Charlaine looked at her. "I still don't see what business this is of yours."

Deb, suddenly, felt angry: her patience snapped. "Look, if you don't see that it's my business, fine—whether you like it or not, I'm *making* it my business. And I know you're here because of that boat—right?"

Her anger, at last, seemed to get through to the other woman; the tension eased in her face, her manner suddenly became more natural. "Something's going on, isn't it?"

"Yes," said Deb, "something's going on. And I'm going to find out *what*."

There was a long silence; then Charlaine said, "Those people are disgusting."

Deb nodded. "Yes. Disgusting."

Deb didn't say anything more; after a moment, Charlaine smiled, then looked away, resting her hand on her palm. Deb listened; but the old people had fallen silent, presumably occupied eating . . . *Conurbation*. That's the word she'd been trying to think of; it chose that moment to drift into her mind. *Urban conurbation* . . . It was crazy to remember it now, but she felt a sudden sense of satisfaction anyway, as if, at last, she was getting somewhere. The silence stretched on. Deb watched Charlaine, whose admission of fear hadn't seemed in any way to diminish it. On the contrary; she seemed more anxious. Face turned, she looked over the water; for the first time, it seemed, she'd noticed the osprey.

Quietly, Deb watched her. Charlaine's head, held at this particular angle, was for a moment perfectly steady, like a sculpture, and Deb thought of the museums in Paris where her parents had taken her as a girl. There'd been sculptures of black people, "negresses." She wasn't sure why, but she seemed to remember that they'd all had a certain quality of exaggeration. Charlaine's beauty, however, was exactly the opposite, a kind of *concentration*. Her skin was so perfect. And perhaps it was this beauty, or perhaps it was the suspicion Charlaine had displayed, or perhaps it was a sense of something false in her own position—but Deb now felt the depth of the gulf between them. How different they were. Different races, different nationalities, different people. They'd led completely different lives, grown up in different worlds.

Deb tried to imagine what Charlaine had been like as a little girl. In school, daydreaming, looking out the window at the June sunshine with only the last few days to go before the holidays— what had she dreamed? She was a doctor, a black woman doctor. Was that a big deal? Presumably. Probably it was a very big deal. Of course, being so beautiful would have helped her. Or maybe that wasn't true, Deb thought, maybe it was just the reverse. Her beauty could have been a temptation. It would have been so easy just to marry someone, or try to become an actress or a model, not that there was anything wrong with that, but somehow that would have been the easy way out. And she hadn't taken it. It was amazing, though; despite all their differences, they were connected. Giacomo was a connection, of *some* kind. And Deb was pregnant and this woman was an obstetrician or a gynecologist or something. And both of them had known Curtis Price. Both of them were sitting here now, at this particular moment, with those old people sitting behind them. *You can't escape anything*, Deb thought. She took a sip of her beer. Then Charlaine turned back, and now for an instant Deb saw the gulf from the other side, for Charlaine's face was filled with the question, *who the hell are you?*—though in fact she said, "All right. Look—you tell me . . . what's going on? Or what do you *think* is going on?"

"I don't know. I only know that Curtis Price was murdered just after he'd given me an order for a big chunk of Xynex stock."

"And that's suspicious?"

"Maybe. Yes. The way it happened. The police think it could be. At the time, I wondered. I thought he knew something . . . that he might have inside information."

Charlaine thought for a second. "Well, I don't *know* . . . about that, or much else. But it wouldn't surprise me. On the other hand—he wasn't a crook."

Deb said, "I agree with that."

"Is anybody saying that he was—or that you did anything wrong?"

"No, not directly. Not so far."

"But you're worried?"

"Yes. And then . . . there are connections. Nisram Singh. Xynex. You. They all, somehow, *connect* to Giacomo. Valli. My boyfriend."

"So—just to worry out loud—it would look real bad if ten thousand shares of Xynex stock showed up in your boyfriend's account?"

"Yes. It won't—but it would."

Charlaine, then, gave her a little smile: "That never occurred to you, did it?"

"No. I guess it didn't. I've—I've had other worries. But now you tell me—what do *you* think is going on?"

"I have no idea. I just know that Curtis was murdered and I don't want to have *anything* to do with it."

"You don't know who murdered him?"

"Of course not."

"Or why?"

"No."

"But you're afraid you might become involved."

Charlaine poked her salad with her fork. "Well, I don't want to become any more involved than I have to be."

"And what you're looking for on the boat—never mind . . ." But then Deb added, "You realize, Bannon does know that you and Curtis were friends?"

"Of course. That's why he called me. They want to interview me."

But you were more than friends, Deb thought. Or there was something more. But she said, "Do you think they know about the boat? I mean, I'm sure they know he owned a boat, but . . ."

Charlaine was shaking her head. "I don't think they've got

around to it. That's why I thought . . ." She shrugged. "I thought there might be time."

For what? Deb thought. But she didn't want to press. There was so much suspicion in Charlaine's face—Deb wondered if distrust was her natural state, but then she thought, no, that was unfair. But she kept her voice neutral. "Do you have any idea where his boat is?"

Again Charlaine shrugged. "That last time we were out, he brought it into the yard, this one over here. They had to do something to the engine. And something else—I forget what. Anyway, when they were finished, they moved it to a mooring. I asked—that's what he told them to do."

"Moorings are a lot cheaper than the slips in boatyards."

"This is his own. He bought a piece of land, right by the water. He was going to build on it, he said, but what he really liked was how protected it was. We anchored there once. There's no road, you can't get at it. And even if you could, you'd have to swim out to the boat."

"Do you know where this place is? Is it far? This side of the Bay? North . . . south?"

"No, it's not far. And north, I guess—toward Washington."

"But on this side?"

"Yes, on this side."

"All right . . . tell me what you were going to do. Let's say you found this boat. It must be locked—"

"But it's a combination lock, and I know the combination." She smiled, a shade ruefully. "It's my birthday, day, month, year. I guess, in a way, I was *his* girlfriend." Then she added, "In a way."

This last comment hardly clarified matters, but Deb just smiled, and then turned, trying to catch the waitress's eye. She came over and said, "Would you like coffees?"

Charlaine nodded, and Deb said, "Yes, I would too. And I was wondering, is there a place here I could rent a boat? Just a day-sailer, I mean. It's such a beautiful afternoon."

The girl thought a moment. "I don't know about the boatyard," she said, "but there's Eastern Charter just here on Bank Street."

As the girl turned away, Charlaine leaned forward. "Look . . . I don't know."

"Don't worry. I told you, I know how to sail."

Charlaine hesitated. "Are you sure you want to do this?"

"Sure." Then she said, "My name is Deborah, by the way. Deborah Graham." She felt idiotic. "I don't know why, but it suddenly occurred to me that you might have forgotten."

Charlaine smiled. "No, I didn't. And thank you—Deborah."

But there was something grudging in this thanks, and Deb found she was feeling embarrassed. Quickly she said, "We do have one small problem. I can't rent a boat looking like this—in these clothes."

"What about sweats? My workout stuff is in the car—fresh washed, I promise. They'd fit you okay."

"Shoes? I need running shoes of some kind."

"There's a pair in my bag . . . size eight."

"That'll be all right—"

"And come to think of it, I think there's a pair of old Topsiders in there too. They'd be even better."

Deb sat back. The two ducks circled, squawking, and Charlaine tossed them a little bread. Behind them, one of the ladies was saying, "It really ticked me off, I can tell you. I was supposed to get that cheque in December, so they made me count it for my last year's taxes, but I didn't actually get it till January, almost February come to that. I mean, it's their fault, it's their own darn cheque . . ." The osprey lifted off its piling, circling and climbing, and Deb followed it higher—and, way up, spotted the contrail of a plane. She remembered herself that morning, looking down. She thought: "If they've still got ospreys, it can't be hopeless," although as soon as she thought this, she remembered from the guidebook that the Chesapeake had been dying for a century—the great shad runs were failing in the 1830s, the oyster harvest peaked in 1880, and the Bay's true riches are now the cadmium, chromium and other heavy metals that coat its bottom. But the waves still danced in the sun, it still *looked* good. Watching the ducks, Deb felt the excitement she always did at the prospect of a sail.

The waitress brought their coffee; she and Charlaine began poking through the creamers, looking for the ones with milk.

They didn't find Price's boat until almost three o'clock that afternoon—and even then, they almost missed it.

They'd poked their noses into a dozen coves and arms and in-
lets, gunkholed into any number of creeks and streams—this last,
nameless indentation on the map didn't appear to hold special
promise. There were a few scattered moorings along its southern,
settled shore, and one decent boat: a Hinckley Sou'wester. Deb had
sailed up to it, giving Charlaine a look, for she was still trying to get
a clear idea of what Price's boat was like. Charlaine, looking at the
Hinckley, nodded. "Pretty close. But I'd say his was chunkier. Flat-
ter at the end. And navy blue." Gradually, during that afternoon,
they'd narrowed the possibilities. It had a single mast, so was a
sloop or a cutter. Its hull was blue, and more or less traditional in
its lines—definitely not a reverse transom because, when Deb had
pointed one out to her, Charlaine thought it was ugly and she remembered Price's boat as beautiful, "a real boat" was the way she
put it. As for size, Deb was guessing around forty feet, but not
much over; according to Charlaine, Price never had a captain, and
even though he was clearly an experienced sailor, he was an older
man. So a Sou'wester, at forty-two feet, was about right, and in fact
as they turned around, and headed back toward the main channel,
Charlaine said, "Yes, it's about that big. I can remember sitting in
the dinghy, looking back, and that's the way it looked." And then
Deb had glanced back herself, mainly for the Hinckley—not as
beautiful as a Bermuda 40, she thought, but still very nice—but had
also looked over to the opposite, northern shore. This was heavily
wooded, and there were no houses; it was probably too narrow to
build on. Beyond it lay another bay. And then she realized the
shoreline here was deceptive. She'd assumed this bay, the one they
were in, had ended just beyond the Hinckley, curving around gently on itself; but now, she realized, a little hook of water continued,
cut into the shore on that northern side. What she'd thought was
the end of the bay was really just a little point.

"Could I see the chartbook?" she asked.

Charlaine had it open across her knees—though, as she said, she would have done better with a roadmap: she simply couldn't match the picture on the page to what she could see around her. But even as Deb took it, she caught a flash through some pines... that section of the shore was indeed a point, with a narrow cove behind it. "Didn't you say it was all woods, where you were? That time you anchored?"

"That's right."

Deb pointed. "What's wrong with that?"

"But I don't remember this side at all."

"Look there . . . you see, it looks like the shore just runs straight around, but there's actually water behind those trees. And I think that's a mast."

Already, Deb was tacking. When she'd rented their boat, she'd expected something like a Sunfish or a Laser, but she'd got to chatting with the man about her father's boat, a Niagara 35, and he'd mentioned that he had a couple of Nonsuch catboats—they were built by the same company. "Of course," he added, "I couldn't let you have it for the hourly rate." Deb had jumped at it anyway. It was twenty-two feet, and had a little cabin; she knew it would be a lot more comfortable. And, assuming they found Price's boat, they'd have to get on board, which would be a lot easier if their boat had a deck and some freeboard. A Nonsuch was also a wonderfully easy boat to sail; to tack, all you did was turn the wheel. Now, quietly, the sail swung over; and in a moment, they were cutting across their own wake. They glided past the Hinckley, and then Deb rounded up, beyond the point, so they were looking behind it into a small cove, like a forest pool, which the shore had hidden.

A sailboat swung to her mooring there, her navy hull so bright she reflected her reflection back to the water. *Royal Palm* was neatly lettered in an arc across her transom: her home port, *Sag Harbor*. And Charlaine, excited, said, "That's it!"

Deb was excited too. But she kept her voice calm. "You're sure? That's a ketch. Two masts . . ."

She looked at Charlaine, who frowned, but then shook her head. "I'm sorry. I just got that wrong. *Royal Palm*—now I even remember the name."

"Okay." In fact, she didn't doubt it; the boat was a Shannon, a very fine fibreglass boat, exactly the kind of boat Price *would* own. A rich man's boat. But a real boat. As she'd guessed, it was a little under forty feet, probably thirty-eight. With her hand, Deb eased the boom out, letting the sail catch the breeze, and they drifted slowly down on it. As they came closer, she flipped up the seat locker. "Take those fenders and tie them to the stanchions. Let's try not to scratch his gelcoat." She said this lightly, but her voice was already dropping to a whisper—guilt and anxiety taking over. Going on board another person's boat—you just didn't do that.

Now, quickly, she went up and dropped the sail, then stepped over the lifelines, leaning back, waiting for the two boats to come together, her foot ready to absorb the impact . . . but it was only the gentlest nudge. Pushing with her hands, she worked the little Nonsuch down to the Shannon's stern. But its hull, even here, was still well above her, and of course there was no boarding ladder. Holding a rope, she had to reach up, then pull herself up, and slip underneath the bottom lifeline. Awkward. But she managed it. Then tied off the rope around a winch. Pointing, she looked down at Charlaine. "Toss me up that line, and I'll pull the bow in." Gently, she drew the two boats together, simply looping the second line around one of the lifeline stanchions. Happily—a simple luxury—*Royal Palm* had boarding gates both port and starboard; Deb slipped off the pelican hook and called down, still whispering, "Okay. Come on."

Charlaine looked up, uncertainly.

Deb beckoned with her hand. "Don't worry. Just pull yourself up."

Charlaine didn't move. "Listen," she said, "if you don't mind I'd rather do this by myself."

"What do you mean?"

"I'd rather—I told you, I want to look by myself. Maybe it would be better if you came back down here."

Deb was furious. "Hurry up," she said. It was hard to control herself. "We don't have all day. In case you haven't guessed, you're not supposed to come aboard other people's boats unless they ask you."

"Look—"

"*Come on, come on.*"

Charlaine pulled herself up, and Deb reconnected the gate behind her. She was so angry now she couldn't speak: what more did she have to do to earn this lady's trust? And then she blurted it out, "Didn't I find the damn thing for you? *Come on!*"

But Charlaine said, "I told you this was personal."

"Personal?" said Deb. "I guess so. Top secret is more like it. Maybe—" But then she broke off. She stared at the main cabin hatch. "I thought you said there was a *lock.*"

The door from the cockpit to the cabin was neatly closed—the hasp of the latch was over the staple—but there was no padlock.

Charlaine looked too. "There *should* be. He had a big brass combination lock. They must have forgotten it. From the boatyard."

Deb shook her head. "No, they didn't." Because, she knew, the guys in boatyards could screw up a hundred ways—but not *that* way. Instinctively, she glanced into the water. The padlock would be lying on the bottom. Yet, for a moment, the precise meaning of this didn't hit her—she just wasn't used to thinking this way. And then, before Deb could stop her, Charlaine stepped quickly forward, tugged open the hatch, and started down the companionway.

"Charlaine—"

But she was gone. Deb went to the open hatch, and swung herself through and down, onto the companionway ladder. The cabin, for a second, was all dark shadow.

"Are you all right?" she called out.

"Of course I am," Charlaine called back.

Deb stayed where she was. The boat moved gently under her; a crow was squawking on the shore. She felt uneasy . . . because, now, it had registered: someone had broken in. But, she told herself, they wouldn't be here now; no, the cabin hatch had been closed too neatly. *Someone had come and gone.* And she knew who it was. That man, from Giacomo's apartment, the same man who'd tried to frighten her with the car last night, that man in his stupid baseball cap ... but who was he? what was he doing? what did he represent? A whole bunch of questions, which she'd never precisely asked herself, now came rushing at her. *And what did this have to do with Giacomo?* Blinking, she peered down, into the cabin. She wanted to go down ... although clearly Charlaine didn't want her to. By this time, though, she didn't like doing what Charlaine wanted her to do even by default. Besides, despite everything, she couldn't help admiring the interior—she'd never been inside a Shannon before and it looked beautiful. Of course, there was too much teak, but then there was always too much teak. She preferred mahogany. She let herself down another step. She could hear Charlaine moving about in the forward cabin. Maybe it *was* underwear ... But then, just as quickly, she came out again. She looked worried, throwing a quick, irritated glance in Deb's direction. Then she began poking through the shelves above the settee. Was she looking for a book?

Deb said, "You can't find it?"

Charlaine looked at her. "What do you think?"

And then she ducked into the aft cabin. The hell with her, Deb thought. She came all the way down the ladder. Just to her right was the galley, with a great little chart table tucked in, right aft of it. There were a lot of electronics, Horizon VHF, an Icom SSB radio, Loran, the works. Except radar. Of course, if ordinary thieves had broken in, these items would have been their main objective, assuming they weren't trying to steal the boat itself. Or, she mentally added, the inflatable. And she couldn't remember— had there been one? The question was sufficiently interesting that she went back on deck and looked over the stern ... but in fact it was lashed to the lifelines amidships. And in the second cockpit locker was a twelve-horsepower Merc. So, rule that out.

She slipped back through the hatch and down the companionway. Charlaine was still poking about in the aft cabin. For a moment, Deb sat quietly on the bottom step of the ladder, but then she couldn't resist, and slipped into the little bench seat of the chart table. She ran her fingers over the wood; it was a simple, perfect piece of joinery. Of course, she thought, everyone knew that chart tables were really a waste of space—certainly she always did real chart work on the salon table anyway—but was there a better place to play captain? The top lifted up, like an old school desk. Inside, she found the usual clutter, a box of navigation instruments, a cheap plastic protractor, a couple of pencils, the AAA roadmap for Maryland and Delaware, and a zippered plastic envelope for the various licences and legal documents every yacht has to carry. Plus assorted elastic bands. Plus a beer coaster from the Waterfront Restaurant, Camden, Maine. Plus a book of matches from Croft's Marina in Kennebunkport, plus . . . plus a newspaper clipping. It was folded, but she could read part of the headline—"Rescue or Salvage?"—and immediately knew what it was. This was the article from *Soundings* that Price had told her about—this was how he'd learned about the death of the research man from Xynex, the man Nisram Singh had replaced. *The boat was spotted drifting in Florida Bay, due south of Flamingo, by another pleasure craft, which radioed the Coast Guard. They found no one aboard, immediately instituted a search, and the next morning the body of Donald Peterson, 54, was picked up by a fishing boat. An autopsy revealed a very high level of alcohol in his blood, and at the inquest the Coast Guard testified that when the body had been discovered, Peterson's fly was open, indicating that his death was "the most common type of boating accident." But what of the boat? A Krogen cutter, the Coast Guard towed it to Marathon, and then took steps . . .*

Curtis Price had underlined all the relevant details in pencil, and at the bottom of the page was a photograph of Peterson, a big, bearded man, standing on the deck of his boat. *Double Helix*, the caption read, *Lost and Found, or Government Property?* Clearly, there'd been some sort of legal dispute about the boat, but presumably this had been resolved; stapled to the clipping was a boat listing from a broker in Palmetto, Florida: apparently Peterson's boat was for sale, and Curtis Price had taken the trouble to find out about it. NAME: Double Helix TYPE: Sailboat BUILDER: Kady Krogen MODEL: Krogen 38 Cutter LOA: 38' 2" LWL: 32' 1" BEAM: 12' 8" DRAFT: 3' 2"/6" 8" . . . But Deb stopped reading. Charlaine was coming out of the aft cabin. There were no pockets in the sweatpants, so she tucked the clipping and the listing under the waistband—Charlaine was too preoccupied to notice. Turning in her seat, Deb said, "Still can't find it?"

"No."

Deb thought, *Because someone found it before you.* But she said, "Well, I can't help you look, if I don't know what it is." And then, stopping herself, she held up her hand. "Sorry—I didn't mean it to sound like that."

She *had* sounded pretty snarky, and for a second Charlaine's face had started to tense; but her expression softened and she shook her head. "No, I'm the one who should be apologizing. You've been very kind, and I've been rude. I'm sorry. It wasn't . . . I didn't mean anything personal, okay?"

Even in this apology, there was a hostile edge; she was obviously upset. Turning, she went into the main cabin, and slumped down on the settee. Deb followed her. It was wonderful to walk on a boat; to feel it move ever so slightly beneath her. She sat down on the other side of the cabin and waited. She could feel the boat swinging slightly. She felt very tense. On the other hand, she felt completely at ease here on the water. *Floating.* In your own world. For just an instant, as an indulgence, she let herself sink into it. She thought of Giacomo, who *said* he liked sailing, though he hadn't really done it a lot. And no cruising. Well, she thought, he'd better like it! She sat quietly in the silence . . . except it wasn't silence; it was a question of tuning your ears for the small sounds, line stretching, a halyard slapping the mast, the run of a wave on the smooth hull. For an instant, she simply sat there, suspended in herself. Then Charlaine looked up slowly and said, "You're afraid I slept with your boyfriend, aren't you?"

Deb looked at her. "Actually, no."

"Really?"

"Yeah. If he had, you'd be just a *little* happier than you are."

For a second, Charlaine's face was expressionless. Then she grinned: "I kind of like that. This guy must be quite a guy."

"Yeah, he is."

"Well . . . anyway, you're right. I didn't sleep with him. I didn't sleep with Curtis, either—I suppose you must be wondering." She shrugged. "Maybe now I wish I had." And then, looking directly at Deb, she added: "I'm gay, actually." And then, after a little pause, she amended this: "I don't know, maybe that's just a way of being celibate. A couple of years ago—this was the last time—I let a guy pick me up in the Water Street Exchange, and it was so disgusting I swore I'd never let one touch me again."

Deb was shocked. It was as simple as that. She didn't know what to say. But she *had* to say something, even if it sounded dumb. "Men must come on to you all the time."

"You want to know something? They don't. No means no—I guess they're finally figuring it out. And I'm a walking No."

Now they were both silent. Deb felt the boat swing, almost as if she was trying to gather way . . . but then stop; like a breeze dying on a too-hot-day. She waited. She had, she realized, completely lost the initiative; everything was up to Charlaine. Charlaine had to make up *her* mind. She must have; because, finally, she said: "I don't know why, but I guess I'm going to tell you. What I'm looking for."

"Maybe you shouldn't. Not if you don't trust me."

"I guess I'm saying I do." She shrugged. "I'd never have made it out here, not by myself. Besides . . ." She smiled. "I like you."

"I like you too."

"It's just that—when you get right down to it—I don't have that many friends. I guess I'm not used to it." And then, before Deb could respond, she added, "The one thing is, I'm still not sure why you're here, how come you turned up."

Deb said, "I have to find out what's going on. I can't pretend that Curtis meant that much to me. I don't even think I liked him. But I have to find out what's happening, and I have to know about Giacomo."

"Your boyfriend? I wouldn't worry about him. He's okay."

"That's a relief, somehow—that you think that."

"What happens if . . . well, you just ask him?"

"That's not so easy. He's . . . vanished."

"What?"

"Well . . . at least nobody knows where he is."

"You're frightened."

"Yes. Beginning to be."

"Well . . . what I'm looking for is a file."

"A file?"

"A regular file folder, blue. It's got Amy Everett Health Clinic scrawled across it in Magic Marker."

"This is the clinic where you—the one Xynex was funding, and Nisram Singh—?"

"Right . . . It's got some papers in it. Say it's half an inch thick."

There were a hundred questions Deb wanted to ask, but she kept her voice calm, as if the file and the papers were the last things she was interested in. "Are you sure it's here?" she said. "Maybe Curtis took it back to New York."

Charlaine shook her head. "The last time we were out, he brought the boat into that yard, and it's been there ever since—he hasn't been on it. I asked them. And that day, when we finished with the boat, we drove back to the city together and he realized he didn't have it in his bag. He was going to drive back right then—I had to stop him." She shook her head again in frustration. "It *has* to be here, but I've looked everywhere. It's not."

"Boats are full of places to hide things."

"I was with him. If he'd hidden it, I would have seen. And he was going to give it back to me, not keep it. He forgot to put it in his bag, that's all."

"You're sure?"

"Yes—what do you mean?"

"You know what's in that file, not me. You know why he was interested in it, I don't. Maybe he wanted to keep it. Maybe he lied to you. Maybe, when you weren't looking, he hid it away—"

"No. There was no reason for him to lie. And he *would* have driven back here that day, I'm sure of it. I don't know. Maybe something happened to it when they were working on the boat."

"I doubt it," said Deb. "They're very, very careful about stuff like that. Price was a good customer—the kind they love. A rich man. Paid his bills. Didn't want to work on his own boat. They'd be very, very particular not to screw up, especially over something like that." Finally, she couldn't help herself. "This file . . . I guess it was pretty important?"

Charlaine took a moment before she said, "In a way. It might be embarrassing. If the police—or—"

"You mean, it's about patients—records?"

"No, not exactly." And she began to get up, reaching out for the overhead grab rail. But then she stopped herself. She sat back again. "Did your boyfriend ever tell you about the clinic? Or maybe Curtis did."

"No. He never talked about it. Neither of them."

"Okay, it's in the ghetto, or at least on the edge. Just about the worst section, an area called Harlem Park. Do you know Baltimore?"

"No."

"Well, that part's ninety-nine per cent black. Two-thirds of the families are headed by a woman. A third of the population is under nineteen. It's . . . well, you really can't describe it."

"It's like the Third World," said Deb.

"Exactly. Which is probably why Nisram Singh thought your boyfriend's foundation might be interested. Anyway, our clinic does everything. But we do a lot of abortions. You have to understand, illegitimacy, teen pregnancy—that's the *norm*. In a couple of the high schools, statistically speaking, every girl gets pregnant before she leaves. Actually, that's not exactly true. A few girls *don't*. But plenty of others have two, even three, to make up for them."

Charlaine's tone, somehow, was one of justification, and Deb said: "I'm not against abortion. Although I guess what you want to be *for* is birth control."

"Don't worry," said Charlaine, "we do a lot of that too. And a lot of straightforward public health work, nutrition counselling, prenatal care, *post*natal care—if they're going to have all these babies, they might as well be healthy, we might as well give them that much of a chance."

"Of course."

"Okay, part of that is just basic immunization, making sure kids get their shots. A lot of them don't. Most of the mothers in Harlem Park *try*, let me tell you, they *try*, but it's almost impossible. So many kids drop out of school—and that drops them out of the health system too. So they miss their shots, or they only get some. A lot of the girls, for example, miss their rubella shots, or at least part of the series. What we've found—in fact there's been a number of studies about this—is that a good time to catch them is when they present for abortion. We developed a program around this. We'd test them for immunity, and if they didn't have it, we'd give them the shots."

Deb nodded. "Kumari explained—I told you, she's Nisram Singh's fiancée. And Xynex is interested in all this because they make vaccines."

"That's right. They funded the whole thing. They did some training, took care of the testing—for the rubella—and gave us vaccine kits. As part of the program, we did follow-ups. We tracked all the patients, and retested them six months later, then a year later, then two years later." Charlaine took a breath. "And that's what's in the file, the results of the follow-ups."

"But why would that be embarrassing—did the vaccine have some kind of side effect?"

"Not exactly. But we did find something strange. Twenty-two per cent of the women who went through that program got pregnant again, and all their babies had one thing in common." She looked at Deb. "They were boys."

"What are you saying?"

"I'm saying, if you had those shots, and you got pregnant, you had a boy."

"Only boys?"

"Only boys."

"I'm not sure I understand . . . The shots were really a kind of contraceptive? In a way?"

"Right. But sex-selective. Once you had the shot, you could still get pregnant—but only with a boy."

"That's incredible. *Only* boys?"

"Only boys."

Deb was silent for a moment. Charlaine said: "You're getting the picture, aren't you?"

"My God. No wonder Price was buying Xynex stock. In China..."

"Exactly," said Charlaine. "And somehow, I bet, that's why he was murdered."

Somehow. "Those tests—if that's what they were doing at your clinic—"

"They'd be illegal. Absolutely. In fact, I don't think you could get the FDA to approve testing something like that in a million years. Not in America. Not on American women. Not even on American *black* women."

"So Xynex Corporation... they'd be in big trouble, if it got out?"

"You're damn right they would be."

Deb shook her head. "In one way, though, it doesn't make sense. Curtis Price wasn't going to tell anyone—he'd be the last person to cause them any trouble. He was buying their stock."

"Well, I don't know about that. And of course it doesn't make much difference, anyway. I couldn't prove anything. All I have are some statistics, and you can prove anything with statistics. Or disprove anything."

"Only you don't want anyone to know you've got those statistics," said Deb. "Isn't that it?"

"I just don't want to be involved. Period."

But you are, Deb thought. And so am I. *And so was Giacomo.* But exactly what were they involved *in*? She leaned forward. "Do you want to look more? For the file?"

Charlaine shook her head. "It's not here. I know it's not here."

Deb looked at her; had Charlaine, she wondered, worked out the implications of the broken lock? But Deb knew—now—that she couldn't leave her in the dark.

"Charlaine, there's no use kidding yourself. You're right—you're not going to find it, because someone's already taken it. That lock up there—someone broke in. Like I told you, with rich men's boats, boatyards will make some mistakes, but not others."

Charlaine's face was very still. And then she looked sick. "So they know..."

"Yeah... whoever *they* are."

"Jesus."

"Whether you like it or not, you're involved."

"Jesus, Jesus," she said again. Then, as she stood up, she turned to Deb. "I know this isn't going to sound very good . . . it's going to sound selfish, conceited—"

"What?"

"You have to understand. I've got a lot to lose. I think I've got more to lose than you."

Deb thought about that for a moment—she thought of Giacomo; and then she shook her head. "No, you don't. But it doesn't bother me that you think so."

They went quickly up the ladder. Deb shut the hatch behind them; no one would know they had been here. Quickly, Deb helped Charlaine down to the Nonsuch—for one moment, holding her by the hand—and then stepped outside the lifelines herself. She fastened the hook behind her. The boat was swinging gently around, toward the shore. In fact, they weren't so far from the shore at all, the lovely reflection of the boat merging with the shadows of the trees. And Deb sneezed. Then, more violently, she sneezed again.

"You okay?" Charlaine whispered.

Deb nodded. Some pollen must have blown out from the land, she thought. "I've got allergies," she said, as her foot reached down for the little boat's deck. And then she sneezed again—Giacomo's shots, it seemed, only worked for cats.

CHAPTER EIGHT

*I*n case they were separated, Charlaine told Deb how to get to her house in Baltimore, but in fact Deb was able to follow her without once losing touch, the two cars working their way in orderly tandem down the interstate and then through the city. Coming off the highway, they went around Camden Yards, and then headed along North Calvert Street—Charlaine wanted to look in at her office.

Deb had never been to Baltimore before, but it was a lot like Toronto, better actually, because it wasn't so flat, and she liked it, the way it looked down from a gentle hill upon all the folds and shiny intricacies of the harbour. It had plenty of trees, there was a nice, easy, open feel, and something cheerful in people's strides as they hurried along. Waiting for a light to change, one of the municipality's trucks pulled up beside her, and she noticed the motto printed across the door, "The city that reads." And when she parked outside Charlaine's office, she found herself almost opposite the main building for the *Baltimore Sun*, which proclaimed its own motto above the entrance, "Light to All." The place was like that, quirkily progressive, spirited in an old-fashioned way, with a connection to a history that wasn't just for tourists like the

Constellation in the harbour, but ran back to a time when cities had neighbourhoods and big shots and funny accents, to a time when cities were something more than freeways and plazas and condos. Charlaine lived in a beautiful area called Bolton Hill, and when she got out of the car, Deb had a memory flash of her European trip, a trip that had ended in Venice—that had ended with Giacomo—but had begun in Dublin. She'd only stayed three days, but one afternoon she'd gone for a walk, just wandering around, ending up at some house where Oscar Wilde had lived; and this district was kind of the same, fine streets with broad sidewalks deeply shaded by old, lovely trees, and rows of elegant eighteenth-century townhouses: some had gracefully arched windows, others classical pediments, all a fine sense of privacy and calm.

But now that calm was ominous, the quiet ghostly. Charlaine's apartment was on the third floor; there was no elevator, just a panelled, freshly varnished staircase with rattan-bladed fans slowly turning above every landing. As she climbed, Deb imagined Price coming up these stairs. And the apartment itself—modern, expensive, tasteful, in a neutral, impersonal way—seemed to harbour echoes. Secrets. As if she's just moved in, Deb thought. As if she deliberately hasn't brought any of her previous life with her. In the bedroom—vaguely Italian in style, with big wrought-iron loops for the headboard of the bed—she changed out of Charlaine's sweats; back in the living room, a cappuccino was waiting for her on the glass-topped coffee table. "Your foam is great," she said. Then: "Did you ever want to be a dancer?" she asked, because the only decoration in the room was a row of posters—reproductions of Degas's ballerinas and one from some old film about Isadora Duncan, starring Vanessa Redgrave.

"I just needed pictures." Then, harshly, she shook her head. "Look, we can't do this."

"What?"

"Chat. Socialize . . . as though nothing has happened."

"I know."

So Charlaine was feeling it too. "Curtis is dead," she said. "He was *murdered*." And then she added: "And someone broke into his boat . . . if you're right about that."

"I am."

"Yeah . . . I'm afraid you are."

Someone was very, very close . . . As close, Deb thought, as she'd been to the man in Giacomo's apartment. "The question is," Charlaine went on, "what can we do about it?"

"What I still don't see—I was trying to work it out driving back—was why anyone would want Curtis killed."

Charlaine shrugged. "He knew something. He was going to tell something."

"I know, that's what it looks like. But you still have this problem—you don't buy the stock of a company you're going to blow the whistle on."

"That's *logical*," said Charlaine, "but maybe you're being too logical. Maybe there was some stupid argument, maybe killing him—in a way—was a very dumb thing to do. Maybe—"

"But he wasn't killed like that. It was . . . neat, cold-blooded. It *was* logical—I just can't see what the logic was."

"Well, he was killed for some reason," said Charlaine. "Maybe it was because of this." She slid a thick, spiral-bound report across the table. Deb picked it up. It was called *Measles-Mumps-Rubella Immunization in a Clinic Setting*. "This is the original of what I was looking for on the boat. That's the official report. The stuff I pulled out for Curtis is all stapled in the back."

Deb flipped to it. There were a lot of tables and charts. "I'm not sure there's much point in my reading it—I wouldn't understand it anyway. *You* don't have any doubt, though, about what it means?"

"No. Of the women who received that vaccine and later became pregnant, one hundred per cent had male children. Because the sample's fairly small, you could argue it was an anomaly, but it would be absolutely extraordinary. And there were other things, looking back . . . about the way the whole study was conducted."

"You don't think it was legitimate?"

"I wouldn't say that. At one level, it was perfectly legitimate. MMR—measles, mumps, rubella—is a real problem. Those diseases are all coming back—we never 'conquered' them, you know, the way *Time* likes to say. For measles, the low point was sometime in the early eighties, but by 1990 there were epidemics across the country, a wave of them. There was something to study, all right, and in fact there've been a lot of studies—it's pretty easy to get funding."

"So, what you're saying is, there's nothing startling about this—about doing a study like this in the first place?"

"No, not at all. And we had our own slant, of course, because we were doing it with poor people. They drop out of the system—they don't have family doctors, they quit school—and so they miss their shots, or at least don't get all of them. One place to pick them up is at our kind of clinic, and with the women that means you're usually seeing them when they're pregnant, usually wanting an abortion. Then they *have* to see a doctor. And they're thinking about pregnancy, the consequences of it—hopefully. Besides, a woman who wants an abortion will do pretty much what you want."

Deb wondered if that would be true of her—she *might* want an abortion. But she said, "Tell me something . . . did Xynex approach you, or was it you—"

"They came to us. But that didn't make me suspicious. Of course, I knew they had an angle, but that was reasonable enough—they manufacture vaccines, and this kind of study just demonstrates the need for them. Also, they knew their stuff. They knew the science—I mean, they were obviously a perfectly legitimate company."

"This is when you met Nisram Singh."

"Not then. It was another man. Peterson his name was."

"Curtis Price met him—Nisram Singh replaced him at Xynex. I think—Curtis thought—Peterson was pushed out."

"Well, medically speaking, it didn't make much difference. They were both top of the class. They knew what they were talking about. I never felt it was a hoax. I mean, it wasn't—that study, as far as it goes, is perfectly valid."

"Tell me how it worked—in a practical sense."

Charlaine leaned back against the sofa, squeezing her hands between her knees. "Let's see. Actually, from our point of view, it wasn't much trouble. Normally, when a woman comes in and wants an abortion, we give her a questionnaire and a medical exam—we just added a couple of points to each. For example, on the questionnaire, we asked them if they had been vaccinated. That was something we wanted to establish. Do women know if they're immune? They don't, actually. Whether they are or they aren't, they usually don't know when you ask them ... which is perfectly consistent with what other studies have found. And then, during the physical, we took an extra blood sample—that was to establish their immunization status. Xynex gave us a kit, and we couriered the samples directly to them in Boca Raton."

"Don't you have a regular lab?"

"Sure. And of course, looking back, that makes me suspicious. In a way, though, it made sense. They had a lab. They were paying for it. They wanted to be absolutely certain of the results."

"And do you think the results they gave you were accurate?"

"That's a question, isn't it? But I think they were. I've gone through half a dozen studies, more or less similar to the one we were doing, and the rates of immunization fit."

"So ..."

"Well, if they said a woman needed the shots, she probably did. They weren't just *saying* patients weren't immune in order to have an excuse to give them a shot."

"Did you ever check up on that? The women you immunized, did they in fact become immune?"

"I checked some of them, afterward, when I became suspicious. And they were immune all right."

"So, this contraceptive vaccine, which we're saying Xynex gave them, had to be mixed in with the other ... the legitimate one against measles and so on?"

"Yes."

"Is that possible?"

"In principle, yes, but who knows? It would depend on the nature of the vaccine."

"Which is? But of course you don't know."

"No. I've tried to check, but it's hard. The geneticists I've spoken to all say it's possible theoretically but they've never heard of any direct work on it. On the other hand, there are some areas, which you can see being connected, that people are investigating. For example, about sixty per cent of men who have vasectomies develop an immunological reaction to their own sperm—they produce antibodies against it. That's one of the reasons they're so hard to reverse. Even if you can hook up the plumbing again, it doesn't do any good. The man's effectively sterile."

"So maybe you could have started with that problem and found something else?"

"Yeah. Possibly."

"Could this have all been a surprise to them? I mean, maybe it was a legitimate rubella vaccine, and then they discovered that the contraceptive part was a side effect."

Charlaine shook her head. "That's hard to believe. There's just no connection . . . maybe, I suppose, you could imagine it making women sterile—but this doesn't. And it's *selective*—it couldn't be an accident."

"Well, is anyone—out in the open—working on a contraceptive vaccine?"

"Yes, but again they're not sex selective. They're simply contraceptive."

"How do they work? In short words."

"Do you know what the trophectoderm is?"

"Of course not."

"Well, it's the layer of the developing embryo that attaches to the uterine wall. It produces hCG—human chorionic gonadotropin, a hormone. There is a vaccine which is built around a synthetic peptide that causes the uterus to reject it. But the vaccine is very complicated to make, it doesn't last long and I don't see how you could make it sex selective."

"What company's working on it?"

Charlaine shook her head. "There's no company. Actually, there's almost no commercial research on contraceptives—most of it's organized and funded by the World Health Organization. There's no money in it for the big drug companies. The Food and Drug Administration makes testing for anything to do with contraception so complicated and expensive that it would take at least fifteen years to get a new contraceptive approved, and cost you millions and millions of dollars. That's why there aren't any new ones. Even Norplant—which is really just a different way of delivering the same old thing—took years to get approved here. It was already accepted in forty or fifty other countries first."

"Before the United States, you mean?"

"Yes."

"But it's not one of those American things . . . like . . . well, abortion."

"Isn't it? A lot of these right-wing Christian groups don't see it that way, they say it's blurring the line. Like that trophectoderm vaccine—the rejection takes place *after* fertilization, so is that a contraceptive or an abortifacient? You see . . . you get all kinds of problems like that. Then, on the other side, you have the feminists. When it comes to contraception, all they see are side effects, exploitation, whatever. Who makes them? Who profits by them? But who *uses* them? They love to chant that sort of thing—you know . . . they're almost paranoid. The FDA just chickens out. They don't actually ban research, but they effectively make it impossible."

"Okay, but side effects are important. A lot of women in my family get breast cancer. My mother has a friend, barely fifty, who had a stroke and they're pretty sure—"

"Side effects are real important if they affect *you*. It's the most important thing in the world, *then*. But the birth-control pill is actually one of the safest drugs ever invented, and it's a hell of a lot less dangerous than having babies. It makes me so angry! If people in this country were really concerned with illegitimacy, teen pregnancy and all those other things they make speeches about, the first thing they'd do—this is what your feminists would really be campaigning for—is to get the pill taken off prescription. And before you go out of your mind, just remember that all the women who've ever suffered side effects from the pill or anything else— the Dalkon Shield—anything—including your mother's friend— they all had a prescription. Every one of them. From a doctor."

"Maybe. But just the same—"

"Don't be so wishy-washy! What it comes down to is, your nice, white middle-class lady, she's got all the contraception she needs. Poor people, black people, young people... they can 'say no', can't they? Or use condoms. Sure!"

"I don't think I buy that—but never mind, I see where you're going. What it all means—if you're Xynex—if you've worked out some kind of sex-selective contraceptive—is that you're going to get it from all sides."

"You're not kidding. The right-to-lifers will hang you, then the feminists will cut off your head. Besides, in the most straightforward way, if they were testing something like that, it would be illegal—as is in *going to jail*."

"In fact," said Deborah, "there's really no way they could develop a contraceptive like that in the U.S."

"No. Not in a million years."

"But outside—"

"That would be different. And they'd make... God only knows what they'd make. Millions, *billions*. As you said, maybe we should all be buying their stock—"

"Okay, but it would be different, in the end—outside the U.S.— because governments would ... well, at least they wouldn't oppose it."

"I don't see how they could ... China, India, Pakistan, Egypt, Mexico, Brazil... those countries are drowning in people. They've got so many children, they literally get rid of them, like garbage. It's part of keeping the streets clean. And there's no doubt, a lot of those children are born because their families want boys, and they just keep having them till they get a boy. Or the women just die, I guess. There've been all kinds of studies ... well, take Taiwan. *Small* families are *boy* families—they have two boys, then stop. Big families, though, have lots of girls, because they keep trying to have a boy, because the parents have to be buried by a son to get to heaven. Or something. And it doesn't make any difference what *we* think about it—"

"By 'we' I assume you include nice *black* middle-class—"

"Okay, I plead guilty. But what you always have to remember is, girls can do everything boys can do, *and one thing more*. They can get pregnant. The fewer girls, the less your population in the future. And some of these countries, Vietnam, Kenya, places like that, half their population is under fifteen—think of it, all those girls who haven't even started getting pregnant yet. Do they want any more? I don't think so."

Deb sat back. "It almost sounds like you're in favour of it."

"Actually, to tell the truth, I don't know. But you have to face the facts, you *can* make a case. Say you only had one girl baby for every *other* woman—that would bring the population down, real quick. You see? And from the point of view of a company like Xynex . . . well, maybe there'd be risks, but there'd also be rewards. You know, that good old capitalistic *risk-reward ratio*."

Deb said, "I don't think I like it. At all."

"Well, I'll tell you what I don't like. Since 1940, the population of the U.S. has about doubled. In the next fifty years, it'll go up by another fifty per cent—it'll be way over three hundred million, if you can believe it. And almost half those people won't be white, they'll be black and Asian and Hispanic. *Over* half of young people will be coloured. Maybe, thinking of the history of this country, you could imagine that white people might not like moving toward minority status. They *might* want to do something about it. One thing they could do is limit the number of coloured women, because that automatically cuts back on the number of coloured *babies*."

"That's disgusting," said Deb.

"Has that ever stopped anyone? And it's not just the blacks, even *mainly* the blacks. Let me tell you, the rise in the Hispanic population in this country makes the baby boom look like the tiniest ripple."

Deb was silent; then she said, "You've been thinking a lot about this, haven't you?"

"Thinking, reading—yes. Since Curtis told me what was going on—I was figuring it out, but he confirmed it all—I haven't been thinking about much else."

"And now he's dead."

"Yeah. He's dead. Because he *knew*. And now I know. Now *you* know."

146 • ANTHONY HYDE

Deb thought about *that* for a second, then said: "So ... what do we do about it?"

"I don't know. I told you, I can't prove anything."

"What if you could?"

Charlaine shrugged. "I guess, when you get right down to it, I still don't know. I told you—I've got a lot to lose. Let's say I could prove it, let's say I took the whole story to the *Sun*—it's not necessarily the best thing, getting your name in the papers."

"Right, you don't mind sounding off to me, but you're afraid—" But Deb stopped herself. "Never mind."

"What do you mean?"

"Nothing. Forget it."

"No, what were you going to say?"

"I was going to say you don't mind making speeches at me, one of your nice *white* ladies, but you're afraid ... you know ... I *was* going to say that, but it wouldn't be fair. You do have a lot to lose. You *do*." Yes, Deb thought; her career, which she must have fought so hard to have; her reputation; even this apartment ... which maybe looked a little barren, as if she'd just moved in, *as if she hadn't brought any of her previous life with her*: because, probably, there hadn't been a lot to bring. "Besides," Deb added, "someone murdered Curtis—we can't forget that." *And someone had been on that boat.*

Charlaine nodded. "No, we can't." Then she added, "Sorry about the speeches, though. And I will admit, some white ladies are a hell of a lot better than others."

"I *think* I'll take that as a compliment."

"I'm not so great at compliments ... but I want you to."

Deb was quiet a moment; it made a certain sense, she decided, that she and Charlaine edged closer to each other through these little touchy moments. In the end, how much did they really have in common? They pretended to live in the same world, but were actually a universe apart. She got up and went to the window. Outside, the day was fading; below, in the street, shadows were gathering in a big old chestnut tree. She glanced at her watch, and Charlaine said, "Look, don't worry about your plane. You can stay over here."

"Are you sure?"

"Absolutely. All I've got is the couch, but it's pretty comfortable."

Deb hesitated; she wasn't quite sure why. But then she said, "Thank you, that would be great."

Charlaine smiled. She seemed pleased that Deb had accepted. "Why don't we go get some dinner?" she said.

Deb hesitated. "Okay," she said.

Charlaine said: "Maybe, though, you want to call Toronto first?"

"Yes. If you don't mind. "

But the Marsh Foundation still hadn't heard from Giacomo. *Frankly, we're a little worried. If he calls you, could you tell him . . .*

"Yes, of course I'll tell him."

They walked over to Mt. Vernon and found an Afghan restaurant, deferring to each other in a tentative, awkward way as they ordered their meal—did Deb want wine? Yes, but only if Charlaine . . . Red or white? It doesn't make any difference, whatever *you* want . . . It was as though the two young women now pulled away from each other so that they could meet all over again, but this time more conventionally, which allowed them to account for themselves in a more straightforward way. So they told each other about their different upbringings, in Kingston and Baltimore, and exchanged details about their siblings—Deb's older sister, in Vancouver, who was a lawyer; Charlaine's three brothers, one a sales representative for Honeywell, another back in school studying industrial design, the third simply not mentioned—and then the course of their respective academic and professional careers: Deb, who'd studied history, and had stumbled into the securities business almost by accident—a summer job that turned permanent; Charlaine, who'd decided on medicine after someone at school made a class presentation about Lois Young, the first black woman to graduate from the University of Maryland's medical school. Again, as they talked, Deb was struck by the gulf between them, the very different worlds they'd come from. And at one point a memory flashed through her mind, and she smiled—purely to herself, but Charlaine noticed, and cocked her head to one side.

"What are you thinking?" she asked.

"I was just remembering something . . . One time, up at my parents' cottage, I came across this huge pile of old magazines, a great stack of ancient copies of *Chatelaine*, I guess from the sixties, maybe even before that."

"*Chatelaine* is—?"

"Oh, like the *Ladies' Home Journal* . . . but different. Anyway, what I can remember is this one picture of a woman. She looked— you could almost say, *unnaturally* happy, *unbelievably* happy . . . I mean, you couldn't believe it, how happy she was. I can just see her. Her hair wasn't exactly long, but longish—all around her face—and she was wearing this skirt, fairly long, gathered at the waist—I don't think there were pleats, but it was long, swishy, probably mid-calf—"

"Like a dirndl skirt?"

"Almost, but I don't think that's what they called it."

"No. Probably it had a pattern of—what? Polka dots?"

"*Exactly*," said Deb, "*polka dots*. It was incredible." Deb knew, now, why she was remembering this; the distance between herself and the woman in that picture was some measure of the distance between her world and Charlaine's. She said, "She seemed so different, she could have come from a different planet. I don't know—she almost seemed childish. Maybe people were more childish then, at least the women were treated that way."

Charlaine shrugged. "Maybe they were. Maybe they *are*—more childish. Just the style has changed." She laughed. "Now they're kind of *militantly* childish."

Deb said, "I keep thinking—assuming—you're a feminist, but you're not, are you."

"Feminism is for nice, white, middle-class ladies. I don't have the energy to waste complaining. Let me tell you something, anyone who complains about the world is admitting they don't understand it. Take your lady in the polka-dot skirt, maybe she's ahead of us. To you, she seems unbelievably happy. I don't know. Maybe you should believe it. At least she had an idea of what happiness meant."

By this route, it seemed, they'd worked their way back to this afternoon. Deb leaned forward, "As a nice, white, middle-class lady, let me ask you something."

"Okay."

"If you were going to have a baby, what would you want, a girl or a boy?"

Charlaine laughed, "As long as it was one or the other, I don't think I'd care." But then she shrugged. "Actually, I probably would. As a doctor, I can tell you—whatever they may tell the Gallup poll—women want to have boys, at least the first time."

"You said you were pregnant once?"

"Yeah.

"So you . . . ?"

"Yeah, I had an abortion. Which proves I don't *always* do the dumb thing."

Afterwards, as they walked back through the first moments of darkness, Deb wondered about what Charlaine had said. And she could understand it. It was true, she felt it herself, *I'm pregnant*, this sense of being taken over, *occupied*. But you could get used to it, she thought. And would it really be any different if she'd wanted to be pregnant? Every woman probably felt the same way to begin with. That was probably the first thing you had to do, make it *your* pregnancy. That was the first step, the first decision—and she realized that her fears about Giacomo, which she'd been holding at bay all day, were part of this, that he'd shifted subtly in her mind: he wasn't her boyfriend, her lover, he was the father of this baby *and where was he* . . . was he in danger? where could he be? If the Marsh Foundation didn't know where he was— But then they were outside Charlaine's building; and just as they turned up the walk, Charlaine touched Deb's arm and said, "Wait a second." She turned back. Her car was parked at the curb; a folded sheet of paper was stuck under the wiper. Charlaine unfolded the paper and Deb read it over her shoulder:

DR CHARLAYNE I NEED TO SEE YOU. CLINIC IS CLOSED TONITE BUT IT IS VERY IMPORTANT. YOU WEREN'T AT HOME. Callie

"Who's Callie?" asked Deb.

"Callie Devon . . . She's one of the clinic women . . ." Charlaine hesitated. "It's interesting, actually. You might like to meet her. They worked it out, you see. Some of the women who got pregnant—they realized, they were only having boys. Callie came and talked to me about it." But then Charlaine stood silently a moment, holding the note in her hand. "I wonder what's wrong," she said.

"Maybe you should call her."

Charlaine shook her head. "She doesn't have a phone—only a pay phone."

"So what do you do?"

"I'm not sure. She lives in Harlem Park. It's not the kind of neighbourhood where you want to be wandering around at night."

Deb said, "I don't think you should go."

"Why not?"

"I don't know. It's just that . . ."

In fact, Deb knew why she was nervous; she just couldn't quite admit it. *Someone had broken into Curtis Price's boat. Someone had almost run her down last night. And it was the same man . . .* it was the same man who'd been in Giacomo's apartment. That was *her* problem; it all led back to Giacomo. Somehow, he was involved. He knew something. *Or somebody thought he did.* "Everything makes me nervous now, I guess." *Since everything was falling apart.*

"I don't blame you. I don't really like it either."

"No. Maybe—"

"But I *should* go. She'd never trouble me like this—she'd never come over here. Not unless it was important. But you don't have to—"

"No, no. Of course I'll come. You're right, it might be interesting to meet her. Is she sick? Does she have some sort of problem?"

"She's got—"

But Charlaine was already walking around the car and getting in, with a kind of nervous haste, as though the unease that had touched Deborah had touched her too; but she couldn't admit it either, and there only seemed one strategy available, *get it over with*. Deb, in a way, was surprised; she wouldn't have guessed that this was how Charlaine would have responded to a medical emergency. Or was it that? In any case, Deb certainly didn't *want* to go—but she got in anyway; she couldn't see that there was any other choice. Charlaine stared straight ahead, putting the car in gear; Deb, beside her, caught her perfume, a scent of high-rises and boutiques, the glossy pages of expensive magazines: a different smell, she thought, than the one they were heading to. But of course nothing was going to happen; nothing ever did—she thought of all the times she'd been afraid, and all the times her fears had been completely groundless. As they drove, Charlaine told her about Callie, four kids, three different fathers, "Once I asked her why and she said, 'It just seems to *happen.*' The problem is—well, she has a lot of problems, but number one is father number three. The last one. He can be a little rough, *fucking* rough."

"Jesus."

Somehow, though, Deb almost found this information reassuring; it at least provided a convincing explanation as to why Charlaine would have responded as she'd done—what else could she do? And she herself clearly had no choice but to come along. Still, she still felt nervous, all the more so because she was soon completely lost; they seemed to be travelling in circles, reconnoitring, tracing some perimeter. Each corner seemed identical to the last. Waiting at a stoplight, she realized theirs was the only car; in every direction, the streets ran off in empty, lonely darkness. Charlaine said, as if explaining, "Whenever I come down here, I like to stay on the main streets as much as possible."

Deb saw a sign—*Fremont*—but after that none of the streets were *main*. Dark, narrow, desolate rows of houses stretched to empty corners where black faces, upturned in their headlights, stared blankly after them, ghosts or zombies, disembodied in the darkness. Another corner: a storefront, gloomily alight, *Caplan's Discount:* Money Orders, Patent Medicine, Ice, Beer, Wine, Liquor, and lottery tickets, the daily, Scratch Offs, Match 5, every kind... Obscurely, a park drifted by, and Deb thought she saw pale figures passing though the gloom, and she smiled nervously, remembering a late-night drive-in show from when she was a kid, Krazy Kult Klassics, hours and hours of pictures like *The Night of the Living Dead* and *A Nightmare on Elm Street* and *Friday the 13th*. They turned, turned again; for a moment, Deb thought Charlaine was lost, for they seemed to be turning back upon themselves— maybe it was a nightmare—and in fact Harlem Park is like that, only a few blocks square—approximately enclosed by Fremont, Franklin, Monroe and Laurens—but the desolation is so uniform and monotonous that it's like a maze or Mobius strip and there seems no way out.

"It's just up here," Charlaine finally said.

The car's lights raked across a dark block of row houses, each with a narrow cement porch; up and down, many of its neighbours were boarded up.

"Don't worry, it's not as bad as it looks."

But it did look bad. They both fell silent as Charlaine turned one last time, and slowed, looking for a parking spot. She found it underneath a streetlight. It was a very bright light, presumably as safe a spot as you could find; but Deb felt more like an illuminated target.

They got out of the car; Charlaine hesitated, but then reached behind her seat for a rather old-fashioned-looking medical bag. The snap of the car locks made Deb jump. She found herself remembering an article from some magazine, "Do You Walk Like a Victim?" which in turn made her think of the woman down the hall from her who was convinced, every time she went out, that some man was "stalking" her. Peg, her name was, Peg Robson. She could just hear her voice, *It was really really scary*... And precisely then she perceived one element of danger—not understanding it, but knowing nonetheless that it *was* danger: the two identical Ford sedans, parked one behind the other; and the third, exactly the same make and year and model, parked two cars further down. She took a step with that in mind, *something's wrong*, and then from behind a huge hand closed on her face and a great arm seized her at the waist, dragging her to one side. For two seconds, she was so startled, she was paralyzed; she didn't react at all. It just *happened*. Then she screamed. She screamed in terror. But the hand over her mouth was so big and strong that her scream was pressed back down her throat, and she choked, and then really she panicked and kicked and twisted, losing all control, or tried to twist and tried to kick, but nothing happened—she only managed to hit her shin on something. Pain shot up her leg; tears started in her eyes. And the pain of this penetrated her terror sufficiently that she was at least aware of being dragged up steps. And then she heard, *felt*, a grunt and so was aware too that *someone*, unseen, unknown, was doing this. But her awareness, such as it was, didn't make the slightest difference. There was nothing she could do. A door had opened. She was thrust forward into darkness, she staggered. A light wavered over ripped-up walls. The blank, grey, cockeyed screen of a television stared at her from a filthy corner. An arm pressed down on her neck and her arm was twisted back behind her. *"Don't!"* she shrieked, and gasped. Music blared. The light came around again as she was pushed to her knees, and forward, *down*. Face down. A hand grasped her hair and jerked her head right back, and a voice behind her whispered, surprisingly low and calm:

"No, baby. Don't *you.*"

The music was so stupid. It was so loud and stupid. You couldn't help but hear it and maybe she'd heard it before. It was one of those songs where you couldn't even tell if it was a boy group or a girl group, or if they were white or black, or maybe they were just electronic, because that's how they were trying to sound.

Black midnight

This town is gettin' hot

Sweet as my baby

She stared. She wanted to shake her head and have it all go away.

"For Christ's sake, hit her," a voice said somewhere, but no one hit her, she just heard a groan. *Charlaine.*

"Oh my. Do look at that. Look at *that*!"

The light wavered again, then steadied. Deb gasped for breath. A weight—solid, substantial, warm, alive—pressed on her back and shoulders, and a knee thrust up between her legs. She smelled aftershave.

"Don't move now, honey. Don't you move. All right?"

As if she could. Her head was pulled right back; any more, her neck would break. Like this, she could barely breathe.

I'm packin' just for you
An' you're comin' just with me
You wait and see

She stared and panted. A hand thrust between her legs. She screamed and the music kept on beating. Other hands pulled her by the ankles, and her panties were ripped aside. Oh God.

Black midnight
An' the dark is cookin' all around me
Like my baby

"Know what this is, honey? Pepsi. *Diet* Pepsi. The *family* size." She didn't move and a smooth, hard shape pressed against her vulva. She closed her eyes. *Her baby.* "Okay now? You going to keep still now? Tell me now? You gotta voice? Tell me."

"Yes." *Her baby.*

"You keep still?"

"Yes." *They'd hurt the baby.*

The bottle pressed inside her and she closed her eyes, *it's okay it's okay* but then the hand jerked her head, commanding, and she opened them and stared, obedient. A warm presence panted over her. "You watching? *You watching?*"

"Yes, I'm watching," she had to whisper.

Hey you gotta know
When they close that door I'm OK

Ahead, torn linoleum on a floor, rubble scattered everywhere, bars... But they weren't bars, they were the studs of a torn-down wall, there was another room beyond. The light was there. She saw Charlaine, and shapes. Her mind resolved them into men. *The bottle pressing into her, don't move, two men.* She didn't move. Absolutely, she didn't move. *You can't move you can't do anything.* She stared. Charlaine's face flashed as one of the men hit her; it was Charlaine they'd been hitting. They'd been raping her. The first of them had already raped her, now the other one was raping her, while the first one held a flashlight. The beam of the light jerked—Charlaine was still struggling—and the light swung across the blackness of the room, and around and down, glinting on the television, which, she saw, teetered on a wire stand, like a dead-drunk rummy propped up in the gutter. The man raping Charlaine gave out a grunt. Someone behind Deb, more or less over her shoulder, said, "You done, son?"

A warm breath panted. "Guess, what, Miss? You listening? My name's Boyd. My real good friends all call me Gerry, but maybe we don't know each quite that well. But you like the show? Look over there now. Look over there. Isn't that awful? Isn't that just too bad. Look at that. What's the world coming to? A nice lady goes out at night to lick up her lezzie friend, and just see what happens. There's a lesson in that."

The man with the flashlight said, "For Christ's sake, finish her, no one's paying overtime for this."

She was thinking the men were black, because of their voices, but she couldn't see.

Nothin' I can do

If you wanna be with me

Behind her, Boyd's voice was low and calm. "Stay home. Stay out of things. That's the lesson you want to learn. Understand, Deborah?"

I'm goin' to bend you down

The bottle pressed hard and a sob caught in Deborah's throat and she was nodding, "Yes, yes," *he knows who I am.*

"And when you get back, I want you to call this number. Listen. *Listen.*"

"Yes."

She listened. He hissed a number in her ear. "*You say it.*" She said it. "*You say it again.*" She said it again, and then he backed away, and jerked her head up, so she had to see as the man who was on Charlaine heaved himself up, and caught his balance and made a little grunt. And Deb saw Charlaine's eyes flashing in the dark. Kneeling, the man panted and caught his breath. Then he said, "Hey, Gerry, didn't you say this one liked the taste of pussy . . . I was thinking maybe she'd like to taste her own." He sort of waddled his way along her, straddling her chest. Then he cleared his throat and he leaned down . . . "What the hell, open up . . . Jesus Christ, you open up . . . open up now." Charlaine's face jerked around, *she's looking at me,* and Deb saw Charlaine's eyes again, white, looking toward her and calling, *help, help*. But Deb didn't move. *She couldn't move.* There was a gun, now, in the hand of the kneeling man, and he kept on saying, "Open up, open up . . . that's it, that's it, not so bad now, not so bad . . ." Oh God, Deb thought. And then he chuckled, "That's it baby, you doing good, real good." Deb saw him pressing the gun against Charlaine's head and she could hear him chuckling, "Colt .45, works every time." Deb closed her eyes. "Works every *fucking* time." She had to close her eyes. As the music drummed out so stupid—

Hey you gotta know

She waited, eyes shut.

After a time, the weight on top of her, the pressure, lifted.

When they close that door I feel OK

Her neck was aching. She strained to hold her head up. It was the music that kept her where she was.

They'd raped Charlaine but not her. Because . . .

And now, without actually looking, her eyes just staring stupidly in front of her, she saw the dark, filthy room all around her, the plaster and bits of wood, the TV set and the stand in the corner, and in this corner a strip of wallpaper dangled down, the old life of this place persisting like a dripping drain. She smelled plaster. There was a smell of urine. She could smell charred wood. A long time passed; and finally she knew the men were gone. Her hands came up and caught her weight. For a moment longer, though, she still didn't move. She didn't quite dare. She stared ahead. She looked through the bars of the studs to the room where Charlaine lay curled up in a ball. Yet she didn't move even then. She waited quite a while like that.

Then she stood up; she was certain that the men were gone— the music was still going, the tape had gone all around, *Black midnight, this town is gettin' hot,* but the light was gone—and she heard Charlaine groan. So she stood up; and then there was a moment, horrible, when she had to pull her panties up. She couldn't see very well. She stretched her arms ahead of her and called, softly, "Charlaine? Charlaine?" Her hands touched the rough, spiny wood of the studs of the wall as she felt along, searching for the opening; and then, very cautiously, she stepped forward. "Charlaine . . . you okay?"

Charlaine was now sitting up in the middle of the filthy floor. When she looked up, and looked around, she didn't seem to know where she was; and when Deb knelt down beside her, she wasn't sure that Charlaine even recognized her. She was whispering something, "Callie," she whispered, over and over.

"It's all right," said Deb.

"Callie . . ." Charlaine said again, and she was almost sobbing.

It was only then that Deb precisely remembered about Callie, *her lezzie friend,* and the note on the car. And that started her mind working, figuring everything out. Yes, the note. And they'd known exactly who she was . . . Gradually, the logic of what had happened began to come together. Gently, she touched Charlaine's shoulder—she wasn't sure, somehow, that her touch would be welcome *oh God it's all your fault,* Deb began to think—and she said, "Don't worry about Callie, they just used Callie to get us here." *Your lezzie lover . . .* But that was something else: *they'd known all about Charlaine too.* "She'll be okay."

Charlaine, for quite a while, didn't move. Then Deb took her arm, pressuring lightly, until finally Charlaine got up. She didn't seem to be badly hurt. They'd hit her; but she wasn't bleeding anywhere and nothing seemed to be broken. But her blouse was ripped, her bra was half off. Her slacks were lying on the floor. Deb handed them to her, and for the first time, in her own voice—her adult voice, *her* voice—Charlaine spoke. "It's so disgusting," she said. She sounded exhausted.

Deb didn't say anything. But all at once, anger surged through her, for some reason it was the music that set it off, because the music was still blaring—blaring out from a big ghetto blaster, lying to one side, and she found it, feeling around with her hands, pushed buttons, trying to turn it off *why had they played music like that so loud* but she couldn't find the switch, there were hundreds of buttons and finally she kicked at it, kicked it away *it should have made people come* but of course it hadn't, she kicked it again, and then again—it kept on playing—*they were warning people, stay away, something's going down* until finally, thank God, the music stopped. She panted in the silence. Then she said: "We have to get out of here."

Charlaine, on her feet, was a little unsteady, and put one hand on Deb's shoulder. Slowly, they felt their way through the darkness. At a certain point, they could feel a draft of air and they moved toward it. As they stepped outside, Charlaine said, "Oh God," and Deb said, "It's all right. Let's just find the car." As she said this, she was aware of a sense of obligation; she was the one who had to get them through it.

They made it down the sidewalk, and when they reached the car, Charlaine leaned against it and said, "I don't have my keys, my purse is still in there somewhere."

"It's okay," said Deb, "just wait here. I'll get it."

So she went back. For a moment, stepping inside, she was scared, but then she was all right; it was just the shell of an old slum house, the most frightening thing might be a bat. She stumbled and stubbed her toe and swore. She found the purse. Back at the car, she said, "Let me drive."

But Charlaine wouldn't let her. She shook her head and said, "You don't know the way." Then she opened the door, and the inside light came on, and Deb could see that there was something awful on Charlaine's face, semen or something, but by the time she'd gone around and got in herself, Charlaine had wiped it away. Charlaine started the car; they drove in silence, staring straight ahead. But when they reached Charlaine's place, and parked, Charlaine took the key out of the ignition and said, "I don't want anyone to see me like this."

"It's okay," said Deb, "there's no one around."

"There might be someone on the stairs."

"It's okay. I don't think there will be."

Charlaine leaned forward, over the steering wheel, as though she was praying. She said, "I just need a minute."

"Charlaine, I really think you should go to the hospital."

She shook her head. "That would only make it worse." She

leaned back now, against the headrest, and closed her eyes. She didn't move. Then a weak smiled played across her lips, and with her eyes still closed she said, "Funny. I once took a course about this. Rape. Trauma. Either you're hysterical at the time, or you're okay, and then fall apart a week later."

"You're not going to fall apart. You're too strong."

"Really? I don't know. You, on the other hand, are definitely in the week-later category. Right now, you see, you get to look after me."

"Shit," said Deb. "Those bastards. Those . . . *fuckers.*"

Charlaine said, almost wearily, "They are animals."

For another minute, neither of them spoke. A car passed, and Charlaine opened her eyes then, and turned her head, to watch it go by. When it was gone, she said, "I'm okay now. Let's go."

They went inside, and up. They didn't meet anyone. Deb took a breath and looked at her watch; it wasn't even that late.

Charlaine slumped back, leaning against the wall by the door. "Oh God, that was awful."

"Are you sure—maybe you should go to the hospital?"

"No."

"Do you want to call the police?"

"No. Don't be crazy." Charlaine pushed away from the wall, and they went into the living room. "Listen," she said, "are you on the pill?"

"No. But he didn't . . . actually . . . do anything . . . If you know what I mean."

"I do. And the first one *did*, with me anyway. And I'm not taking anything." But then she said, "I think I've got some," and she went over to her desk, which had a computer on it, which for some reason she turned on, flipping angrily at the switch, and then she banged through the drawers. Finally she found what she was looking for, a round birth-control dispenser. She began popping out the pills—to Deb's surprise, a lot of them; she put one in her mouth and swallowed. "Samples," she said.

"But it won't do any good," said Deb.

"Of course it will. If you take enough—the right combination . . .

It works as a morning-after pill, about three-fourths of the time."
She kept swallowing the pills. She said, "Doctor's secret. University
woman's *clinic* secret."

"Let me get you some water."

Charlaine shook her head. "Any taste in my mouth but *that*."
Then she added: "You're absolutely certain?"

Deb nodded. "He just put a bottle . . . there."

"You're not bleeding?"

"No."

"He didn't force it in—it didn't tear?"

"No. He didn't put it that far in. They were just trying to
frighten me."

"Oh *yeah*. They were telling you, be good, *white* girl, or we'll do
you like the *nigger* girl."

Deb looked at Charlaine, could see the hate and fury in her
eyes. But now she was remembering something else, and she got
up and went over to the phone. *I want you to call this number.
Listen . . .* She dialled. Charlaine got up. "What the hell are you
doing?" Deb held up her hand, as a recorded voice came on, saying
the number was long distance, she had to dial "one" before the
area code. *"What the hell are you doing?"*

"Just wait a minute."

The phone was ringing, then a voice came on, a man . . . For a
moment, Deborah didn't believe it, but then she did: it was some
detective, in Long Island . . . *Of course.* In the background, she
could hear an office, humming. She kept her cool. "I'd like to
speak to Detective Bannon, please."

"I don't want the fucking cops in this."

Deb pushed her off. "He isn't here. Been reassigned."

"What do you mean, reassigned?"

"Who is this?"

"I want to speak to whoever's investigating the murder of a man
called Curtis Price."

"The hell you do—"

Deb jerked away, even as she could feel, at the other end of the
line, a palm come down over the mouthpiece, and hear a muffled

voice, "She wants Bannon." *Just tell her we're off the case. It's been federalized, tell her to call the FBI, we don't know anything about it—*

"Miss?"

But she was already hanging up. *Call this number . . .*

"You stupid bitch."

"Charlaine, it's okay." Reassigned . . . federalized . . . off the case . . . *Call this number.*

"It's okay. You think this is okay?"

Deb backed away. She could see the wild, hurt fury in Charlaine's eyes. A puffy, livid bruise was coming up across her cheek, her lip was bleeding—

"Charlaine, I'm sorry."

"Sorry? For what? *Sorry that you're white?*"

"Charlaine—"

"You want to be the nigger girl? You want to trade? You want to be the one they rape?"

"Charlaine, this was not my fault."

But then Charlaine reached out and slapped her across the face.

"You goddamn stupid bitch!"

"Charlaine, listen—"

And slapped her again.

"I told you I was sorry—"

"You *white* stupid goddamn *bitch*!"

For a second, Deb stood there, too stunned to move. Was it her fault? Had she brought this whole catastrophe on Charlaine? Perhaps she had. She hadn't really told her about the *danger* . . . the man in Giacomo's apartment, the car last night. And they raped *her,* not me, she thought. So when Charlaine slapped her face, she simply stood there, and began to cry, and when Charlaine slapped her again, she simply turned the other cheek. But then—*no!*

"I didn't rape you. I don't care if you're white or black!"

And this time, as Charlaine drew her arm back, Deb grabbed her, and they struggled. Deb pulled Charlaine down, but Charlaine got free and she began to swing and slap and hit until Deb grabbed her arm again and this time punched *her,* one punch that sent a red splash of blood spurting from her nose. *"I told you I was sorry, but I'm not that sorry!"*

They fell back, out of breath, and lay there, gasping.

Blood trickled down Charlaine's face and she began to cry, and Deb, quite soundlessly, began to cry too. "Oh God," Charlaine said, "oh God, oh God. *Fuck, fuck, fuck.*"

Neither of them moved. They just lay there, breathing in the darkness.

Quite a long time passed. Outside now, it was very dark; a car passed down the street, and a faint reflection of its headlights touched the room.

Finally, Charlaine whispered, "The bastards. Those fucking bastards..."

Deb said, "It's okay."

They lay there in the dark some more, and then Charlaine said, "You okay?"

"I'm okay."

"I'm sorry. That was stupid—I just... Shit. *Shit.*"

"Yeah," said Deb, "exactly."

Very softly, Charlaine chuckled. "Yeah," she said. Then she said: "You don't know who they are?"

"No. They're not the police—"

"Maybe they work for Xynex."

"Maybe. *For* them, yes. But maybe that's not who they are."

"I don't know what you mean. I'm really not sure of anything."

"I'm not, either." And then Deb reached out and touched Charlaine's arm. "Listen, you have to be careful," she said. "They know who you are. They knew that note would make you come."

"But they know who you are too."

Deb didn't say anything, and after a moment, in the darkness, Charlaine sniffed back blood and then said, "What about your boyfriend?" Which was funny, because Deborah had just been thinking that whoever *they* were, they knew so *much*. About her. About Charlaine. About Callie. And what tied it all together? *Who* tied them all together?

"Charlaine, you said... before... that it was possible to mix in this vaccine with something else?"

"Yeah. Theoretically. Why?"

Deb closed her eyes, and then, slowly, trying to keep her voice from trembling, she said, "I haven't told anyone else, except Rosie, but I'm pregnant."

"Pregnant?"

"Yeah."

"My God. Are you sure?"

"I'm sure."

"You've been pregnant all this time?"

"Yes. The point is, Giacomo has this cat . . . he's great, actually. Henry. But every time I went over there, I'd start sneezing and my eyes would get all red . . . I was allergic."

There was a long silence and then Charlaine said, "Right. You're allergic to cats, a lot of people are—"

"Well, Giacomo's a doctor . . ."

"I know that. I met him, remember."

"Right. You met him with Nisram Singh."

"So?"

"Well, he's a doctor, I was allergic, so he gave me a series of allergy shots. They started a couple of months before I got pregnant."

There was another long silence and then Charlaine said, "*Jesus.* My God. You don't really think . . ."

"Of course not," Deb said. But then she stopped herself. "Of course I *think*—I have to *think*. He's involved. And it all looks so suspicious—even the way we met . . . Everything. I just don't know. If this is a test, maybe he's part of it—and maybe I am, too."

"Jesus—"

"I'm sure he's not—but I can't help *thinking*. I love him, but I have to *know.* I have to find out, I have to find *him*. My God, I could be one of their guinea pigs."

"And if you are, what will you do?"

Deb didn't answer. She sat there, exhausted. She thought about Giacomo. She thought about the baby. *Tonight she could have lost the baby, but did she want the baby if—*

And then Charlaine reached out and touched her shoulder. "Okay, you're going to have to find out . . . and you're going to need some help."

"Charlaine, listen—like you said, you've got so much to lose."

Gently, keeping her head tilted back, she shook her head. "It's too late for that. I'm in this. What the hell, I'd rather help you than fight you anyway—you pack quite a punch."

"I'm sorry."

"Forget it. We'll do better if we're friends."

They lay there in the dark. After a time, they reached out and found each other's hands, while outside in the street, a car door softly shut, and a woman and a man laughed happily together—sounds that carry easily through the darkness of an early summer night.

FLORIDA

CHAPTER TEN

*A*t *9:28 the next morning,* Deb called the Marsh Foundation
from the phone in Charlaine Daniels's kitchen; when she put it
down, about ten minutes later, Charlaine said, "Didn't sound like
any good news."

Deb was quiet a second, her hand still on the phone; then she
shook her head. "Not really. They still can't find him, but they
think he flew to Brazil."

"Brazil?"

"They have a project there, a couple of them. Some sort of
clinic. Apparently they've had problems. So they think . . ."

Deb's voice trailed off. Charlaine said, "But they don't know
where he is?"

Closing her eyes, Deb could hear the executive director's
smooth, carefully modulated voice: *I'm sure there's nothing to worry
about, but frankly . . .* She turned to Charlaine and shook her head
again. "They've no idea. He's just disappeared. Vanished." Deb sat
very still for a moment. "Something's happened, Charlaine. He's in
trouble."

Charlaine leaned forward. "He's in trouble, *you're* in trouble."

Deb tried to smile, but couldn't. "I think he's in a lot worse trouble than I am. It's just not like him. Sometimes it's hard to keep in touch—when he's travelling like that, in countries like that. But he always manages. Even if he can't get me, he can always get a message to them—the Foundation, I mean. And I don't like the way they're talking—you can tell they're worried."

"Watch that, Deb. As a doctor, you get it a lot, patients trying to figure out what you mean rather than simply listening to what you actually *say*."

"Yeah, but somehow this *does* connect to him, everything. Maybe he doesn't even know how, but it does."

"Of course. You're connected. You knew Price—he bought his stock in Xynex through you . . . and you know Giacomo."

Deb hesitated a second. "To tell you the truth, I never looked at it that way—but of course that's true. I meant something more, though. I didn't tell you this, but I think the man from last night—the one who called himself Boyd to me, who told me to phone that number—I think he was snooping around Giacomo's apartment. I was over there. He hid, but I saw him sneak out. And I think it was him. He wore that same kind of cap."

"A lot of men—"

"I know, I know. But right now it's hard to put things like that down to coincidence. And Giacomo knew you, he knew about your clinic, he knew Singh, and anyway that's his whole world—what's this whole thing about? Babies. Overpopulation. The Third World . . . it makes sense in so many ways that he'd be connected."

Charlaine leaned forward, pouring coffee into Deb's cup. "And guess what?" she said. "You're having a baby. *His* baby."

Deb managed to smile. "I thought you weren't supposed to drink this stuff if you're pregnant?"

"Don't worry about it. Know what they used to recommend? Beer. For the vitamin B." Then she added: "Tell me something though . . . about what you said last night. Those shots he gave you . . . Does that worry you along with everything else?"

"No. Not really. Of course not. But . . . I don't know, there are so many questions."

"Do you trust him?"

"Yes, I trust him."

"It's just that there are all these questions?"

"Don't, Charlaine. Please."

Charlaine reached out and took Deborah's hand. "No, Deb, you *don't*. Don't ask those questions—you can't answer them, so forget them. Listen to me. You're pregnant. And I'm the doctor. I'm telling you, what you want to do right now is take care of yourself, go home to Mother and have your baby. It doesn't matter what you *think*—that's what you *want*."

"No—not go home to Mother, not that part. And it doesn't matter what I *want*. He *is* in trouble, and I'm the only one who can get him out of it."

"Okay. Except the pronoun is wrong. We. We're the only ones who can get him out of it. From now on, you have to count me in. We are the Dynamic Duo, the Dangerous Divas, the Daughters of Doom—after last night, I think I want a little revenge."

"Charlaine, listen . . . yesterday. It's true what you said—you've got so much to lose."

"I do. But I'm not sure it makes much difference now. I've probably lost it—what I have to do is get it *back*."

"I don't think—"

"Deb, this is settled. Okay? *We* are in this together. What *you* have to do is not panic, especially not about Giacomo. You love him, you trust him—all those other questions don't matter. Okay?"

"You're sure?"

Charlaine shrugged. "I sort of regret it, actually . . . I mean, I wouldn't mind sowing a few doubts. In that nightie, you're out of this world."

Deb had slept on the couch. The nightie, which Charlaine had lent her, was lavender, slinky and very short. Deb looked down at herself and smiled. "Charlaine, listen—I'm terrified out of my mind. So don't make me nervous."

Charlaine laughed. "It's a deal." She leaned forward. "So what do we do?"

"Well, I think I've got one idea . . ."

Deb was feeling better; it always did help if you talked. She wasn't any less frightened, but she felt calm. And she was incredibly grateful for Charlaine's offer to help . . . Charlaine, whose face was still bruised, whose hand shook as she lifted her cup of coffee—which she used to wash down three Valiums. For her part, she threw the last of her coffee into the sink and then—what the hell—got some milk from the fridge. She poured some. Drank it. And it didn't matter what she did, she always ended up with a bit of a moustache.

She leaned back against the counter. "I think what we have to do," she said, "is start with what we know—at least, what we can be pretty sure we know. Xynex Incorporated. They're a small biotech company, but somehow they've come up with a major discovery: a sex-selective contraceptive vaccine. You get a shot, and you can only have boys. They want to keep this a secret, but they also want to test it, so they mix it into rubella vaccine and distribute it through your clinic."

Charlaine nodded. "That works. It would even make sense, from their point of view. There'd be risks. But if they went through all the usual steps, even trying to do it outside the Food and Drug Administration, it would be bound to get out. They'd be better off proving it worked and was safe—then you pull off the wraps and say here it is, what the hell are you going to do about it? The trouble is, somehow Curtis Price figured out what was going on."

Deb shook her head. "Not *somehow*. We know a little about that, too. We know *how* because he told me. He's in Carolina, walking through some yacht basin, and he meets a man called Peterson, formerly the top scientific guy at Xynex. Then, later on, he meets him again, here in Baltimore. Now maybe that wasn't exactly an accident—maybe he was lying about that—but it doesn't make much difference. It was meeting Peterson that got him started."

"And Peterson let the cat out of the bag because he'd been fired—"

"Replaced by Nisram Singh—"

"Your boy-wonder scientist. That all makes sense. People who get fired can sometimes shoot off their mouths."

"Yes. Then he connected with you—how did that happen, by the way?"

Charlaine shrugged. "A fundraiser. A sort of auction thing we do for the clinic. He gave some money—real money, but nothing *too* much, if you know what I mean."

"So," said Deb, "he gets close to you, and finds out even more, or maybe just confirms what he already suspects."

"Then he starts buying their stock and gets himself killed, but your point is—he started with Peterson . . . It was Peterson who gave him his first hint."

"Exactly."

"Therefore . . . you want to talk to him."

"But we can't."

"Why not?"

"He's dead."

Charlaine hesitated. "That is not good."

"Not usually, but let me show you something." She went into the living room and found her purse, then came back into the kitchen. "That's a boat listing—same thing as a real-estate listing—for Peterson's yacht. Curtis Price kept it in the chart table on *Royal Palm*."

"And this article . . . ?"

"Peterson supposedly drowned, fell off his boat."

Charlaine scanned the article from *Soundings*. "While taking a *pee?*"

"Yeah, it's definitely a guy thing."

Charlaine looked up at Deb. "But you said *supposedly?*"

"Well, I wonder. Why was Curtis Price so interested? I know it's nothing definite, but it makes me curious. Price began with Peterson, who supposedly died in an accident—and Price seems to have gone to a lot of trouble, finding out the details."

Charlaine flipped the listing over. "Palmetto, Florida . . . That's where it is, this boat—*Double Helix?*"

"Yes."

"Curtis had a place in Florida. He was always going down there."

"Which would have made it easy to check things out. That's what I want to do. What *he* did."

Charlaine thought for a long minute, then nodded. "Okay, it's a place to start. At least it gets us doing something."

They knew they had to be careful.

They'd been warned—now it had to look as though they'd heeded the warning. Calling Bannon's office last night had been a good first step. Deb had done exactly what Boyd—or whatever his name was—had wanted her to. By now, as far as he was concerned, she was frightened out of her mind and knew that the police weren't going to help her—they'd succumbed to the "funny pressure" Bannon had talked about. So what would any good, sensible, terrified girl be likely to do? Shut up, go home, and keep her head down. And so they tried to make it look like that. Charlaine called her office, said she wouldn't be in: natural enough, under the circumstance. Then she drove Deb to the airport—again, what you'd expect—in time to catch the first flight to Toronto. But, in fact, Deb bought a ticket to Tampa, a flight leaving forty minutes later. This wasn't perfect, obviously, but it was the best they could do, and at least it *looked* right. Charlaine, meanwhile, drove out of the airport, but doubled back. She wouldn't be able to make the Tampa flight, but there was one not long afterward to Orlando. She'd rent a car there, and meet Deb—the drive from Orlando to Tampa was barely an hour.

Deb, in any case, needed the time: she had some research to do.

Peterson's boat had been a Krogen 38, and for the plan that was beginning to form in her mind, she needed to know a little about them. In truth, before she started, all she knew about Krogen was that they made a trawler, like the Grand Banks. But the library had a copy of Janet Mauch's *Sailboat Guide*, an alphabetical listing of virtually every yacht a prospective buyer was likely to find offered for sale. The Krogen 38 was there. A line drawing gave a general sense of the boat's appearance; it was a cutter, with a clipper bow and a raised deck. Sitting in the library, studying the picture, Deb wasn't sure what she felt about it—the raised deck made it look a little "funny." Instead of a separate cabin, with side decks to take you up to the bow, the Krogen had a flush deck that ran straight from one side of the hull to the other. It looked a little less "yachty." Still, it meant you had a lot more room inside, and more air circulation. The interior plan also had pluses and minuses. The galley looked okay, so did the main salon; not as luxurious as the Shannon, but very pleasant. On the minus side, the main sleeping cabin, which was aft, had an athwartship berth, i.e. it ran across the width of the boat. It wasn't a common arrangement, and Deb had never slept in one; but she remembered that Eric Hiscock, who was probably the greatest modern cruiser, said to avoid them like the plague—and it would be strange, sleeping like that, given the way boats usually moved. As for the boat's construction, that seemed pretty good. "The KROGEN 38's hull is of fibreglass sandwich construction with closed-cell PVC foam core . . ." To save weight, almost all fibreglass hulls were cored with something, usually balsa wood or some kind of foam, like Airex. They all had problems; balsa could rot, Airex turned soft in the heat, and PVC-cored hulls were said to delaminate easily—the fibreglass could pull away. But not if the work was well done, Deb had always believed, and PVC would have been her personal choice. So, all in all, that was a plus for the Krogen, and just the sort of technical detail she wanted to know. And there was one other interesting point—there were two centreboards, an unusual arrangement that allowed the boat to be trimmed very precisely, and made it just a little different. All together, Deb thought, that was point about the Krogen: it was slightly out of the ordinary.

When she was finished with the *Guide*, she began checking other references, old copies of *Cruising World* and *Sail*. She found a couple of reviews—middling—and photos—she still wasn't sure about the esthetics—and the sort of "advertorial" that went into the Boat Show issues of all the magazines: *"The KROGEN 38 is yet another quality cruising sailboat developed in this country and built in the Far East with U.S. supervision. She's been around for a couple of years, but with little ballyhoo. It's time to turn that around, for she has all the makings of a perfect live-aboard boat."* Perfect? She didn't know about that. All the same, by the time she was through, Deb was confident that she could pass herself off as a genuine Krogen enthusiast, a potential purchaser of *Double Helix*.

When she was finished, there was nothing to do but sit outside the library and wait for Charlaine—who showed up around half past two in a Toyota Corolla that looked as if it had seen better days.

"Don't worry, though, she moves."

"Where did you get it?"

"A real small place. Not even a franchise. They wouldn't take Amex."

That's what they'd wanted; someplace that wouldn't be linked to a national, computerized reservation system, so they'd be hard to trace.

"Great. Now if we can manage to find Palmetto. Did you get maps?"

"Yeah. It really shouldn't be hard. The I-75, then we look for Route 41."

Charlaine was a good, quick driver, and Palmetto was barely twenty minutes away, a tiny place quietly sheltering in the shadow of the bridges that carried the big coastal highways over the long, blue bay formed by the Manatee River as it reached the sea. It was quiet, lazy, asleep in the afternoon sun—bungalows with haphazardly cut lawns, sidewalks that petered out, backyards with swings and doghouses.

"Pure *Father Knows Best*," said Charlaine, slowing down.

Deb laughed to herself and Charlaine gave her a look: "What's that about?"

"Actually, it makes me think of my *mother*. She grew up in a place like this called Willowdale."

"Willows, palms . . . big difference."

"I remember one time, I had some friends over—my mum showed us how to do The Twist."

Charlaine laughed. "My word, did you ever see so many beauty parlours . . ." And then she slowed down as they came up to a tiny cemetery, one of whose headstones they could read from the car:

J. ovial

A. ctive

C. onscientious

K. ind

Charlaine said, "I'm not sure if I like this place, or if it gives me the creeps—I wonder if Stephen King has ever been through here."

"Don't say things like that. We have to find a motel."

They turned into the second one they came to. It wasn't very good; the room had a lingering scent of air freshener, and when Charlaine looked into the bathroom, she made a face. "We should have brought thongs." Still, the towels were okay and when they turned on the air conditioner, it produced a wonderful refrigerated gale. They lay down for twenty minutes, then hit a McDonald's, and then headed for their real objective, the Regatta Pointe Marina. It was getting late—almost four.

If Palmetto had a hot centre, the marina was probably it: brand new, it formed a complex of piers and buildings stretching along the Manatee River, all done in a quiet grey colour that was probably called "barnboard" but really tried to suggest "Mercedes." The river, Deb guessed, was pretty shallow here; the main pier stretched well out, then formed a T—at the junction, there was a floating restaurant—with more docks extending even farther.

Charlaine said, "Now there you have a lot of boats."

Deb pointed. "And those are Krogens . . . the trawlers."

"Like fishing boats?"

"Right, but that one is a Krogen 38—with all the stuff piled up beside it on the pier. Someone's working on it." And then Deb added: "I think I want to look at it."

"But maybe," said Charlaine, "I won't come with. Around here, I expect I'm kind of exotic."

Deb grinned. "Just a little. Why don't you sip a Bloody Mary in the bar, and I'll do my thing."

"Got you. And good luck."

Deb watched Charlaine go into the restaurant, then walked out on the pier, feeling the muggy warmth of the river enfold her as she left the shade near the shore. There weren't many people around, despite the size of the place; a man was walking up a stairway to the second storey of the restaurant, and an older man—who reminded her of those people in Oxford—slowly shuffled down the dock to her left, carrying a blue Igloo cooler. Under the pier, waves slapped at the pilings with a soft *chunking* sound; the water here had a muddy, leaden tone, not very pleasant, and it threw the light back with an ugly glare. Shading her eyes, she looked at the Krogen; she had a big, flat transom—the proverbial girl with a bottom two axe-handles wide—and across it, in dark red letters, was *Double Helix*. So this was Peterson's boat—and Deb had an anxious moment, thinking it might have been sold. But she went out to the T, and turned left; and as she drew closer to the boat, she could hear voices coming from the interior. She was too far away to make out exactly what they were saying, but they were clearly angry; and instinctively she stopped. But then she thought, No, that was being polite, and from now on she had to *stop* being polite. She went on, and a woman's voice yelled,

"For Christ's sake, quit trying to sell the damn thing, *give* it away!"

"All I'm asking is that you wash out—"

"I've never seen such filth!"

"Okay already, I'll do it my goddamn self!"

Deb stepped back—then held her ground. The voices stopped, and though something banged below, no one actually came on deck; so she went a little closer. She realized what they were doing—they were cleaning out hatches and cupboards, delving into the horror of the bilge; ropes, boxes of food, books, blankets, foam mattresses, dishes, a fishing rod, a roll of fibreglass mat . . . the slip beside *Double Helix* was littered with the kind of junk any boat picks up over time.

Now that she could see it better, the Krogen gave Deb the impression of being a bigger boat than thirty-eight feet; her clipper bow, and her bowsprit, made her seem longer, and her raised deck gave her a massive feel—which was emphasized by the smaller boats moored on either side of her, an Island Packet 27 and a thirty-foot Hunter. Do I like this boat, Deb wondered? The answer was yes, although asking the question probably meant it wasn't *the* boat for her; it wasn't making her heart beat faster. But the esthetics did work; the Krogen 38, in her own way, was a handsome boat; she was big enough to carry the clipper bow, and the raised deck—though "different"—was still nautical and not "funny"—which, as far as boats were concerned, was what you wanted to avoid. At a glance, she seemed well-equipped. A Danforth anchor was lashed to the pulpit, with a chain anchor rode. The chain ran to a heavy windlass, Sampson at a guess . . . Both foresails were roller furling—Furlex, which was supposed to be good. Sail covers. Cockpit cushions—they were lying on the slip. Dodger—probably a bimini: in any case, a great pile of canvas and plastic was heaped up in the cockpit. There was a pair of davits in the stern, with an inflatable pulled up on them: just your average Zodiac knockoff, but the outboard was a Mariner, and they were endlessly reliable. The more she looked, the more Deb liked what she saw. The boat had character; it wasn't imitating anything else. You had to take it on its own terms. There would, she suspected, be lots of things to discover as you sailed her. She could see one of them right off; forward of the main deck was a small foredeck, a neat little well—just the place to go with your book. But the female voice, emerging through a hatch from approximately that position, didn't exactly sound mellow.

"What do I do with this? God!"

"Just wash it with the Spic and Span, and then dry it off with the paper towel. It just has to be clean—it's no big deal." This voice, young and male, probably thought it was being conciliatory.

"No big deal? Jesus Christ—"

Deb decided to retreat. She went back to the shore; here, the main marina building housed a couple of marine supply stores, a restaurant and the broker who'd sent Curtis Price the listing for *Double Helix*. Deb looked in the window; it was stuck all over with listings and snapshots of boats, but through an empty pane she could see a small, modern office with a tall man hunched in front of a computer. She hitched her bag up on her shoulder, opened the door, and stepped inside; the man immediately looked up and smiled. "Hi."

He was wearing glasses, which he immediately took off, folded, and slipped into the breast pocket of his golf shirt. He was very tall—stooped. He had a big head. Somehow, with his height, this made him look older than he probably was, but also very friendly, like somebody's grandfather. He smiled expectantly. Deb smiled back and said, "I bet you're not going to believe this, but I'm looking for a boat."

He laughed. "Well, I'll *try* to believe it." Rising and coming forward, he extended his very big right hand. "Dick Fowler."

"Deborah Graham."

Her hand was lost in his; he held it rather delicately, almost chivalrously . "Any particular boat?"

"A Krogen 38. I was just taking a look at the one you have out there."

"Well, they're two, actually. This was—?"

"*Double Helix*. Someone was on it—they seemed to be cleaning . . ."

"It could do with some. Did you speak to him? Andy Peterson his name is. The lady's his wife, Kelly."

Deb shook her head. "They didn't seem to be expecting visitors." Then she added: "I wonder how many divorces have been caused by sailboats?"

Fowler laughed. "A couple," he said. He was now half-leaning, half-sitting on the edge of the desk; even so, he was still taller than Deb. "Actually, that boat has a story, but it's not quite that. But tell me—why a Krogen? Not that it isn't a good boat—in fact it's a great boat. But it usually takes people a while to get around to it."

"I should explain. I'm really looking for my father. He's retiring down here—he's a Canadian. He has a boat up there, at least he had—he's sold it—and he wants a new one. The place he's buying in the Keys has a slip."

"Wonderful. Whereabouts—in Canada?"

"Kingston."

Fowler folded his arms on his chest, and squinted, turning his head to one side. "That's west—no, *east* of Toronto?"

"Right."

"Hamilton . . . Niagara Falls, Windsor—*that* would be west." He folded his arms on his chest. "And you said your dad had a boat—what kind?"

Dad. "A Niagara 35—"

"Great boat. Perfect for down here."

"I think he was a little tired of it . . . No, that's not fair. It's just—well, he'd done a lot with it—"

"No reason to explain. If a man wants a new boat, great—remember, I sell 'em. So he decided on a Krogen—?"

"Well, he has a friend who owns one of their trawlers, but he keeps saying he's not ready for that yet—"

"He's a sailor, and a real sailor never is. Not really."

"Well, you're right. He is a sailor. So am I, for that matter. Anyway, I think he met a few people who owned them through him . . . and they kind of intrigued him. There was some English yacht designer who did raised deck boats . . ."

"Oh yes. Maurice Griffiths his name was. Great! Your father knows his sailboats."

"Yes. Anyway, he's been looking into them. He's got a couple of listings, one of them's private. And the one from you."

"Us?"

"That's right . . ." Deb opened her bag, and pulled it out.

But Fowler was already circling the desk. "Graham? From Canada? I should remember that . . ." He folded himself carefully into the very small chair in front of the computer, then took his glasses out of his pocket, opening them with great care, as though they were an especially complicated device. But on the computer he was surprisingly dexterous. His big hands moved over the keyboard, and then he shook his head. "Funny. Nothing on him."

"David Graham, from Kingston?"

"Nope. Nothing. Not that it makes any difference. The idea is, you're going to look a few boats over for him?"

"Right. I'm supposed to say whether it's worth his while making the trip. They're going a little nuts, my mother and father. They've sold the house, but they have to arrange for the moving, and of course the place down here isn't quite ready . . . you know how it is."

"I get the picture." He was still sitting in the chair, but had turned it around, and was tilting back, hands folded now on his stomach: one way or another, Deb thought, he had to fold some part of his anatomy. But now he was getting down to business. "Krogens," he said. "I told you, I've got two of them. The second one, she's a beautiful boat, clean, perfect shape, everything on it, Stoway main, all the buttons you can push—"

But Deb was already shaking her head. "My father would never bite. It took me and my mother years to convince him on roller furling. There's no way you could sell him on a Stoway main."

"*Long View*, she's called. One owner, *superbly* maintained, and considering the quality, the price is very reasonable. *Very* reasonable." He gave her a wink. "One ten, but of course that's negotiable."

"Mr. Fowler, my father wouldn't want it if you gave it to him."

Fowler shook his head ever so slightly, as though he found this impossible to believe; but then lifted his eyebrows in resignation. "Well, that leaves *Double Helix*. Fine boat. Great shape. You saw her. No blisters, in fact she's got an Imron bottom. What's the price on that listing you've got?"

"Eighty-five thousand."

"They're down to seventy-five. If you offered seventy-two, you could sail away." And then he looked at her significantly, as though he was now expecting to hear a great secret.

Deb smiled. "Well, I'm not going to offer anything, but if you're wondering, 'Could my father afford that?' the answer's 'No problem.'"

"Look . . . you know what I'd like to do? Give you all the stuff on *Long View*—I know, I know—but there's even a video. Deborah, seriously, I wouldn't want your father *not* to see it."

"I really don't see the point, Mr. Fowler." She did, of course: several thousand dollars in commission.

"Sure," said Fowler, "but it wouldn't hurt, would it?"

"Okay, I'll give it to him . . . on condition that you tell me about *Double Helix*. You said there was a story."

"Deborah, you're not going to regret it. This fellow's almost made her a custom boat, and he lived in the Keys, so it's really perfectly set up for your father. Cruisair—16,000 BTUs. You don't know how *hot* it can get until you've spent time in the Keys. You *need* air conditioning on your boat. The fellow's asking one ten, but in my opinion *Long View—*"

"*Double Helix*, Mr. Fowler—"

"Just one thing more—"

"Mr. Fowler, I really do have to stop you there. Do you know what I do for a living?"

"Well . . . no."

"I sell stocks. As in stocks and bonds. Let's you and I make a deal. I won't sell you any gold mines—any *Indonesian* gold mines—and you'll let *Long View* go. Okay?"

Fowler closed one eye and tilted his head to the side. "They really have gold mines in *Indonesia?*"

"Of course. You can buy them for just pennies on the Toronto Stock Exchange, or Vancouver, or Alberta—"

"They have a stock market in Alberta?"

"Absolutely. Maybe I *should* tell you about one of them. It's called Bre-X. It's trading around two dollars, and it's a speculation, no doubt about it, you'd have to know that going in—no promises, right?—but I've got a little of my own money in it—and what we're looking at here is a property—"

Fowler grinned. "Maybe I should tell you about *Double Helix.*"

"Maybe you should."

Rocking back in his chair, he closed his eyes. "Right. Well. This fellow was from Carolina, Beaufort. Donald Peterson, father of Andy. Tried to sell her, didn't like the offers he was getting, so took her down the Intracoastal Waterway and had her listed in Miami." Fowler opened his eyes, and gave a matter-of-fact little shrug. "He worked for a company in Boca Raton, I think, and he was going to buy something bigger and live on her. But that fell through. So he took her out to bimini—"

"Did you ever meet him, Mr. Fowler?"

"No, to tell the truth. Just the son."

"Right. So—well . . . what happened?"

"He cruised her out to the Keys, I think all the way out to the Dry Tortugas, then back to Sanibel Island on this side."

"That's a sail."

"It is."

"You say you didn't meet him . . . I don't get it. How did you end up listing the boat?"

"Well, that's the story. There was an accident."

"God. The boat *looked* okay."

"Not that kind of accident. One evening, all by his lonesome, he decided to sail to Key West and just plain fell off." He made a face. "For the usual reasons."

"That's horrible, Mr. Fowler. It's the sort of thing you hear about, but never really believe."

"Maybe. But that's what happened. The boat has an Autohelm— Datamarine, Apelco Loran, Icom VHF—she's really well-equipped . . . mind you, she doesn't have air conditioning and down here—"

"So the autopilot was on, and she just kept sailing?"

He nodded. "God only knows how far . . . well, actually, they worked it out, the way they can. He had some people on the boat that afternoon—of course they were drinking—and they left around half past four, and sometime after that he sailed. The Coast Guard figured he was almost halfway when he went over, but they didn't find the boat till the next morning . . . the wind shifted or something, the autopilot quit, I don't know . . . it was just wallow-ing. The real miracle, though, was that they found his body."

"I guess." Then she added: "Of course, it's the sort of story that would put some people off. The boat, I mean."

He squinted at her. "We talking price now, Deborah?"

"Not to me, my father. About halfway, you say—when he fell over?"

"About fifty miles out, they said. They figure he left around six. There was a great breeze—probably why he left. He would have been doing at least five knots, so you can figure it. Has some booze in him from the afternoon—"

Deb nodded. "And a few more beers to wash down his supper."

"Uh-huh. Then he puts on the autopilot—"

"And dozes off."

"That's it. But he wakes up, around three . . . you know."

"Sure," said Deb. "He needs to take a leak."

"Deborah, you are a sailor, God bless . . . and so he unzips his fly . . . tried to hang on with one hand . . . and over he goes."

"Mr. Fowler, on a boat, sexual equality reaches its max—*everyone* should sit down."

"Well, amen to that."

Deb wondered if Fowler was making a pun; it was possible—she was beginning to suspect he was a man of secret vices. But she'd been sufficiently duplicitous during their conversation that she didn't think she could be too judgmental. So she merely nodded and said, "You know . . . despite all this, I'd still like to see her."

"Sure enough. And—do you mind?—let's take one quick peek at . . ." Deb turned her mind off as Fowler rose in a single, oddly sinuous motion, like a Slinky Toy, and came around the desk. He held the door. Stepping out, Deb felt a kind of instant exhaustion as the heat and humidity hit her. The sun was beating down fiercely; she needed a hat. Florida, in the summer . . . the Manatee River oozed like a sluggish stream of molten lead. Boats, rocking in their slips, seemed abandoned: certainly no one wanted to be out here now. Certainly Peterson's son and his wife didn't; they were now sitting sulkily in the cockpit of *Double Helix*, drinking Snapple and studiously not talking to each other.

"Hi there," said Fowler, giving them a lazy wave. "Meet Deborah Graham, all the way from Toronto. Her father's looking to buy a boat, and is all gung-ho on Krogens."

They exchanged names and waves and smiles. Deb said, "Lovely boat," and Andy Peterson, finishing another slug of his drink, managed a nod, while his wife, Kelly, summoned a positive facial twitch. Deb tried not to grin. Of course, there's nothing more horrible in the world than a sailboat—if you don't like sailboats. Even cleaning them was hell. And the slip, by this time, looked like a poorly organized garage sale; Deb recognized, beside her foot, one of those "slow cookers" that had been all the rage with mothers when she was a kid—for some reason, they'd all been decorated in a garish plaid. "*Double Helix*," she said, "that's DNA . . . or something."

Andy smiled more genuinely. "Or something. I'm an old-fashioned arts major . . . my father was the scientist."

"Permission to come aboard?" said Fowler, who then quickly stepped on deck, as though fearful this permission might in fact be denied. He unsnapped the lifeline for Deb, then added, "Andy's father was one of those biotechnology men . . . what would you say, 'biotechnologist?' "

Andy didn't seem much interested and just had another gulp of Snapple. Deb said, "I'm an arts major too, so of course I sell stocks and bonds. Did your father work for one of the biotech companies?"

Andy squinted and nodded, "An outfit called Xynex. They're in Boca Raton."

Deb cocked her head to one side. "They're traded, aren't they? Vaccines or something?"

"Or something . . . yes."

Deb wanted to prompt him, push for a little more information; but he seemed completely bored by the subject; besides, she wasn't exactly sure what sort of information he could offer. And then Kelly said, "This is awful. We can't even offer you one of these. And the damn boat's a mess—"

"Now don't worry," Fowler cut in, "Deborah knows boats. She knows what it's like. Don't you, Deborah?"

"Of course. No problem. I must say, this cockpit's great—really big. You could have a party out here. Have you done a lot of sailing in her?"

Andy shook his head. "Not on this one. My father bought it after he and my mother were divorced. But the one he had before this, we sailed a lot. A Lancer." Then he added: "I don't sail any more." And then, not too convincingly, he concluded: "If I was going to sail, though, this would be a great boat to do it in."

"She is a great boat," said Fowler, following up this sales pitch. "Real solid. Well-equipped. Everything you need—"

Deb couldn't resist. "Of course, she doesn't have air conditioning, and this is the sort of day when you could really use it." Hurrying on, before Fowler could recover, she added, "But I was wondering, you've got your inflatable in the davits—doesn't she have a hard dinghy too?"

Deb had noticed this when she'd first looked at the boat; it wasn't a big point—even though davits were more often used with a dinghy, a lot of people carried their inflatable in davits too. On the other hand, these davits looked especially substantial—they would certainly have been intended to carry a dinghy.

Andy said, "I don't know. Maybe he had one, but not now."

Deb pulled the listing out of her bag. "Here it is," she said. There was a section headed HULL AND DECK EQUIPMENT, and she read it off: "Bow pulpit with rails, stanchions with lifelines . . . three rodes, Simpson Lawrence 555 manual two-speed windlass, dinghy davits, eight-foot Trinka sailing dinghy . . .'"

Fowler leaned forward, extracting his glasses from his pocket. "You're right," he conceded, with a grunt. He looked at Andy: "I don't remember any dinghy, though."

Andy said, "Don't look at me. I don't remember much about this boat at all—I was only on it a couple of times . . ." Andy looked from Fowler to Deb: "He told you about it? The accident, I mean?"

She nodded. "I'm sorry . . . it must have been awful."

"Sure," he said, then pointed at the listing. "That's all taken from the place where he was trying to sell it in Carolina. And I think he tried to sell it in Miami too. It probably just got lost along the way."

"Too bad . . . a sailing dinghy would be great. But it's no big deal . . ." She stood up. *The dinghy was missing.* "Look, do you mind—could I go below?"

"Sure," said Fowler, "sure, that's what we're here for."

"God," Kelly said, "it's such a mess."

Deb gave her a girl-to-girl smile, told her not to worry about it, and then slipped through the hatch and down the companionway, with Fowler coming along right after her—though, from the corner of her eye, she saw him give a quick sign to Andy and Kelly not to join them.

Inside, she paused for a moment, letting her eyes adjust to the darkness. It was hard to pretend now; she could feel that her palms were sweaty. Fowler loomed behind her, only halfway down the ladder—God, he was irritating, she thought. She longed to be rid of him, but of course she was as chipper as a chipmunk. "Nice galley."

188 · ANTHONY HYDE

"The main cabin's just here."

But Deb was already stepping forward, into the saloon. A lot of stuff was piled on the settees; one of the bilge hatches was open, presumably to facilitate Kelly's cleaning efforts. "Boy," said Deb, "she's really doing a job." God—she sounded totally mindless. "Is that the head?"

"Right. Real nice—" But Deb was already inside "—shower." *The dinghy was missing...*

She leaned back against the door, unzipping her bag. She was sure her voice was trembling, that she was giving herself away; she sounded so phoney. "Yeah, for me that's really important. I have to wash the salt off, or my skin turns something awful."

But she was almost sure—she had to check. Hands shaking, she unfolded the clipping she'd found on Price's boat, the article from *Soundings*. There was a photo: Peterson, beside *Double Helix*. She studied it quickly. The photo could have been taken anyplace there were palm trees, but this had to be Florida—maybe Miami, but definitely Florida. And even though the background was a little out of focus, there was no doubt about it: a dinghy was hoisted in the davits, *not* an inflatable. *A sailing dinghy...*

"You okay?"

"This has one of those Nauta flexible holding tanks, doesn't it?"

"I think so. Uh-huh."

"My father would want to replace it—I told you he was an engineer? One of those Class 1 systems ... you know, a macerator, those chemicals." She opened the door. "I just wanted to make sure there was room to put it in."

"A great waste of time, you ask me."

"But the Coast Guard doesn't."

"I know, I know." Fowler shook his head. "I agree with you, tell the truth, no matter what anyone says, those bags always smell, just a question of time."

Deb opened the door into the forward cabin. Vee berths, a washbasin. Nice. Lots of light, air ... *I need a plan.* She turned, stepped aft into the main cabin again. It felt immense, because of the cabin roof extending right out to the hull. Bookshelves—of course there were never enough. And a good quality dining table. In fact, the finishing was all first class—not in the same league as Price's Shannon, but very good nonetheless. A little fireplace . . . But she was hardly noticing now.

"As big as a ballroom," Fowler said.

A plan. "I guess there's no chance of taking her out—maybe tomorrow? The day after?"

"Well . . . yeah. Stupid to put everything back until they're done, I guess."

"Right." She stepped around him, into the owner's cabin, aft. Again, very big. A washbasin, with a chart table folding down over it—neat. But the athwartships berth still bothered her.

Fowler, behind her, cleared his throat and dropped his voice. "Of course, if you want, *Long View*'s all set—"

"Forget it. Really. If my father goes for one of these boats, I expect it will be this one."

And before he could reply, she was around him, and up on deck again.

In the cockpit, Kelly and Andy had their heads together, whispering. They looked up in unison and smiled, though Andy's effort was a little weak. Then Kelly said, "I know it doesn't look so hot down there, but it really is a *great* boat."

Andy nodded. Then he managed to get out, "She really is."

Deb bobbed her head obediently, and then said, "Your father never had any trouble with her?"

"No, no. He really loved her."

"But he did want to sell her."

"Oh, that had nothing to do with the boat. His whole life began changing. He got into a big thing at Xynex . . ." He shrugged.

Deb tried to prompt him. "I'm just trying to think . . . I don't buy a lot of biotech stocks—just Amgen, you know, or Chiron, the big ones—but I think I remember our analyst talking about it—they'd hired some brilliant young guy . . ."

"Yeah," said Andy, "that had something to do with it. My father had developed something, and he thought they were giving credit for it to this other guy, some Indian guy."

"It was all quite gross," said Kelly. "Apparently men who've had vasectomies can develop a kind of reaction to their own sperm, they sort of became immune to it or something—"

Andy cut her off: "It was all complicated. They couldn't really fire him because he owned a lot of stock in the company, but he didn't like working there any more, so he pretty much quit. Anyway, he was talking about doing a lot of travelling, maybe moving to Europe—it just didn't make sense any more, you know, owning the boat."

Deb nodded. "Well . . . Mr. Fowler can explain—I'm really checking things out for my father. You'll have her ready to sail in a couple of days? I think I'd like to look at her again. Maybe he could come down."

"Sure. That would be great—you should take her out."

She gave both of them a quick wave, then stepped down to the dock. Fowler was now working a little to keep up. He was, she decided, easy to keep off balance; given his height, he was especially vulnerable in that direction. But that's how she wanted him, and as she strode quickly ahead, she said, sternly: "Forget about *Long View*."

"Right."

"Do you have a fax machine?"

"Sure we do. Of course."

"Could I use it?"

"Sure. Fine."

"Great."

Duplicity, thy name is Woman . . .

They'd reached Fowler's office; he held the door. Inside, he brought her a fax cover sheet and a blank sheet of paper. "Here you go."

So you might as well take advantage of it . . .

Deb made a little motion with her hand, shooing him away. "This has to be just a little private. You know, confidential."

Fowler rose to his full height, apparently a certain proof of his rectitude. "Absolutely. Tell you what. Forget about me. I'll head down to the coffee shop—okay? Let me get you something."

"Actually, I wouldn't mind. Just coffee. Cream, no sugar."

"You've got it. Say ten minutes? The machine's in there . . . you can work it?"

"No problem."

"Great."

When he left, she started to write her message—but then realized she might not need it. Instead, she picked up the phone and dialled Toronto.

Rosie was at her desk. "Oh God, Deb—"

"Rosie, you have keep it under control. Just shut up. I don't have time. And I'm all right, perfectly fine, safe—"

"But where the hell are you?"

"Near St. Petersburg. Tampa. Florida."

"*Florida!*"

"Rosie, no. *None of that.* Get a pencil. I'm going to give you a phone number, a fax number. You're going to send me a fax."

"Something's happening, isn't it? Okay, I've got it. What happened in Baltimore? What about that woman?"

"Area code 813, and the number is 749-2294. And Charlaine is great. Shut up, listen. The fax is supposed to be from my father. Send it on Orme stationery. It's to me—dear Deb—and you better type it up. It doesn't have to be formal or even especially businesslike. But your handwriting's too feminine."

"Really? Thank God something is."

"Shush. You're supposedly replying to a fax I've sent you, my father that is. It's about a boat. Put in it something like, The Krogen sounds great—K-r-o-g-e-n—and I don't think the berth is a problem. Of course we have to discuss the price. Ask Mr. Fowler if he has, or can get, a set of plans. I have to be sure that I can put in a decent waste system—"

"Is this some kind of code?"

"No. The next important bit is—the wording isn't that important—something like, I can't possibly get down there till the end of the week. How about Saturday? There's an Air Canada flight that gets into Miami just after eleven. Could you meet it?"

"Deb, what does all this mean? *Please.* A hint? A penny for your thoughts? A *loonie*, for crying out loud?"

"Well, I'm not exactly sure what it means, but I think I've

figured out what Curtis Price figured out, or part of it. Have you fed Henry?"

"He's fine. *What* did he figure out?"

"Somebody's getting away with murder."

"Deb, please say that's a figure of speech?"

"Sure. That's a figure of speech. Are there any messages?"

"God! I hate you! No!"

"Rosie, listen, I want you to do one thing more. I just thought of it. You know those keys I gave you? The big silver-looking one, with Dominion on it—that's for Giacomo's apartment. I want you to go over there, to his building—they're pretty tough on security, they won't want to let you in, but show them the key, tell them about me—anyway, they'll probably send someone up with you—in fact, make sure they *do* send someone up with you—"

"And then what the hell do I do?"

"You go into his study. His computer's on—he always leaves it on. There'll be a screen saver, but I think after that his File Manager thing will be running. Are you following me?"

"Sort of, yes. The security desk. Begging and pleading. The File Manager—but that will just show a list of files."

"Right. And I want you to tell me *what* files."

"All right. Should I be doing this now? And how do I get in touch with you?"

"Well, not right now, necessarily. After work's okay. And what you do is call my number and just leave the message on my voice mail. I'll get it the next time I have a chance."

"Deb—listen. I have to know where you are."

"Stop trying to sound like your mother. And I don't have time to explain. But I'm okay. I'm going sailing. I'll be all by myself, out in the Gulf of Mexico. Check the weather channel. As long as there're no hurricanes, I'll be fine."

"How long—"

"Look, I've got to go. Really. Send the fax, right now. I'll call you as soon as I can."

She hung up just as Fowler's shadow—long enough to give her plenty of warning—appeared at the door. He'd brought her coffee. They chatted boats and sailing. Then the machine began to whistle, and the fax came through. It looked good—so good, that Deb slipped it across to Fowler and let him read it.

"Saturday," he said, "that's great. Miami's a ways, but you can drive up here, then take her out, late afternoon."

Deb looked pensive; perhaps a little too theatrically pensive, but Fowler was so busy calculating his commission, he didn't notice. After a moment, Deb said, "That's what we'll do . . . though I guess it means I've got a couple of days on my hands."

It couldn't have worked out better: he actually suggested it. "Why not get a boat, go for a sail? You could go out right here."

"That's an idea. Or . . . what about Sanibel Island . . . if I promise not to drink. Isn't the sailing down there supposed to be pretty good?"

"Sure. I know a couple of places. Billy Gillum. An old friend of mind. They have Odays, Calibers, that sort of thing. If you like, I'll give him a call."

Deb smiled. "Mr. Fowler, it's been a real pleasure doing business with you."

Charlaine said, "This sounds like *sailing* sailing."

"That's it."

"I don't think I'm so good at that."

"Charlaine, in a boat, all you have to do is lie back in the cockpit and look great. But right now, we have to move fast."

In fact, they almost didn't make it. The Coast Guard office in Fort Myers was just closing as they arrived—but Deb was cute and polite, and they dug out all the weather reports for the night Peterson had disappeared off his boat. Then they hit a Publix for a box of groceries, and a Wal-Mart for two Florida Marlins baseball caps. Even so, it was almost seven when they found Gillum's boatyard on Sanibel Island. But a handsome young man, with a great tan and wonderful blond stubble, was waiting for them.

"Dick Fowler called, said you'd be coming."

Good ol' Dick, thought Deb—he sure wanted that commission. The blond young man was very attentive, as he checked her out on a twenty-eight-foot Caliber sloop, the biggest she could wangle.

"I guess you'll be heading out in the morning?" he said.

Deb smiled, cute as a button, like a real nice Canadian girl. "I don't know. Maybe it'd be fun to anchor out overnight."

The young man smiled. "I can show you the perfect place, if you like."

Charlaine, whom Dick certainly had *not* mentioned, gave him a look. "Thanks, I think we can manage."

"Expect you can."

He was hopeful, though, right to the last, giving them a wave as they sailed off. And of course it never occurred to him that they would have plans of their own, that they'd sail at night—that the moment he slipped the rope off the dock, they would be gone.

CHAPTER ELEVEN

*D*eb *took a last look over* her shoulder and saw that the slight westward swing of the channel had dropped the charter company's dock behind a low, cedar-covered spit; no one could see them now, even if they'd wanted to look.

"We have, I think, made good our escape."

"He sure wanted to come with us."

Charlaine had herself wedged in a corner of the cockpit coaming and now watched, quietly but with admiration, as Deb throttled back the engine, then swung the boat around until its bow was into the wind. Sounds changed: waves thunked against the bow, water smacked softly under the stern. Slipping the engine into neutral, Deb stepped quickly up to the mast, uncleated the halyard and hoisted the sail.

For Deb, this was always a great moment. Even now, under these less than favourable conditions, it was wonderful—the way the muscles in her back and shoulders remembered, *pull*; the way the breeze pressed her cheek as she looked up the mast; the way the rope creaked on the winch as she tightened the halyard. All that was the same; and the way the sail filled as she eased the

196 . ANTHONY HYDE

sheet, and how the bow came right around, and the jib with one smooth ripple took its share of the wind: and finally that last moment of hesitation (the last quick press from the edge of your skis that tilts you over the hill)—and then they were sailing.

"That looked pretty good," said Charlaine. "You know what you're doing."

"I do."

"So I hereby nominate you captain of the good ship—what's it called again?"

"*Melody*. And you just shush now. You'll make me self-conscious."

She eased out the mainsheet and trimmed it back against the wind, which was coming out of the southeast; since she was steering about 125 degrees, this put her on a nice close reach. In fact, with Charlaine sitting there, she did feel a little self-conscious, and told herself to calm down and steer, since she was still more or less in the channel, which was fairly narrow. Staring over the port side, she picked up a flasher, and fell off, angling a little more south, until she saw a green buoy, number 3, which she definitely wanted to keep to starboard; north and west of it was a big shoal area. But soon she was beyond it, and there wasn't much trouble. She felt herself relax and gave Charlaine a smile. "Okay, this is going to be fine."

"I hope so. I hope you understand it—because I'm not sure I do."

"Well, we're going to follow Peterson's boat."

"How can you follow something on the water—especially months later?"

"Because, when you sail some place—and he was sailing to Key West—you don't just sail around, you follow a course. And everybody pretty much follows the same course." As she said this, she was swinging even more south, easing the sheet. She pointed. "Look over there."

Charlaine twisted around and shaded her eyes. "Don't see a thing."

"Keep looking. There . . ."

"No. You must have good eyes. All right—I've got it—something flashing."

"It's a beacon. Now look at the chart." Deb turned it around, and put her finger on the spot. "That's the beacon you're looking at. With the box around it."

"Okay. Something something north latitude . . . something something west latitude. And, right, *To Key West* . . . 106.3."

"That's it. And it's really pretty simple. Steer a course of 180 degrees from that marker, and the channel into Key West harbour is 106 miles away. Anyone who wants to get to Key West from Sanibel Island will come up the channel the way we did—you'd have to, or you'd run aground—pick up that beacon, and then steer due south until they reached the harbour buoys around Key West."

"What about the winds, and tacking . . . all that sort of thing."

"Well, as a practical matter, probably no one ever makes this sail unless they've got a wind that lets them steer this course. And even if the wind wasn't right, you'd keep coming back to this course. But that's all academic. The night Peterson sailed, the wind was a little more out of the east, but that's fine, and stronger, so he would have made better time—and he had a bigger boat, so that means he would have gone faster too. But that isn't important. He would have sailed this course."

As she'd been talking, Deb had gently eased the wheel around, watching the compass needle swing, oversteering just a shade, then bringing it back.

"Due south," she said. "It wouldn't be a hard course to steer, even if you were drunk. And his boat had an autopilot. He would have come out here, set things up, and let the boat steer herself."

"While he had another drink, you mean."

"Exactly."

She eased the jib a trifle—she was sometimes inclined to starve her sails. At once she felt a stronger *press* of the bow into the waves. The wind ruffled the hair over the back of her neck . . . and they were following *Double Helix*'s track over the sea.

For a time, they just sailed.

Soon Deb had the feel of the boat and the sea. The boat was quick enough, though nothing special; a standard production fibreglass sailboat. Like most such, it had a tremendous beam for its length, but a very sharp entry. It moved easily, with a gathering, eager rhythm. The sea was very gentle; small, fussy waves that actually smoothed out as they moved away from the shore. The wind, still out of the south and east, might have been twelve knots or a little more—conditions more or less perfect for this size of boat. If it held, Deb knew, they'd be sailing about as fast as they could; but since that would be five knots, six knots max, this trip would take the better part of a day. But they'd been lucky, she thought. The wind was not only a perfect strength, it was also very steady; and their course would keep them on a close reach. With luck, if she trimmed the sails properly, she'd be able to rig the boat to steer itself, at least for short periods. With Charlaine watching curiously—there really wasn't much she could do to help—Deb tensioned lines, adjusted sails. With a rope, she rigged a sort of vang to the boom—to hold it down—but decided that this was more trouble than it was worth. Finally, when she had everything set, she took her hands off the wheel.

"What's this about?" said Charlaine.

"We'll see. Maybe it'll work, maybe not. Why don't you go fix us something to eat?"

Charlaine laughed. "Oh, *yes*. I knew it was your lowly able-bodied seaman who got to do the woman's work."

Deb kept one eye on the sails, the other on the compass. The wind was steady . . . and the little boat quite happily held her course. After ten minutes, she went below.

"Below" was perhaps a little grand, and perhaps the wrong word; the Caliber 28 wasn't very nautical. In fact, it was a confusion of styles, also eras—the boat would have been anachronistic at any point in its life. It was "modern"—as opposed to "traditional" in the boating sense—but its definition of modernity harked back to the days when "Danish modern" and "dinette" were new; in the same way, its inspiration not only came from the world of automobiles rather than ships, it also recalled a time when "sedan" still meant something and when automatic transmissions had names like "Select-a-Drive." Still, given its size, it was comfortable enough.

"Running water," said Charlaine, "but no Fridgidaire—we make do with an icebox."

She'd set out a little picnic from the stuff they'd bought—stoned wheat crackers, cheese, olives. All the dishes were plastic, including the wineglasses—they'd found a bottle of Mouton Cadet, which Deb had thought was pretty good for a supermarket. When they were finished, they took the bottle up to the cockpit, although, as Deb put it, "We don't want to do a Peterson."

Charlaine laughed, "I'm not sure we can—though I guess we could try."

The boat was still dead on course, which was excellent. They sipped their wine, enjoyed the sun, fading now into evening. But it was a perfect time to be sailing, and the water was dotted with sails. A couple of guys in a forty-foot Beneteau gave them a wave and when they raised their glasses, they began waving bottles, beckoning madly. Deb felt relaxed. She tweaked the sails a little, but they were going along fine; the boat had found a nice easy groove. She was keeping one eye on the chart, and after a while she said, "We are now leaving American territorial waters."

"Really?"

"The three-mile limit, anyway."

"You know, I've never been outside the U.S.A."

Deb smiled. "Believe it or not, there's a whole world out there . . . people who *don't* drink Coca-Cola for breakfast."

"You got to be kidding."

"Charlaine—please tell me you're having me on."

Charlaine got up, bracing against the cabin top, and grinned. "I am having you on. And now I'm going to go do the dishes."

Alone, as they moved farther away from the shore, Deb watched the water turn a deep, sumptuous blue—this was now the sea—and the waves flashed with gold in their crests, entirely befitting the *Golfo de Mexico*. It made her think of the Spaniards and galleons and pieces of eight, and Cortez, *silent, upon a peak in Darien*. Which, for some reason she couldn't immediately locate, made her think of *Swallows and Amazons*, the favourite books of her childhood; she'd always feared that there was a little too much Susan Walker in her, whereas what she definitely needed now was Nancy Blackett. But at least she wasn't John, she thought.

Although that was definitely unfair. Maybe, being in America, she should be one of the Bobbsey Twins, though they never seemed to have quite as much fun. In any case, she finished off her wine and then took the helm—there was an area here marked as full of obstructions, to which she wanted to give a wide berth—and by the time she swung back on course the wind had moved around to the east, so she was on a full reach, and the boat wouldn't steer itself. But they were going faster now, rushing on, gently heeled, really making time, *sailing*, and every so often a bigger wave flicked spray over the bow, catching her face. Soon, there were fewer sails, more widely scattered. She could sense how the miles and the time had passed from the burn on her face, despite her hat, and the way the sun now seemed to hang in the sky. Then, at last, they were alone: there wasn't a sail in sight. And only then did she realize that Charlaine had never come back to the cockpit. She'd gone off to wash the dishes, but had never come back up. "Charlaine!" There was no answer. She swung the helm over, until the sails flapped in the wind and the boat stalled out, then ducked through the companionway.

Charlaine was lying on the settee, her legs drawn up, her hands squeezed between her knees.

"Charlaine? You okay?" Deb sat down, leaned closer to her. It took a moment for Charlaine's eyes to find her. "You're not seasick?"

She smiled weakly. "No, no. I kind of like that, actually, the way the boat moves. No . . . I guess it's just the Valium wearing off—and I don't want to take any more."

Deb took her hand—long fingers, a soft, pink palm. "It was pretty awful."

Charlaine smiled. "Pretty awful. I'd like to kill those bastards." Then she shrugged. "On the other hand, I don't want to kill anybody at all."

"No. Of course you don't."

"But you know, I was thinking . . . the worst of it is, what if they're right?"

"What do you mean? They're not right."

"No, no. We talked about it. Maybe their drug is the greatest thing in the world. The world is drowning in people. People all start as babies. Ladies have babies. The fewer ladies, the fewer babies. You can't deny it."

"No. I hate it, but I guess you can't."

"I told you I looked into it . . . it's incredible, the way the numbers add up. Take Nigeria. Since my mother's not around, I'm free to tell you that this place is the asshole of the earth. The capital's a city called Lagos. In a few years, they figure its population will hit 25 million. Unbelievable . . . so you have to do something. And how do you argue against it? People should take what they get? Let nature take its course? You can use all those arguments against contraception and abortion too, it's just the usual horseshit recipe for irresponsibility. Family planning, population planning—maybe this sort of thing, planning for the number of women, is just one more part of it."

"Charlaine, let's not argue about that—it still wouldn't make what they did right. To you. To me. And maybe they're doing something to Giacomo—that's not *right*."

Charlaine, with a little grimace, pulled herself up. "I know. Whatever these people are doing, it's not for the betterment of the human race, but the bottom line. They are truly bastards." She ran her fingers back through her hair and smiled. "And if I'm going to do anything about it, I guess I have to get myself together—maybe I *should* take another Valium."

"No—listen—can you swim?"

"Sure."

"So let's . . . you'll feel better."

"Are you serious?"

"Of course. Come up and see—we're entirely surrounded by water."

Deb didn't wait; she darted up on deck. The boat had now rounded up, and she backed the jib so they were properly hove to. Then she tied a long rope to one of the cockpit cushions and threw it over the side, hitching it to a stanchion. Charlaine, blinking in the sun—which still stretched away magnificently in the west— looked dubious. "You're serious about this?"

"Yes."

"My God, where are we . . . I can't see any land."

Deb laughed. "Don't worry, it's over there, somewhere."

And then, quickly, she stripped off her clothes and dove over the side.

It was wonderful, so cool and clean. Bobbing up, she rolled onto her back, gave Charlaine a wave, then dove again. She swam down and down, then treaded water, keeping herself down, and opened her eyes and looked up at the golden light above her; finally, gasping, she shot up into it.

She came half out of the water, venting like a whale. She waved again to Charlaine, "It's wonderful!"

"Sharks!"

"Only a couple of little ones!"

Then, breast-stroking, she swam back to the inflatable, which they'd been towing behind the boat.

She dived under it, bobbed up on the other side, then she climbed up into it, and checked the knot in the line. She watched Charlaine—who abruptly made up her mind, stripped her clothes off . . . stood one moment at the side of the boat, and jumped.

Deb laughed. Charlaine bobbed up, black and glistening; then as she tried to swim into a wave—which almost rolled her over—the sun flashed all copper on her back.

"My God!" she gasped.

"You okay?"

"I think so! Oh . . . it's wonderful!"

"Don't worry—I've got all my lifeguard badges!"

But Charlaine hung onto the safety line a moment, catching her breath. Finally, setting out in a calm spot, she swam back toward Deb, in the inflatable. Floating on her back, she said, "I always loved to skinny dip."

"Me too."

But she was still a little worried. "You're sure, though, this is really safe? I mean, we're here, the boat's over there . . ."

"Well, I admit, I can just hear my mother, quote *Deb I'm worried sick* unquote, but we're okay, the boat's not going anywhere."

Charlaine grabbed the side of the inflatable, and Deb helped pull her over.

"I guess I don't care anyway; that was wonderful."

Deb said, "I know. It's always the first thing I do, if the water's warm enough."

Charlaine, sprawled in a corner, was panting, goosebumps coming up on her breasts and shoulders. "I wouldn't say that was *warm*."

"The sea almost never is. But it's not exactly *cold*."

"And tell me there aren't really sharks!"

"Well, there could be—fairly shallow water, in fact pretty warm . . ."

"*Please.* Have you ever seen one?"

"Two. Together. Scared me out of my mind."

"God. What I'd love to see is a whale."

"When you were sailing with Curtis—"

"That was just around the Chesapeake."

"Well, I've seen plenty of whales. They're really something." Then she laughed. "Listen:

> *The whale, improbable as lust,*
> *carved out a cave*
> *for the seagirl's rest;*
> *with rest the seagirl, sweet as dust, devised*
> *a manner for the whale*
> *to lie between her thighs."*

Charlaine laughed, "Now what is *that*?"

"A poem Giacomo found. He wrote it on my birthday card."

Charlaine nudged Deb's knee with her foot. "Okay, this has worked. I'm getting over it—but now you're worried."

Deb, leaning back, felt the wind on her shoulders and the hot fabric of the inflatable across her bare back. "Yeah. I was thinking about something you said . . . something I hadn't thought of before."

"Which is?"

"That Giacomo is connected to all this—but only because of me."

"So?"

"That's what could have happened . . . somebody wants to scare me away. Maybe the way to do that is through him. He's vanished, right? Maybe they've—"

"Deb, you have absolutely no reason to believe that. Don't make up things to worry about—there's enough without that. Do what you said this morning, start with what we know . . . and we don't know that. Your friend in Toronto . . . maybe she's already heard from him. Okay, you don't know. But that just means you don't know one way or the other. Right?"

Deb smiled. "Okay."

"That's what we'll do—take turns getting down."

"Yes."

"But somehow, when we're both not too far down, we also have to work out what comes next."

"Well, we keep going . . . until we reach the spot where Peterson went into the water."

"And then we play this hunch of yours—which is?"

Deb smiled. "I'll tell you when we get there."

"How about a hint?"

"Okay. *Double Helix* carried an inflatable . . . which it's still got, back in Palmetto. But I'm pretty sure it also had a sailing dinghy, in those davits. So—what happened to it?"

And then, with a quick roll, Deb went over the side of *their* inflatable, into the sea. As she started swimming back to *Melody*, Charlaine called, "Now you wait for me!" She tried to stand up—then a wave caught her, and she was swimming too.

Together, drying in the cockpit, they watched the sun go down, a sunset as corny as a postcard: a soft line of pink clouds hovering over some paradise beyond the horizon, a shimmering streak of gold across the purple sea. It was magical, a spell, like "once upon a time," or "forever more." Despite herself, Charlaine held her breath and Deb could feel her lips part in silent expectation. Then, an orange ball surrounded by a rosy halo, the sun was gone, down below the hard line of the horizon. Then came the afterglow. And then the dark. It fell quickly, but softly; a drawing-in; so that the world seemed closer. But this was only dusk, a quiet expectation of the night, which, when it came, was sudden, as befits a revelation, for this is one of the true wonders of the world, the moon and the stars above a tropic sea.

Charlaine whispered, "I didn't know the night could be so bright."

That was always a surprise, Deb thought, the way you could see for miles and light years, long curling crests of waves shining in the light of Orion's Belt, streaks of phosphorescence streaming toward the moon. She grew calm, her mind fell still. In that extraordinary clarity, her senses were almost too alive for thought. The wind lifted the hair from the back of her neck the instant before it pressed the sails, there was the spray to taste, and her nostrils flared with all the sea smells of salt and iodine and her own damp skin and Charlaine's silent warmth beside her, and all around were the sounds of the waves, each so individual she could name them, the low, heavy rush of a big crest running up behind the stern dying gently in a trough as they raced ahead, or a long, quartering swell so far away she was watching it long before it crested and toppled in the rush of its own small waterfall, and everywhere the small quick burblings, the flashes and winks in the water as the hull pressed on. After a time, in the dark, she began to hum, and then to sing, dumb songs like *There's a Hole in the Bottom of the Sea*, or sad songs like *Farewell to Nova Scotia*, and finally a whole lot of crazy Irish shanties. Not long after midnight—ahead of schedule, in fact—the knotmeter told her they'd come halfway down the track to Key West, and somewhere on this stretch of water ...

"Just in here," she said aloud.

Earlier, Charlaine had dozed; but she must have sensed Deb's tension because now she was awake and said, "These waves look all the same to me."

"But this is where it happened. If the Coast Guard got it right— and they usually do."

"Now you have to tell me. *What* happened?"

"Peterson went into the water, that's definite. But I think some-one helped him."

"Helped him?"

"As in *pushed* him."

Charlaine said, "But that means there had to be someone else on the boat."

"Exactly."

"But they found the boat. There *wasn't* anyone else on it."

"Yes, but the sailing dinghy was missing too."

"Jesus . . . You mean someone killed him and then just sailed away?"

"Charlaine, that boat had davits, and at some point there was a sailing dinghy that was hanging in them. It's in the picture in *Soundings*, it's part of the equipment in the listing—*something* hap-pened to it."

"He sold it."

"But it's not the sort of thing you sell, not when you're trying to sell the whole boat. Yes, he *could* have. Or it *could* have been stolen. But it's much more likely, the night he left, that it was exactly where it should have been, in those davits."

Charlaine was silent a moment as their own boat tracked easily on its way. "Deb, you're assuming a hell of a lot."

"I'm not so sure. I think everyone else has been making the assumptions, except maybe Curtis Price. It *looked* like a routine boating accident, so that's what everyone assumed. But was it? No one actually saw Peterson sail off alone—he'd had people on the boat earlier—"

"And one of them might have stayed."

"Right. And we know that Price was killed, and that something very funny is happening with the company that Peterson worked for. Was fired from."

Charlaine was silent a moment. "Okay. I see it. As a long shot."

"I don't know. Medium."

"All right . . . whatever. This guy—Mr. X—he kills Peterson . . ."

"I think he's pretty cool. He has to be. I will make one assump-tion—he planned it. Maybe not weeks in advance, but as they were sailing away from Sanibel, he was working it out. No one knew *he* was on *Double Helix*—that would have been absolutely crucial. They'd been having a party, he'd left, but came back after everyone else was gone . . . something like that. Since they'd already been drinking, getting Peterson a little smashed presents no problem. It's night. They're sailing along. Eventually Peterson has to go to the good old taffrail, starts to unzip and you just push."

"I guess it would be easy enough."

"Absolutely. Once Peterson was in the water, he was dead."

"Why not play it out like that . . . pretend it was an accident, I mean?"

"Because you'd have to answer questions. What happened? How come you couldn't find him in the water? An investigation might turn up the fact that you had a motive. Also—in *Soundings*—they say that Peterson definitely drowned, but that he also suffered contusions . . . so maybe he put up a struggle. If there'd been someone on the boat to struggle *with*, the police might have gone into the whole business a little harder."

"Deb, you have a suspicious mind."

Deb laughed. "No, I don't. I have a sailor's mind. I mean, I can see how he *could* have done it. He'd have to be a real good sailor, at least as good as me, and have real guts, but he could have done it. If he did, right around now—after Mr. X had killed Peterson—he'd have one big decision to make."

"Just a sec, I think I can see this. He's going to take this little dinghy and sail it . . . where? To one of the Keys—he couldn't go back—"

"Right."

"But that has to be dangerous, a real risk—in a little boat—so what you'd want to do is stay on Peterson's boat to the very last minute."

"Not too long, though. As long as possible, but not too long. If someone finds you in the open water, sailing along in a little dinghy—"

"Would it have the name of Peterson's boat—*Double Helix*—would that be on the dinghy?"

"Probably. And you're right. That would be disaster. So you'd want to leave early enough that you could reach land, or get real close, before anyone would spot you—before morning, that is."

"And what about the wind, all that kind of stuff?"

"Well, that night, it would have been a problem, but not a big problem. This course we're on now, due south, takes us right to Key West, which is at the very tip of the Keys. What he'd be afraid of was any wind that would push him west. Then he'd miss the Keys all together—he'd end up in the Gulf of Mexico. What he'd want to do—given the winds that night—was stay on *Double Helix* as long as he could, but get off far enough north so he could reach them sailing a course that would be more south than east."

"You're losing me."

"Well, look at the chart, the way the Keys bend, like a banana—"

"If he misses the tip, he ends up in Mexico or Texas—"

"He ends up in open water and the sun fries his brains, actually. So what he wants to do is sail south—toward the tip—but also enough east that he hits the banana sort of where it bends."

"Okay, I think I get it."

Deb turned her flashlight on the chart. "And what that means, I think, is that he leaves the *Double Helix* right *there*." And she put her finger on a spot on the chart where a number of wrecks earned the warning "dangerous to surface navigation." Deb shrugged, "Anyway, thinking like a sailor, I bet that's what he'd do. He'd want a reference point—he'd want to know where he was when he started. That would be a good one. He'd have enough time to get well away from *Double Helix* before the sun came up, get pretty close to land—but the sail itself wouldn't be too far, not if you were a decent sailor and had a little luck."

"So that's where we're heading for now."

"Uh-huh. And you know what . . . I think I'd like a break. So why don't you steer a bit."

"Jesus, Deb—"

"It's a great, steady wind. Just hold the wheel like that . . ."

The night and the miles wore on. Oddly, from that clear, star-studded sky, a shower fell, two minutes of dew—fresh on their tongues—that left the mainsail shining silver like the moon. Once, Charlaine spotted a light in the distance . . . a white light, then a wink of red: a powerboat. It disappeared almost before Deb could spot it. Then she managed a lovely forty-minute nap, waking from it when Charlaine grew anxious at the way the sail was moving. But that was no big problem: she reset the jib, dozed again. Then the dawn woke her, pearly, rosy, milky blue like the inside of a mussel shell across the eastern sky: she pointed for Charlaine— the Keys were somewhere over there. But she had to look the other way, staring to the west, into the last of the night, to spot a wan, bleak, lonely light: the light at the end of a dreary tunnel. A wreck. *The* wreck. Mr. X's wreck. Deb took the helm, and sailed up closer, till they heard the horn, a groaning, honking sound, and then watched a herring gull drift down and perch upon the tower.

Charlaine said, whispering, "I'm impressed. Jesus, you said it was going to be there, and there it is. But isn't this wrong? I mean, according to your theory, he wanted to be hell and gone before the sun came up, and it's almost light."

"Sure, but remember he was in a bigger boat, and the wind that night was a little stronger. He would have made it here long before this . . . it would have still been dark."

"Okay . . . so he gets in the dinghy . . ."

"And that wouldn't have been easy, let me tell you. But he does it, and *Double Helix* just goes sailing on . . ."

"And so how does *he* sail?"

"Nothing fancy. He's in a dinghy. The best he can do is a simple reach . . . like this . . ."

And she swung the wheel . . . not quite on the reach Mr. X would have tried to sail, because the wind, as the dawn stretched out, was just a trifle different: but she could guess the course he would have headed, south-southeast, carrying them over an area marked as dangerous on the chart—*Area is open to unrestricted surface navigation, but all vessels are cautioned neither to anchor, dredge, trawl, lay cables, bottom, nor conduct any other similar type of operation because of residual danger from mines on the bottom*—and then into shallower water, forty, fifty feet deep, which would have finally taken him down the Keys. Deb, steering so carefully now, tried to think along with him. What relief he'd feel! What terror! How desperately he would have stared over his starboard bow, knowing that if those low, dull shapes were not the Harbor Keys, he was probably done for, had probably drifted too far west. But if he'd made it—and Deb had to assume that he had—he would have kept on for those last few miles into the great dotting of keys and islands, cuts and channels, east of Boca Chica... Now, like Mr. X, she peered ahead, into the dawn. The boat was still moving well; but an hour later, unaccountably, the wind just died. Reluctantly, she kicked the Iron Jenny—a Yanmar diesel—into life. It banged away. Mocking it, jets snaked contrails against the washed-out denim of the sky. She locked the wheel—with the motor, the boat would steer a reasonable course itself. They made coffee, even took turns in the little shower, and then as the morning sun threw down some heat, they saw a sail, three sails, then more sails, and then, at last, the land.

Land...

As always, Deb sensed it before she actually saw it. The sea changed. And the wind. And the colour of the sky. For the first time in a long time, she looked at the fathometer; she was still in forty feet of water, but it had been fifty something the last time she checked. Birds. A lot more of them. And then a hardening of the horizon, a chalky line—those were the Keys. *Land...*

Charlaine laughed, "I don't believe it!"

"What do you mean, you don't believe it!"

"I don't know—you do all that, and you actually end up where you said you would."

"Of course. To tell you the truth, the hard part's all ahead of us."

She was right. In about twenty minutes, it seemed, they'd gone from a world in which there was no land, to a world in which there was nothing else. Land was everywhere, surrounding them, a bewildering universe of dots, lumps, smudges, humps, bars, patches—none of which, in some profound failing in the order of things, was provided with a proper sign, a big billboard, say, proclaiming *Mud Key, Florida, U.S.A.* Deb kept checking the depth. There was still a lot of water under them; sometimes, changes in the depth provided a help to working out where you were, but here the bottom shoaled up in such a regular fashion that it didn't offer a clue. Half the trick, she quickly realized, was to learn how to see this unique, beautiful landscape, to tell the mangrove islands from the land, to pick out where one key ended and another began, to catch the hard ripple of the wind across bonefish flats where the water was knee-deep at best. It was landscape of pure Impressionism, light tracing form and changing constantly with the wind, with the sky, with the shifting sea—a brilliant *pointillisme* that Deb had to reconcile with the old-fashioned realism of the chart. And she did it. Gradually. Slowly. With a determination to see what was there—not what she hoped would be there. And in fact, she realized, she'd done terrifically well.

She pointed for Charlaine. "That's Mud Key over there, and those have to be the Snipe Keys."

"Yeah, well what's that?"

"Shit!"

A small island—even "islet" was too grand a word—had suddenly bumped out of a broad patch of water between the two larger groups of keys. "It's some kind of flat," she said. "Look—don't panic. In water like this, you're going to run aground. It's no big deal."

But she swung the wheel and headed in . . . and slipped right through and didn't run aground once.

On the other side, though, she didn't press their luck. Between the Mud Keys—which were strung together like the vertebrae in your tailbone—there was a small channel of deep water; Deb nosed into it and dropped anchor. And then, rather than backing down on it with the motor, she took off her clothes and jumped in, and dived down—feeling along the rode, for the water was inky with mud and tannin from the trees—and set it by hand. It was wonderful to get cool. Deb guaranteed no sharks and Charlaine jumped in, too. After another shower, they opened a tin of tuna fish, lay back in the cockpit and worked out a plan.

Everything depended, of course, on what Mr. X had done.

From the cockpit, they were looking out upon a strange and wonderful world. It was a small world, a world of details: the world of naturalists and fishermen, the world of a single summer in the life of a child that lives forever in memory. It was a world where knowledge becomes lore, explanations turn into yarns and legends. Squirrel Key, Old Finds Bight, Rattlesnake Lumps, Jim Pent Point, Happy Jack Key, Old Dan Mangrove—every one of the names on the chart would have a story, and someone, somewhere, would be able to tell it. Right now, they were looking out on Waltz Key Basin. The deepest water here might have been ten feet; most of it was five or six or seven; a lot of it was under three. And people here would know every change of depth and bottom, and how it all changed with the seasons and the hours of the day: so if you put your fly just *there*, you'd find a bonefish.

"So what do you figure?" said Charlaine.

"Well, there's no point getting our hopes up. He could have come in here—but no guarantees. Look at the chart. Jewfish Basin ... Turkey Basin ... They would have worked just as well."

"So he could have got to shore in a million places."

"No ... not a million. Not quite. Think about it. Okay, job one is getting here, making it to the Keys. But now he has to hide the dinghy—and really hide it, because if anyone finds it, Peterson's 'accident' turns into murder."

"Yeah, but look out there—all those little islands—he could have hidden it on any of them."

"But then what would he do? Because he has to get to the mainland. That's the highway over there—that's what he'd be aiming for. And remember, he's exhausted, probably looking pretty beat up—he wouldn't want to be seen, if he could help it. So he didn't have as many choices as you think."

"What he would really want was someplace out of the way—so he could hide the dinghy—but also connected to the highway, the mainland."

"And there aren't actually *millions* of places like that."

"But you know what, Deb? There're *hundreds*."

Shading her eyes, Deb scanned across the blue-white water toward the green-black land, and carefully, with a pencil, began marking up the chart.

Twenty minutes later, she put the outboard on the inflatable. Cowled in a sheet—the sun was fierce—and provisioned with three jugs of water and peanut butter sandwiches, they headed off.

It was going to be a long, hot afternoon, Deb thought.

"This is going to be one hell of a hot day," Charlaine pronounced.

And they were right.

They saw a hundred white herons, and a thousand mangrove trees. They saw bonefish and parrot fish and a thirty-inch barracuda. A lovely, gaff-rigged sharpie sailed up the channel; a dozen Boston Whalers went shooting by. Up on the highway, ten thousand cars must have driven past them and overhead they watched the high acrobatics of the fighters from the Boca Chica naval air station. They drank all the water. They ate all the sandwiches. And didn't find what they were looking for—until the next morning, just after ten.

That night, in search of rest and recreation, they'd putt-putted the inflatable around to the next basin, where they'd found a marina, and then hitched a ride into Key West and civilization: truly excellent margaritas, a big Publix, and a Wal-Mart where Deb had picked up a pair of cheap binoculars. The next morning—for the twentieth time, or perhaps the hundred and twentieth—she raised those glasses and slowly scanned the broad half-moon of glittering water in front of her.

A bay . . . although here in the Keys, they seemed to prefer "bight."

They were trying to be systematic, doing every possible island, islet or section of shoreline in order. This one was perhaps half a mile wide, with a hard, rocky shore. Quickly—because she was now getting good at this—she passed over all the places where Mr. X could *not* have hidden the dinghy. In fact, as experience had now shown, that included most of the territory she was looking at: Mr. X's problem was more difficult in practice than it seemed in theory. An eight-foot sailing dinghy is a lot to hide. In the mangroves, it would have been easy enough to screen; but screening wasn't good enough. Someone was bound to see it, and then would come a host of fatal questions: where had it come from? how had it gotten there? Another possibility, burying it, was even more difficult. An eight-by-three-by-two-foot hole is a very big hole, especially if you're digging by hand; besides, there was almost no place here with enough soil to dig in. Filled with flotation material, the dinghy was virtually unsinkable; made of fibreglass, it would have been very difficult to break up, even with an axe. So Mr. X needed to find a very special spot. His only advantage was time. A dinghy, sailing quietly through these shallows, would have attracted little attention; so he really could have looked. But even then, there were limits—he had time, but would have preferred to be as quick as possible.

"What about over there?" said Charlaine. "Not too many mangroves. And isn't that a road, in behind those palms?"

Mangroves—which at first had seemed to create the natural hiding place—were just the opposite; their roots created an impenetrable floor, and though their trunks and branches made an effective screen, dragging a dinghy far enough into it would have been virtually impossible. And they were still assuming that Mr. X would have been aiming for a road, the quickest exit he could find.

Deb swung her glasses, searching the shore where Charlaine was pointing.

A few palms; but immediately behind them, a thick growth of other trees, cedars and pines. She focused on the trees; caught in her binoculars, their branches waved in the wind, back and forth, in silence, as though the sound had died. Slowly, she panned across them, then back, twisting her body and steadying the glasses as the inflatable rocked gently under her. And now she could make out an opening, a little gap. As if someone had taken a bite out of the shore—but they must have had a jagged tooth.

Charlaine, in the bow, was studying the chart. "The road's on here ... you could get up to the highway from it."

"I think it could be a ditch, there's a funny gap. Or maybe it's just the way the trees are growing. But we should look."

Gently, she opened the outboard's throttle. The inflatable eased ahead. The bottom here was hard sand, with long, trailing patches of pebble in the hollows. She had the prop shaft raised up as high as it could go, and she was okay, to about a foot. In the bow, Charlaine navigated, "Right a little . . . little more . . . deep spot up ahead, you're okay . . ." But then, a hundred yards from shore, they began to bump. Charlaine said, "Your turn to row."

The inflatable had two nasty aluminum oars with two nasty plastic paddles stuck on the ends of them—nasty, but they worked, after a fashion. She rowed with her back to the shore, looking out toward the entrance to Waltz Key Basin. Beyond, she glimpsed the sea, incredibly blue, except for long, hard, white streaks, glittering like quartz. She watched a white heron, neck tucked, long legs trailing, as it flew out toward Mud Keys. Earlier, she'd seen a skiff, with two fishermen; but they were gone now, and she couldn't see a soul. She rowed for another few minutes, but then turned around, pushing on the oars, with Charlaine ducking out of the way so Deb could look past her. In many places, the trees came right to the water. There were only a few mangroves; usually, they were more massed than this, not mixed in with other trees. She sculled ahead, but was still twenty or thirty yards off when the oars began to catch and the inflatable—with their double weight— began to bottom. Deb said, "Your turn to pull."

They both stepped out of the inflatable into the shallow water, warm as a bath, the sand like concrete beneath their feet. Charlaine led the way, pulling on the inflatable's towline, with Deb walking alongside, steadying it in the water. But after a moment, Charlaine stopped:

"Deb, this is disgusting."

"What is?"

"The bottom. It's some kind of muck."

"Don't be ridiculous. I told you. No snakes. No sharks . . . It's just leaves, they've blown out from the shore, those trees."

"*Worms.* I'm telling you, it's truly yucky."

"Charlaine? Yucky. *Jesus.*"

"Deborah, it's like a fried egg with a runny yolk—"

"Charlaine, *move.*"

"Shit. *Shit, shit, shit.*"

But she started off again, then angled to the left, which made Deb smile as she followed along—because, in that direction, the bottom changed to sand once more. They ended up about thirty or forty yards from the funny gap she'd seen.

Charlaine made a face. "You go. That's where all the muck is. I'll guard the boat from all those Amazons."

Deb grinned. Last night, in the cockpit, she'd told Charlaine *Swallows and Amazons* stories, mystifying her, except for the dirty bits. "I can't believe you'd really call a little girl Titty."

"Okay," said Deb, "but give me the Evian."

You had to drink a lot in this sun. She started off, along the shore, wading about twenty feet out: the water was barely above her ankles. Walking slowly, sipping at the water bottle, she searched for a spot where Mr. X could have gone *in*, but mostly it was too dense, too dense if you were trying to drag a boat, no matter how small. Trees. Bushes. Brush. He would have needed an axe, or a machete.

She stepped closer to the shore—the trees gave a narrow band of shade. Even this early, it was really very hot. She sipped more water. She went on like this for a hundred feet or so and didn't see anything, but after a time she angled out farther into the water, because she was coming level to the gap. It was the best spot, she thought. *She'd* seen it, and from way out there; Mr. X might have, too. Now the water got deeper; maybe there wasn't a stream, but some crease in the land probably caught the run-off, and took it out here. Directly opposite, she was up to her thighs.

She stopped there. Shading her eyes, she looked into a deep, narrow cove.

It was quite dark: the trees, even at this late hour of the morning, completely covered it with shade—the water looked almost black. Maybe cove wasn't the right word. It was only about ten feet wide at its mouth, and angled sharply back about twice as far. Really, it was just a cut in the shore of the key. Big mangroves, with those great arched roots—as though they were standing on tiptoe—covered the banks, all around; and there were other trees, farther back. Yet—it was open, too. There were spaces between the trunks, openings, streaks and patches of sunshine dappling the shade.

She started to wade in, but when she reached the spot where the shade began—where the water turned very dark—she stopped and took a sip of Evian. She wiggled her toes. Leaves. Bark. Twigs. She went closer to the shore. And then she saw the first sign: grooves, crushed into the roots of two mangroves. Pushing ahead, she ran her finger over them . . . it was as though someone had cut . . . But of course they hadn't *cut*; he'd lifted his boat up, and run it back—it would have been easy, the roots made a kind of slide . . .

She scrambled over the roots herself, onto the shore. There was a lot of growth, and undergrowth, shrubs and trees, but you *could* get through, just by staying in the ditch, and barely ten yards on she could see the stern of the dinghy, though he'd pushed it way under some brush.

She bent down . . . lifted a branch.

Double Helix, burned into the fibreglass.

"Charlaine?" she called. "Don't give me any bullshit! You come here!"

"Jesus," said Charlaine. "So you were right."

Deb nodded. All at once, she was trembling—she *had* done it. She sat down on a mangrove root and sipped more water, then wiped her mouth. "We were lucky, though. To find it. This quickly."

"Yeah. But you worked it out." Charlaine took the bottle from her and drank some too. She grinned. "Come on now! You worked it out!"

Deb, suddenly exhausted, smiled. "Well, I guess I did." On the side of the dinghy, painted, were the call numbers for *Double Helix*. "We should write them down, I guess." She had her "sailing wallet," fastened to her belt loop by a chain; she always carried it in her purse and it was big enough for everything, money, change, passport, and a little notebook and a pen. Now she jotted down the state registration number of the boat—in effect, its official identity.

"So what now? Charlaine said.

"Well, I guess we just keep going." Deb pointed. "The road has to be right up there."

After Deb caught her breath, they made their way up the ditch. Beyond the boat, it petered out in a patch of reeds; but then, on the far side of that, it deepened again, and there was actually a metal culvert. A path ran over this, and they followed it along for thirty feet until it hit the road. Directly in front of them, it was gravel, but not too far ahead, as it curved back toward the highway, it became paved.

Charlaine still had the chart. "I'd say the highway is barely a mile."

"I'm trying to think what he would have done."

"Got the hell out, fast."

"Yes. Except it would depend what shape he was in. After a sail like that, he might be pretty rocky."

Charlaine pointed toward the highway. "Why don't I go on this way, and see what's up there, and you check out the other direction. Maybe there's a house, something . . ."

"Okay. But don't go too far. Say we meet back here in twenty minutes?"

"Right."

Deb headed down the gravel part of the road, which bent sharply about twenty yards down; and once she reached the bend, she could in fact see a house, or, more exactly, something glinting behind some trees. As she walked that way, she realized it was a truck, a new, shiny, bright red Ford 250 with fancy side mouldings and flashy alloy wheels, and little antennas sticking up all over the place: cell, CB, God knows what else . . . Interesting. If Mr. X had come this way, this was the first thing *he* would have seen. Moving closer, Deb realized that this new, expensive 4x4 was parked on a patch of scraped ground in front of a ramshackle wooden fence. Behind this, she could see the smooth, round end of a polished aluminum Airstream trailer—it looked like the nose of a plane—with a wooden cottage—shack, really—built onto the side of it.

There didn't seem to be anyone around.

She walked past the fence. So far as she could tell, there were no more houses—or dwellings of any description—farther down the road. The fence ended in a stand of scruffy Scotch pines: the trees were all stunted and twisted, but they grew in regular rows, as though they'd been deliberately planted—for Christmas trees, however improbable that seemed.

She walked through them, over dried-up brown needles that crunched with each step, until she reached the side of the Airstream's property line; here, the fence was just wire, a single sagging strand; all she had to do was step over it. She crossed a patch of dry hard ground that someone had scratched at, even planted a few rows of scraggly beans, and went over to the shiny trailer. On this side, a low, wooden lean-to had been built onto it. It was made of plywood, all streaked with lime and paint and cement, which Deb guessed had been stolen from a building site where they'd been pouring concrete. There was one window. To her surprise, it had a curtain, a gauzy strip of white cloth, tacked over it. But she could see through it well enough. A small room. With a metal cot. A brown blanket folded neatly on one end. She realized then that the walls of the room were made from card-board cartons, she could tell by the folds, though they'd been care-fully painted white. There was a door . . . into the Airstream, she assumed . . . and by the door was a hook, and on the hook . . . a yel-low storm suit. Or the jacket, at least. It caught her eye. Because of the colour. And because it's the sort of thing sailors wear . . . the sort of thing you might put on if you were planning to spend the night in a small, open boat.

She stepped back from the window.

Certainly, this would have been the first place Mr. X could have reached, she thought. Say he'd been exhausted. Well, he *would* have been exhausted. But it might have been worse than that. He could have been in real bad shape—after all those hours in the little dinghy. Mr. X might have been half-dead, in fact. Deb stood there, working that out. And then she thought of that very expen-sive truck outside . . .

"And what can I do for you today?"

Deb gasped.

She jerked around.

A short, fat, loathsome man was standing in front of her. The thin, greasy hair on his head came down to his neck; the thick, greasy hair from his nose came down to his lip. He was five-foot-five in every direction. He wore black cowboy boots, black jeans and a stretched, faded xxxxl T-shirt that said Roy Rogers Family Restaurants across the front.

"God," said Deb, "you frightened me."

"Uh-huh." He smoothed his hair back over his head. He wasn't young, Deb realized. In fact, he must have been fifty. "You're tres-passing," the man went on. "Usually, with trespassers, I rape 'em, kill 'em, then cut 'em up and FedEx the pieces to their loved ones." He smiled. With his right hand, he smoothed the T-shirt down over his belly. "Don't worry, though. That's a joke. But who the fuck are you anyway?"

"Look, I'm sorry—"

"Don't be. Just tell me who the fuck you are."

"My name's Deborah."

"Great. So what are you doing here, Deborah?"

"I'm looking for someone."

"Like who?"

"I'm not sure exactly, I—"

"You mean you're looking for someone but you don't know who you're looking for?"

"Look, I was just fooling around in my boat . . ."

"Uh-huh."

"The ocean's right over there—"

"Deborah, I know where the ocean is. You got a boat?"

"Yes."

"Come on. Like what kind of boat? A Zodiac?"

"Yeah."

"Okay, so you left it down there? On the shore?"

"Right."

"And then you walked up here, and then you started looking for someone, but you don't know who, except you're on my property. You think I'm going to believe that?"

"Listen, this is no big—"

"Yeah, it is. A big deal. A real big deal. Maybe you should come inside. Maybe we should have a talk."

222 · ANTHONY HYDE

"I don't think so."

"But I do." And then, with a funny lurch—but a movement of great quickness—he reached out and grabbed her arm. His hand, in some particular way, dug into her muscles and pain flashed up to her shoulder and she wanted to be sick.

"Let me go!"

"Deborah, I don't think so."

Despite the pain, she pulled back. "For Christ's sake, let me go!"

Deb was frightened; he must have heard that in her voice. All the same, the pressure of his fingers eased. "Okay. How about this. I let you go, you come inside. All on your own."

"Okay," she said. There was no point resisting; he was too strong. "Okay, okay," she said again.

He grinned. "What the hell, we can have a beer. It's early, but it's going to be a hot one, isn't it?"

"Yeah, I guess so."

He stepped aside. But not very far. He smoothed his belly with his hand again, and she could see the big shadow of his navel under the cloth. Tentatively, she stepped past him. He walked with a limp. *I could outrun him*, Deb thought. But maybe not. He walked with a limp, but he'd walked with a limp for a long time; he knew how to compensate. He smiled at her. She wondered if he could read her thoughts, because his smile seemed to say, *You're right, not too many get away from me.* Around the front, she could see the top of the brand new pickup over the fence. There was a long wooden addition at the end of the trailer, but the front door went into the Airstream. It had a little porch, built out of poles, tree branches. This was almost pretty, an arbour; you could train vines to grow up it. But there weren't any vines: instead, hundreds of fishing lures dangled from the bark of the branches.

Behind her, the man said, "Door's open. Sometimes she's a little sticky. Just give her a push."

He was right behind her as she opened the door, and she could smell him, the smell not directly unpleasant, just the thick, sweaty odour of all his flesh.

She stepped in. It was dark, and she blinked. He was right

behind her and he said, "The morning, you know ... somehow that always means you sit in the kitchen."

She had a glimpse of the living room, though. A big, puffy couch, grubby beige in colour; a La-Z-Boy chair, the footrest extended. The TV was on, but muted: a smiling lady was mouthing words and squeezing Cottonelle. Had he been watching it? Had he heard her? Or was it just on all the time? But she was already turning into the kitchen, the trailer's old kitchen, cabinets neatly built in, a Formica counter, with a small propane range but a great big fridge. It made Deb think of a little kitchen room on the floor of a hospital; when you began to feel well, you could make yourself coffee. The metal table was like that; a vinyl top, with gold flecks. The idea was, it wouldn't show the dirt; but it was an idea that didn't work, at least not here.

"You wouldn't mind a beer?"

"Sure, that's fine."

"I got Schlitz and Bud."

"Bud's okay."

He opened the fridge. "It's cold, anyway." He slid a can across the table toward her, and zipped one open for himself. "Billy," he said. Deb looked at him. He took a sip of the beer and said, "That's my name. Billy Mayfair."

"Hi."

"Like the golfer."

"Right."

"You follow golf?"

"Not really."

"What do you follow, Deborah?"

"The stock market, actually. I'm a broker." She wasn't sure why she told him the truth—her brain just wasn't working fast enough to come up with a lie. But Billy gave a little nod, believing her, but also saying, 'I hope you don't think I'm too impressed.' He took a long pull at his beer. "Listen," said Deb, "I'm sorry about coming onto your land, but I didn't mean anything."

"Sure. Forget that a moment. Just tell me who you were looking for."

Deb took a sip of her beer. "That's a bit of a story."

"No rush. Go ahead."

"Well, there were these friends of my parents . . ."

"Your parents?"

"That's it."

"Where'd you say you were from, by the way?"

"Toronto." She sipped her beer. "Canada," she added.

He nodded, also drinking the beer. "I know where it is. Spent a little time there. More in Vancouver."

"Right."

"I'd say I prefer Vancouver."

"A lot of people do."

"That was after I picked up this limp. Just after. Took a bit of a trip up there."

"Really? You hurt your leg?"

"Yeah, I hurt my leg. Surprised you didn't notice." He tilted back his can of beer and drained it. "Like another?"

Deb had barely started hers but she said, "Sure." Really, she didn't know what to say. He wasn't crazy, she thought; but he was something else—something she didn't exactly have a name for.

He turned to the fridge. "San Diego. I was in the army." He was talking about his leg. Deb glance toward the living room; from here, she could see the door. *You could outrun him.* Billy turned back, a can of beer in each hand, and closed the door of the fridge with his elbow. *No.* "A pallet fell on me. Upper thigh. A bad break, and a worse doctor, so you limp. You know?"

Deb nodded. Billy came over to the table. He leaned forward heavily, with his full weight on the beer cans; and then he squirted Deb's over to her, and pulled the chair out and sat down, but awkwardly, because he had to drag his leg in. He opened his beer and said, "So these friends of your parents . . . ?"

"Well, they'd chartered a boat. This was last year."

"Okay."

He was drinking his beer. Deb took a sip of hers, holding it in her left hand, and taking the new unopened can in her right, and resting it on her bare knee, under the table. She realized then that she'd been jogging her foot up and down; she stopped.

"Anyway," Deb said, "they'd rented a boat..."

"And whereabouts was this? Here, you say?"

Deb shook her head. "I think it was Florida City."

"Okay."

"But they sailed here. I'm not sure what happened. No one is. They went down. The Coast Guard thought it happened somewhere off Mud Keys."

"Really? So they could have washed up here?"

"Well, I didn't really think so, but... I guess I was just curious."

"Maybe you could have found some wreckage? A lifeboat, say?"

"I guess."

"*Personal effects*—isn't that what they call them?"

"Right," Deb said. And she thought of the bright yellow foul-weather gear she'd seen hanging in that little room. *He knew.*

Billy drank his beer. He seemed to be considering things, and Deb tilted her own beer back, watching his face around the edge of the can. Finally he said, "Look, Deborah . . . can I tell you something?"

"Sure. Go right ahead."

"Okay. Let me tell you how the Keys work."

He seemed to be changing the subject. "I'm not sure I know what you mean," she said.

"Let me tell you. Forget the tourist shit. You got three kinds of people in the Keys. First, people on pensions—insurance companies, they pay a fortune into here. People like me, you know. On disability. You going to collect money, this is as good a place as any, better than most."

"Absolutely."

"And number two, you know, are the drug people. You know what a Florida key is, Deborah? It's an uninhabited island waiting for a bale of cannabis to come ashore. We can be proud, Deborah. These tiny islands support ten thousand federal agents. They're all here, the FBI, the DEA, the ATF. Even the navy. You know that blimp, over the highway? Fat Albert, people call it. Seriously . . . Drugs. That's what they're looking for. People bring the stuff in by your light plane, your high-end speedboat—anything. And everything. Cannabis, coke, heroin."

"I believe you, Billy."

"Good. And lastly, you got the trust-fund people, you know, the coupon clippers, the automatic monthly deposit types—"

"Maybe that's you, Billy. That's a real fancy truck outside." Deb tried to smile. Billy ignored her. He just nodded and went on:

"They're all different, these people, but they all got something in common. You know, they're collecting disability but they got a job on a side, or they don't just use their boat for bonefish, or there's that little capital gain they didn't *quite* declare . . . what they all got in common Deborah is they don't like snoops, they don't like people pushing their nose in where it's none of their business. And you see, Deborah, that story you told me, about your parents' friends and the boat from Florida City and the shipwreck, that's about the stupidest fucking story I ever hear in my motherfucking life, *so tell me what the fuck you're doing here or I'm going to shove your face down your throat.*"

At which point he leaned forward and grabbed her left arm, squeezed it so hard tears jumped into her eyes.

"Billy, I'm telling you the truth."

"No, Deborah, you're not."

"Billy—"

"Let's cut the cackle. A little bird told me to keep an eye out for you, at least that you got as far as Sanibel Island, and if I found you . . ." Billy grinned.

"What little bird, Billy?"

"That's good, Deborah, you're keeping your cool." His hand tightened on her arm. "You know something, Deborah . . . you have very nice breasts. Expect your boyfriend really likes them. Understand, though, they have him locked away in Brazil, so . . ." He was incredibly strong; he began to pull her toward him, over the table, closer and closer. She was so close—staring into his eyes—that she was just as startled as he was when the voice came from behind him.

"Let her go. *Let her go right now!*"

He did—and spun around. And as Deb fell back in her chair, there was Charlaine, with a gun in her hand. A rifle. She pointed it at Billy, who took one slow look into its barrel and said, "Who the hell are you?"

"Never mind who the hell I am." She looked at Deb. "You okay?"

Deb nodded—her throat was too tight to speak.

Billy smiled . . . and slowly stood up.

"Don't you move," said Charlaine.

"That my gun?" Billy said.

"That's right. Found it right there, that little hall. *Don't you move.*"

Billy was slowly getting to his feet. He smiled. "Expect you think I'm some sort of dumb, greasy redneck, don't you?"

"Yeah . . . maybe I do," said Charlaine.

"I tell you, though . . . I'm not so dumb I keep a loaded gun in the house. Go ahead, pull the trigger. Cock it first—*then* pull the trigger."

Charlaine, for just an instant, looked uncertain. Then her face went fierce as she stared at Billy and her finger squeezed down on the trigger . . . and the hammer made a very loud *click*. "Oh, shit," said Charlaine. But then she stepped back, twisted the gun around and swung it like a club, a tremendous, vicious cut right at Mayfair's head . . . except he stuck up his hand and caught it, as easily as a piece of dandelion fluff floating in the breeze.

Billy had the rifle's stock; Charlaine gripped the barrel. Billy grinned. He was standing now. Slowly, deliberately, like a tug-of-war, he began to pull Charlaine closer. And closer. His voice was surprisingly mild, as if he was enjoying this contest. "Don't worry, I got enough for both of you. You got real pretty breasts too."

"*Billy!*"

Deb's voice was a scream.

Billy jerked his head around, facing her. "Billy," said Deb, "this Bud's for you"—and she threw the second beer can he'd given her, the full one, right at his head.

It struck him directly between the eyes, creating, for a single instant, the perfect impression of a half-moon in his forehead. Then his whole face gushed blood as he dropped straight down, like a poleaxed pig.

Deb and Charlaine just stared at him.

Blood and beer were everywhere. Deb was trembling. "Jesus," she said, "his natural element. God, he's disgusting."

"Throw me that cloth," said Charlaine, kneeling beside him. "Yucky's a problem—disgusting I can deal with." A dishtowel was stuck through the handle of the fridge and Deb tossed it to Charlaine, who started mopping his head. "Looks worse than it is," she said. "Still . . . this man is severely concussed. Thank God . . . I saw through the window the way he was grabbing your arm—"

"Where'd you find the gun?"

"I came in the back. There's a little hall, an alcove—through there." She pointed. Deb ducked through the doorway. In a gloomy little space, she found a cabinet, began opening drawers. In one of them, she found a box of rifle shells. Back in the kitchen, she loaded the gun, pressing cartridges into the magazine until it wouldn't take any more. "You know about guns?" said Charlaine.

"Not really. But my father took me hunting once. It's pretty horrible. But he showed me how to shoot." She cocked the hammer. "Charlaine—now it *will* fire. If he comes around . . ."

"Jesus, I'm not sure I could actually shoot him."

"You're a doctor. Just point it someplace it will really hurt."

"All right. Yeah . . . his other knee. That would be good."

"He knows who Mr. X is . . . He must have come up here, and Billy helped him, and then got on the payroll—Mr. X paid him off somehow."

"Okay, but who's Mr. X?"

"Watch him. I'm going to look around and try to find out." She stood in the doorway. "They've got Giacomo," she said. "He told me that. In Brazil."

"Shit."

"Yes."

Charlaine looked at her. "Deb—you okay? No, of course you're not, but listen . . ."

"I'll be okay. You watch him and if the bastard moves—"

She stepped back into the little alcove, going through the drawers in the cabinet again. Nothing. In the living room, the TV was still on, still muted: squinting hard in the Florida sunshine, a man with a toothbrush moustache was selling used cars. She kept going, into the lean-to where Billy had caught her. Just inside, on a hook, was the jacket she'd noticed; and it definitely wasn't Billy's—he could diet for a year and still not get into it. But there wasn't much else to see, and so she quickly walked on through, into the big addition on the end of the trailer.

There was a small hall, a room on either side. To the left was a bedroom; a mattress took up half the floor, with a midden of Schlitz and Pepsi cans and plastic takeout trays built up around it. A bureau was shoved into one corner, another TV on top of it, which was also on, also muted: now a girl in a tank top was marching ahead on a NordicTrack. Deb turned away, stepping across the hall. This room was smaller, a kind of office. A metal desk. A phone . . .

From the kitchen, Charlaine shouted, "Find anything?"

"Not yet." She looked around. A slab door had been attached to the wall with angle irons, making a big bench; on this Deb recognized a single sideband radio, a ham radio, a frequency scanner, and a multimeter and some other test gear—and there was a lot of stuff she *didn't* know. She took another look at the desk. The drawer was locked. She knelt, to look more closely; it was a standard metal desk, grey, like a government desk, and the lock was nothing special. Locking it seemed an odd precaution—especially since there was an assortment of screwdrivers handy on his workbench . . . although it took a surprising amount of effort to force it open. Finally, with a grunt, she levered it back. Looking inside, she was surprised. Everything was neatly arranged—not something you expected from Billy Mayfair. In the little tray at the front, each with its own compartment, were two sharpened pencils, a Magic Marker and an assortment of stamps. Two block tablets of writing paper—compliments of the First National Bank of the Florida Keys, in Marathon—were lined up with one corner; opposite, held in a paper band, was a package of envelopes.

There were manila envelopes, the expensive kind with a clip to close them, and all carefully labelled with black marker. "Bank": cheques and statements, beginning with January of the current year. "Bills": paid and unpaid, carefully separated. "Dorschen": this was the Ford dealership, in Marathon, where he'd bought the truck. He'd bought it in January and apparently paid cash—the bill of sale was stamped "paid" and there were no financing documents. Three work orders, routine service checks, were clipped together. "Personal" included a current passport, birth certificate, discharge papers from the U.S. Army, a letter from a lawyer—Billy's father had died in 1982. Billy's full name was William Holden Mayfair, and he'd been born July 14, 1951, in Stearns, Kentucky. Deb flipped through the passport, and found entry stamps for Curaçao and Venezuela.

She kept going. Two fat files were labelled "First American" 1 and 2: this was an insurance company. He was, indeed, getting a disability check—$442 per month. She checked back, with the bank statements. There it was, every month; but there was another regular deposit, too—$1,500. Deb wondered when *that* had started. It was there in January. In fact, financially, January had been an interesting month. His balance had been over $50,000 at the beginning, but then he'd bought the truck; and he had definitely paid cash, because there was a debit memo for a certified cheque from the bank. Quickly, she went through all the other statements—but his balance had never been so high again. Because... sometime *before* January he'd deposited an exceptionally large sum. Of course, that was a guess. Maybe he'd been saving his pennies for years. But the coincidence was just too great—Peterson had died in December, Mayfair had bought the truck in January, and now every month money was being deposited in his account. Either Mr. X had landed here in such bad shape that he'd needed Billy's help, or Billy had caught him hiding the dinghy and worked out what had happened.

But who was Mr. X?

Two minutes later, Deb had the answer.

Almost literally, it fell into her lap.

She'd pulled the drawer right out, to see if there was anything at the back... and she pulled it so hard that it came off its runners. She couldn't quite catch it—the files, everything, spilled. But now Deb realized that the drawer was lined with brown paper—a corner had flipped. She peeled it back... and underneath discovered half a dozen newspaper clippings.

She took it all back into the kitchen.

Charlaine was sitting at the kitchen table, sipping the remains of Deb's first Bud. "He's not dead," she said. "At least, he's got a pulse."

"Charlaine, he was being paid off. One big cheque, fifty grand, and then fifteen hundred a month . . . and look at all these clippings I found . . . they're all from Florida newspapers, trade magazines.

Charlaine read through them. "Norman Danson, president of Xynex Incorporated, named Biotech Executive of the Year . . . Norman Danson, president of Xynex Incorporated, delivers speech to symposium on AIDS, Norman Danson . . . look at this one . . . Norman Danson greeting potential investors from Hong Kong, Malaysia and Pakistan—"

"Just the people who'd want to invest in his sex-selective contraceptive vaccine."

"So," said Charlaine, "Norman Danson is our Mr. X?"

"Yes. Here he is, presenting a cheque, on behalf of Xynex, to the crew of *Cresting Wave*, one of the entries in the America's Cup."

"So Danson is a sailor . . . it fits, then. He could have sailed that dinghy."

Deb nodded. "And he was a *rich* sailor, the kind Curtis Price would have known. Danson killed Peterson and ended up here, in bad shape. Our friend on the floor helped him, maybe looked after him for a couple of days—"

"But of course he had to be paid off," said Charlaine.

"Exactly. That's where he got the money for his fancy truck . . . He's probably on the Xynex payroll . . . security consultant or something."

Charlaine thought a moment. "Do you think Curtis figured this out?"

"I bet he did. Not the way we did—but somehow. He was buying Xynex stock because he wanted it to go *up*—I still can't see why anyone would kill him for that. But if he knew something about Peterson's murder—"

Just then, on the floor, Billy moaned.

Charlaine gave him a look—but then fished another clipping out of Billy's pile. "Deb, look at this . . . it's the sort of write-up they do for fundraisers . . ." Deb looked. It was a photograph, glossily reproduced from a trade magazine, the kind of photograph that's usually taken at an awards banquet or charity function: smiling men in tuxedos holding drinks, very skinny middle-aged ladies dripping with jewels. Charlaine read out the caption: *"Norman Danson, president of Xynex Inc., chats with Mrs. John S. Nelms, Honorary President, Children All Over This World, and Mr. Giacomo Valli of the Marsh Foundation. Xynex Inc. supports many—"*

Billy moaned again.

"Oh, God," said Deb—but she was thinking of Giacomo.

Charlaine took her hand. "I know . . . but listen, unless we do want to shoot him, we should get going."

Deb didn't say anything. They moved to the door. Outside, they ran up the road, throwing the rifle away into the bush. But they'd barely reached the ditch where they'd found the dinghy, when they heard the roar of a powerful engine.

"Get down!" said Deb.

They wiggled into the grass as Billy's 4x4 came toward them, weaving from one side of the road to another.

Charlaine said, "He really shouldn't be driving, the condition he's in."

In a cloud of dust, he roared by them.

"But where the hell is he going?" Deb wondered.

Charlaine propped herself up on her elbows as he disappeared. "Didn't you say Xynex had a big lab in Boca Raton?"

CHAPTER THIRTEEN

*C*harlaine, *driving, peered* into the gloom.

From Key West's little airport, they'd flown to Miami—they'd just missed a flight to Fort Lauderdale—where they'd rented a car and driven north. But everything had been more complicated, and taken longer, than Deb had expected.

Deb, with the map, murmured, "Up here."

"Yeah, I think so."

Boca Raton slipped by, masked by a violet dusk. It was increasingly hard to see, and the place, in any case, almost seemed an illusion, so discreet it scarcely seemed to exist at all. Even people's faces, reconstructed with superpulsed lasers and glycolic peels, expressed the same subdued, homogeneous perfection. Here, privacy was the greatest luxury, and so addresses were deliberately obscure; most people were residents of "parks" or "estates" or "landings" or simply "communities," where the high, flowering hedges cunningly masked the barbed wire, and the "ways" and "lanes" and "bridle paths" finally merged and passed out through a single gate, guarded twenty-four hours a day. They'd managed to get lost three times; everything looked exactly the same. "*That* has to be the golf course," Deb said.

Sprinklers flashed delicate streams of water against the darkening sky and a few ghostly figures still moved on a green. The trouble was, there were golf courses everywhere; but Charlaine said, "I think you're right this time." She speeded up; and a mile further on they finally saw the discreet brass sign, set into a stone wall: Fairway Industrial Park.

And it almost was a park. How many tons of grass did they cut in Florida every day? Low, modern structures nestled amidst carefully sculpted mounds of grass, bougainvillea, wisteria, rhododendron. The road curved around endlessly; the light was almost artificial—shadows stretched out of nowhere. It was weird, Deb thought, not quite real. "It reminds me of an old Star Trek episode," she said. "You remember? They land on this planet, where everyone's died, killed off by a thing like a rubber fried egg."

Charlaine laughed. "Right. One of them jumps on Spock's back. But he figures out that the way you kill them is with intense light, so they rig up photon bombs around the planet. The only trouble is, during the test, the light made Spock go blind—"

"Except he's okay in the end, because of his Vulcan internal eyelid."

"Yeah. We all need one of those."

"Slow down. We'll miss it." Deb peered out the window. It was like a maze in here, like some sort of crazy shopping centre. The buildings all looked the same; you could only tell them apart by the logos in front of them, but even they were all worked out on the same principles, so they could have been divisions of the same huge super-mega corporation. She began looking for the Xynex logo, the *X* and the *Y* emerging one from another. But Charlaine saw it first. "There . . ." The entrance, and the sign, were discreetly lit by lights set into the surrounding lawns. There was a security gate. A big tractor-trailer was coming out of it. Charlaine kept going, then turned into the parking lot of a small complex of buildings down the road—"units" where smaller local companies made custom windows, installed swimming pools, fabricated modular greenhouses. The parking lot was empty; in fact, since they'd turned in, Deb hadn't seen a soul.

They looked back toward the entrance of the Xynex lab.

"No sign of Mayfair," Charlaine said.

"He must have got here hours ago."

Sitting in the car, they watched the big truck slowly turn out from the entranceway onto the road; with a lurching of gears, it rumbled away. "Wonder where *he's* going," Charlaine said. And there was another one behind him. Then she added: "We can walk back there . . . no one will see."

As pedestrians, in such a place, they stuck out like sore thumbs. But there was so much vegetation—hedges, plantings, ornamental trees—that they were able to move from one patch of shadow to another until they were directly across the road from the Xynex gate. Sheltering behind a low brick wall—the entrance to a company that manufactured specialty lenses—they were out of sight, but could look straight into the Xynex compound. This was hidden by a wall of vines, which of course were masking a security fence, while the entrance itself was guarded by a security gate, with a guardhouse and a pole barrier. Already, the pole was going up and another truck was leaving—two guards were checking the driver's papers.

"I wonder what's happening," Charlaine whispered.

"I don't know. It almost looks like they're moving."

"Give me those glasses."

Charlaine, focusing the glasses, stared across the road.

Deb said, "Of course, they make vaccines. They could just be shipping them."

"At this time of night? Besides, you don't move vaccines like that . . . *Hawthorne International Forwarding* . . ." Charlaine put the glasses down. "They *are* moving. *Of course*, that's what they're doing."

"I don't get it," said Deb.

"Sure you do. It's just what we talked about. Listen—remember those 'international investors' in that clipping Mayfair had? They can't develop their drug in the States, we know that. So they're taking it all somewhere else. That's their lab equipment, test stuff

... They're getting out. And listen, Deb... that's where Giacomo comes in. The Marsh Foundation sponsors clinics in Brazil, medical clinics, right?"

But Deb was already there. "Yeah. And Xynex has been running tests in *those* clinics, just the way they did in Baltimore. He found out about it, or suspected something—just the way Curtis Price did." Then Deb stopped. "Oh, Jesus."

Charlaine took her arm. "You're thinking, And they killed Curtis..."

"Yes. Oh, God, yes—"

"Hang on, now. You don't know anything. A day ago, you were even thinking he could be in it with them. If they were going to kill him, why didn't they just do it? Think, now—"

Deb closed her eyes. She opened them again. "Okay... okay. God, it's so horrible... The trouble is, we can't *prove* anything."

"I know. Even finding out about Peterson doesn't really help—they'd find some way to explain that dinghy."

"If we only knew why Danson killed Peterson, that might help."

"Maybe Curtis knew." Charlaine looked at Deb. "Of course, you realize the only way we're going to find out anything...?"

"Charlaine... listen. No fooling. This isn't a game now... some kind of puzzle. Those trucks, what's going on over there... you're talking a hell of a lot of money, those folks are *serious*... and this is my problem—"

"Deb, we've been through all this."

"Charlaine, it's different now. You saw Mayfair. This could get—"

"*Shut up.*"

For a second, Deb was silent. Then she said, "The trouble is, I feel like such a hypocrite."

"Hypocrite? Now I don't get it."

"Because I know you shouldn't do this, I'm telling you not to do this, and I mean it... but I also know, if you don't come with me, I don't have the guts to do it on my own."

Charlaine grinned in the darkness. "Look, we've been through all this before as well. You're pregnant. You've got a little baby in there. To hell with Giacomo. To hell with right and wrong. To hell with everything except keeping that baby safe . . . I told you, you just want to go home to Mother. *In fact*, a young pregnant woman such as yourself, in good general health, is perfectly capable of carrying on a full range of normal activities, including fairly vigorous exercise. It would probably do you good to take a quick jaunt over there." Deb thought a second. They were both kneeling behind the wall. Deb reached out and put her arm around Charlaine, and kissed her lightly on the cheek. Charlaine didn't move. Then she raised the glasses and said, "The trouble is, I don't see how we *do* get over there."

"Well, actually," Deb said, "I don't think it's that hard. All we have to do is cross the road . . . we'll just go down a little ways . . . then we get against the fence. There's so much shadow there, no one will see us. Then we just wait for another truck to come out. They have to lift the pole, but the truck is so long it completely blocks the guardhouse out—we just keep the truck between us and the guardhouse and sneak right in."

Charlaine looked at her. "I think you're right."

"Charlaine—"

"Deb, enough of that shit. In ten seconds, I'm going to say *come on*. I'm heading across this road, and I'm not looking back—not once. Which means, if you don't come, I'll be in there alone . . . which wouldn't be fair *at all*. Ten, nine, eight . . ."

It was even easier than Deb had thought. Crossing the road, it was true, they were right out in the open; but only for five seconds, and there was no one around to see them. Once they reached the fence, they were lost in shadow—even in the time they'd been talking behind the wall, the darkness had deepened. Then they had to wait, crouched down, until the next truck emerged. It was so long that its back end projected behind the barrier as the guards checked it, and its heavy engine, grunting and idling, would have drowned out a marching band. Running alongside the truck in a low crouch, they darted inside the Xynex compound. Here, they were again in the open, although even so there was a good deal of cover; the road, branching around, was edged with palms, pools of shadow, waving, stretching. Beyond, dimly lit, they could see a low, modern building—light-coloured brick, softly glinting glass. But Charlaine, still in the lead, stuck to the road, which took them around behind it. A parking lot. Charlaine stopped and Deb pressed up beside her.

"Look at that," Charlaine whispered.

"There's almost no one here."

The lot, if full, would have held several hundred cars; there were no more than twenty or thirty.

Deb said, "That's Mayfair's truck."

In fact, it was too dark to be certain, but a 4x4 was sitting in the first row of parking spots, right against the back wall of the building. Against the building itself was a low, raised walkway with a railing; every so often, they could see the dark shape of a door. And then, from the far corner of the building—from around the corner—there was a flash of light. It was obviously the headlights of one of the large trucks they'd been seeing and Charlaine said, "There must be loading bays around there."

"Yeah. I think we have to try those doors."

The third was open: someone had wedged it open with a rock. They slipped inside. A short, dimly lit corridor: another door.

Charlaine whispered, "Not the best security."

"But they're moving. There's some kind of crisis—"

"I think you're right."

"But whoever put that rock there will be coming back—get going."

They went though the second door. A corridor. The hum of ventilation. They stopped a moment, whispering, trying to work out where they were, at least in terms of the general orientation of the building. They decided they were moving toward the front, and kept on. Another corridor cut across theirs, but it wasn't lit. Doors led off, left and right; Deb tried one, but it was locked. And yet another was standing open—inside, they could see a large, open-plan office; but the computer terminals at all the desks were covered, with only one exception . . . its dim glow casting an eerie, lonely shadow.

"It's weird," Deb whispered. "Something's up, but the place is almost empty."

They went on a little farther—and then heard voices, indistinct, echoing . . .

"Deb, down here—" Charlaine tugged her toward a door. It was marked *Women's Locker Room.* "Quick!" As the voices came closer, they stepped inside.

The room was large, tiled, lit with a bright fluorescence. Rows of metal lockers stretched away on either side, with wooden benches in front of them. Water dripped. Deb sniffed—cigarette smoke? But almost at once, they heard low voices. Quickly, they stepped down one of the aisles of lockers and stood very still.

From three or four aisles over, someone said: "You're sure the alarm is off?"

"Don't worry. Not that anyone would notice . . ."

A woman laughed. "I know. They're going out of their little minds."

"But it's nice to see the suits doing some real work. I actually saw Danson loading boxes into the back of one of those trucks."

"And I believe I detected the slightest hint of—could it actually have been perspiration, *sweat?*—around the armpit of Ray Garvey's shirt."

Another laugh. "Yeah. The obsessive-compulsive personality of our time."

"What a prick."

"Come on. Deep down, wouldn't you love to darn his socks?"

Just then, the door to the room swung open: "Michelle?" someone called. "Michelle?"

One of the women who'd been talking called back, "In a minute."

"They need you for those records."

"In a minute . . ."

The door swung shut. Michelle said, "What the hell . . ."

"Put the fan on first."

A fan, with a surprisingly loud rush, came on, and the odour of cigarette smoke dispersed a little. "That should be okay." Now there was a loud *thunk*—a switch had been thrown. And a second later, two women, walking briskly, flashed past the lockers and went out of the room.

Deb held a finger to her lips.

She started down the rows of lockers. They all had combination locks. She gave each a tug; halfway down the third aisle, one opened.

"Come here," she hissed.

Inside the locker was a lab coat, hanging on a hook; at the bottom, a pair of low-heeled shoes; on the top shelf, a pile of books, manuals, a large appointment diary. Charlaine slipped the lab coat on. It had a name tag, with a picture. "Too bad," she said, flipping it up. "ROBERTS, Beverley, is a blue-eyed blonde."

"Listen . . . an attractive black woman in a lab coat—no one's going to stop you. You're a doctor. You look the part."

Charlaine looked skeptical—but said, "If I could actually get into the lab, I might find something."

"At least you'd be able to recognize it if you did—I wouldn't."

"Deb, I don't like this. You're saying, we split up?"

"I could try to find Danson's office. Or a computer that was on—like that one we saw—it might tell me a lot."

Tentatively, Charlaine tucked the manuals from the top shelf of the locker into the crook of her arm, straightened up . . . she made a face. "I never wear these things. I always feel like one of those TV doctors in a toothpaste ad."

"No. You look perfect. And these people are running around like chickens with their heads cut off. No one's going to stop you."

Charlaine still looked dubious. "What happens if somebody stops *you*?"

"Don't worry about me. Look, if we're going to do this, we have to *do* it. I'll meet you back here in half an hour."

They left together. A few steps down the corridor, they found an elevator. The building had only three floors; Charlaine decided to try the basement first, giving Deb a little wave as the doors closed in front of her. Deb, alone, was suddenly very nervous—her legs seemed made of straw. And yet almost at once, she had a reassuring test. A man stepped out of an office right in front of her, a floppy stack of computer paper looped over his arm. Before he could speak, Deb said, "Have you seen Michelle? Danson's going crazy about those records."

He shook his head. "No, but I thought I heard someone calling for her."

"That was me. I thought she was in the can. Shit!"

But he'd already turned away, marching quickly down the corridor. Yes; everyone was in a hurry, too concerned with their own business to be worrying much about anyone else's. She hesitated. The man was leaving—but for how long? She tried the door to his office. It swung open, and she stepped inside. The office was small, desk, chair, two file cabinets, a small table . . . The computer was on, all right—but the man wasn't going to be gone long, certainly not permanently: his suit coat was draped over the back of his chair. Quickly, leaning down, she looked at the computer monitor. When it came to computers, she wasn't exactly a dummy—if somebody showed her, she was okay. But she didn't recognize this at all. It wasn't Windows, nor whatever it was Macs used. The technical analyst at Orme ran os/2, which he'd showed her—there was something intriguing about it—but this was quite different, probably Unix or something, the kind of thing—as Rosie once put it—that men talk about now instead of cars. Tentatively, she tried one of the function keys, F6. Why not? The computer emitted an irritated beep. F2. F4. More beeps. But then she hit F5, and the screen changed. A box said: *Search Term (case insensitive)*. She hesitated; for Help, she could press F1. But instead she simply typed *Valli, Giacomo*.

She held her breath.

God, they've even got a picture of him.

Her heart began sinking as the pixels collected themselves but she told herself to calm down. It was just a picture. She recognized it—the standard picture the Marsh Foundation had, the one they'd run in *The Financial Post* when they'd made him executive director; he looked so *politely* bored. She read the biographical material underneath, and it too was absolutely standard. She tried to be relieved. So what? They had him in a database. They'd have hundreds of other people too. It didn't mean anything. But then she clicked one of the buttons at the bottom, "Bibliography," and the screen flickered. He'd written a lot, more than she realized; here, four items were highlighted. *Economic Expectations and Family Size: Local Factors. The Sex of Siblings and Girls' Reproductive Goals. Contraceptive Strategies: Tunisia and India. Marriage Age and Contraceptive Choice* . . . Involuntarily, she ran her hand back through her hair. She hadn't realized he'd written so much about all this. *And that's why they were interested in him.* But then she froze: she'd heard something. *Somebody had walked right past the door.* But they went on by and she steadied herself, hit F5 again, and this time entered Danson's name. His picture . . . The biographical material was PR stuff, although there was confirmation of his sailing experience—he'd won various cups, even crewed on an America's Cup boat . . . but that was nothing new. In fact, she only found one useful fact: he was in office 100. Still, that at least gave her something to look for . . . F5 one more time. This time, she tried Peterson's name, expecting to get "not found." But he was there; picture, bio. He'd been the company's first scientific director, but was listed as having retired the previous year. *But he was still on the board of directors.* That was interesting . . . She thought aloud, "He quit or was fired, but still stayed on the board . . . how come?" She shrugged. Of course. "Because he owned a lot of stock." She let out her breath. Maybe, here, was the answer to *one* question. Maybe he'd owned enough stock to prevent Danson from doing what he wanted—and so Danson had finally killed him. She felt frustrated, though. She was sure, if she only knew more about their computer system, that she might find more than this—but she looked toward the door. She didn't have time. She hit "Escape" to get the screen back to where she'd found it, then ducked outside. Office 100. She started down the corridor, now noticing the numbers on the doors, and realizing that she was being led to one corner of the building. Of course. The CEO would have a big corner office. And there it was.

In fact, there was a pair of heavy glass doors, with *Executive Offices* engraved across them. One of these doors had been propped open with a cardboard box. Of course—when you're moving stuff, you want doors open. Beyond was a reception area, two big desks. Both were deserted but a light was burning on one of them, and a lot of papers were scattered about—Michelle Kincaid, read the nameplate. Michelle, obviously, was still chasing down records, or off on some other errand; but she wasn't going to be gone forever. Deb knew she had to move fast. In front of her were two more sets of doors. Both were large, and made of polished cedar. The pair on the right led to the offices of R. Bennet Garvey, Executive Vice-President; those to the left, Norman F. Danson, President & CEO. She stepped up to the doors leading into Danson's office, took a breath, listened—she couldn't hear anything from the other side—and pushed.

She let her breath out. The room was empty.

It was also huge. It wasn't just the office of a CEO; it was the office of a man who owned a very big piece of the company. The floor was all carpet, except for a big square of beautiful red quarry tile in the centre, with Danson's huge desk—all glass—sitting right in the middle. All the walls were lined with the same cedar as the doors, and there were built-in bookcases, and a bar. Two doors opened in the back wall, presumably to the CEO's personal washroom and—there was a push-button private elevator. It was all very plush. But it was a mess, just the same. Cardboard cartons were stacked up everywhere, including some already loaded on a dolly. Even in the executive suite, it seemed, Xynex Inc. was on the move. But Deb was barely taking this in. This was a big, fancy corporate office, but she'd been in lots of them, and she knew where the secrets were buried: in the CEO's desk.

In fact, in this case, on it.

Perhaps this was yet another indication of the rush they were in, a rush that was close to panic. Because this was the sort of thing you'd normally put in a safe, or at least slide under your desk blotter. It was a single piece of paper, one corner held down by a small box of polished wood.

CONFIDENTIAL it said, in the upper left corner. There was a title, PRESS RELEASE, with "draft" written in pen beside it, and, also in pen, "Xynex Inc. Announces Self-Tender Offer." Underneath this, printed out from a computer, was the main body of the text:

Xynex Inc. today announced a self-tender offer for all of the company's shares, as listed on the National Association of Securities Dealers Automated Quotations (NASDAQ). The offer, at $16 per share, is conditional on at least 90% of shares being tendered, and will be open to the end of this month.

Norman F. Danson, CEO, said that the offer will be financed internally, and with additional funds provided by a number of leading Middle Eastern and Hong Kong banks.

"Our shareholders have been very patient with us," Danson said, "but we feel this is the best way to surface the fundamental value of our proprietary technologies in the areas of vaccine development and production."

Xynex Inc., based in Boca Raton, Florida, is a leading . . .

Deb closed her fist.

So much, over the past few days, had been so mystifying; but now she was back on her own turf again. *This* she understood. Here, at last, was the information Curtis Price had known or guessed. Xynex was taking itself private . . . that is, they were buying up all their own shares on the stock exchange, and so ceasing to be a public company. Once their offer was accepted and concluded they wouldn't be much different, legally, from the corner hardware store. There were a lot of reasons for doing this, Deb knew—but she could guess the ones that interested Danson. Private companies don't need shareholder approval for major corporate decisions—like relocating operations to another country; and they're not subject to much official scrutiny at all. In a physical sense, Xynex was getting set to disappear—that's what this moving was all about. The self-tender offer would be the equivalent, financially and legally. Later, they could resurface as a completely different entity . . . And who, she thought, would bother to object. Because they'd be taking themselves private at a very rich price— very, *very* rich, since sixteen dollars had been stroked out, presumably by Norman Danson's pen, and eighteen dollars written over it. Deb needed Danson's scratch pad to work it out. Curtis Price had wanted to buy two hundred thousand shares at five dollars and change—so he would have been looking at a profit that was north of two and a half million dollars; real folding money, as her father liked to put it. In fact, anybody who had a big position in Xynex stock—Danson most definitely included—stood to make a fortune out of this. Was this the real reason that Peterson had been murdered—because, somehow, he was standing in the way of the sale? And she could also guess the reason for the current panic. Maybe they'd been able to bury Bannon's investigation. But Price's murder, coupled with his purchase of the stock, would have set off a Securities investigation as well—they would have been forced to reveal a "significant corporate development" earlier than they'd planned. But, all at once, these questions seemed rhetorical, hopelessly abstract and totally theoretical—because she could hear someone outside the door.

And the elevator, behind her, descending.

This happened so suddenly, and quickly, that Deb could only freeze.

Something was clattering outside in the corridor.

Deb whirled around. But there was no place to hide. The door to the washroom was too far away—and she couldn't even get under the desk since it was as clear as a microscope slide.

With a little bump, the elevator arrived.

Her mouth gaped open and she almost screamed as the elevator doors opened and there, *right there*, was Billy Mayfair.

But there was something terribly, terribly wrong with Billy.

He was, in a clumsy way, squatting, but all jammed up, and his neck had been so completely broken that his cervical column no longer gave any support to his skull or his bulging, swollen face. There was no blood, just a yellowish foam around his mouth. And as the elevator settled back slightly, his weight shifted forward and he slumped, slid, *oozed* between the elevator doors into Danson's office. The elevator doors tried to shut—squeezed Billy's neck—bounced back.

And then something banged against the door of Danson's office. Swung slowly inward . . .

Deb took a deep, quick breath. There was only one thing to do, and her guts were just going to have to look after themselves. She went over to Mayfair's body, tugged an arm; and just stepped between the elevator doors as they automatically came together . . . caught Billy's foot . . . bounced back . . .

She kicked his foot away and squeezed her eyes shut . . .

Danson was already turning—but his eyes were glued to Billy. "Oh, Christ," he said. And then, as if by magic, the doors slid shut.

And quietly, soundlessly, the elevator began to rise.

Deb didn't move. She couldn't have moved to save her life. Slowly, smoothly, with the dignity appropriate to an executive's ascent, the elevator rose. Then jiggled to a halt. The doors slid open—and a foot, clad in a Nike running shoe, jammed against it: and then a cardboard carton slammed down, taking its place.

Deb pressed herself back . . . but no one appeared.

Although her body no longer worked—it was someone else's body, a body made of sticks—she managed to step to the door and stick her head out.

She was looking down a hall. And at the end of the hall, she saw him again, the same man—was his name really Boyd?—in the John Deere cap or whatever the hell it was, whose shadow she'd first seen in Giacomo's apartment. Now his body turned—for a terrible instant she thought he was looking around—but then he headed left, down a side corridor at the far end of this one.

Deb was trembling. *Run the other way.* It was all she could do. So she ran, though her legs didn't want to work and her lungs didn't want to breathe, running as fast as she could until she slammed into the door at the end of the corridor, as if to embrace it. It was a heavy grey steel door with a very secure lock, and she was shaking now, shaking inside and out; but when she twisted the handle, it turned.

She jerked it open. She stepped inside, and leaned back against it, almost sobbing. Then she looked around. Her mouth opened. She so wanted to scream. Because all she could see were rats, thousands of them.

And then the lights began to dim.

CHAPTER FOURTEEN

*D*eb *stretched an arm out* in front of her and moved forward in the gloom. She was terrified—desperate to get away from the door, but expecting each step to plunge her into horror. All around was the soft, intimate rustling of the rats—on every side and even, it seemed, above her head: aisles of cages, rack upon rack, reached up toward the ceiling. She actually closed her eyes and stepped ahead; *that* darkness seemed almost safer. But then a subtle alteration in the atmosphere, a slight current of air, made her stop. And she realized that beyond the pressing, fussing restlessness of the rats—and she could smell them too, a warm, acidic scent like vinegar—a mechanical hum had commenced—some fan. She hesitated, trying to get her bearings. The room opened up to her left, the aisles of cages running off that way, almost like the stacks of a library; in front of her was an open lane, a kind of corridor. And then, another step farther on, she saw a light. It came from under a door, along to her right; presumably there were rooms on that side. She went forward, listening—there didn't seem to be anybody there. Then she stopped again. To her left, among the rats, a different light glowed, the flush of phosphorescence from a computer screen. It flickered; below it, she saw a small red light—a hard drive whirring. She made out a table. And then the light was blocked out, as something moved in front of it. She stared . . . "*Charlaine!*"

"Deb!"

With a tremendous rush of relief, Deb ran toward her. "Thank God!"

Charlaine put her finger to her lips. "Keep your voice down," she whispered, "though I don't think anyone's around."

"Are you all right?"

"Sure. But we have problems. You'll never guess who I saw—"

Deb nodded. "I know. He's just out there."

"But I don't think he'll come in here. No one will, at least till morning."

"What *is* this place—some kind of lab?"

"Exactly. A test lab. I don't know whether you've noticed, but you're surrounded by rats."

"I've noticed, believe me."

"We did a little of this in med school, but I'm not quite sure how it works. It's automatic, though . . . this computer probably runs the lights, sets the temperature, even waters and feeds them." The screen now flickered, producing a graph. "That shows the gases in the atmosphere . . ."

With the light from the computer, Deb could see a little more. Charlaine was right; this was obviously a monitoring station. On the table were various pieces of test equipment that she didn't recognize, a clipboard dangling from a nail. The racks of cages were all linked together with plastic tubing, a network of wires; each cage, as far as she could tell, held a single rat—she watched one watching her with its small pink eyes. "What's that?" she said. Against the back wall, reaching to the ceiling, was a different rack with pieces of loose plastic hanging in front of it, like plastic raincoats or plastic bags—they had arms and funny gloves for hands.

Charlaine said, "Some kind of isolation chamber, I think. But never mind. Look what *I* found." She picked up a small blue box that had been sitting beside the computer. It had a handle, and was about the same size as a lunchbox.

Deb said, "You're kidding. That's not—"

"It is. Twenty-four doses."

"You're sure?"

"Almost positive. It's labelled rubella but the lot numbers are all in the same series of the stuff they sent to Baltimore . . . And don't worry, I don't think they'll miss it. I put another box in its place. These people are in a panic—"

"Yes, I know. I got into Danson's office. The whole business with Curtis Price has forced their hand. They're taking the company private—buying their own stock back on the stock exchange—but it's all happening just a little faster than they planned."

"No kidding. They're running around like crazy. No one noticed me, I swear."

"But we have to be careful, Charlaine. They killed Mayfair . . ."

Charlaine made a face. "Good riddance—"

"Yeah," said Deb, "but they killed him because he knew too much—"

"Like Curtis."

"Like *us*. I think what we have to do—"

But she never got a chance to complete this thought; both she and Charlaine froze—a door was opening; a patch of light spilled into the room. Indistinctly, they heard voices. Charlaine tugged Deb's arm, leading her down the aisle of cages to one end. They pressed back against them, as a voice said, "Jesus, there's a lot of them."

Deb cautiously peered around the corner; she could now see Danson and the man who'd called himself Boyd standing at the far side of the room, where it opened up. For the first time, in fact, Deb could see Boyd properly. He was tall, heavy-chested, and had a broad, rough-skinned, weather-beaten face, an outdoors look, but the real thing—not L.L. Bean and a Jeep Cherokee, but pickup trucks and construction sites. In a suit, Deb thought, he'd look like an aircraft pilot, or at least the way they're supposed to look—his face seemed intelligent, his expression had an *executive* cast. Danson, in a white shirt—his sleeves rolled up—stood beside him, making a gesture to take in the lab. "We call this the Genesis room. Unto the generations, you know . . . All the animals in here were born from parents who'd been given the vaccine, even while they were pregnant."

"You're looking for birth defects?"

"Right. And there aren't any. In the next room, we've done the TD50 studies."

"And what's that?"

"Simply put, it's establishing the daily dose rate—x number of milligrams of the drug per kilogram of the animal's body weight— that halves the probability of the animal remaining tumourless over its standard lifespan."

"In other words, that room is full of rats with cancer."

"But it's not. There are no more cancers in that room than you'd expect to see in that number of rats, of that age."

"All right. So, let's say, if a cat were to snack on a few of your rats, he wouldn't start growing extra ears?"

"No. On the other hand, if a good lab got hold of a few of our specimens, they'd have a fair idea of what we were up to. They'd definitely know we were up to something."

"What about inspectors, records, that sort of thing?"

Deb could see Danson shake his head. "That's not a problem. The Animal Welfare Act doesn't cover rats, mice or birds. Of course we're registered with the USDA because we use primates in the other labs, and they inspect us annually, but they never bother this lab. All the records have been destroyed or moved—they were in the shipment that went yesterday."

"What about the technicians, people who know about this?"

"I think that's okay. We were always very careful. Once we knew what we were doing, we made this lab extra secure. Top people only. Need-to-know. The only technicians who *do* know are in Malaysia now, setting things up."

"All right. All the other records and equipment you want moved are ready?"

"Yes. Or gone. Most of it, thank God."

"So once we get rid of the rats—"

"And Billy—"

"For Christ's sake, I don't want to know his name. It's bad

enough that he exists. It's bad enough you didn't *tell* me he exists ... Never mind, though. You know how to work all this?"

"Yes. I can turn the ventilation off, seal the place, right from the computer."

"Okay. And what about the cages?"

"I'll set it up. All you do is hit 'enter.' "

"You're sure they'll come out of the cages?"

"They haven't been fed in thirty-six hours. Spread some food around, they'll come."

"All right—"

"Boyd—what about that stockbroker? The one Price was screwing around with?"

"Don't worry. So far as she's concerned, we've got insurance. Just get your ass in gear—I don't want any more surprises."

Charlaine and Deb held their breath—for as Boyd turned to leave, he actually glanced down the aisle where they were hiding; but it was too dark to see. Then he was gone and Danson disappeared, moving toward the computer at the end of the aisle that they'd just left. Charlaine didn't move. Deb gave her a little nudge and led the way ... down the aisle to the open area. It was very dark. Reaching back to keep Charlaine with her, she quietly stepped forward, and now could see Danson, bent over the monitor. Then they were by him. They reached the door where Deb had seen the light—it was still on. But it was not an office. There was a swing door, that you pushed. She pushed—and, behind her, heard the ventilating fans begin to die. Then she was blinking; it was suddenly quite bright: they were in a small foyer—a door to the left had the universal sign for men; to the right, a skirted figure ... Together, they stepped into the relative familiarity of the Ladies' Room.

Charlaine took a breath and whispered, "That was close."

"Yeah. What do you think they're doing?"

"No idea. But they're old-fashioned American men. They'll never follow us in here."

"The trouble is," Deb whispered, "I think Boyd is coming back."

"Who was the other guy? In the white shirt?"

"That's Danson. President. CEO. He's Xynex Inc."

"Ah . . ." Charlaine was gripping the box of vaccine with both hands. She said, "I've never actually seen a murderer before. But did you notice—? Boyd was angry."

"Yeah, about Mayfair. As though he hadn't known."

"Right. I don't quite follow. We know Danson killed Peterson—"

"I've got that worked out. Peterson owned a lot of stock . . . which is no surprise. He was the scientific guy, but when companies like this start up, they give out a lot of options. He probably could have stopped Danson doing this, or at least made trouble. And then Mayfair helped Danson—"

"Except Boyd didn't know about that. Right? So you almost have to think that Boyd's from *outside*—"

"Shhh! Quiet . . . Listen . . ."

All at once, a loud clanging sound reached them from the other side of the door. They both went over to the door and pressed against it. Another metal clang . . .

Charlaine said, "They can't move all those cages. God knows how many there are out there . . . they've got breeding cages, those isolation boxes, everything."

Deb said, "It sounds like something *rolling* . . . maybe they're on wheels."

Charlaine frowned. "No, they're not on wheels." Then, urgently, Charlaine gripped Deb's arm—because she could hear the first door, the one into the little entranceway to the washrooms, swinging open. And then the light that had been on outside went out—someone had stepped in and turned it off. They both stood there, absolutely still . . . and then Deb, touching Charlaine's arm to hold her back, opened the door, and stepped into the foyer. It was very dark. She had to feel her way ahead. But there was light outside now, in the lab—or at least there was a narrow strip of light up the side of the door, though not *under* it. She pressed her eye against a crack. She couldn't see very much, one row of cages: in the light, they were even higher than she'd thought. Then a figure passed through her line of sight—he looked so strange that she couldn't quite take him in. Boyd. It had to be. Because it was a big man . . .

and then he came by again. It was Boyd all right. But he was wearing a strange mask on his face, and a small tank was strapped to his back. It was a respirator. And he was wearing high rubber boots . . . He disappeared. Deb didn't move. But now she understood, and she waited for the sound she knew she was going to hear: the hiss of gas.

Gas.

She turned in panic and pushed back into the Ladies' Room. "Charlaine . . . it's gas. I saw him. He had a gas mask on."

"Jesus. Of course. They're going to gas the rats."

"He put tape around the door, partway up the side."

"Jesus, Jesus. To keep the gas in *there* . . ."

"But it's not going to *all* stay in there."

"Come on," Charlaine said, "hurry."

Now, with fumbling hands, they flicked on the light—fluorescent, dazzling. And there was another switch.

"Charlaine—a ventilator . . ."

But Charlaine shook her head. "No. Just a minute. It will only suck the gas in here."

They looked around; high up, they spotted a long, low, frosted window. Charlaine said, "If we stood on one of the toilets—you're taller than me."

Deb began to move, then stopped herself. "But you couldn't even stick your head out—it's too small—*shit!*"

And Charlaine, in any case, had already moved on, pulling paper towels out of the dispenser, and running water in the sink. Deb saw what she was doing, and without a word began to help, soaking the towels, then jamming the wet, wadded-up paper around the door, working into the cracks, pushing it in as though she was chinking between logs. Charlaine helped her, and every few seconds one of them would sniff, but then Charlaine leaned back:

"Don't bother, Deb. If I remember my chemistry, cyanide is odourless, colourless, invisible."

"Is that what you think it is?"

"I don't know." They were listening. Deb pressed her head against the door. Was that a real *hiss* she heard, or was it only in her mind . . . but then Charlaine, also pressing against the door, pressed too hard—it moved. And all the towels they'd stuffed into the cracks fell out, a wretched cascade of soggy paper.

"*Oh fuck oh fuck oh fuck—*"

Deb could see that Charlaine was on the edge of tears, and put an arm over her shoulder. "Shush. Oh *fudge,* oh *fudge—*"

Charlaine gave her a look. "Jesus. Okay." Then she smiled. "That was stupid. My God, that was stupid."

"It's okay. I don't think it was going to work anyway. I think we have to run for it."

"Yeah, I was coming to the same conclusion."

"One deep breath and then a lot of giant steps."

"Just a sec . . ." Charlaine slithered across the floor, and grabbed the vaccine. "I'm taking this with me, no matter what."

"Okay. Ready?"

They both took deep breaths, pushed through the door into the foyer, and then the second door into the lab—and as Deb pushed that second door, she could feel something *pull*, the tape that had sealed it up. But then she stepped into darkness and horror, for there were things around her legs, things she couldn't see. Oh, God, she thought. She felt something. She could feel things around her legs, everywhere, against her legs, and she kicked out, but as soon as she took a step she felt them again. She stepped on something, she felt something squash under her foot, and kicked at it, and then she remembered, they'd killed the rats. Now the floor was covered with rats. She was walking on them. There were so many. She stepped forward—onto something hard. *The hard little head of a rat.* And she couldn't step down, she hopped, or tried to. And then she had to step down, and her foot came down hard. They were everywhere. They came over her feet, over her ankles, and then she remembered, he was wearing rubber boots, and she gagged, she couldn't help it, and she panicked and tried to run, and although most of the rats were dead, they were not all dead and she must have stepped on one that was still alive, because it squealed, and she tried to run too fast and she skidded and fell. They were all over the floor, thousands of them. She managed to turn and land on her shoulder, but they were all over. She could feel the dead bodies of the rats against her back, and she had to kick with her feet, because they clung to her there. She tried to get up, and managed to, but almost immediately she slipped again. She broke her fall with her hands, and she could feel a rat's hindquarters under her right hand and another rat ran over her left. She rolled over. She could feel one against her face, moving. They were everywhere; they were all against her legs. One began crawling over her hip, and she just couldn't move, she couldn't bring herself to touch it. She closed her eyes. She was close to fainting now, though she didn't know it, since she'd never fainted before in her life. She didn't know where the door was; she didn't know how to get out. She'd gone the wrong way. One was against her hair, she could feel the warmth of it. She tried to calm herself . . . She closed her eyes. She felt suddenly sleepy . . . as though she was a little sick, in bed, and about to doze. It was okay now. She didn't even have the energy for anything, let alone being afraid. It was okay, she thought. It wasn't too bad. Right now she couldn't feel any of the rats actually touching her, although she could smell them, sense them, she could sense the heat of their bodies, and she knew that if she tried to get up—as soon as she tried to move—she'd touch them again. So she didn't move. She lay there. She grew even sleepier . . . but then a rat, quite innocently, crept against her and touched her ear, and the feel of it there, so close to her face, sent a jolt of adrenaline through her—

"Deb! Get up! Get up!"

It was Charlaine, pulling her up by the arms, knocking the rats off her shoulders, her breasts, and then hugging her, keeping her up, and pulling her, dragging her across the floor, through the piled-up bodies of the rats. "It's okay," she was saying, "it's okay. *Breathe.* Take a breath. Stand up. *Up.*" And then she pushed Deb up against one of the racks of cages, now empty, holding her in a standing position. "Breathe," she said. "Take a good deep breath . . . it's not bad if you stay on your feet . . . it's not a gas . . . or it *is* a gas but it's not really poisonous—look . . ."

She turned Deb's head to one side, and made her look out

across the dark sea of dead rats, and dying rats—for some still crawled about, aimlessly, slowly, creeping over the corpses of their fellows—and as Deb tried to make her eyes and brain work, she vaguely took in a long green canister, in fact several of them. "You see that? See what it says on them? CO_2. It's carbon dioxide . . . it's heavier than air, it *sinks*—it's suffocating the rats, but it *sinks*. Anything below your waist, you're dead, but up here, it's okay. You understand? Just take a breath . . . I remembered, that's how they kill lab animals, just suffocate them like this—but breathe, slowly, slowly . . ."

"Oh, God," said Deb. She gasped. But her head was clearing. She closed her eyes, opened them slowly. The rats, long swirls of them, banks of them, like drifts where they'd crawled up on each other trying to breathe, stretched across the floor of the lab, interspersed with the lethal green canisters of carbon dioxide. But now she began to feel okay.

"Move," said Charlaine, "start walking."

"Oh, God."

Because she could still feel them.

"Just don't step on them. Don't fall down." Deb reached out her leg—set her foot down with a little *flick*. She could feel their bodies, and once her heel came down hard and she felt one squash, but she understood now—*they're dead, just don't slip*—and then they reached the door. They had to tug—it was all taped up. But they made it through; on the other side, the lights were on, but the hall was empty.

They both coughed and gasped; still light-headed, it took them a moment to figure out where they were. Down the hall, they found an elevator; inexplicably, there was no button to push. Then Deb remembered: "That's Danson's private elevator . . . it goes right into his office." She closed her eyes, thinking this: they'd be waiting there, Boyd and Danson, in corporate splendour, waiting for the rats to die.

"There has to be another one," Charlaine gasped, "because I came *up*."

But they found the stairs first, and headed down, breathing

deeply, working to get their heads clear. At the bottom, they stopped; a door led—where? They were still too befuddled to work it out, so they slumped down, each into one corner of the stairwell; a couple of panting minutes passed. Then Deb took a deep breath, gave Charlaine a look, and Charlaine nodded. Opening the door, they stepped into a narrow hall with bare concrete walls. Charlaine, who'd gone down to the basement at the start of her explorations, started one way, but Deb stopped her—she was always good when it came to direction. "We want to get to the back, don't we?"

"I think so. The parking lot."

"This way, then."

Deb was right; the corridor led past various utility rooms, but ended in a door: beyond this was an open basement with ramps and loading bays. It was deserted—though it was a moment longer before they realized the significance of this. They were too eager to find a door; as they stepped into the cool, clear night, both of them gulped great breaths of the wonderfully fresh air.

"Jesus, that feels good."

Deb said, "As long as you've still got the box."

"You're damn right, I do."

They sat, leaning back against the walkway that ran around this part of the building. Charlaine clutched the box of vaccine against her stomach and for a few minutes they soaked up the feel of freedom. The sky was black but full of stars; the wind whispered gently, rattling in the palms. All at once, Deb felt fiercely thirsty. She licked her lips. And Charlaine finally managed a long, easy breath. Then she said, "Now all we have to do is get out of here."

That's when Deb understood: "The trouble is," she said, "I don't see any trucks."

They both sat up—looked; listened. The parking lot wasn't empty—they could still see a few cars—but there was no sign of the big trailer trucks that had been coming through here when they'd arrived—and which had given them the cover to sneak by the guards. Deb said, "I think they're finished. They've all cleared out."

"Jesus, Deb, we can't stop now. I'm not going to get this far—"

"No. And there has to be some way—"

"Could we just sneak past them? It's dark. Until you get up to the guardhouse, there's no one to see us. And they're so flustered . . . all that time in there, no one asked me a single question. They were afraid I was going to stop *them*."

"I know, but it would be real risky—this time, they might be looking for us."

"Why would they be looking for us?"

"Well, think a minute. The tape around the doors, when we got out—we pulled it off, remember? When they went in, they must have noticed."

Charlaine considered this. Then: "We could wait till morning. Walk out then. There'd be people around."

Deb was quiet, and after a second Charlaine murmured, "I know what you're thinking . . . What Boyd said, or whatever his name is. *So far as she's concerned, we got insurance.*"

Charlaine reached out and touched Deb's hand, and Deb nodded in the darkness. "That's the trouble. If they caught us . . ."

"Yeah," Charlaine said. "I know." She patted Deb on the tummy. "How are things down there?"

"No complaints."

"That comes later."

They leaned back against the walkway in frustration. But it was just then, in fact, that they did hear an engine—a sudden roar. And headlights spilled across the parking lot, swinging in a wide yellow arc across the shiny asphalt. A vehicle, which they'd missed in the dark, now came toward them—they had to scurry back along the walkway to get out of sight. Then they realized what it was. "That's Mayfair's truck," said Deb.

They watched as it made a three-point turn, then backed into one of the loading bays. It sat there idling, its lights still on.

A moment later, they heard voices. Outside the glare of the truck's headlights, the night seemed even darker—slowly, cautiously, they crept closer. And they heard someone say, "Just leave it running, it's full of gas."

For a few more minutes, they watched in silence. Nothing seemed to happen. When it finally did, it was only a sound: a soft, cushioned *thump*. This was repeated—but almost more gently. Only after a time—there was a quick gleam in the night—did they understand what was happening. Mayfair's 4x4 was being loaded—with green garbage bags. And then it registered.

"Oh Christ," said Charlaine.

"Yeah."

A soft *plop* . . . a sigh of air escaping . . . green plastic garbage bags . . .

Charlaine refused to look but Deb kept watching. "I suppose it makes sense," she said after a moment. "They had to get rid of them. That's what this all about. Destroying the evidence—cleaning up, covering up."

"I guess. It's just that I don't think they're taking those . . . bodies . . . to the dump." Now, the bags made a definite pile, bulking over the side of the pickup's box. Deb watched; she couldn't actually see any of the men doing the loading—they were down the ramp, at the bottom of it. Charlaine insisted: "You know what I'm saying, don't you?"

"Yeah, I know what you're saying. There are only two things in a Florida swamp at night—alligators and alligator food."

"Exactly. That's *exactly* what I'm saying."

But then Deb was quiet, thinking. She finally said: "Listen . . . Charlaine. Can you drive a pickup?"

"I don't think so. No. Can you?"

"Yeah. I have."

"What are you getting at?"

"Well, the truck . . . the engine's running. It wouldn't be hard. We can just sneak along here, slide into the cab . . . we'd drive right through their barrier."

"No. Don't be crazy. They'd catch us—for sure. It would be some sort of stupid hot-rod chase and maybe you can drive that thing but they'd catch up—"

"Just a minute. What are they doing here? *Covering up*. Destroying the evidence. Those . . . bodies . . . are the evidence. You heard them in the lab. If someone examined those rats they'd find out what was going on."

"Deborah," said Charlaine, "are you thinking what I'm thinking?"

"You get in the back. I drive. Okay, they'll chase after us, but all you have to do is start throwing those bags off the truck and they'll have to stop to pick them up."

"Deb . . . seriously. I don't think I can do that. What you're saying is . . . I jump over the side of that truck and land right in the middle . . . no, somehow I don't think so."

"Well, I'll do it then. You drive. Just remember, don't stall the truck out. It's a Ford. The parking brake's a little lever under the dash—they'll have set it, because of that ramp. All you have to do—"

"Shut up. I can't possibly drive that thing and you know it."

Deb hissed, "Well, think of something else then."

There was a moment of silence. Then Charlaine sighed—and pushed the box of vaccine over to Deb. "I think you better take this."

"You're sure?"

"No, but come on," she said, "or we'll be here all night." And before Deb could say anything more, she started forward, running in a crouch along the walkway. They were well hidden in the darkness, but there was no one to see them anyway; as they came up to the 4x4, they could hear the steady whoosh and plop of the garbage bags softly settling on each other, but the men were still out of sight, at the bottom of the ramp. There was only one problem: they were approaching the truck from the passenger's side—Deb would have to crawl across the cab. "You first," hissed Charlaine.

"Okay. Bang the cab when you're ready."

Charlaine nodded and Deb skittered forward, opening the door, making the high step up. For an instant, the interior light came on: but she got the door shut quickly and was relieved as two garbage bags, sailing up from the ramp, bumped in mid-air, then settled into the pile, slithering down a little; clearly, they hadn't noticed. Bent down, she squirmed across the seat—which smelled of beer; why was she not surprised? Sitting up behind the wheel, she felt with her feet. There it was, the pedal—like a tiny clutch—which set the parking brake. Okay. And then, reaching under the dash, she found the lever that released it. A thump . . . against the window . . . Deb glanced into the rear-view mirror. Charlaine's face appeared; she looked almost out of her mind, but not entirely demented, so that was all right—although one of the bags, bulging oddly with its contents, loomed up behind her and nearly hit her in the back. *Don't look*, Deb thought. No; she stared across the gleaming hood, down the path of lights . . . Thomasina, one, two, *three* . . . and with her left hand, she released the lever while her right foot fed a little gas . . . and the truck rolled easily forward. She simply drove away.

Since the men loading the truck hadn't even been alerted by the engine starting, they didn't know what had happened until one of the bags—Deb watched in her side mirror—hit the ramp and split, cascading rodent corpses back to them. But she was halfway across the lot by then, and all she had to do, she told herself, was keep her nerve, and she did, turning easily down the lane of palms and coming up to the guardhouse at a normal speed—actually slowing slightly, as if about to stop. As the guards came out, she hit the gas and shut her eyes and smashed through the barrier—her body flinched but the truck barely noticed—and then she began to twist the wheel, so the truck rocked through a tire-squealing turn onto the main road.

For some reason, *then,* she screamed: as if she was afraid the truck would flip, and she kept screaming as she put her foot down on the gas, hard down, until the screaming engine drowned her screaming out, and her mouth finally stretched open in silent horror as she watched Charlaine in the back, like a windmill, throwing the green bulging bags off the truck, into the elegant lanes and avenues of Boca Raton. Lights in the mirror: but they stopped, slewing across the road. She turned. Turned again. Took one big gamble: turned off her own lights, glided ghostlike through another turn. Finally, ahead, she saw a sign pointing toward the highway—and hit the brake.

Deb was trembling. She could barely work the door to let Charlaine in.

"You okay?" she gasped.

"Yes. No. Hurry up. They had to stop just like you said, but for Christ's sake—oh my God, just get going . . ."

She was beside herself—she kept brushing at her clothes, as if a dead rat might be clinging to her. And Deb kept saying, "It's okay, it's okay," and raced up the on-ramp. After that, they drove in silence—Deb flicking glances at Charlaine, watching her compose herself—and then there were lights and cars, and big trucks, and McDonald's and Levitz stores and Amoco stations, and they passed into that extraordinary landscape, south Florida, the end of the world just before you went over the edge, flat, dun, stretching out to nowhere: a sand dune, with concrete.

"Charlaine . . ." she said.

"I'm okay now . . . and don't ask. Mostly, I kept my eyes shut." She closed them now, and shivered. "I tell you, I never smoked a day in my life, but right now I'd *love* a cigarette."

"Don't you dare."

She pressed herself back in the seat, as if revolted. "There's one thing. God . . . Mayfair was in there too. He *still* is."

"Jesus. I didn't think."

Charlaine shrugged. "I suppose it figures . . . just another rat."

Deb couldn't help it. She had to laugh. And then Charlaine laughed, and they both laughed, the horror and relief spilling out of them in equal measure. Finally Deb said, "I can't believe you. All that—and getting us out of the lab. But you were frightened by some yucky leaves, in the Keys."

Charlaine gave Deb a look. "Deborah," she said, "that was yesterday. Today I could walk through yucky leaves up to my hips, and I'd consider myself blessed."

A few minutes later, a sign for Miami International flickered by the window. Neither spoke. They both knew it was where they had to go.

In the airport, over coffee, it didn't take long to settle the obvious points. This time, no matter how she looked at it, Charlaine had to admit she shouldn't come. The vaccine was *their* insurance, the only proof. She had to hide it, keep it safe. Deb squeezed her arm. "And keep yourself safe, too."

"Listen, you're the worry. They'll know it's you, Deb. They'll be looking."

"Don't worry. That might help. And I'll be looking too."

"But there's one thing . . . We didn't settle this. Boyd—he's been around from the start, hasn't he? And I'm not so sure he works for Xynex . . . I mean, he didn't know about Mayfair. He's from *outside*."

"I'm not sure I understand."

"Well, I'm not sure I do either. But I wouldn't be surprised if he has a nice shiny set of credentials . . . you know, the kind with a picture and initials, like FBI or CIA. Anyway—listen . . ." And now she opened the box of vaccine, took out one of the tiny plastic vials. "I want you to take this. It might help—it proves that we really have it. And that might come in handy."

Deb nodded. It was so small—it seemed extraordinary that it could do so much. She slid it into the breast pocket of her shirt. Then she smiled, squeezed Charlaine's arm again. "You better get out of here," she said, "they'll be searching for that truck."

Charlaine leaned forward, kissed Deb's cheek. "When you find this guy of yours, that's from me."

She turned away. Deb watched her disappear . . . and began listening for a flight announcement to Brazil.

BRAZIL

CHAPTER FIFTEEN

R$_{io}$.

Deb coughed, gasped for breath, and turned her head away from the smoke and noise of *Avenida Atlantica*—the diesel fumes in Rio, she'd discovered, were almost as bad as Paris; people here were suffocating, just like those rats in the lab. And the water— which she was now facing—was even worse. Even from the tap, you couldn't drink it, and you didn't want to swim in it, either; Guanabara Bay, with Christ looking down upon it, was the great symbol of the city, and sparkled now in the early morning light, like a lagoon in paradise: in reality, it received one and a half million tons of waste every day, and its glorious blue was the colour of cholera, dysentery, polio, hepatitis—in Rio, *E. coli* counts were part of the weather forecasts, like UV readings. The previous afternoon, sitting in a café, she'd overheard two Frenchmen—her ears reached out to a comprehensible tongue—who'd chatted cycloserine and ethionamide over lunch. They must have been doctors and she'd wondered if they were here to attend the conference that Giacomo was supposedly organizing; it wasn't due to begin till the next week, but they might have come early to enjoy the sights.

Turning away from the road, she headed across the beach . . . the beach at Ipanema. It was impossible, as she walked, not to hum the famous melody.

But she didn't feel lighthearted. Today, she thought—tomorrow at the latest . . . *If it's going to work at all . . .*

Waking up this morning—she'd slept in her rented car, in the top level of the parking garage at Galeão Airport—she'd wondered again if this was the right strategy, but she couldn't see anything better.

They'll be looking for you, Charlaine had said; *I'll be watching for them*, she'd replied, to be reassuring.

But coming down on the plane, she'd wondered, *maybe that's exactly what you should do*. They already knew about her; they'd guess it had been her in the lab. They'd also know where she was going . . . they'd guess, they'd eventually find the truck at the airport; and they were certain to follow her. So the easiest way to find Giacomo might be to double back on her tracks, follow *them,* and let them lead her to him. They couldn't let her go; they couldn't just let *him* go—the only new fact she'd discovered seemed to bear that out. From the airport in Miami, she'd called her number in Toronto and Rosie had left a message, as promised: she'd been to Giacomo's apartment, checked the computer. File Manager was still running, with half a dozen files highlighted. They were all letters about "some clinic in Brazil and a couple of them from Nisram Singh"—Rosie's voice had been full of excitement, making the connection. It all made sense, Deb thought. It was just one more link in the same chain. From the beginning, they'd been covering up; Boyd had simply been making sure that Giacomo wasn't a threat— or, more exactly, establishing the degree of threat he represented. Except that thought, whenever she had it, always made her shiver a little. In the lab, Boyd had said *insurance*, which seemed to imply that they weren't worried about Giacomo directly, but only as a way of getting to her. But what if they decided they had to get rid of him, no matter what?

But she couldn't think about that. No, all she could do was make her plan work. She stopped, digging her thongs into the sand, and then turned right around, looking back the way she had come—she'd parked the car, bought a *café com leite* from a guy on the street, then walked here. Had anybody seen her? Was anybody watching? Following? Because, of course, that was essential—that Boyd, or whoever, *not* find her first.

But there was no one paying her any particular attention. And here, on the beach, a young, single, attractive woman was wonderfully well hidden. Sun, sand, skin: the sheen of tanning lotion—shouts and whoops, happy screams: the morning was as glossy as a colour spread, a *Playboy* layout come to life. And she fitted right in. Even the beach required a disguise, and in this case there was only one choice, near nudity, the "near" being provided by the Brazilian version of the bikini, the *fio dental*—which translated, more or less, as *perineal floss*, and she'd in fact bought hers in a place called Bum Bum. As a garment, it had some advantages. For example, it did cover enough that you could hide an Amex card and a few bills down the front. On the other hand, there were problems, such as the way it attracted amorous males, one of whom now approached her, grinning, babbling in Portuguese, gesturing in a more universal tongue. She'd found there was absolutely no way to discourage them except to run away, but this revealed another of the *fio*'s disadvantages, the way *everything* moved—and not necessarily in the same direction, or in the same frequency of oscillation. But that, presumably, is what jiggling means, and now, irritated, she jiggled her way through volleyball games, soccer drills, frisbee contests and various stages of amorousness until she hit the harder, darker sand at the water's edge. *Boys*—she hadn't given the word that particular intonation in her mind since she was eight. Turning, squinting against the sun's hard glare, she peered into a kaleidoscope of colour and nakedness, but the jerk had already moved on to another target. She waded into the water. There was nothing too obviously disgusting in it, so she washed.

When she was finished, she stayed in the shallows, walking along, letting the backwash of the waves tug at her ankles

She wondered what time it was. She'd spent most of yesterday at the airport, and now had all the Miami arrival times committed to memory; but she wasn't wearing a watch. You don't, on the beach, in Brazil. It was one of those Brazilian "don'ts" you learn. No watches. No jewellery . . . Her watch, and most of her money, and in fact most of her stuff, were all out at Galeão, the airport: she'd left a skirt and T-shirt, and a little money, in the car; but that was it. All she had with her was a string bag with a towel, and a bottle of water. Knowing the rules of Brazil, in fact, was one of the few advantages she had, and she knew the rules because she'd been here before. In her very first year as a broker, she'd sold a staggering amount of mutual funds, and one of the fund companies had offered a week in Rio as bonus. The whole thing had been disgusting, really; the contest, Rio, everything. But at least now she knew that you didn't drink the water, except bottled, or eat the food, especially the vegetables and the shellfish, and you assumed that everyone was a thief.

After a few hundred yards, she began angling up the beach. It was hard to walk. There were so many people—the sand was always chewed up with footprints; every step, you slipped. It was already hot, even in thongs. There was no room—you couldn't take two steps in a straight line, there were so many people on towels, chairs, chaises, under the umbrellas. It was amazing, she thought, how exhausting the beach could be; she could feel herself making a face. But it was okay; she wanted to get going. So she made her way straight back toward the road. She'd found a place to leave her car that was, of course, illegal, though also reasonably safe; but she didn't want to lead anyone to it, and so before she left the beach she again took a quiet look around.

And that's when she saw the little boy.

A street kid.

Pepsi T-shirt, *Lara Cardinale* baseball cap, no-name runners— but shoes, at least.

Her first guess at his age was six, but more likely he was nine or ten, just small. He smiled at Deb and she smiled back—and then she hesitated. Because she'd seen him before. Around, and just hanging around. Maybe two or three times. Maybe following her... Normally, they worked in pairs. Excuse me, a bird did something nasty on your shoulder let me brush it off... and then, as you turned and loosened your grip, the second one would snatch your bag. They probably wouldn't go after her string bag, she thought, but she didn't like it; she especially didn't want to lead him to the car.

The little boy smiled again.

She knew he was one of the twelve million abandoned kids who live on the streets of Brazilian cities, many of them in Rio; she remembered the newspaper stories from a few years ago, how death squads had hunted them down like vermin.

"Hi," she said.

"Hello, Miss America," the little boy replied.

He had a beautiful smile, all white teeth and big brown eyes. "Hello," Deb said again.

He kept on smiling. "Hi, there," he said.

"Right. Hi, there." She smiled again; he was hard to resist. "What's your name?"

"Renato."

"Where did you learn English, Renato?"

"Oh, men. On the beach." He grinned. "Whatever."

Deb nodded, trying not to imagine what this could mean. "I've see you here before," she said. "On the beach."

He shrugged. "My beach."

"Are you here all the time?"

"Mostly, around here." He made a gesture, up and down the beach. Then he grinned. "Let's go to your hotel."

"I don't think so."

"I come and shine your shoes."

She lifted up her foot, and dangled a thong.

Renato looked at her, "What are you doing here, Miss America?"

Deb hesitated. It seemed a funny question for him to ask; as if he'd already noticed something peculiar about her. Deb said, "Renato, what if I asked you to find someone on the beach. A lady?"

"Who?"

"Anyone."

He seemed to consider this, though Deb wasn't sure he understood. But he understood one thing, apparently: "Five dollars," he said.

"Okay," she said, "I want you to find a woman called Susan Randolph. She has dark brown hair, and she isn't wearing a *fio*—just an American bikini. Okay? She's from New York."

Renato nodded. "Okay."

She kept a little money down the front of her *fio*; she took out a couple of bills. "Here, then. This is for you. And if I need you for any more errands, I'll always know where to find you."

He nodded, and smiled—unfortunately, Deb realized, the prospect of finding some particular individual in that great mass of humanity didn't seem to daunt him; but at least it got rid of him. He ran off, in search of the fictional Miss Randolph, and Deb started across the street. Cautiously, she made her way to the car. It was her one major worry. She was not registered in any hotel; she'd changed all her money at the airport, coming in, and was only paying cash. So her name appeared on only one document, created only one link: to the car . . . which was some kind of Brazilian VW, which you fed methanol. But everything looked okay. She got in, and put on her skirt and blouse over the *fio*, and turned into the traffic.

After four trips, she knew the route to Galeão Airport like the back of her hand: through the Rebouças Tunnel, and then all the way around one arm of the bay, and out to *Ilha do Governador*. She was at the airport before ten, which left her plenty of time; she got more money from her locker, put on more clothes and had a pee, then drank her *cafezinho*.

She sat quietly, sipping.

She thought about the little boy, Renato.

He was such a cute kid. Did anyone love him? Look after him? She wondered who his mother was; he probably didn't know himself. Her hand went to her own belly, but then she took it away. It was incredible, to think of her baby and Renato, in the same world. But they were. Would be. *If* . . .

Now, suddenly, she felt frightened. In a certain sense, despite

Mayfair, despite the lab, despite Baltimore, she hadn't felt this frightened since the beginning, in Toronto. Because she was alone. Because of the baby—yes. But because of Giacomo, mostly. It had started on the plane, the long flight toward the bottom of the world. It had given her time to think, imagine. Where was he? She wondered if they'd hurt him . . . But why would they? It was funny. Somehow, they'd lured him here, made him come here. Why? What did they want him for? Of course, she tried to phrase these questions so they reassured her—if they simply wanted to kill him, what was wrong with Mexico City, or even Toronto?—and told herself that neither of them posed a threat, *now* . . . Xynex had won. She'd read Danson's press release in *The Wall Street Journal*, in a box under "Company News." Curtis Price, Peterson—they could have stopped it happening, but she couldn't; it had already happened. Xynex had effectively closed itself down as an American public company, would soon disappear; when it resurfaced, it would have a different name and be located on the other side of the world. The trouble was . . . she knew what the trouble was, all right. She knew—*everything*; and that was much too much.

She fought off these thoughts until quarter past ten, then went down to Arrivals: the American Airlines flight came in at ten-thirty. She watched the people stream out. *I'll be watching for them* . . . but he wasn't on it.

Turning away, she realized she'd been holding her breath the whole time. She went into another of the airport bars, ordered a *cana*, and started to worry again. She was meeting only flights that came in direct from the States. But perhaps he'd flown to Buenos Aires and come in from there. But why would he bother? And when it came to joining A and B, she suspected, a man like Boyd probably preferred a straight line. So she ate a sandwich and calmed herself down, and when the United flight came in, late, just after noon, she was back in the hall again, watching, as Boyd came off.

She almost missed him—he wasn't wearing his hat.

And yet, in another sense, she recognized him instantly; she knew it was him, something about the way he moved, before her brain supplied details. She could feel herself shrink a little. And she stared. Of course. No hat. But him. Now, though, he was just one more well-set-up American, in a decent tropical suit—linen, to judge by the luxurious wrinkles. In fact, he looked fresh, First-Class fresh, as he weaved through the crowds, giving a smile as he pushed by.

And he never noticed her, because a man stepped out of the crowd to greet him: older, in a grey suit, tall and slim—they shook hands, and then this second man led Boyd over toward the Hertz counter.

That was enough for Deb—she took off, because she'd worked it all out beforehand, where you picked up your car from Hertz or Avis or Localiza, where the lots were, how you got out. There was only one difficulty; to make sure she didn't lose Boyd, she had to park right there, on the service road, and let him drive right past her. But he was talking to the man who'd met him—who sat back, casually, his elbow resting on the open window—and it was clear they weren't looking for her, or anyone, and she slipped in behind them as they headed for town.

It wasn't hard. The road in from Galeão was long enough, but straightforward; as long as she stayed behind Boyd when he came up to the exits, he wasn't going to get away. In the end, they retraced her earlier route, then went on a little more, along the beach to Copa—closer to *centro* than Ipanema, also more crowded, and a shade down-market. His hotel was even off the *Avenida*, and he had to park his own car in a building two blocks farther in. Deb kept close to him. Again, this wasn't difficult. He didn't seem the least concerned that he might be followed, walking along, chatting to the other man without a care in the world. By the time they reached the hotel, she'd taken nine decent photos of Boyd and his companion with the disposable camera she'd picked up at the airport the previous day. She walked out to the *Avenida*, then along to a café. It was hot; she asked for ice coffee, sipped it. Smiled: *Yeah, you need to be cool.* Then she arranged the frosty glass of coffee, her sunglasses and her big wallet in a semicircle, a kind of tableau: carefully, she propped the vial of vaccine in the middle—the brown leather of the wallet made a good background. She snapped four shots, just to be sure, then took the camera to a one-hour photo store.

By three-thirty, she had the prints back.

She examined them on the beach, in the shade of a palm—here and there, near the road, palms were still allowed to grow and created scruffy oases of shade. The pictures had all come out pretty well; Boyd was clearly identifiable in every one. And the shots of the vial were good enough—you could read some of the lettering, the Lot Number, stamped on the plastic. She had no way of knowing whether they'd discovered that some of the vaccine was missing, but even if they hadn't, she thought, this wasn't a chance Boyd could take.

Now, in a funny way, Deb felt frightened and relieved, all at the same time. Okay, she thought, you've done it—and she found herself remembering the pleasure, and amazement, Charlaine had expressed when they'd actually come upon the dinghy. This was the same sort of thing: she'd made her plan, and it had pretty much worked out.

Yeah—but now, really, came the frightening part.

She had to make her move; she had to reveal herself. But at least she was going to be in control. Boyd *had* to meet her—and she was going to set the conditions.

She selected two of the photos, one of Boyd, the other with the vaccine; and on the back of the Boyd photo, she printed: *the bar in the Costa Brava 9pm alone.* She was going to underline "alone" but then she didn't; somehow, it looked weaker like that. But then, at the bottom, she did add: "D.G." Then she slipped the shots into an envelope and sealed it up.

As she did this, she heard a voice behind her:

"Hello, Miss America."

The street child, the one she'd spoken to before, swung around one of the palms. He smiled. That irresistible smile. *"Bom dia,"* Deb said.

Hanging onto the trunk of the palm, he replied, *"Tudo bem."*

"I don't speak much Portuguese."

"Renato. You forget my name?"

"No," she said, "I didn't forget your name. Deborah, that's my name."

"'Deborah.'" Renato smiled, then laughed, as though there was something funny about her name; or he was just embarrassed.

Deb said, "Who is the team? On your hat? The cardinals—"

"Yes, yes. *Cardinale*. From Caracas."

"Ah. *Caracas*. It sounds wonderful, when you say it."

"Caracas!"

"Caracas!"

They both laughed. Then Deb pushed her sunglasses up on her forehead. "Listen," she said, after thinking a moment, "would you like to earn some money?"

"Of course."

She hesitated. She wondered if this was really a good idea. But then she said: "Can you get to Copa?"

"Of course."

"It's a long—"

"No, no. Of course."

"There's a hotel there. The Amer-Continental."

"Of course.

"Not the Inter-Continental."

"I know, I know. Of course."

"There's a man staying there. His name is Boyd. I want you to give him this." She held up the envelope—but didn't quite give it to him. She'd intended giving it to a cab driver—would Renato be more, or less, reliable? But then she thought of something else, which actually tipped the balance toward Renato. "Actually, Renato, it's possible that he won't be called Mr. Boyd. He may be using a different name . . . Look, here, you see . . ." She brought him closer, so he could see one of the other photos of Boyd. "That's the man. You have to give it to him, no matter what he's calling him-self. You can take this picture."

"Of course," Renato replied. It seemed to be his expression of the day. But still she hesitated. Was there a better way to do this? If the envelope was left at the hotel desk for Boyd, he'd never get it, not if he was using a different name. And that was very possible; certainly "Boyd" wouldn't be his real name. Still—

"You're sure you can do this?"

"Of course, of course."

"Well, did you ever find that lady from New York?"

He suddenly looked sheepish, remembering. He thrust one hand into the pocket of his pants, brought out some coins. "I have this much left."

"That's okay, you can keep the money. But this is very important—this envelope. You understand?"

His eyes brightened as he took it. "Very important? Twenty dollars."

Deb didn't hesitate. "Yes. Twenty dollars. *That* important. Here."

She gave him the money and his eyes went very wide. "I come back soon."

"No, you may have to wait," Deb said. "You may not find him right away. But I'll be here tomorrow."

He ran off, like a rabbit. Deb, watching him, felt somewhat anxious, but decided that he'd actually solved a problem. She'd forgotten that Boyd might be using a different name, and finding out what it was—that intermediate step—would have been difficult and dangerous. And she had no doubt that Renato would find him, one way or another. So it was done. She closed her eyes: she was suddenly remembering Giacomo, his awkward excitement the first time he'd brought her home to meet his parents. But she'd been disciplining herself, trying not to think of him, because that was *remembering*, as if he was gone—and he wasn't. No. He was close. All she had to do—

That was all right, remembering what she had to do, keeping her whole mind on that. And she had to do things now, small things, but everything was important. If she was going to sit in a bar, she wanted to look halfway respectable, so she bought herself a new skirt and a light jacket, something to cover her shoulders, and a new pair of sunglasses, something fancier, the style Brazilian girls wore . . . just to blend in a little. Then she drove out to the airport, one last time, to pick up her things, and to wash her hair— you could manage, in a sink. By the time she headed back to town, the first hint of twilight was settling slowly over the day, but she took her time, dawdling past *Flamengo*, *Botafogo*, beneath Sugarloaf

Mountain: and then, with a whoosh, she entered the tunnels that took her over to *Leme*.

She parked—in a small sidestreet; it left her a long walk to her own stretch of beach, but she always felt safer away from the car; besides, when she came back to it, she'd take a taxi.

Walking slowly, she headed toward Ipanema. It was too early, but she ate anyway. She chatted with the waiter, had a second cup of coffee. By the time she left the restaurant, it was almost dark, and she crossed the *Avenida*, to the beach side, and joined the throngs of Cariocas in their ritual evening walk: couples, parents with their kids, old people nodding together. She tried to relax. She took a long, deep breath. She made herself walk slowly, mingling, meandering. Lights twinkled in the gloom. Lights rose and rocked upon the sea. *Ipanema* means "dangerous waters" in the language of long-dead aborigines, and the surf was up, smashing in—Deb could almost hear the rip, a nasty undertone behind the soft sounds of the cars on the broad, dark road. Yet, even with the breeze, it was warm; she took off her jacket, carried it over her arm. *You're nervous but that's okay—*

"Deborah!"

She turned—and there was Renato, running through the sand toward her.

"Renato!"

She was glad to see him—though that was probably crazy. But his smile, white as bread, flashed in the gloom. He was out of breath as he came up, and she stepped off the sidewalk, into the sand. She bent down. He was so out of breath, he teetered a little, and she held his shoulders. "Are you okay?"

"Of course." He took a breath. "I had to find you!"

"But did you find the man? Did you give him the envelope?"

"Cable. Mr. Porter Cable."

For an instant she was alarmed, but then understood. "He was calling himself Mr. Cable—but you did give him the envelope?"

"Of course."

"Well, that's all right. I knew you would, Renato."

"You must give me fifty dollars."

"Fifty dollars! Why?"

"More than twenty-five."

"Why more than twenty-five?"

"I like you."

"I like you, too, Renato. But why—?"

"*He* gave me twenty-five American dollars."

"He gave you twenty-five dollars?"

Renato put both hands in his pockets, a gesture of stubbornness. "Fifty dollars," he said.

"Why?"

"Forty dollars."

Deb hesitated; she was, in fact, running out of cash. But as she looked at the little boy's face, she saw not only stubbornness but desperation. She took out her wallet. "Okay? Thirty dollars. That's more than twenty-five. That's enough."

He took the money. "Okay. He asked me where you were . . . where you lived. I didn't know. But for twenty-five dollars I told him the car. The number."

"You told him—you knew the number—?"

"Yes. But I like you better, so now I tell you."

She thought a second . . . At some point, he must have followed her to the car, and she just hadn't noticed. But did it really make any difference? She was, in any case, going to reveal herself to Boyd—but she hadn't planned on going to the car before she met him in the bar. Afterwards . . . well, she'd just have to abandon it, get another. It would be no more than inconvenient.

She smiled at Renato. "It's all right," she said. "Thank you for telling me. But you should go now—all right?"

Renato said, "When are you going to America?"

"I'm not from America, actually. I'm from Canada. Toronto."

"Toronto Blue Jays?"

"Exactly. Toronto Blue Jays."

He looked directly into her face. "We are friends, Deborah?"

"Sure, Renato."

"I *like* you."

"I like you, too."

He looked thoughtful, almost puzzled; then his face lit up with a big smile, "*Trigo*," he said. "*Trigo!*"

"*Trigo* . . . I don't understand."

"*Trigo* . . . *Pao*—" he made a twisting motion with his hand, then a motion of eating. "Bread!"

"*Trigo* is . . . bread?" He almost nodded, then shook his head.

"*Trigo* . . ." His face was full of consternation . . . "*trigo* . . ." but then Deb understood.

"You mean wheat—*trigo*—"

"Wheat, yes. *Wheat.*" He pronounced the word very carefully, and looked very pleased.

Deb smiled; it seemed a rather old-fashioned symbol for the country, but it would certainly do. "You're right, Renato. We grow a lot of wheat in Canada."

"Of course. You see, I already know."

"Good. That's really good . . . but you have to go now. You know? You have to go, and stay away. It's not safe now. Go away."

"Of course. I will go now but when you go back to Canada, I will go with you."

Deb had only guessed what he was going to say in the split second before he said it; she could hardly think how to respond.

"I'm sorry, Renato—"

"I will come. Please!" He smiled. "Please?" He wasn't quite sure of the word. He rushed on: "I can work. I can go to school!"

"Renato, I'd really like to—"

"Good!"

"But I can't. You know I can't."

He shook his head. "I can come. Of course!"

Deb looked at him, and then reached out and took him by the shoulders. He was serious. He was absolutely serious. She said: "I can't take you with me. Do you understand? I *won't* take you with me." He looked at her. He simply kept staring, and smiling, as if what she'd said hadn't registered.

"Canada," he said. "Toronto!"

"No, Renato." But how could he take "no" for an answer? There was no way, she realized, looking into his face. There was no profit in "no." What good would it do? So he just ignored it. Yet she had to get rid of him. For his sake. For hers.

"Renato..." Yes, she absolutely had to get rid of him, and fast... so she lied: "Renato, in three days—three days—come back here to the beach and find me."

He grinned. As if he'd won. "Of course!"

"We'll talk about it then."

With his finger, he wrote in the sand, 3. "Three days!"

"Until then—you promise—you stay away?"

"I promise."

She stood up quickly, wanting to get it over with; but when he grinned, not knowing how to say goodbye, she was so overwhelmed with guilt that she leaned forward and kissed his cheek. With a big smile, he ran off.

For a moment, watching him disappear, Deb stood quietly in the gloom.

People drifted past, like ghosts. Behind her, the sidewalk was crowded; beyond, muffled by the surf, the vendors on the *Avenida* beat their drums and whirled their wooden rattles and shouted their wares.

How could she have looked into that face and lied?

Of course she hadn't had any choice; it was *for his own good*... God! How could she think that!

She wondered if he'd really believed her? Did he really think that she'd be back here in three days? It seemed incredible. He lived by his wits, survived by knowing the score. But she'd seen his face, and he *had* believed her. But then, she thought, maybe that made sense, in its own way. He had nothing real to believe in—so, by default, he could only believe in lies and miracles.

But what was *she* to do? Her own wits—that was all she could count on. *They knew about the car.* Yes, they knew about the car; but she thought it through again, and came to the same conclusion: she didn't like it... it had been the one link to her, and she guarded it so carefully... on the other hand, it wasn't the end of the world; after all, she was revealing herself anyway. There was no reason to change her basic plan. She checked her watch. She still had over an hour.

But then she hesitated; she'd left the car in a narrow street, near the Lancaster Hotel, in *Leme*, the part of Rio where the great beaches begin. Had they found it? Would they be watching it? Now, as she started to walk, she let herself be pulled that way. After a time, the character of the crowd began to change; this was a night-time, nightlife throng, fashionable, boozy, smelling of money. For the most part, she was working against it: Leme has long passed out of fashion, and when she came up to the Lancaster and turned off the *Avenida*, she was entering Copa's red-light district, though this early in the evening the only excitement was the flicker of neon, a few desultory hookers gathering in the shadows.

The *Rua Do Conjueiro*, where she'd left her car, was only a block long. But she stopped two streets away; a side entrance into a small hotel gave her cover. From here, she could only make out the very back of the car, and only because she knew where to look. But she didn't dare go any closer; and traffic was so jammed into these sad, narrow streets that it was hard to see. She kept watch-ing. Five minutes passed. There was no sign of Boyd. She couldn't be sure—she was simply too far away—but she began to conclude that they hadn't found the car. After all, they'd only known about it for a couple of hours ... and, looking at her watch, she knew she ought to be going; it was a fair walk to the Costa Brava.

But that's when she saw him ... stepping from behind a garbage bin, walking quickly down the street—toward her in fact—and then leaning down, speaking to someone in a car. They talked quickly; they might have been arguing. An elbow protruded from the car's open window, and that reminded her of the tall man who'd met Boyd at the airport—but she couldn't really see him. Boyd pointed at his watch. But of course. He, too, had to get to the Costa Brava. For some reason, that gave her a sense of satisfac-tion, to see him following her instructions. And then she realized, as she straightened up—as she had a sense of his bulk and strength—that she loathed him, that there was some quality to him physically, a beefiness, that revolted her. He crossed the street. She didn't move. He would walk right past her, but on the other side . . . rather fussily buttoning his jacket.

Buttoning his jacket . . .

It was a hot night; here, away from the water, even hotter. All the men she'd seen were in shirtsleeves; those with jackets wore them open, or carried them looped over the shoulder. But not Boyd. His jacket was on, and now carefully done up. He had a gun. *They'd found the car and he had a gun.* And all at once she could see Charlaine, sitting in the airport. Who was Boyd? Who was he working for? He'd been able to stop Bannon's investigation of Price's murder, but within a few hours he'd been able to find her car in Rio. And he had a gun.

Fancy credentials. The kind with a colour photo and impressive initials underneath. *Except that doesn't change anything for crying out loud, you don't have any right to be surprised.*

Maybe not; but it left her shaky, as she followed him onto the *Avenida*. And even the lights and crowds, and then the classy hotels as they got to Ipanema, couldn't reassure her. Yes, she was frightened. *Don't kid yourself,* she thought. No; she couldn't afford to do that. It was all about money. *How much do these guys stand to make?* It was all about power. They'd kill her if they had to. They'd kill Giacomo. Why? In the end, just because it was convenient.

She watched him turn into the Costa Brava—there was a separate entrance for the bar.

She hesitated—took a deep breath . . . and went in, straight in, saw him looking around the room, smelled his shaving lotion—kept her stomach down at the vileness of this intimacy—and stepped right around him *as bold as brass* as her mother would have said:

"What's wrong with the table by the window?"

And marched over to it before he could move. Then sat there, watching him, as if he was some sort of fool.

"Are you going to sit down, Mr. Boyd . . . if that's what you want me to call you."

"It'll do . . . Deborah."

She shook her head. "I don't think so. I'm not sure we're on a first-name basis."

"Miss Graham, then. Or Ms. if you like."

"'Miss' is fine. I'm a real old-fashioned girl."

"My favourite kind."

"You know, I could really care less about your opinions on women. Tell me something—do you work for the CIA?"

"Is that important?"

"Why don't you just answer the question?"

"Would you believe me if I did?"

"Look, Mr. Boyd, you came here because I've got something you want. If I want you to answer a question, maybe you should." She sat very still; she had her hands in her lap—so he couldn't see them trembling.

He shrugged. "Let's say I work for an agency of the United States government. Are the initials all that important?"

A waiter hovered. This seemed to allow Boyd to regain his composure. "I think I'm going to have a beer," he said. "Antarctica?" He looked at Deb and she nodded. Now, suddenly, her mouth was too dry to speak; she turned her head so he wouldn't see her swallow. They were sitting by a window, but it was covered by filmy white curtains; behind them, lights drifted by . . . cars on the *Avenida*, a few ghostly glimmers from the pale beach. She looked back at Boyd. He was adjusting his arms on the table, as if his wrists were caught up by the cuffs of his shirt. He was that kind of man; the kind who always seems too big for his clothes, whatever he wears. Then the waiter returned with their beer, in the very large bottles you get in Brazil—600 millilitres, almost the size of a bottle of wine. Boyd stopped the waiter—poured for both of them. He leaned forward slightly, kept his voice down.

"Let's try to put this on a little more friendly basis," he said. "You've got something I want—"

"Twenty-four of them to be exact—"

"But I've got something you want. One of them—to be exact. Your boyfriend. So we're going to do a deal. Right? The important thing to remember . . . we don't want anyone getting hurt."

"Really? I was under the impression some people had already been hurt. Me, for example. I was thinking, that's where I'd seen you before—Baltimore."

"Look, I'm sorry about you, that black girl—"

"Mr. Boyd, that black girl is my friend—and it's taking all my restraint not to throw this beer into your face."

"Listen—we were trying to warn you. If you'd been smart enough—"

"Smart enough? Really. I've been smart enough to get you into that seat. But that's interesting, the warning part—how did you warn Curtis Price?"

Boyd held up a finger, a small gesture of menace. "He was getting greedy, Miss Graham. Make sure you don't."

"Funny. I sell stocks for a living. And you know what they say about the market—greed and fear. That's how it works. All Curtis Price wanted to do was make a little money."

"Not exactly. He wanted to make a *lot* of money."

"I don't believe it. You killed him because he knew about Peterson—that Danson had killed *him*—"

"Take it easy. Keep your voice down—"

"Don't tell me about my voice. If I want to scream, I'm going to scream. And if people ask me what I'm screaming about I'll show them this little vial of vaccine I've got in my pocket. And I don't believe you'll be able to cover it up."

"Okay. Relax. But what you've got in your pocket doesn't prove that anyone killed Peterson. You can't prove *anything* about what happened on that boat."

"I'm not so sure. I think that's where it starts. And I think Price found out."

"Sure—it starts with Peterson. He discovered the vaccine. On his own. He started to test it secretly . . . the idea was, he was going to quit the company, use it to set up on his own. There you have your greed—a couple of billion dollars' worth . . . let's say a buck for every Chinese, and we won't even count India. Or Pakistan. You follow?"

"Why don't you tell me something new, Mr. Boyd?"

"I don't have to. What's new about a deal? What's new about

trying to do down your partner? But it didn't quite work. Danson caught him, forced him to resign, replaced him—and maybe he did more than that. I repeat: I don't know, and neither do you. But Peterson owned stock in that company, a big piece—and who do you think got it after he died? His son. Price was buying a lot of stock, but that was just the first step. He was going to tell Peterson's son what had happened, and together move in on the company. Everything would have come unglued."

Deb didn't say anything for a moment. All this, she suspected, was true. Or true enough. It explained enough. In a funny way, it even calmed her. She *knew*. And now she knew what she knew ... She let herself take a small sip of beer. "I suppose that's where you come in. Trying to glue it all back together."

"Well, maybe we came in a little earlier. The financial side of this Danson could do on his own, but there were other issues. Technology transfers, for example. There's a lot of law around that."

"And so a U.S. government agency helped an American company break U.S. law."

"Sometimes national security can't be held hostage to a narrow view of legality."

"Really. And that's what this is? National security?"

"Look, I don't want to get in over my head. I work for a living. I don't have to justify anything. You think I'm disgusting. Fine. It's a disgusting world out there. And it's a world drowning in people. You have countries, dozens of them, whose populations are doubling every twenty years. So the water's filthy, you can't breathe the air, and millions starve. But it's not even a question of resources—long before you run out of natural resources, you run out of social resources, political resources. Society gets swamped. It can't cope, governments run out of money, people run out of will. Things break down. Destabilization—that's the fancy word. But it just means that everything falls apart. In Africa, you don't care. People starve, you see awful pictures on TV, so you send in a cheque. But some of these countries—India, China, Pakistan, the Arab countries—they've got the bomb. And they don't even have to drop it on us, just each other—think what that does to the cancer rates in

Newark and Dallas. So it's a security issue for the United States government. Or that's what they tell me. I just do as I'm told."

"My God, Mr. Boyd. You almost sound like a liberal. Are you
sure you don't work for the UN?"

"No, but I liaised six months with the border control—I know
how quick poor, desperate people can get across borders. This isn't
something for the future—it's happening now. And what Danson's
company discovered won't solve the problem, but it will help. And
if it helps, we want it out there. Whether you like it or not . . . So if
you don't mind, I'd like a turn. You say you've got those vials of
vaccine—where?"

She looked at him over the table, and as she raised her beer
with one hand, she took the thin plastic tube of vaccine out of her
pocket. "This is one of them." She put it on the table. He leaned
forward. She said: "This is strictly look, no touch." He looked up.
"If you want," she said, "I can read off the numbers."

"That's okay. I've got good eyes." He took a long slug of his beer,
draining the glass. Now, in a different way, he seemed to be all
business. "I guess you're worried about your boyfriend," he said.

"Yes. I'm worried."

"Everybody says he's a real nice man."

It was very hard, to keep her voice level, but she knew she had
to be cool. "I say so especially. Where is he?"

"São Paulo. Or near there. That foundation of his supported a
clinic, something called 'Rosalita.' There's been a lot of trouble."

"That's how you got him there?"

"Yeah. This is perfectly genuine. The people were going nuts.
They beat up some of the workers—one of them's in hospital,
might not make it."

"They were using this clinic to test the vaccine?"

"Yes. But the women began talking. At first they thought it was a
miracle, only boy babies, then they said it was the devil or voodoo
or something—a way of getting rid of all the women."

Casually, from the inside pocket of his jacket, he brought out a
photograph. "I think this was taken yesterday, maybe the day
before."

It lay there on the table. She knew, if she tried to pick it up, that her hands would shake uncontrollably. She knew, if she tried to speak, that she'd cry.

The way his head was turned . . . she had to close her eyes. One time, he'd taken her up to a cottage, a place on Georgian Bay. He'd been looking out the window, and then had turned his head, just like this, and told her to come, quickly, and she'd come and stood beside him: outside, in a tree, a great white owl was preening itself in the shade . . .

Boyd said, "I suggest we work it like this. We drive up there, now. We get him. We go to the airport in São Paulo. I've checked— Canadian Airlines flies out of there. We all go through, and before you get on the plane you give me the vaccine you've got, and tell me where the rest of it is. Simple. And like I said at the start, no one gets hurt."

She made herself drink a little beer. Then she said: "Sounds like you're trusting me, Mr. Boyd."

"I thought that might appeal to you. But I have a little insurance. You might not remember this, but when you were in Baltimore you opened an account with Merrill Lynch. You deposited a treasury bill for a hundred thousand dollars—you had it on you, you know that wonderful paper they print them on? Surely you remember. You signed the back of it—and don't kid yourself, every handwriting expert in the world will swear that signature is yours. Anyway . . . well, maybe you can guess the rest."

"You bastard."

"I don't know. We made you a lot of money, Deborah. And not in Xynex, by the way. Some little company in Alberta that claims to have a cheap way of getting oil out of the tar sands. Let me tell you, that stock ran . . . in fact, it ran so well that if anyone looked into it, they might conclude that a certain bright young lady manipulated it up, and up, and up. Are you getting the picture? I'm telling you, Miss Graham, if you ever breathe a word of this— a word—you'll be covered in shit. *Shit*. You understand?"

She leaned back. If she leaned back and looked just over Boyd's shoulder, she couldn't see the picture of Giacomo, could just keep control of her feelings. She said. "All right. It's a deal." She let her eyes, for an instant, pass over Boyd's face. "When you say 'now'—that's what you mean?"

"If you want to leave it till morning, that's all right with me."

"No. Now." Then she got up from her chair. "I'll be back in a moment."

She walked across the room; Boyd looked briefly anxious until he'd understood that she was just going to the toilet. But she had to be alone. She could feel the pressure of tears as she pushed through the door . . . and yet, inside, they wouldn't come. They couldn't. She couldn't let them. She washed her face and stared in the mirror, and thought as hard as she'd ever thought in her life. Did she believe Boyd's deal? It sounded so convincing. It was convincing right down to the final detail, the way they'd set her up. Yes, it was all so very believable. She was supposed to believe it. She was supposed to see how reasonable it was from every point of view. But she didn't believe it. She didn't believe it, in the end, because they so counted on her belief, so confidently took it for granted. Those men with their guns. Those men, finally, who couldn't possibly take the risk that she'd talk . . . *Two dead in Brazilian riot* . . . It would be so easy. Easier than Price. About as easy as Mayfair . . . *I don't believe it I don't believe a single word* . . . But she knew she had to be so very careful, that whatever chance she'd get, she'd only get one . . .

Coming out of the washroom, she managed to fix a neutral, businesslike expression on her face, sufficiently natural that Boyd smiled as she came up, even, in a half-hearted way, lifted out of his chair.

"I'm all set," she said.

He hesitated. "Maybe that's not a bad idea . . . it's a long drive."

"Around the other side of the bar."

He wasn't halfway across the room before she waved to the waiter and told him the gentleman wanted another beer. He brought it, and she paid, and when Boyd got back, she was already on her feet, the little jacket draped over her arm. "You made me so rich," she said, "I took care of the cheque."

She followed him out. "My car's up here."

Deb didn't move; she was terrified now, her legs stiff as posts. "You walked. I saw you."

"Right. But I left it here earlier—I wanted to make sure I got a spot." When she still didn't move, he said: "Stay here if you want, I'll drive it around."

But she took a step then, she was thinking, *they won't do anything till you get to São Paulo,* although she kept a half step behind him, all the nerves in her body poised to turn and run. And after that it was easy. He couldn't see her hands, under the jacket, and the car was in a short, dark street, as dark as that Baltimore night.

He came around, to open her door.

"Shit."

"What?"

"I dropped my bag."

He didn't bend down, but he looked down, and that was all she needed. As she swung, his face just began to turn *up*—so the big, heavy bottle caught him flush on the temple. It made a dull, soft sound, like the first stroke of a sledge driving a post into the ground. Boyd gasped. He staggered, his hands flailing out for the car. *Now* she started to cry, as she hit him again, and the bottle smashed, and she threw herself against him, in a strange, desperate embrace. And found his gun, in the small of his back.

He didn't quite go down, ever.

She stepped back, cocking his pistol, though her arm was trembling.

She was panting, scarcely able to breathe through her tears. "You heard it cock," she said, "now all I do is squeeze down on the trigger."

In fact, he probably didn't quite take this in—he was too stunned, there was blood all over his face.

But finally he said, "You little bitch," in an almost neutral tone, as though this was merely an observation.

Deb nodded. "That's right," she said. She was thinking of Charlaine. "From now on, you better bear that in mind. Get in the car."

CHAPTER SIXTEEN

*O*n the outskirts of São Paulo, Deb started to see them, all these beautiful, wonderful children—and, very calmly, she thought, *If Giacomo's dead, you're going to have this baby.*

But he wasn't dead. She made that as a promise to herself. And looked at the children.

They were all colours, gold to copper, obsidian to ivory, sand, bark and loam, and their faces were as bright as pebbles in a stream—which was literally true, for it had rained all night on the road from Rio so now the whole world was wet and shining. The small chests of the boys glistened as if they'd come out of the sea, and the hair of the girls streamed glassy smooth. Looking up, their eyes were filled with a friendly, eager incomprehension—did they speak less English here?—but finally Deb found a young girl who understood. She could have been Renato's sister; ten or eleven; gawky; a white T-shirt was plastered to her narrow chest, but her hips, under a long cotton skirt, had a saucy, jaunty tilt.

"Yes," she said, "I know where the Rosalita Clinic is."

"Could you take me there? Show me?"

"Take you?"

"Yes. Come with me, in the car." Deb held up some money. "I'd give you this much—five American dollars."

"But you are a woman."

Of course—as Renato might have said—she knew the difference between the sexes, and so found the money and the car understandable enough, but not with a woman. She was, at least, that innocent. Deb said, "I just want you to take me the clinic. That's all. Do you understand?" She leaned across, and opened the passenger door, and pushed it open. For a moment longer, the girl looked dubious but then she went around the front of the car and climbed in. "You're sure you know where it is?" asked Deb.

"Yes. The women say it puts the devil in their babies."

"What do you mean?"

She shrugged. "The devil . . . you know, the devil."

"When they're born, you mean . . . ? There's something wrong with them?"

"No. Not like that, I don't think . . . They think there's magic there." As she said this, the girl was turning her head, noticing Boyd in the back seat. He was under a blanket.

Deb said, "You see, he's sick. He needs to go to the clinic."

"A man?"

"Yes."

"I don't want—"

"No. Absolutely not. Just show me the way to the clinic. Here's five dollars. And when we get there, I'll give you five more. All right?"

When the girl didn't say anything, Deb leaned across her and pulled the door shut. She started up, and as they pulled back onto the highway, Deb asked the girl what her name was. She smiled; she was pleased to be asked. "Vera," she said.

Vera. A pretty name. It sounded old-fashioned—but maybe that's how they named their little girls in Brazil. Deb leaned back; she was exhausted. The drive—which should have taken five or six hours—had been a nightmare. Almost as soon as they were clear of Rio, it had started to rain; then the rain became torrential, something truly tropical and terrifying. The highway was jammed with trucks and buses; half the time, they could have been driving through a waterfall. And on top of all this, she'd had Boyd to deal with . . .

To begin with, this hadn't seemed much of a problem—less of a problem than shooting him, however great a temptation that might be—and he was potentially a bargaining chip, exchangeable for Giacomo. And everything had started well enough.

In Rio, he'd been stunned, wobbly, but he never lost consciousness, and she'd made him drive—the gun, pointed at his ribs, seemed to help his concentration. But the second time she'd hit him, he'd been cut, and by the time they reached the outskirts, they'd gone through the box of Kleenex in the car and he was sufficiently a mess that she was afraid someone might notice. So she made him pull over and gave him her jacket to clean himself up with—there was nothing else. They went on; the rain began—it began to come down very hard. And then, an hour out, he said that he felt sick, he was going to throw up; at first she hadn't believed him, but his face had turned deathly white and he began to sweat—she was afraid he was going to lose consciousness, and when he pulled over, she didn't try to stop him. He just got the door open before he vomited. And that effort was apparently the end of his strength; he went down to his knees beside the car, gasping and gagging. She'd had a desperate minute then. It was obvious he couldn't drive; he was just able to get himself into the back seat—she actually had to take the risk of helping him, pushing him in. And then he didn't move.

When she'd found a set of booster cables in the truck, and began to tie his legs, he didn't resist her, in fact he probably passed out—after she tied his arms behind him, she felt his pulse. It was light, racing; his breath was quick and shallow. She waited about ten minutes, afraid that he'd be sick again and suffocate himself, but his eyes opened, and his face looked better. She drove on. And in some ways, this was actually easier; there was no way he could free himself quickly enough to make a move on her, so with the gun up on the dash in front of her, she drove into the incredible night, the rain and the spray making a ceaseless inundation. She

294 • ANTHONY HYDE

only stopped once, at a big truck stop. She had coffee, bought a blanket—Boyd was starting to shiver; and then went on. As a weak, watery dawn rose around her, she sensed a change in Boyd's breathing, and realized that he'd actually fallen asleep.

But that had been hours ago; now, with the little girl beside her, Deb checked her watch and realized it was almost eleven o'clock in the morning.

The rain, at least for the moment, had stopped. But the sky was grey, ugly; the Brazilian sun, moving toward noon, gave the atmosphere a livid cast. Water lay in pools everywhere. Her car, every car, was splattered with mud, and she looked out at the city through half moons of greasy clarity.

Or she supposed this was São Paulo.

As she drove on, it was hard to know. She'd left the highway miles back, but perhaps she hadn't actually entered the city yet. In any case, already, it exhausted her. There was nothing to do but keep driving. The streets were jammed; the smell of diesel cut like acid in her throat. Of course she was lost—but in this place, she wasn't even sure what it meant to find your way.

"You're sure you know where you're going?"

"There. Up there." Vera pointed.

The city was vast but seemed to lack definition. There were no rivers or mountains or bays, or much discernible landscape; it wasn't a city, so much as a populated accretion, spreading and rising, like an anthill. At one point, before she'd thought about asking her way from the children, she'd stopped and bought a map, but it was useless; it was impossible to follow. She managed to pick out a street sign, so maybe . . . but in fact she had no idea where she was. Her only clue about the clinic was the obvious one, that it would be in a slum; and actually, even if she didn't know it, that was a piece of luck. São Paulo is well-supplied with slums, but the greatest—not *favelas* here, but *cortiços*—crouch around the city, forming its principal suburbs. They are a world in themselves; in the last hundred years, São Paulo has grown from about seventy thousand people to seventeen million, and today about five million of those live in the tin and cardboard hovels of these dark hills and valleys

. . . a population about double the size of Chicago, and which boasts thousand of miles of open sewers, and hundreds of thousands of abandoned children.

"Are you sure this is the way?" she asked Vera again, after a time.

"Oh yes." She considered a moment. "You could go more quickly in a different way, but not with a car, only if you are walking."

"Okay," said Deb, "I understand. But you've been there—to see the doctor?"

She shook her head. And when she didn't offer anything else, Deb said, "Do you believe the stories about the devil?"

She puckered up her lips and frowned, which seemed to indicate skepticism—but before she said anything, she pointed out the window and said, "All of those people are going," and then she actually waved at someone, and began mugging at the window.

It was true: there was a vaguely purposeful trickle of people winding down the street ahead of them.

"They're going to the clinic?" Deb said.

Vera nodded. "But we will be there first . . . of them."

I'll exchange Boyd, she thought. Of all the possible plans, this was the one that had now taken clearest shape. She had Boyd, she had his gun. *I want Giacomo, but then I won't make any trouble.* She'd make them believe her . . . She glanced into the back seat. He'd come around a couple of times, and moaned; but he hadn't actually spoken. Still, she thought, he wouldn't need much convincing.

With greater concentration, Deb looked out the window. And now, at least, she *was* somewhere; or she had that impression. Or perhaps she was just getting used to things, so that this strange, jumbled agglomeration of structures had a certain coherence. The streets were narrowing. There seemed to be more of them—a ceaseless branching and dividing, without apparent pattern, but which nonetheless drew you on. Hovels rose out of the mud, and collapsed into the mud. They were made of wood and cardboard, and cast-off pieces of metal and plastic, although most had metal roofs, sheets of corrugated steel, or flattened oil drums, or stolen road markers: an acknowledgement of the power of the rain, Deb decided.

"Not far now," said Vera. "It's good. I don't have to climb up the hill!"

Deb drove carefully on these wet, slippery streets. This was worse than Baltimore—there was a connection, but this was worse. Everything was patched. Each piece was laid over another. Everything seem jammed together. These buildings, this whole neighbourhood, were intricate structures of inertia. Something nudged at her mind, and then she recalled what it was, images of the Great War, the trenches, the mud-covered men and the rats, with rain-sodden skies overhead. Here, actually, there was a little more colour; bright swatches of advertising were built into the hovels, many of the people in the streets wore clothes advertising Coke and Nike and Fuji and other great names. And there were many children. They played in the gutters. They played with garbage. In the jog of a fence, a slight suggestion of privacy, a little girl squatted, and urinated, then ran away. A baby, left in the mud, was crying. But other children played in the mud, and seemed happy. The streets were running with mud, and now Deb realized she was climbing, there was in fact a topography to this misery: a hill to ascend, as Vera had said. This became quite steep. Her wheels slipped, and she felt her stomach tense—*to be trapped here.* That was the fear.

"Is there no other way?"

"I think so," said Vera, "but this is the way I know."

The wheels caught, finally; twisting the steering wheel, she straightened around. Leaning forward, she peered through the window. What would it be like to live here? To be born here? Faces passed, beyond the window. Ultimately, their expressions were all the same. Under the exhausted, sad face of an old man—anger. His one life: he'd lived it here. A younger man raised his eyes, his expression roused from a listless vacancy by something that Deb couldn't see—now they looked wary; then sullen; then fierce . . . with anger. His one life: he would live it here. Young women, as they walked, were alive in their hips and their breasts; the old women moved like zombies . . . The living dead—was that part of the religion? Voodoo. No: *candomblé* . . . that's what you called it.

But you could certainly believe anything here, or nothing; one thing was as good as another.

In fact, ahead of her, the crowd was something like a religious procession. They ambled along, snaking back and forth over the road, only reluctantly letting Deb's car pass through; and she was fearful, somehow, about blowing the horn . . . although there was no direct act or even look of hostility. And up ahead, a truck *was* honking, a man leaning out the window and shouting at the people around him. Reluctantly, Deb came to a full stop. She set the parking brake, couldn't quite lift her foot from the gas. *Don't get stuck.*

But she tried to relax. She twisted around, to look at Boyd, then reached down, pulling the blanket back. His eyes looked angrily up at her.

"We're almost there," she said.

He seemed to shrug.

"Boyd? Can you hear me? *You better hope he's alive.*"

He made a sound, some sort of grunt.

"That's the deal, you see. You for him . . . do you understand that? And if he's not alive—"

She thought she could make out, "He's alive," and she pulled the blanket over him again and said to Vera: "Is this where you live?"

The girl shrugged, wiggling in her seat, and didn't answer. Maybe the question made no sense. Did you have an "address" in a place like this? Another war image came into her mind, pictures of the blitz in London, or the war in Sarajevo, whole sides of apartments peeled off so you could look in, like a doll's house. In a funny sense, it was all the same—and all at once she felt very fearful, claustrophobic, shut into the little car, encased in mud, lost in this dark, filthy place with all the people around. She closed her eyes. Hurry up, she thought. *Please.* And after a moment, when she opened her eyes again, the crowd did start to move, slowly, still climbing the hill.

She looked in her rear-view mirror; faces, bodies pressed in.

The car, she realized, was surrounded by people and she stiffened in her seat and must have spun the wheels and splattered people, because now they began to bang on the roof, and some bent down to the window, looking in at her. She stared straight ahead. The car inched forward. They were still climbing, even more steeply, which added to the impression that this column, huge now, had some religious goal; they seemed to be ascending in that way. And as they neared the crest of the hill, the angle of the car let her see the sky, which had broken up a little, the over-cast swirling into black bulges of cloud shot through with pale rays of sunshine, as if she was climbing into the background of some lurid religious painting. People were shouting, too. Everyone was making noise. Some banged on metal cans, or shook them on poles over their heads. Others simply hit sticks together, or whooped, and just before the top, when the car began slipping in the mud, one whole section of the mob descended on the car and pushed, heaving her up. Then they all cheered and shouted as the wheels caught, and this time, as the mud splashed them, they seemed to take it as a wonderful joke, laughing, yelling and point-ing. Vera, sitting right up in her seat, clapped her hands together; and then the car ran on, and they could see down, into a valley.

For just a second, oddly enough, Deb felt reassured.

Perhaps it was simply because she'd finally arrived; she wasn't lost—she wouldn't be stuck someplace, out of gas. Her body relaxed—and she realized she'd been straining, pressing forward to keep the car going. She slumped back. *All you have to do is let out the clutch* . . . even if there wasn't a clutch.

But then she wasn't so sure.

For one thing, even with her foot on the brake, the car slipped forward, slewing. The way down, she realized, was even steeper than the road up, and the whole steep side of the hill was covered with people. For a moment—the crowd was so dense—she couldn't see where they were going. All she could make out, at the bottom of the ravine, was a railway line, apparently abandoned, because two rusting boxcars were knocked over on their sides and the track itself ended in a low, wide mound of garbage which then rose up into a higher plateau . . . it was a dump of some kind. Gulls circled above it, hundreds of them. The dump blocked the ravine at the end. The far side—opposite her—was a high, deep cut, with the raw, red earth hollowed away near the top—too steep to build on.

But on this side, the hovels continued, slumping down the muddy hill, washed over now by the huge crowd. The car, slipping, pushed into the people. Now Deb blew the horn, but the noise was so great no one could have heard, and faces turned back angrily toward her. Deb yelled, "Stop!" She was screaming at the car. "Stop!" And then it did stop, with a soft, sticky lurch. "Oh, God," Deb said.

"*There* is the clinic!" Vera called, pointing.

"Where?"

"There!"

She peered out through the filthy windshield and could see it through the crowd. It was near the tracks, a low, squat building, but more solid in its outline than the shacks and hovels—it was made of cement blocks, painted a dark, runny green.

It took a moment to grasp what she was seeing—that the clinic was surrounded by a huge mob, a vast horde. The people they'd been climbing the hill with were stragglers, the tail end of a greater mass of humanity that had already arrived. They surged around the building. And then one clump of this mob disengaged itself, and she realized what they were doing, rolling a car over on its side... it went over and everyone cheered. A lot of people leapt up and down, and then a kid with a bucket ran up and threw it over the car. Then a stab of red flame flickered up, and they cheered again. People pressed around the burning car. They were carrying signs, posters held up on sticks, emblems Deb didn't recognize. People were throwing bottles and rocks at the clinic. Everyone was yelling. The noise was deafening. And people began to bang the top of her car again, although they didn't seem angry, it seemed just a way to join in the noise-making. She let the car roll forward, and she made herself touch the gas, but then the back end began to move again... she closed her eyes and got it to stop.

And then Vera opened the door and fled, without even asking for her second five dollars. At the same moment—the movement of the crowd, like the shutters of a thousand cameras opening in a particular order, allowed her to see this—she realized that many of the people closest to the clinic were children. It was as if they'd been pushed up to the front.

She was shaking. Trying to turn, her seat belt grabbed her;

angrily, she pulled it apart. Then she leaned down behind her. Boyd, still stretched across the back seat, was terrified. His eyes were wide and staring. "Do you know what this is? *Do you know what this is?*"

He tried to pull himself upright, but fell back. "You stupid little bitch," he gasped.

"Boyd, what's going on?"

The car rocked as people banged the roof, and Boyd's face turned red as he shouted, "I told you. There's been a lot of trouble here."

"*They're trying to burn the clinic!*"

"Oh Christ ... Look, you've got to untie me."

"You said there was some sort of trouble—"

"Yes, you stupid—"

"Shut up. *Do you know what they're saying?*" Accidentally, her arm bumped the wiper stalk, and the wipers came on. The car was rocking. A black face stared in the window, mouthing words; and then a hand grabbed at the wipers, and ripped one off.

"I'm not sure ... something about the clinic being ... a whorehouse of the devil. For Christ's sakes, untie me. Can you turn around?

"We're not turning around—listen ..." She leaned over, into the back seat, and undid his legs.

"The rest of it!"

"No way—tell me what they mean—"

"They worked it out—they realized some sort of experiment was going on. I think we have the local priest to thank for that ... he was suspicious ... he thought they were doing abortions, which they weren't, but he began to figure things out—one of the local people who work there showed him some of the records, and if you work backwards, of course, you could get a rough idea what was going on."

"Where's Giacomo?"

"Down there, or at least he should be. He knew the priest ... some of the community leaders, I think they call them. He was supposed to work it out ... and then, once we had him there, it seemed very convenient. He figured out what was going on fast enough, but there was nothing he could do about. And he gave us insurance . . ."

"Because of me?"

"You couldn't talk as long as we had him—you had to do a deal."

Deb closed her eyes; she knew, now especially, she had to hang on—she couldn't lose her cool for a moment. "So somebody's with him . . . guarding him?"

"I don't know. There should be. The Indian left yesterday—he cleaned out the records, there was some vaccine . . . There should be another agent there, Carter. *Look, you've got to get turned around.*"

Carter. An agent. Well, he'd let something slip, after all . . . For the rest, she didn't bother to answer; turning around was ridiculous; they were surrounded by people, and the car had virtually no traction. She peered through the muddy windshield. This high on the slope, she could still see the clinic, although the crowd around it was huge, had almost engulfed it. The car they'd set alight still flickered and smoked; people were throwing things. Yet there was a kind of hesitation, a tentativeness, as if they didn't quite have the nerve to go further. They surged closer—but held back. At the same time, it was apparent that soon enough someone *would* dare . . .

She had to get down there.

She'd come so far . . .

Part of her wanted to get out of the car and run, run down and find him . . .

No.

She'd never get through that mob—a mob that was on the edge of turning murderous.

Boyd shouted something. She didn't even glance behind her. *Now.* She touched the gas, and the car slipped ahead. She pressed the horn, flattened the heel of her hand against it. She picked up speed. The car skidded forward, and people had to jump out of the way. Behind her, Boyd was yelling; he was sitting up, but with his hands tied behind his back, he could only lunge at her with his head. She screamed at him to get away. People leapt to the side, and a woman hit out at the car with a stick, which flew out of her hand and away. Ahead, people ran, looking behind them as she careered down the slope—and then a rock hit the windshield, and something big jolted against the passenger door. As they pulled back, some of the people turned and threw rocks at the car, or sticks, so she was running a gauntlet, and as the way opened she could see a boy with a burning bottle of gasoline run forward and launch it at the clinic. *He* dared: he would live his life here, but he dared. And then a second hit, and a third, until flames washed across the front of the building, the yellow flames turning the green building black. And then more flames leapt up from behind the building, and the roof began burning. Deb clung to the wheel of the car, trying to keep it on the road, but she could see that someone was trying to come out of the clinic—except, as the door opened, a dozen rocks hit it, and the door shut again. Yet no one could stay inside. Smoke was pouring out of the windows, and pressing heavily down from the roof, and as she braked hard and slewed in the mud, the door swung open again—then shut as a flaming bottle of gasoline hit, spreading a curtain flame across the cement apron in front of the building.

She stopped in an open spot, near the burning car—the wind had blown the smoke in this direction, driving the people off, but had now shifted so the area was clear.

It was a small chance. A clearing. An opening. And either the two men inside saw this, or it was purely fortuitous that they now opened the door a third time.

For an instant, two figures stood in the doorway, ghostly behind the flames that flickered around them. But now they had no choice. Behind them, the building was burning; a thick, heavy, black smoke blew down from the roof. They gathered themselves. They took three steps, and jumped, and then dashed forward, ducking down, and just as Deb saw him, *yes, it was Giacomo,* a rock hit him in the head, and he went down, skidding down in the mud. She was yelling then, leaning across to get the door open, and he somehow got up, his momentum carried him up, and he slammed into the side of the car. And then another man appeared, hitting the car full on, and going down, almost sliding beneath it. Deb jerked the door open, and they both swung themselves in, and Giacomo shouted, "Drive! Go! Go!"

But there was, in fact, nowhere to go.

As the crowd rushed at the car, Deb accelerated down the last few metres of the road in front of the clinic, and then the road ran out and the car bumped over the tracks—then hit the sea of mud and garbage that spread out thickly, like lava, in front of the dump.

The wheels spun, then sank—the car stalled.

Giacomo said, "Okay, get out." Blood was pouring down the side of his face. He said it again: "Get out."

They got out. Deb was gasping, suddenly remembering, "Boyd's in the back. *He's in the back!*"

But he wasn't; somehow, he'd pushed himself out. But his hands were still bound. Giacomo saw him and yelled at the other man, "Carter, get him loose."

In front of them, the garbage was as high as a mountain, with the white gulls wheeling over it, lifting in the rising wind, and looking down.

Giacomo took her arm . . . and then he held her, squeezed her tight. "I never thought I'd see you again—"

She pressed herself even closer into his arms. "If they'd hurt you—" But then she drew back; his face was covered in blood.

But he said, "I'm all right."

"Who is he—"

She meant Carter, who was now struggling to get Boyd free. "There were three of them. He's the last. They were holding me and Father Gonzales . . ." But even as he said this, he was looking around. "No," he said, "we'll never make it up there."

The clinic was now blazing, and an odd, black column of smoke—tulip-shaped—rose up from it. The excitement of this spectacle had given them a moment's respite, for most of the people were watching it, and only a trickle as yet had moved down toward the railroad tracks. Many of these were children. They seemed uncertain. They stopped, and looked toward the people standing by the car. Overhead, the gulls screamed and Deb had to steady herself against a hard gust of wind. But then the crowd turned.

"We have to go across," said Giacomo, "over there."

Yet Deb didn't move, nor did any of them; they regarded the crowd. Men, women, the children. They were together, all massed together; yet they didn't quite keep together, as if some inward pressure was pushing them constantly apart—as if, at any second, they might break into smaller throngs which would attack one another.

Boyd looked at Deb. "You stupid bitch."

Carter said, "You okay?"

"No, I'm not fucking okay."

Giacomo had already grabbed Deb's arm. "Come on," he said. "Don't run—not yet. But as fast as you can."

So they got ahead of Carter and Boyd. Deb looked up; in front of them, the far side of the valley or ravine loomed up, like a wave . . . literally, for the ground was actually hollowed away, under the top. Presumably it had been cut like that when they'd built the railroad. They hurried on, but did not quite run. Then Deb saw Giacomo look back, and he said, "Hurry," but she didn't look back, she couldn't bear to, and then he said, "Okay, just run a few steps, hurry, hurry . . ."

She did look back then. The crowd, having gathered itself, was over the tracks, pushing toward them, a great mob of children in front, running so fast, some of them, that they fell; but they all got up, scrambling, slithering across the slick ground. The ground was very wet. Water lay in pools. The mud sucked down with each step Deb took, it was hard to run, and then even harder, for now the ground sloped up. She bent forward. She was climbing now. She kept sliding back, and began to lose her breath. Giacomo caught her arm again. "Okay," he said, "just a second. Don't worry. We're going to be okay."

They both straightened up, looking back.

Carter and Boyd were still behind them, but closer now. About twenty children, older than the rest, had broken away, running ahead toward them. They were definitely older, taller, gangly; Deb could see the dark, intense expression of their eyes, but it was impossible to know what they were seeing. They were quite silent. Everyone else was yelling and screaming, but they were silent. One of them threw a stone at Carter and Boyd, but it landed in front of them. And then, behind, the crowd surged forward—yet, oddly, almost away from them, toward one of the derelict boxcars, as if something had attracted its attention there.

"Carter's got a gun," Giacomo said, as he tried to catch his breath.

Deb could see that Carter was holding a gun at his side.

"I've got Boyd's gun," Deb said. "Are you okay? You're bleeding."

"I'm okay. Come on."

Deb looked up. It was a high, steep slope, all red slippery mud except for the one huge rock closer to the top. Looking up, all she could see above the ravine was the dark sky and the circling, screaming gulls. And then, blown by the rising wind, a piece of plastic from the dump—the wind whipped it away. She began to climb again, reaching up to take Giacomo's hand when it was very steep. There was a huge, low sound; glancing over her shoulder, she could see that the mob had turned away from the boxcars, had seen them again.

"Hurry," Giacomo panted. "They can't all climb up here."

But already the leading edge of the mob, mainly children, were at the bottom of the slope, starting to climb. And they were as quick as monkeys. They scrambled up, on all fours.

"Oh, God," said Deb.

They were very close to Boyd. Clearly, he didn't have much strength. His arms flailed as he tried to pull himself up, clawing at the ground with his hands. But the ground was so slippery he made little progress.

A stone hit him in the back.

He turned around. He stood up quite straight, but was weaving, tottering. The children were pelting him with rocks; the rocks hit him, and bounced away. He put up one hand, trying to keep the rocks away, but then he reached behind him with his other hand . . . and Deb thought, *I have his gun.* But he was reaching for his wallet, in fact; he pulled it out, and shook it, scattering money in the wind. The children leapt up, jumping to catch the money, then scrambled for the bills as they fell. For a moment, Boyd was free. He managed to struggle a little higher up the slope. He gained a few yards, and as the children, some now clutching his money in their hands, came after him again, he threw out the change from his pockets and gained a little more. But he was too weak. The great churning mob of children were too close. Now they were all around him, shrieking and yelling, pulling at Boyd, hitting at him with their sticks. He fell. Deb thought of boys fighting in the schoolyard at recess. Carter, a little further on, saw what was happening and fired his gun in the air; but with the shrieking of the mob, and the wind, the shot was barely audible. And it was too late in any case. For the children were all around Boyd, jumping on him, pounding at him with sticks and rocks—jumping in and hitting, then leaping back. They were all over him, and then they began dragging him by the arm, and with his arm stretched out like that, one of the children chopped at him with a piece of metal and blood spurted up. They tugged harder at his arm, and chopped at it, and Deb knew—

She turned away. As she turned, as she started to close her eyes not to see the horror of what they were doing to Boyd, she saw Carter with his gun in the air.

But he didn't fire.

He must, then, have realized the perilousness of his own situation.

He was only fifteen or twenty metres higher up the slope than Boyd, and by now the whole mob was much closer. Most of them, the nearest, were still children, but it wasn't just a question of the smaller, advance group; there were dozens and dozens of them, wild and frenzied. Carter had his gun, but there were just too many. Moreover, they were circling around him; some were as high up the slope as he was, off to one side—it must have been easier to climb there. Carter had seen them, too, as he looked around, and now he stopped, turning this way and that. It was obvious that they would soon surround him. Below, Boyd's body, abandoned, was a lump the mud. Deborah watched. Carter, turning, levelled the gun in his hand. But the children kept coming. They knew a simple truth, *he can't shoot all of us at once.*

"Giacomo, he's going to shoot those kids."

"Deb—come here. Hurry!"

She climbed up, and then he pulled her up beside him. "Over here," he said. He tugged her along. There was a faint path, a track; it wound up the side of the slope, and it was a little easier to climb because stones had been ground down into the mud. She climbed, following Giacomo, and then they were under the big rock that jutted right up over the edge of the ravine.

And then she heard a shot.

Beyond the gasping of her lungs, and the beating of her heart— on the other side of the hardening wind—it was a wispy little sound. But she turned around.

Carter had shot one of the children.

Deb felt herself stiffen; it was as if her whole body had turned to stone. Her eyes glanced around wildly—and then found the body of a little boy, who was lying face down in the mud. He was wearing sneakers, but no socks; his body had twisted as he'd fallen, his T-shirt had pulled up; she could see his bare stomach. It was shiny, round; a dark honey colour. She could see his belly button. She looked up. The crowd was rushing forward, their faces now upturned to the hillside, their fists raised in the air, shouting out words that must have had meaning, a meaning that they must have understood, but which sounded tortured, incomprehensible, like the sounds of the dumb or the mad. Beyond, a few stragglers came over the railroad tracks; beyond that, on the far hillside, the clinic was burning bright with flames.

Carter shot another one of the children.

Why had he shot that *one?*

Giacomo said, "Deb, get down . . . get down on the ground."

"Giacomo, he's going to kill them all."

He pulled her down.

One of the children, an older boy—higher up on the hillside— charged toward Carter. Turning, Carter shot him, and the boy fell, tumbling and sliding down through the mud, reaching out to stop himself, but then his arms stopped reaching, and he was just sliding.

He was going to kill them all.

He was going to kill them all . . .

This was impossible; Carter simply didn't have enough bullets for his gun. But that was the thought in Deb's mind, that's why she now had Boyd's gun in her hand. Except her hand was shaking; her whole body was shaking.

"Okay," said Giacomo. "It's okay."

He had to pry her fingers off the gun, and he held her against him as he aimed—a way of steadying himself on the slope. His first shot missed, and Carter hardly reacted: he was too terrified of the children closing in on him. *He* knew he couldn't shoot them all. Turning slowly, his face stricken, he perhaps didn't quite understand. His gun was at his side as Giacomo fired a second time, and missed again, and by the time he started to aim his own gun, Giacomo's third shot struck him full in the chest. And perhaps he was lucky; he went straight over on his back, as the children came closer.

And now the crowd surged forward—no one in the middle of such a great mass of people could have known what had happened; they were merely carrying on, the energy that drove them far from exhausted. And then the children, split now into packs—they divided as they approached each of the bodies—began climbing higher up the slope, and any hope that killing Carter would provide a saving grace was erased by the savagery Giacomo and Deb could see on their faces.

Deb said, "Oh, God, I'm too tired."

"No, you're not," Giacomo said.

The mob came on . . .

The children climbed higher . . .

But now everything changed.

It was extraordinary.

Rain began falling . . . rain—

There was something odd about it. The first drops in fact had begun to fall as Giacomo had fired his second shot at Carter; it was as if, finally, the heavens were acknowledging what was happening below. But this was so reluctant, so little interested . . . a few drops, a pattering . . . big drops, but so few that Deb and Giacomo could hear them falling, one by one, around them.

One raindrop hit Deb on the nose.

She looked up, squinting; but it was as if the sky was out of practice, had somehow forgotten exactly what you did with rain . . . there was just those few drops.

But then there were a few drops more.

There was a moment long enough to catch a breath—and then came the deluge.

Only in the tropics does rain fall as hugely as this. It was an inundation. *This* stopped the crowed, or at least slowed it down—for one thing, it was something that they could all experience at once, and understand.

Rain.

Deb, at once, was soaked through. To her skin. Her clothes clung like Saran Wrap, her shoes filled with water. It was deafening, the force of it, falling; and then the heavy hard splash of the drops onto the mud.

She looked out, across the valley, but the valley was invisible behind these great curtains of water—even the flames of the clinic were lost.

Nearer, though, she could see the children. The ones who were climbing the slope, bent forward with the effort, straightened themselves; the others stopped dead in their tracks. In a second, the rain washed them clean, they glistened with a silvery light, and they looked around, as if bewildered, as if not sure what they were doing here. They looked at each other. And then one small boy put his hands over his head, palms up, and jumped up as if he could catch the rain, and whooped. Another little boy took up his call, and a girl lifted her skirt in front of her, catching the rain, and then spun, showering it all around her. And another boy ran up the slope as far as he could go in a single dash, and as he started to slip back, he turned, and came down on the slick mud on his bottom. A girl did it. Most of the girls were wearing long skirts and they reached down, holding them taut, so they were almost like toboggans, and then the boys began sliding on the pieces of tin they'd been banging, and still others began pelting each other with mud pies. They went crazy in the rain, and what was remarkable to Deb was the transformation in their faces, how suddenly bright and happy they looked. Was that Vera? She wasn't sure. And then Giacomo touched her arm, and they started climbing, ignored by the children, invisible to the greater mass of the mob. They climbed higher. They were still beneath the huge rock, and Deb could see that this path reached the top through a gap beside it. They were going to make it, she thought. She felt like crying, she thought, I *will* cry. With a rush of hope and energy, she climbed more quickly—until Giacomo reached out, grabbed her, and held her against him.

He was looking up.

He was looking straight up into the driving rain, this rain that was falling after a day and a night of virtually continuous rain.

He looked up because, above them, the face of the ravine was giving way.

It was very quick. A section slipped, right down, like someone whose feet have gone out from under him. Below, as it slid, more mud broke loose. And then, higher up, a huge section—from the very top of the ravine—came down with such a great roar that it overcame even the pounding of the rain. Then more of the face came away. There'd been so much rain—the ground was already so saturated—that now the mud dissolved, was suddenly no more than a thick solution of water. It all began sliding. Deb gasped; a long tongue of mud arced toward her, struck her like a whip, knocked her down to her knees. Shelves of earth and mud pulled away all around them and only the huge rock protected them . . . but it didn't save the children. Most, at least, must hardly have known what had happened. The great sea of mud swept down on them and over them so quickly—Deb saw two little boys with their hands up, trying to hold the great avalanche back, but in a second they were lost. They were all gone. There was nothing there but a tumbled, churned-up sea of mud.

For a minute, neither moved.

The rain kept falling, and the gulls screamed against it, but there was also a vast, cavernous silence.

"Deb?" Giacomo squeezed her arm. "We're going straight up. *Up.* You understand?" He held her against him. "Okay?"

"Okay," she said.

VENICE

Perhaps the best line of approach to this historical phenomenon may be found by turning our attention to a visual experience, stressing one aspect of our epoch which is plain to our very eyes. This fact is quite simple to enunciate, though not so to analyze. I shall call it the fact of agglomeration, of 'plenitude.' Towns are full of people, houses full of tenants, hotels full of guests, trains full of travellers, cafés full of customers, parks full of promenaders, consulting-rooms of famous doctors full of patients, theatres full of spectators, and beaches full of bathers. What previously was, in general, no problem, now begins to be an everyday one, namely, to find room . . . That is all. Can there be any fact simpler, more patent, more constant in actual life?

—José Ortega y Gasset,
The Revolt of the Masses

*O*n *their fourth night in* Venice, Deb decided about her baby.

Venice seemed the logical choice ...

For two hours, on the plane out of São Paulo, Deb had held Giacomo's hand. It was perfectly restful—there were none of those little twitches she sometimes felt, holding someone's hand, and she'd fallen asleep. When she woke up, he was turned in his seat, sleeping. Deb knew that normally he would have turned the other way; but he wanted to keep her hand in his, and he wanted to be able to see her. When he opened his eyes, she murmured, "Scotty—beam me up."

Giacomo smiled. "Where?"

"Venice, I think."

"Really."

"Why not?"

It was where they'd found each other; there was an unspoken need to start over. Besides, there's nothing more convenient than a town without cars.

But of course it was more complicated than that. Orme Capital, for one thing, had to be paid its dues . . . though this was so easy that Deb wondered if something hadn't been whispered into the Great Orme's ear. There was a distinctly chivalrous undercurrent; he came around from his desk, helped her into her chair, almost as if he knew about her *condition*. She'd been through so much, and she was a woman after all . . . take as much time as you need. Rosie can steal all your clients, heh-heh . . . He was, Deb thought, one of the great assholes of the Western world, but so what—she wasn't going to argue.

Giacomo, when she suggested Venice again, played hard to get. "It's crazy. We should just take a week at your parents' cottage."

"But I don't want to spend a week at my parents' cottage. I want to go to Nice. Then Venice."

"You're serious?"

"Yes. Besides, I paid off my Amex bill . . . and that funny little Indonesian gold mine I bought is really starting to move."

Giacomo was right, of course, it *was* crazy, all that time on airplanes, but the moment they arrived in Nice, she knew she'd done the right thing. She had to be alone with him. It was like Monty Python. *Now for something completely different* . . . Although, in point of fact, the first thing they did was the same old thing, make love, exhausted or not. Afterwards, Giacomo said:

"You know, you can't put it off forever."

Deb, though, was still evading. She said, "Last night, I realized. I didn't think of it as 'it.' It's a boy. I realized—that's what I'm assuming."

"Why?"

"I think it's only natural, really."

Giacomo put his finger in her belly button. "Whenever I hear the word 'natural,' I always prick up my ears. You're going to hear someone's favourite, secret—probably irrational—assumptions."

"I don't think it's irrational. You made me pregnant. No matter what they say, the male is active in a particular way. So thinking the baby's a boy is just an extension of that." He looked amused.

"As long as you don't say that in public, I think we're all right." Deb laughed, and he added: "Tell me honestly, would you prefer a boy to a girl?"

They'd been trying not to think about everything that had happened; for the moment, neither of them wanted to talk about it. But now Deb said, "I don't know. Maybe I should have ten girls."

"The girl part is fine, but forget the ten."

And they didn't talk about it any more.

But the next day, still in Nice, something interesting happened.

It was morning; they were walking along the *Promenade des Anglais* when Giacomo became quite sure someone was following them. They went into a café, had a coffee, left . . . and Giacomo said, "See . . . there he is again."

A man, in a tan suit, vaguely familiar—like an actor you've seen a thousand times in bit parts, but whose name you never remember. He didn't do anything, but it was a sign that someone was watching; and not the first. Charlaine had had some strange visitors . . . but she still had the vaccine. At the same time—they'd agreed—there was no way to stop what had already happened; all they could do was wait for Xynex, in one form or another, to surface again. Meanwhile, they decided to play it safe, and Deb worked out a way to donate the money—the money Boyd was going to use to set her up—to Charlaine's clinic. She was trying to say, "If you don't make trouble, we won't either." It seemed to work. And the man in Nice never appeared again.

"You're not worried?" Giacomo asked her.

She shook her head. "Only a little."

The drive along the Med, through the steep hills on the Italian side, was spectacular, and it was part of the rationale for coming this way; naturally, Deb slept through most of it. In truth, she was exhausted. At one point, though, she woke up with a start, and realized that she'd been dreaming about . . . But she didn't want to remember what she'd been dreaming about. She stared out the window . . . rough brown cliffs with patches of garden, trellises, olive trees clinging to the rock: and then the blue sea.

"You okay?" Giacomo said. The road was narrow, twisting. He had to concentrate.

"I'm okay," she said. And then they went through a tunnel, dark and low. It was so long that she blinked in the sun on the other side. "I was thinking," she said, turning to find the sea again, "I was thinking . . . Let's say I decided that I wouldn't have the baby because . . . well, because the world didn't need any more babies, because the world was overpopulated. What would people think? I bet they wouldn't believe me. That couldn't be the *real* reason. I bet I wouldn't believe it myself. I'd say to myself—you're just using that as an excuse."

"But you'd know—you'd know yourself. Inside."

"I'm not sure I would. Somewhere I'd be thinking . . . you're an idiot. A tree hugger. I mean, unless you're some kind of saint, you can't really believe that anyone does anything for . . . *the greater good*. It sounds so stupid."

"But of course that's what you're supposed to think, isn't it? It's everyone for themselves—if you don't believe that, you're by definition crazy."

"Do *you* think I'm crazy?"

"Only a little." He took off his sunglasses and put them on the dash; they were coming up to another tunnel in a moment. "That's the first sign, though, that things are breaking down. People really start believing that they're not part of a society or a world, anything bigger than themselves. That's what people don't understand. Long before we run out of natural resources, we'll exhaust social resources, moral resources—societies just can't adapt that fast. They break down. They *are* breaking down. It's obvious in Africa, but—"

They hit the tunnel with a rush, and Deb didn't say anything—she was remembering that Boyd had more or less made the same point.

It wasn't till Venice that they talked about the baby directly, *her* baby, *their* baby—without any theory or abstract stuff. She still hadn't been able to figure it out: did Giacomo want the baby or not?

"Giacomo, we have to talk about this. And by 'we' I mean *we*."

"Of course we do. I'm looking forward to it. But you have to say what it is you feel, what it is you want."

"But it has to be mutual. You're involved, you know. It can't be my decision—I mean without you."

"Yes, but the decision, and what you feel, aren't necessarily identical. Look, you know what you're like—"

"Oh, God!"

"Now, now. What you want to do is figure out what I feel, then work out what you feel around it. This is too important for that. You have to say what *you* want, and then we can work out what *we'll* do."

They were walking beside *San Felice*, in the sun, and Deb stopped, and looked down at the gently moving water. "We just never talked about having children. I mean, do you want them at all? I always assumed I *would*, without ever thinking about it much. And we certainly weren't planning it, were we?"

"But ninety-nine per cent of the children born on this planet haven't been planned. Big deal."

"I don't know. Sometimes I think the only moral thing to do is forget about having any of your own, and adopt some little waif like Renato. But I don't know that I'm strong enough—now—ever."

With a cheerfully neutral tone, he said, "Well, it's certainly a possibility."

Deb gave him a look. "You're not being very helpful."

Giacomo smiled blandly. "Listen . . . you remember the first time here . . . who asked you out? who said they loved you—the first time?"

"All right, okay."

"So now it's your turn to go first."

Deb gave him a look. "Grrr!" she said.

"God help me," said Giacomo. "That's just what your mother does when she's peeved at your father."

Later that same afternoon, clouds moved in and the breeze came up—a relief, in fact, in the summer's heat. They'd walked and walked until their feet were aching, but had finally found their way back to the Grand Canal. It was getting late—people were afraid of rain—they were able to find a café with an empty table. They had espresso, and after a moment Giacomo began to laugh gently.

"What is it?" Deb asked.

"Those old guys, behind me." There were two old hunched Italian men, planted like permanent fixtures at the bar—here, if you had your coffee at the bar, you paid less. "They're saying, it was okay for Marco Polo to find China, but did he have to tell them where Venice was?" Deb glanced outside. Tour guides, fairly desperate, were trying to organize a huge party of Chinese day-trippers—part of the great armies which, thankfully, were now heading back to the mainland. Venice once had been in danger of drowning from the sea; now it was sinking slowly beneath a sea of people.

They didn't say anything; they were remembering the conversation they'd had about China the first time they'd been here—the orphanages full of baby girls, abandoned . . .

And then Deb said, out loud: "I hate it—thinking that those guys might be right, even the tiniest bit."

"What do you mean?"

"It's almost saying there's something wrong with women for having babies. It's not our *fault,* after all."

"I don't know. That's probably true for everyone. Population. That's just people. And I'm one of them. Hey, is there something wrong with me? It's never *your* problem. It's all those Chinese, or Indians, or Africans, breeding like flies. Or what would happen—think of this—let's say you go to your mother . . . Mother, Giacomo and I have decided not to have children. There are too many people in the world. The world just doesn't need any more. What does *she* say?"

"She says . . . Well, dear, that's your decision and, of course, I wouldn't want to interfere . . ."

"*But . . .*"

"Right. One of her *buts.* And then . . . Actually, dear, I think you're just the sort of couple that *should* be having children. The real problem is all those people who have children even though they can't give them the opportunities that you could, don't you agree?" Deb took a final sip of her coffee. "That's what she'd say."

"Which is what everyone says. Or, if they don't do that, what they do is translate it into something else, something they do want to talk about. So you get the left-wingers—population isn't the problem, it's capitalism. There're not too many people, just too many *poor* people. And then the right-wingers say . . . if government would get out of the way and let the free market work, no one would have to starve. And all those arguments are true, up to a point. They just forget one thing, the numbers. You could take all the poor people in New York and put them into Porsches and BMWS—but that wouldn't make it any easier to get through the Holland Tunnel."

"God, this is depressing!"

"Isn't it, though? To change the subject . . . violently . . . what are you going to do about this gold mine that Rosie called you about?"

"I don't know. I have to do something. All my clients keep calling her up, wanting to buy. I think they *should* sell."

"Why?"

"Don't you know the definition of a gold mine?"

"No."

"A hole in the ground with a liar at the top."

"And do you own any?"

"Ten thousand, twenty thousand—I forget. It was just a glorified penny stock, but sometimes they work out. This one has, but I'd say it's time to head for the exits."

When they got back, she called Rosie and said she didn't care what the analyst said, she wanted out, and now, and all her people out, and now. "You never go broke, Rosie, taking a profit, especially a *big* profit." Grumbling, Rosie agreed, and Deb lay down. She felt relieved. And maybe, having made one decision, others came easier.

In any case, she woke up around eight.

Her feet were killing her. She said she'd only go out if Giacomo let her wear her Nikes, which she knew was gross, but otherwise she wasn't going to be able to walk, period, and he grumbled but agreed rather than eat any more hotel food, which they both thought was pretty bad.

They headed out, into a cool, pleasant evening. The sky was overcast, but a few stars peeped through, and there was a lovely, steady, sailing breeze. Lights hung in the water, and a soft mist had slipped in from the sea. As they walked along, Deb took Giacomo's hand. "I think I know what I want," she said. "I think I've made up my mind."

"About—?"

"You know."

"What, then?"

She wasn't being coy—not about this. But she realized that she'd said *think* and she wanted to be certain. So she said, no, she wouldn't tell him, not till later. So they went and had dinner, and afterwards both of them had a calvados, and some wonderful, wonderful coffee. Deb realized she was happy. Despite every-thing, after all, you have to live your life, and try to be happy. And she was certain, too. So Deb told him then, and they talked about it, and Giacomo agreed: a child would always be lovely, but if they used their brains, and kept the faith, there might be a better time in the future.